the BOOK of RESERVATIONS

Other Work

The Coat Check Girl

the BOOK of RESERVATIONS

a novel

LAURA BUCHWALD

RADIANCE

An Imprint of Roan & Weatherford Publishing Associates, LLC
Bentonville, Arkansas • Heber City, Utah
www.roanweatherford.com

Library of Congress Cataloging-in-Publication Data
Names: Buchwald, Laura, author.
Title: The Book of Reservations/Laura Buchwald | The Ghost Table Trilogy #2
Description: First Edition | Bentonville: Radiance, 2025.
Identifiers: LCCN: 2025947568 | ISBN: 979-8-89299-077-6 (hardcover) |
ISBN: 979-8-89299-078-3 (paperback) | ISBN: 979-8-89299-079-0 (eBook)
Subjects: BISAC: FICTION/Ghost | FICTION/Fantasy/Paranormal | FICTION/City Life
LC record available at: https://lccn.loc.gov/2025947568

Radiance hardcover edition December, 2025

Jacket Design by Casey W. Cowan
Interior Design by Staci Troilo
Editing by Staci Troilo & Lisa Lindsey

Dedicated to my father,
the only person more relieved than I was
to discover he liked my writing.

d…….I love you forever and a day…….r

Prologue

As autumn descends, the veil between the living and dead grows thin. Those who want proof of an afterlife are sure to find it. Those who don't will have to ignore the clearest of signs.

It takes effort *not* to believe because evidence is everywhere—a tingling on the back of your neck, a high-pitched hum you might be imagining, a creeping sensation you're not alone in the room. Everyone's experienced these phenomena, and many brush them off. Harder to ignore is the concrete evidence—mementos appearing in your path, songs playing with uncanny timing, a long-forgotten scent wafting through the air. Skeptics will concoct outlandish explanations to avoid the truth, but for those willing to see, the proof is all around.

In September 2000, Miss Sylvie's Bistrot in Greenwich Village is hallowed ground. It's a welcoming home for the departed thanks to one of its owners, who created it to be just that. Her partner—in business and in life—is cut off from the spirit world, encumbered by a rational mind. He'll take some convincing.

We'll get there.

Some people already know Miss Sylvie's is haunted, others will come to realize. To the resident ghosts, it's haunted by the living, and that's okay, there's room for us all. Every being who enters these doors comes for a reason.

Including me.

Chapter One

Josie tightened her grip on Derek's arm as they reached the corner. "We're making a right at the end of the block. Thirteenth Street."

"Thirteen—that's some kind of omen."

"When's your birthday?"

"May thirteenth."

"Then you're right. It's a good omen."

They turned the corner, then walked a few paces to the blue-gray door at 230 West Thirteenth Street between Greenwich and Seventh Avenues.

Josie ran her finger down the list of names until she found the one she wanted. She pressed the buzzer for 401.

"Who are we seeing?" Derek asked.

"His name is Quentin Bannister."

"Good lord."

"It's a very distinguished name, Derek. He's British. Or Australian. I can never tell them apart."

"And who recommended him?"

"Boodles."

Derek exhaled an unnecessarily long sigh. "You told Boodles we were doing this?"

When the buzzer sounded, Josie pushed open the door. The tiny lobby held nothing but numbered mailboxes in the wall and a steep flight of stairs. She looked up. It was a long way to the fourth floor.

"No." She let go of his arm to hold the railing as she climbed. "He mentioned he and Bulleit had gotten this great recommendation but decided to see someone upstate by their country house—some old hippie who sees clients out of her garage, which is also her pottery studio. They met her apple picking and 'liked her vibe.'"

"Why do you know so much about those two?"

"I like them. They kind of fascinate me."

Boodles and Bulleit—real names Javier and Daniel, not necessarily in that order—were regulars at Miss Sylvie's Bistrot, the restaurant Josie and Derek owned together. They were named for their drinks of choice, one a Boodles martini, the other a Bulleit Manhattan, and because they bore a striking resemblance to one another—trim, bearded, and bespectacled—spent significant time at their aforementioned country house, and had swapped drinks several times over the years, people weren't entirely sure anymore which was which. Josie was fairly certain the one currently on martinis was Javier, the Manhattan drinker Daniel, but she was not confident enough to say their names out loud. Instead, they were "fellas," "hon," and "handsome." Masking forgotten names with affection was one of many perks that came with working in a neighborhood restaurant where friendliness outperformed formality.

Josie stopped on the second landing to catch her breath. "Wow."

"Yep. If you drag me here on a regular basis, we can cancel our Health and Racquet membership." He patted her butt, and Josie grabbed his hand with her free one.

It was an unexpected reprieve from the tension, and she appreciated it. "I'm not 'dragging you here,' my love. But I think I want to cancel anyway. It's becoming a scene. And I—"

"—don't do scenes. I know. Let's get this out of the way."

Number 401 sat on the top floor, and when they reached it, Josie pressed the button for *Q. Bannister*. Every name on the list had either LCSW or PhD listed next to it as a credential—Quentin Bannister appeared to be the only doctor of medicine in the group practice.

They were buzzed into the homey waiting room of a suite of offices. It had blond wood floors, tweed love seats, a couple of folding chairs, and a large purple beanbag where a boy—roughly nine or ten years old—sat reading *National Geographic* and wearing foam headphones attached to a portable CD player. He looked up when they entered, then moved one of his earpieces to the side.

"Do you want the beanbag?"

"No, thank you." Josie smiled. "We'll take the couch. Looks comfy though!"

"It's my favorite seat in the place."

Josie sat, and Derek went to the magazines fanned out on the covered radiator by the window. Neither of them excelled at sitting still when they were anxious, and both were anxious—Derek because he didn't like to talk about his feelings, and Josie because it was her idea to make him try. And since it *was* her idea, she ceded the standing and pacing to him.

"Are you going to see Doctor Henderson?" the boy asked.

She shook her head. "No, we're meeting with someone else."

Derek clenched his jaw. He also hated small talk when he was tense.

Other than perfunctory conversation at the restaurant, Josie didn't have a lot of experience talking to kids. Even the short exchanges at work left her feeling like she was doing it wrong. But this kid clearly needed to chat. He was plump with pale skin, thick blond hair, and freckles. He had the look of a child who was too smart for his peers and probably among the last chosen in gym class. She felt for him immediately, which was one of the issues Derek had with their relationship—what he perceived as her tendency to prioritize others, even strangers, over him. It was an argument they'd had many times.

At least *this* kid was very much alive, so Derek couldn't make that complaint.

Then again, that was just an assumption. Josie felt tingly as she regarded the kid closely, wondering if she was wrong. One look at Derek, though, put that thought to rest. She was speaking aloud, and he was neither confused nor irritated, so of course the boy was alive. She'd gotten much better at telling the difference. Anxiety was clouding her thoughts, making her doubt herself.

Josie's relationship with the spirit world was another reason they were in this room waiting for Dr. Quentin Bannister. Derek had no interest in something that had become an integral part of her life, and it was taking a toll on their relationship. She'd been working hard to stifle her abilities for the sake of their happiness, and it was proving impossible.

"I like Doctor Henderson," the boy said. "She's really good at Risk."

"Risk?"

"Like, the best board game on the planet, and probably on other planets too."

"Oh! That's a complicated one, isn't it?"

"Not if you're into geopolitics and conflict resolution."

Derek turned to Josie with a trace of a smile.

She winked, relieved by another temporary thaw, then turned back to the boy. "I bet you do well in school. You seem like a very bright guy."

"I am. What's your name?"

"I'm Josie."

"Josie, as in Josephine, the empress and wife of Napoleon One?"

"Something like that." In fact, she'd been named for Josephine Baker.

The door to one of the offices opened. A teenaged girl deeply committed to her Goth phase walked out, followed by a tall, middle-aged woman in a black tunic, leggings, and ballet flats. She wore a shade of apricot lipstick that perfectly complemented her features. Her face was pleasant and open, eyes framed in stylish cat's eye glasses. She *looked* like a child psychologist.

Since opening the restaurant and being viewed more professionally than ever before, Josie had begun to realize she needed to take a vested interest in her appearance. She remembered this whenever she saw a stylish woman, but easily forgot when her mood was mired by daily stress.

Dr. Henderson nodded to them while holding out her hand to usher the boy into her office. As soon as she shut the door behind him, a second door opened.

"When one door closes...."

Josie looked at the back of Derek's head, hoping for a response. A woman she recognized from a police procedural TV show walked out. She smiled at Josie as if to acknowledge she knew she was recognizable, then left. This made Josie feel better. Therapy was so normalized in this city that even the famous—or mildly so—didn't feel the need to go incognito.

A man came out a moment later. He was bald, blue-eyed, and younger than he'd sounded on the phone. Josie started to stand, but he looked around the waiting room, glanced at his wristwatch, then went back into his office.

Derek turned to her, holding a *Conde Nast Traveler* he wasn't reading. "Did you get us here early on purpose?"

"We've been waiting five minutes."

"Okay, I would just really like to not spend my entire—"

She was spared the rest of the complaint by the opening of a third door. A man probably in his mid-sixties emerged, and she knew for certain this was Quentin Bannister.

"Hello." He nodded to each of them. "Quentin Bannister."

"Hi. I'm Josie Gray, and this is Derek Magnus. It's nice to meet you, Doctor Bannister."

He was attractive, if a bit jowly. Silver-haired and bearded, with dark eyes and deep lines etched between his brows. Shorter than average. He looked like a character actor, one who might play the patriarch of a wealthy family on television, and bore a passing resemblance to Derek's father—or so Josie thought—she knew Roger Magnus only through photos.

"Right this way." Quentin Bannister had a kind face but was not a smiler. He led them through the middle of the three doors into his office.

"Thank you for seeing us today," Josie said. "It's an anniversary, so we thought we'd go all in on the romance by dissecting our relationship and hashing out our problems."

Derek and Dr. Bannister both looked at her quizzically.

She cleared her throat. "Thanks for seeing us."

The space looked like a movie set of a therapist's office—mahogany desk at the far end, framed diplomas on the wall, shelves of reference books, and a couple of large plants that may or may not have been real. In the middle of the room sat a glass Noguchi table flanked by a Herman Miller Eames chair that was definitely real and a sky blue mid-century modern sofa that reminded Josie of her grandmother's.

When Dr. Bannister gestured to the sofa, they took seats.

"So, it's an anniversary, you say?" He looked at Derek.

Derek shrugged and looked at Josie. "Sorry, Joze. I'm not sure what you're talking about."

"September eleventh—one year ago today, we decided to move in together."

"Oh. Okay." He nodded. "That makes sense."

Josie addressed the doctor, who began taking notes. "We were in Saratoga for the weekend. The restaurant where we worked was still closed—we were getting compensated but didn't know how long that would last, but it was okay because I had some money I'd inherited from my grandmother. I wasn't being ridiculous with it or anything because I knew I was supposed to do something big, I just didn't know what, but the whole idea for our restaurant was percolating and anyway we'd decided to take a road trip, something I never would have done before Nanette—that's my grandmother—left me money, but it turned out Derek had some money for reasons I'll let him explain to you"—she glanced at him—"if he wants to. But it was like this perfect storm of things leading to that weekend, and I was tired of the Carroll Gardens commute and D was getting tired of the East Village and this apartment was available right down the street, which we found out because our friend Bulleit knows a realtor—"

Dr. Bannister was no longer writing. He stared blankly at Josie, then turned to Derek.

"She does this when she's nervous." Derek put his hand protectively on her knee, which he hadn't done in about a week. "Why don't we let Doctor Bannister lead?"

"Sure." Josie pulled a bottle of water from her bag and cracked it open. "Sorry."

She looked at the doctor, wishing he were a smiler.

He studied her with an unreadable expression. "What brings you here?"

"Well, we've been arguing lately. About little things, mostly, but we can't seem to cycle out of it."

"It's not just little things." Derek removed his hand from her knee.

"Well, no, I mean there are big things going on, but our… triggers? Our triggers are stupid little things." She turned to him. "Like last night, I opened a bottle of liquid soap, and you barked at me in front of Naomi."

"We already had brand new bottles in both bathrooms," he said flatly, having trod this ground ad nauseam the night before. "We can't afford to waste product."

"It's not wasting. It's not like it won't get used or will spoil. It's soap."

"Yeah, and we have to keep track of inventory. Soap is one thing, but what if it's a carton of milk, which will spoil?"

"Then we'll buy another carton of milk!"

"Josie—" He exhaled with frustration.

Dr. Bannister watched the volley, then chimed in. "Why don't you start at the beginning. You said you've been arguing lately. When did 'lately' begin? What's changed for you?"

"Everything's changed in the last year," Derek said. "We've been together about a year."

Josie was glad he was participating. She'd assumed the burden of explaining would rest entirely with her.

"Since 1999—is that when you met?"

"No, we've been friends for years," Josie said. "We worked together at Bistrot, which was a restaurant on Ninth Street—"

"Yes, I'm familiar with it." Dr. Bannister began scribbling on his legal pad again. Josie took note of his automatic pencil, which struck her as an odd choice—why would there ever be need to erase these notes? If they were incriminating, they should either be destroyed, which an eraser couldn't guarantee, or turned over to the authorities, in which case a pen would make a stronger statement.

"We worked together and were good friends," Derek said. "Last summer we decided we were more than that."

Dr. Bannister wrote a few sentences, then clicked the pencil to get more graphite. "You decided how to feel?"

Derek puffed out his cheeks and exhaled loudly.

Josie put her hand on his, urging him to continue.

"We decided to act on the feelings we realized we'd had for a while." He looked at her. "Would you say that's accurate?"

"Accurate." She stared at the pencil tip, waiting for the doctor to click it again.

"There were some… obstacles, so it wasn't the smoothest start. And then, as you might know, the restaurant closed and went on the market. And it was listed for cheap—the last owner took a big loss."

"Why is that?"

"He was ready to move on."

In fact, the previous owner, Chef Eriq Villeroy, had a nervous breakdown and needed to get rid of his business.

"But it was still an investment, and like Josie said, we both came into some money."

"Came into?" *Click.*

Derek squeezed his lips together and nodded slowly. This was a topic he would not be ready to delve into.

"Yes. We bought and renovated the place, and like Josie *also* said, it was a year ago today we decided to move in together."

"So, you're business partners and romantic partners. That can get complicated." *Click, click, click, click.*

"That's exactly it," Josie said, relieved he'd let Derek off the hook for now about the money he'd inherited. "Running this business is a lot of stress anyway, and we're having a hard time getting things off the ground. There's so much potential there—we have an amazing chef."

"Do you have other partners?"

"We have investors, but it's just us running the place. I mean, besides Chef—Naomi—we have staff, obviously. But with operating and managing and all the hiring decisions and creative decisions, every single detail falls to us. Except the menu, but even that we have to approve." She had to tune out the clicking.

"Why don't you simply hire more help?"

"Yeah, there's nothing 'simple' about that," Derek said. "It's been advised we hold off on hiring until we earn back some of our initial investment."

She could hear the acrimony in his voice and hoped the doctor couldn't, though he was in the business of analyzing people.

"We're trying to handle everything ourselves."

"Here's the biggest issue. And one that Josie is either pretending isn't happening or doesn't understand the reality of."

"Wow. That was condescending. And nice to end a sentence with a prep—"

"I'm sorry Josie, but it's true. Doctor, I assume you've heard of Declan Kelleher?"

"The real estate developer?"

"Exactly. The one who's basically going to own Manhattan soon and will sanitize all the character out of it. He's buying up huge swaths of the Village, offering landlords ten times what they paid, driving rents up exorbitantly. He's making it really hard for small business owners. Now there are rumors he's in talks to buy the building our restaurant is in. If that's true, there's no way our landlords are going to pass up on a cash-out like that. Nor should they."

"Of course I understand this," Josie said. "I'm just hardwired for optimism, and my gut tells me even with all the growing pains and struggles, this is going to work out."

In fact, Josie's innate optimism was a relatively new trait, and a hard-earned one after years of unhappiness. But once she realized she could turn her struggles into opportunities to grow, she began to view the world in a different light. In hindsight, she realized even in her gloomier younger days, part of her had always believed good things lay ahead. Now she joked she was a "glass half full" girl, while Derek was a "glass is broken" guy. Lately this rang especially true.

"And I'm hardwired for pragmatism," Derek said. "I follow this stuff, what's going on in the city with real estate and everything else, and every fucking moment I feel like this Kelleher guy is lurking, waiting to make his move. If we don't start making bank, we're screwed."

"Well, your business can't succeed—you can't 'make bank' as you say—if you're running yourselves ragged, right?" Dr. Bannister clicked his pencil though he was no longer writing. "Something's bound to slip through the cracks. I don't know the ins and outs of the restaurant industry, but in my layman's opinion, it seems hiring a manager would be one additional investment worth making. Wouldn't doing so mean you two would *not* have to handle every single detail? Isn't that the manager's role?"

Josie clapped her hand on Derek's knee. "Sound familiar, my love?"

"You've been saying that for a while," he admitted. "But it's still adding another expense."

She turned back to the doctor. "It is an expense for sure, but in the long run it's worth it. Especially for Derek, who does the bulk of what needs to be done outside of business hours—paperwork and inventory, he's just naturally better at that stuff than I am. My off-hours work is more occasional, ordering food and supplies, placing ads when we need help. But still, owning a restaurant is mentally time-consuming even if you're not actively busy. I feel like if we hire a manager, it will free up at least a little bit of time, and then we can have some kind of balance."

"That would stand to reason. Balance is important, of course, and if you live and work together in a high-pressure environment, it can be hard to find. Do you have friends?"

"Friends?" Josie repeated.

"Yes—peers with whom you're compatible—"

"No, I know what friends are. Sure, we have friends."

"Sort of," Derek said. "It can be hard in this line of work since we work nights."

"My grandmother was my best friend."

"Well, a grandmother is its own role...."

"No, you don't understand. Nanette was not your typical grandmother. At all. She was ageless."

She was, to the point that Josie had never found a woman her own age with whom she related better than she did her grandmother. They talked about everything and were closer to each other than either was to the link uniting them—Josie's mother, Alice.

"You have Curtis," Derek said.

"I do. But it's different now."

"Who is Curtis?"

"Curtis worked with us for years at Bistrot and was pretty much my best friend in the city, but I don't see him much anymore. Our situations have changed. I mean, I'm running a business and he's in school and has a boyfriend now."

"Do you have girlfriends?"

"I have casual friends. Acquaintances, women I can meet occasionally for lunch or a drink." She looked at Derek. "Can you name any of them?"

"Josie," he said with exasperation.

"Derek doesn't take a huge interest in my friends outside of the restaurant."

He sighed and spoke in a monotone. "I'll work on that."

"Thank you. It would be nice." She turned back to the doctor. "To be fair, though, the past couple of years, even before Derek and I took over the place, I was always working nights, which makes it hard to cultivate outside relationships. Then I was home a lot helping my mom with Nanette, who was on a downward spiral for a stretch. I was in a pretty bad place last summer after she passed."

When Josie lost Nanette, she lost her compass. Nanette was her sounding board, the first call she'd make with good news or bad. She was the person with whom she'd share movie and book recommendations, and the one she could vent to when she needed an ear. Now she was unmoored, with no one to validate her feelings, and she'd been searching for a connection to fill the void. She thought she'd found one in a new friend the previous summer, but that person wasn't who she'd pretended to be. Just as that relationship dissipated, she and Derek realized they were meant to be together, and she'd hardly had time to mourn the friendship. With things so rocky between them now, she craved an outside connection again. She wanted her grandmother but would settle for a good girlfriend.

"What about you, Derek?"

"I'm kind of a lone wolf. I mean, typical guy, I know. I'm friends with everyone and no one. I don't have time for close friendships. This job was all-consuming before, and now with this real estate stress, it's suffocating."

"Making some hiring decisions will allow you both to find a healthy work-life balance, which would be a good first step. Maybe then you can recalibrate, see the forest for the trees as it were, and Declan Kelleher won't feel like a dragon breathing down your neck. Balance isn't going to come looking for you. You have to be proactive about creating it."

"Agreed," Josie said. "We used to love doing things in our time off—now we don't have any."

"What kinds of things?"

"Going to movies, going out to hear music, even reading—I used to be a voracious reader. I'd love to get back to a life where I have time to do more than just work or worry about work. First, we have to resolve the sous chef situation."

"What's the sous chef situation?"

"We're having a hard time holding onto them. Things keep… happening to drive them away."

"What kinds of things?"

She looked at Derek. "You want to explain?"

"Not really, 'cause it's pretty hard to."

"Try," said the doctor.

Derek uncrossed his legs and bounced one heel up and down. "We've gone through four since opening this past March. It's an old building, and things happen, but there've been rumors."

"I wouldn't call them 'rumors,'" Josie said under her breath.

"What was that, Josie?"

"I said I wouldn't call them rumors. Derek and I don't see eye to eye on this."

"On what?"

"Okay, here's where things get a little dicey," Derek said. "Josie and I are a great match. Like we said, we were really good friends before we switched gears, and we have a lot of common interests and values."

She smiled, put her palm on his knee to stop the bouncing, then took his hand.

"But there is one fundamental difference that gets in the way," he continued.

"What is that?"

"She believes in ghosts."

"It's more than that, Derek!" She pulled her hand away.

"Fine, it's more than that. Which makes it harder. She has this whole… connection to the spirit world."

Dr. Bannister cocked his head toward Josie. For the first time since they'd started talking, a faint smirk appeared on his lips. "How do you mean?"

"I know some people have a hard time with this sort of thing, but it's part of my lineage. My grandmother—Nanette—could communicate with spirits and passed that ability along to me. So yeah, I know for a fact there is supernatural activity in the restaurant."

"For a fact," Dr. Bannister repeated, scribbling and clicking.

"Yes, for a fact. And honestly? That's kind of how I know everything will be fine with this Declan Kelleher situation."

Derek scoffed. "Why? Did Nanette tell you it would be?"

"No. It's not that literal. But I feel a sense of calm when I think about it. It's like I'm channeling her wisdom."

Derek rolled his eyes.

"Anyway, some of our sous chefs—"

"Four of them," he said.

"Four of our sous chefs sensed the energy in the restaurant and got freaked out by it. Trust me, these are not menacing spirits, but I guess it was too much for them. Now we need to find a sous chef. Again."

Dr. Bannister waited for her to continue, a bemused smile on his face. Instead, Derek stepped in.

"The issue is, a lot of people want to believe in ghosts. Or need to believe in them. I don't. It's not my thing, and it's becoming part of my everyday existence that's a serious thorn in my side. It's a liability. With these sous chefs, for some bizarre reason—"

"New Orleans," Josie said.

"Okay—three of the four were from New Orleans, where our chef is from, and that's a 'ghost-friendly' culture—"

When he put air quotes around "ghost-friendly," Josie wished she were holding his hand so she could drop it again.

"—so whether it's the power of suggestion or they're all tapped into this thing I can't sense, it's the reason they all quit. They think the building's haunted."

"We have a ghost table," Josie said proudly.

"A what now?"

"Right," Derek said. "Our restaurant is partially inspired by some places in New Orleans Josie loves, and that's beautiful. She has this whole New Orleans thing—"

She took his hand. "I have this whole New Orleans thing."

"A New Orleans thing?"

"It's a place that's very dear to me, even more so because of a connection I share with Nanette." She toyed with her grandmother's fleur-de-lis pendant necklace, which she wore every day. "She lived there for a while, and I love it there."

"One of the restaurants she likes sets a table every night for their 'resident ghost.'"

Josie dropped his hand at the second set of air quotes.

"Now we have a table set for ours, and sometimes she spends a little too much time with it."

"With them," she corrected him.

"Yeah, see, it's getting fucking weird, Joze."

She flinched. "Wow."

"Sorry. I shouldn't have said that."

"Derek, is there anything you want to ask of Josie? Anything tangible that might make your relationship stronger?"

He turned to her. "Would you consider getting rid of the table?"

"I mean, do you really think that's just going to magically make our problems go away? Because it isn't. And the table is important to me. When we decided to do this, you *said* I could have it."

Dr. Bannister smiled broadly now, any trace of kindness having left his face. In its place was the smug look Josie knew well of a man who wanted to belittle her.

"Now, Josie." He spoke painstakingly slowly. "Is it possible that many of the problems you and Derek are having are rooted in this hobby? Relationships require communication and presence."

"It's not a hobby."

"You seem like a fairly intelligent woman. Surely you understand how… unlikely this sounds."

His use of "fairly" didn't escape her notice. "I imagine those who can't or won't believe consider this unlikely, but this is my world. For whatever reason, I'm saddled with the ability to communicate with the non-living. And even though Derek doesn't believe, it would be nice if he—my partner—accepted that it's *my* reality."

"Josie, you set a table every night in the restaurant we own together for dead people. How is that not acceptance?"

"Because now you're asking me to get rid of it and calling me 'fucking weird.'"

"I didn't call you that, I said the whole thing is. And it's not just at the restaurant. It's everywhere. It's why we don't live in a bigger apartment."

"How is that?" Dr. Bannister asked.

"There were two places for rent when we were looking. One was bigger and on a higher floor. We wound up in the other one because the big one was 'haunted.'" Josie had never known him to use so many air quotes.

"Josie, are you familiar with Joan of Arc?"

"Of course. Would you like to burn me at the stake?"

"Is it possible the reason it's hard for you to keep employees—"

"Just sous chefs."

"To keep sous chefs is that people are uncomfortable working for someone who hears voices or sees visions or however you believe this manifests for you?"

"*Ask him about the time Mister Wigglesworth got into the pudding.*"

The prompt came out of the ether. It was a man's voice, with a refined accent like the doctor's, and Josie knew she alone heard it. She also knew it was probably not in her best interest to follow its suggestion, but she needed something, anything, to wipe the smugness of Dr. Bannister's face.

"What about the time Mister Wigglesworth got into the pudding?"

The tip of Dr. Bannister's pencil snapped, and his legal pad slid from his knees. He stared at her, mouth open.

"Who's Mister Wigglesworth?" she asked.

"My—" He shook his head so rapidly, his jowls danced. "My dog. My childhood dog. My God."

"Okay. What happened with the pudding?"

"Only my grandfather knows this story."

"For fuck's sake." Derek rolled his eyes to the ceiling. "Here we go again."

Chapter Two

"WELL, THAT DIDN'T go as planned." Josie had to trot to keep up with Derek's long strides down Greenwich Avenue toward the restaurant. "And that damn clicking! That pencil! It's like he's trying to ensure he keeps his patients coming back by driving them mad."

"Josie, what was that?"

"What was what?"

"Mister Wigglesworth," he said with exasperation.

"You know what that was. I heard a voice, very clearly."

He muttered something under his breath and picked up his pace.

"Derek, please! You know I can't control when it happens!"

She couldn't. As a child, she'd realized her ability to communicate with the dead in a most terrifying way—alone on a rainy afternoon, when a playful young spirit paid her a visit. Though she quickly learned this was a link she shared with Nanette, who urged her to see it as a gift, she wanted nothing to do with it. It was a terrifying aspect of an already lonely childhood.

"But you *can* control the way you react. You completely freaked that guy out!"

"'That guy' was a condescending prick. Did you hear the way he spoke to me?"

"Yes. He's arrogant. But if you want people to accept you and the things you believe, don't you think you should accept the fact not all of us believe those same things? You shove it down my throat, and I can't stand it! A little restraint on your part would go a long way."

She fought back tears. "Okay, Derek. Jesus. I'm trying. I'm working on myself and on this whole aspect of my life that you don't understand, all while facing the same stuff you are where the restaurant's concerned. Do you enjoy not getting along? Are you just going to keep getting mad at me until our beliefs align and the restaurant is thriving and there's no stress in our lives? Because that's *never* going to happen. That much I can promise you. Perfection is a myth."

She stalked ahead of him and kept up her pace until she reached a *Don't Walk* sign.

"Okay, look." He caught up to her. "Can you stop for a second? I am well aware perfection doesn't exist."

She stared straight ahead.

"And no, of course I don't enjoy not getting along. Something has to give here. I don't criticize you for your beliefs—"

"You don't? Because 'it's getting fucking weird' and 'you shove it down my throat, and I can't stand it' sound kind of critical from where I stand."

"Fine. I apologize for what I've said today, but I never try to talk you out of your beliefs, do I?"

"No, but sarcastically asking about Nanette was totally uncalled for and mean."

"You're right, and I'm sorry about that too. But you're so blasé about this Kelleher prospect that I really don't know if you get what a big deal it is."

"I do, and these are two separate issues. One is the restaurant, which I truly believe is going to succeed, and the other is my connection to the spirit world, which, as far as I can tell, is here to stay, regardless of how you feel about it. You don't get to decide this one."

"I just wish you could meet me where I am. And that there didn't have to be collateral damage—like that guy—while we figure it out."

"Well, I'm sorry for causing 'collateral damage' with him, but I'm willing to sacrifice that relationship. It's not like we're going back."

"Maybe not, but some of what he said made sense."

"Such as?"

"The manager thing might be the right move."

She looked at him, finally. "Do you mean that?"

"It would have to be the perfect fit. We can't just hire anybody—"

"Well, of course not. But this could be a really, really great thing! We could actually have Mondays off. *Completely* off. Like you wouldn't be going to the restaurant right now to do inventory—someone else could do it."

"I don't see that happening for the foreseeable future."

"Eventually, I mean. Once we get this person up and running. Think about it. You could work on other projects, get back to your writing."

"Josie, please. You know better than anyone what a loaded topic that is."

"I'm sorry. I just—you're so talented."

In a former life, Derek was a writer who had sold two screenplays. Neither had been produced, but Josie had read and loved them and wanted him to write more. Plus, the financial success he'd had with them had helped keep him afloat for a while. Only recently, just before they started dating, did she learn of the other thing that kept him afloat. He inherited money when he turned twenty-five in the form of a double trust—his own, and that of the brother he never knew. Alex Magnus had been killed by a drunk driver shortly after his eighth birthday, and one year later Derek was born to a grieving mother and absent father.

Once Josie learned of Alex, she better understood why Derek didn't write much anymore. He'd spent his childhood living in his dead brother's shadow and fled home—Denver—the day he turned eighteen. He'd spent so many years suppressing his childhood memories that it was a shock to Josie when he finally told her about Alex. Privy to the darkness that had shaped him, she understood how hard it must be to lose himself in fiction that wasn't influenced by his trauma, and how hard it must be to write about that trauma. It would mean exposing his deepest self, and Derek Magnus avoided vulnerability at all costs. He seemed to equate grief—his own—with weakness, and as such, he had never really processed the loss of his brother. Though their time on earth hadn't overlapped, he was aware of Alex from the start, his childhood so heavily impacted by his mother's grief he couldn't help but share in it.

This was where their most fundamental difference came into play. The loss of Nanette and return of Josie's ability helped her to reassess grief and understand death is not the end. She wanted Derek to believe in the spirit world because the knowledge Alex was still around might not only help heal him but also lead to his repairing his relationship with his mother. Unfortunately, he was as disinterested in reconnecting with her as he was contemplating the afterlife, and he was as disinterested in *that* as he was in getting back to his writing.

"Josie, if you want to relieve some of our tension, maybe don't nag me about getting back to something I've chosen to give up for now."

"Okay. How about this? We haven't had a vacation in almost a year, and it's showing. Look how stressed out we are. Maybe we could go back to New Orleans, or go out west to Col—"

Sometimes she wished she could swallow the words that came out of her mouth.

"We are *not* going to Colorado, Josie. Just quit while you're ahead."

"I was going to say California!"

He wouldn't believe her. Tears filled her eyes. She was also a crier, now, which had begun when she learned her grandmother's death was imminent. Though Nanette always encouraged otherwise, Josie's mother had taught her by example to keep her feelings in a box. Alice Gray had lost her father, Nanette's husband, at a young age, then lost her husband, Josie's father, to an affair that became his second marriage. Those two traumas made her rigid and vehemently self-sufficient.

To Alice, emotion equaled neediness, and neediness was unacceptable. So, whenever Josie's emotions got too big, she believed she was doing something wrong and tamped them down. The death of the one person in the world she felt understood her rendered that impossible. Now she cried when she was sad, angry, or overjoyed, or when she witnessed someone feeling any of those things. It stunned her how nearly a year and a half later, grief could wallop her when she least expected it. Derek tried to support her but didn't always understand. Their grief looked entirely different—Josie's pure and uncomplicated, Derek's wild, messy, and entirely without rules.

At the end of Greenwich, they crossed Sixth Avenue to West Ninth. Miss Sylvie's was located on Ninth Street between Fifth and Sixth Avenues.

The building dated back to the turn of the century and had been a series of restaurants over the years. When Josie and Derek started working together it was Bistrot, which served elevated French comfort food for a decade before Chef's breakdown. They then bought the business and took over the lease, renaming it after a beloved regular who died the previous summer, an eccentric neighborhood fixture with a long history of holding court at the bar.

It was a beautiful space. A long oak bar with curved ends to accommodate seating on three sides and red leather stools lined the right side of the front room. To the left of the front door was a staircase that led up to the bathrooms.

Throughout the barroom were a half-dozen café tables with chairs upholstered in green-and-white stripes that recalled the iconic awning of New Orleans's Café du Monde. Each table held a tasseled Victorian lamp that emitted a soft glow, as did the fairy lights hung around the room's perimeter. Framed vintage Jazz Fest posters and an old map of New Orleans adorned the walls of the barroom and just outside, by the coatroom and up the stairs, were black-and-white portraits of classic film stars and stills from some of the movies Josie and Nanette had loved and watched together.

Beyond the bar sat the twenty-table dining room lined with red leather banquettes, mirrors, and Art Deco sconces, all salvaged from Bistrot and rearranged for optimum Feng Shui. The two-story room, with the kitchen on the second floor, boasted soaring ceilings and a large skylight. Off to one side was the back staircase the waitstaff used to run food up and down, and on the landing outside the kitchen doors was Josie's ghost table—a round six-top that was set and cleared nightly.

"You said they don't eat or drink, right?" Derek had asked when she first described her plan.

"Right."

"So why do they need gold chargers and cut crystal wine glasses? This stuff is way nicer than what our living guests get."

"As a sign of respect, Derek. They deserve respect and beautiful things!"

"Beautiful things cost money."

"I'm paying for this. It makes me happy. It's how they do in New Orleans."

Eventually he acquiesced, and Josie set places for the restaurant's namesake, Nanette, Derek's brother Alex, and three people who had perished in a fire in 1974 when it was a restaurant called Dave's Continental—two waitresses and the firefighter who tried to save them. Derek never asked who the places were set for, and she never told him.

"I don't have a lot to do here today. Anything you want my help with?" she asked him now.

"Nope."

He pulled out his keyring to unlock the grate over the front door, then raised it with more force than was called for, making it clank thunderously. After holding the door for Josie, he stormed inside and went straight to the bar to turn on the ten-CD player.

John Coltrane filled the air.

"Gonna do inventory." He ducked under the bar, then disappeared through the trapdoor to the subterranean liquor room.

Josie bit her lip. This was going to be a long afternoon.

She stopped to check the answering machine at the hostess stand, which sat opposite the entrance. There were a couple of cancellations, two reservations, and a request from something called *Gotham Guide* for one of its reviewers to have dinner. It wasn't *The New York Times*, but it was something. The past couple of years had given rise to several new guidebooks with websites that reviewed businesses. These were not experienced journalists, and the guides didn't have the clout of the crowd-sourced *Zagat Survey*, but restaurants and shops laminated their reviews and posted them in their windows. A decent one couldn't hurt.

She flipped through the book to erase the cancellations and note the far fewer additions. Most of the restaurant industry used programs for reservations and inventory. While Miss Sylvie's had a computer, Josie and Derek were slow to change, preferring the analog way of keeping track of things. A future technology update was inevitable, but Josie was determined to hold out for as long as possible.

She ducked under the bar and called down to Derek.

"We have a review request!"

He didn't respond.

"D?"

"Yep—heard you."

"Do you want to know who it is?"

"If it were anyone important you'd have said."

Her eyes again filled with tears, and she scrubbed them away with the back of her hand. She couldn't stand the tension but refused to take all the blame. Derek said he wanted things to be better but wasn't doing his part, instead constantly getting annoyed and refusing to cut her any slack. She could as easily stay pissed at him for the way he'd spoken to her earlier, but one of them had to try to keep the peace. What she wouldn't give for a hug.

What she wouldn't give for Nanette.

She walked into the dining room, then climbed the stairs to the landing. Contrary to what Derek had told Dr. Bannister, she *didn't* spend too much time at the ghost table. Not usually, anyway. She went there when she needed comfort, and as long as things were like this between them, she would need a lot of it. The table and what it represented gave her peace, helped her feel connected to something bigger than herself, something on a much higher plane than her daily life.

When she first conceived of the table, she'd hoped it would be both a way to see Nanette regularly and a welcome home for the other honorees. She hadn't factored free will into the equation and quickly learned spirits came around when *they* chose, mostly when they needed something or had a message to impart. While the table hadn't functioned as she'd envisioned, it was important it remain there. To her, it symbolized hope.

She took a seat, closed her eyes, concentrated on her breathing.

Nanette, I need a sign.

Josie had seen her grandmother in spirit form once, on a life-changing day the previous summer in New Orleans. Nanette, who cherished the time she spent there, shared this love with Josie in the form of music, food, and plans to visit together one day. Unfortunately, that day never arrived. Instead, Josie first saw New Orleans after Nanette passed, and it was there she got to once more hug her grandmother.

Nanette told her then she'd always be around, and Josie assumed this would be more literal than it turned out to be. Still, she could feel her presence, often when she needed it most. Nanette sent signs—a waft of her lavender hand cream, the Gardénia perfume she wore, or the jasmine tea she and Josie drank together. Sometimes she sent songs—"What a Wonderful World" in a store that only played pop music or a muzak version of "Do You Know What it Means to Miss New Orleans" at the dentist. Then there were owls—Nanette collected things with owl motifs, and now Josie saw owls far more frequently than ever before. A single owl earring turned up in the restaurant's lost and found, never to be claimed. She fell asleep with the TV on and woke to a documentary about the snowy owl. Once when she was feeling blue in a used bookstore, she asked for a sign—directly in front of her sat a tattered copy of the children's book *Owl at Home*.

Please, Nanette. Send me a sign.

She waited for a shift in the air, a telltale tingling sensation, or Louis Armstrong to come over the speakers. There was nothing. Instead, after a few moments she heard humming. Before opening her eyes, she knew who it was. "Hi, Ruby."

"*Hi Josie!*"

Frances "Ruby" Samuels was the spirit Josie assumed responsible for scaring off the sous chefs. She was a petite redhead with a love of men and mischief, and though she could be a troublemaker, Josie felt for her—hers was a short and troubled life. The fire at Dave's Continental in June 1974 claimed her as its first victim. She'd been passed out in the ladies' room when it broke out.

Last summer she had tormented Josie until she had no choice but to accept her presence, then left her alone for a long stretch. Lately she'd been coming around with great frequency, and Josie wondered if it had anything to do with the fact autumn was approaching. This seemed an apt time for an uptick in spirit energy.

"*Are you in a bad mood*?"

"I'm not having the best day."

"*Did you and Derek have a fight? Do you want me to rearrange his bottle*s?"

Josie fleetingly regretted having greeted her. Spirits rarely spoke first, usually waiting for an acknowledgement, and once Ruby got hers, she was loquacious.

"No. Everything will be fine."

"*Alex has been here.*"

The hair on Josie's arms stood on end.

"Alex?"

"Derek's baby brother. Well I guess he's really Derek's baby BIG brother." Ruby giggled.

"I know, but what is he doing here?"

"Beats me. He only comes when you're not here."

"Okay. Okay. Let me think." She closed her eyes.

If Alex were suddenly coming around, he needed something, and surely it was something from Derek. This was bad timing.

"*What did you fight abou*t?"

She opened her eyes. "Nothing important. We're just having a rough patch."

"*Did he do something bad? Did you?*"

"No. Ruby do you have any idea why Alex is here?"

"*I think he needs to tell you something.*"

"Me? Or me and Derek?"

"*You. He knows* you'll *listen to him at least.*"

Josie sighed. They'd been over this, though Alex had never been part of the equation. "Honey, it's not that Derek *won't* listen, it's that he can't. He doesn't have the thing I have. Will you tell Alex he can talk to me?"

"He's shy."

"Just let him know when he's ready, I'm here." She pushed her chair back and stood. "I'll see you later, okay?"

"*See you later, alligator! And don't be sad, Josie. Derek loves you.*"

Downstairs, she contemplated waiting for him to finish but thought better of it. For one thing, she had no poker face, and her concern about Alex would betray her. But also, this was the pattern when they argued—he'd need space and retreat, she'd need resolution and chase after him. It rarely worked in her favor.

Her instinct to squash conflict as soon as it started stemmed from early childhood. When she heard her parents argue, she'd try to run interference in hopes of magically fixing things. She'd invent an excuse to call downstairs to them and disrupt the conversation. It would work, temporarily—they'd let her know what time it was or which day they were seeing Nanette or the answer to whatever innocuous question she'd asked—then once she returned to her room, they'd resume hissing at each other.

"Time for a new approach," she said to herself.

Out of the corner of her eye, she saw a light-colored streak on the other side of the room, as though a stray cat had found its way inside and was seeking a hiding spot.

There was no cat.

Quick motions like this were another way spirits manifested for Josie. Beings who didn't have a message to impart or a need for assistance might show up as orbs or smudges or flashes of light, making their presence known without lingering. In Josie's experience, in her ever-growing spirit world rulebook, these beings appeared to validate something she'd said aloud—she had a habit of talking to herself. This could be a spirit agreeing that Josie needed a new approach, and it was not Nanette or Alex or anyone she knew. The building was old. If they set a table for every ghost attached to it, there'd be no room for the living.

She ducked behind the bar, then called down to the basement.

"Derek?" She was greeted with silence. "Hello?"

"Yeah. Still working here." His voice was tight, as though he were girding himself for a typical Josie response.

"I'm heading out. See you at home."

He cleared his throat. "You're leaving?"

"Yep, just going to run some errands," she lied. "Love you!"

"Love you too," he said, after a beat.

She wished she had errands to run, or a friend to visit, or somewhere to go so he'd get home before her instead of the usual dynamic where she was predictably available. In describing their hectic schedules to the doctor, she'd misspoken. It was Derek who did most of the round-the-clock heavy lifting, including all of the inventory and much of the paperwork. Josie *did* have free time, and she wished she used it more wisely than she did. She spent a lot of it hanging around the restaurant waiting for him, and that needed to stop. She was an invaluable part of the restaurant culture during business hours, but the administrative details were not her purview. They came much more easily to Derek, so of course he handled it all, and of course he was the more stressed of the two of them. A manager would absolutely help.

Outside, instead of turning right toward their apartment, she turned left. It was a nice day. She could spend a couple of hours browsing the boutiques on Bleecker Street and the Three Lives & Company bookstore on West Tenth. First, though, she would go to one of her favorite spots in the neighborhood.

Across from the restaurant was the triangle where Greenwich and Sixth Avenues crossed at Tenth Street, and nestled within was a tiny urban oasis—a community garden with flowering shrubs and trees, rose bushes, and a koi pond. Park benches lined the path that ran the perimeter of the grounds, which housed the Jefferson Market Library, the prettiest branch of the New York Public Library. This was Josie's sanctuary.

She got an iced coffee, light and sweet, from the bodega on the corner, then gave a small donation to the volunteers positioned at the garden's entry. Her favorite bench was the second one in on the Tenth Street side.

"We meet again, old friend," she said as she sat. Ever since she was little, Josie had anthropomorphized familiar objects, not just dolls and stuffed animals like most kids. The star magnolia tree in Nanette's back yard was a friend, as was the large boulder she sat on in her elementary school playground. Tag sales made her sad for the worn and broken items—old toasters, sets of dishes with missing pieces, Barbie dolls with unfortunate haircuts—being abandoned in favor of shiny replacements or because children had outgrown them. This bench played an important role in her healing the previous summer, and she felt an emotional connection to it.

The sun beamed, and a light breeze blew through the air, cheering her a bit.

She wasn't unrealistically optimistic, she just chose not to share in Derek's doom and gloom mentality. Of course she understood the threat Declan Kelleher posed. But intuitively she believed everything would be okay.

The Alex situation was tough. It would be hard to mask her sadness at her inability to connect him to Derek, but she would figure that out too. She had to because it couldn't be yet another wedge in their relationship. She'd find a new, calm way to approach the challenges between them.

She sipped her coffee and collected her thoughts.

Derek needed space even when they *were* getting along, which meant Josie needed to be more independent. The doctor was right, working together and living together in a one-bedroom apartment was complicated, and they could both use more breathing room. She used to relish her alone time and was surprised to realize she no longer allowed herself any. Never had she expected to be one of those women who gave up her identity for a relationship, but she had to admit she'd let parts of herself languish.

In a book on connecting with the spirit world, she'd read asking guides and loved ones for messages would often solicit answers. The problem came when people mistrusted their intuition and dismissed what they heard as their own thoughts. It was possible, through practice, to recognize information coming from the other side. When she needed Nanette's wisdom, she worked hard to distinguish between her own ideas and external messages, but the book was right—she had difficulty trusting the process of this sort of communication.

She closed her eyes and breathed deeply, rubbing her fleur-de-lis pendant between her fingers.

Nanette, how can I make things better with Derek?

She took deep breaths until she heard Nanette's voice in her mind.

Meet him where he is.

It was a nearly identical sentiment to what he'd expressed earlier. She took a few more breaths and waited again for Nanette's voice. What she heard wasn't exactly audible, more like in conjuring Nanette, the words flowed through her.

You have the gift of communicating with spirit, but it mustn't replace the real gift of connecting with the people in your life. Derek deserves your time and focus.

Whether these were messages or her own thoughts, they contained wisdom. The strife her ability caused made her question whether what she had was a gift at all, but as she'd told Derek, it was here to stay. She had to exist both with and in spite of it. While she would not get rid of the ghost table, she would make Derek her priority. That meant setting stronger boundaries with spirit because while Nanette would always be welcome, she wasn't the one showing up. The ones who did were distractions when what Josie needed most was to focus.

Chapter Three

Josie woke Tuesday morning uncharacteristically buoyant. She was reminded of the early months of her relationship with Derek, when love coursed through her veins and she marveled at their great fortune in walking the earth at the same time. While her mood paled in comparison to those days, she felt she'd at least succeeded in repairing their recent rupture. She envisioned their situation like the Japanese art of mending broken pottery with gold—scars still evident but strengthened in beauty.

When she'd gotten home from the park, Derek was on the sofa reading *The New York Times* and listening to Charlie Parker. She could tell from his rigid body language he was expecting a rehashing of their argument. Instead, she greeted him with a smile, then set to work in the kitchen putting away groceries and humming along to the music.

He glanced quizzically over the top of the paper, but she didn't engage, just kept working and humming.

On her way to the bedroom to change, she ruffled his hair. By the time she came out, he was relaxed and smiling.

⚜

Tuesday afternoons began with a staff meeting. Before everyone arrived, Josie went to the kitchen to see Chef Naomi.

Born and raised in the Tremé section of New Orleans, Naomi Honoré was a beautiful woman with high cheekbones, long braids, and a figure that belied all the roux she made. She came from a matrilineal tradition of excellent cooks. When Josie and Derek met her on a recon trip to New Orleans, she was sous chef in the French Quarter at Antoine's, the country's oldest family-run restaurant. She was craving change and had close friends in Astoria, Queens, so when they proposed she join them in their new venture, she agreed to give it a shot. Naomi reinvented some of Antoine's best-known dishes—Oysters Rockefeller, Pompano Pontchartrain, Chicken Rochambeau—with a New York sensibility, which translated into a little less butter and cream but equal amounts of flavor. Derek liked to say you could taste the love in her food. She managed the kitchen staff—line cooks and dishwashers—with empathy, humor, and inclusion. Everyone on her team was important.

"What's good tonight, Chef?"

"It's fig season, baby." She was quintessential New Orleans right down to her frequent use of pet names. "How does Creole duck breast with fig stuffing sound?"

"Amazing. I love autumn food."

"Me too. I've got a root vegetable jambalaya—vegan."

"Dear God, why? Isn't vegetarian enough?"

Naomi had a deep understanding of food and dietary trends and was a good influence on her bosses. Both slow to change, Josie and Derek had resisted the vegetarian options she'd suggested until they tasted her meatless gumbo and vegan red beans and rice. Once those became two of the most popular menu items, they let her call the shots. At twenty-eight, Naomi was five years younger than Josie, nearly a decade younger than Derek, and far less set in her ways. Change wasn't just easy for her, she welcomed it.

"Girl, I'm telling you, vegan is a thing that's not going away. We gotta keep up with the Great Joneses."

The Great Jones Café was a popular Cajun restaurant in the East Village.

"I highly doubt the Great Jones serves tofu."

"We're not serving tofu neither. Trust me on this, Miss J. I came up in a town that takes the healthiest ingredients on the planet and deep fries them within an inch of their lives. Or smothers them with fat. Or both. I love the challenge of making this stuff healthier. But I promise you, I'll never stop making my roux."

"Good. Balance is important. Speaking of, we've decided to look for a manager."

"I don't know how y'all have lasted this long without one. Most couples would kill each other trying to do it all."

"Yeah, well, we're not exactly a model of domestic bliss lately. What about you? Any sous chef updates?"

"Got someone coming in Friday. Eduardo Quiñones." She pronounced his name with an exaggerated Spanish accent. "I have a pretty good feeling about him. Just have to make sure he's not a believer."

After the revolving door of sous chefs, Naomi figured out a new way to vet candidates—by determining how likely they were to sense spirits. Like most people from New Orleans, she was more than a believer, she accepted the spirit world as fact. She was unable to see them but could often feel their presence. On her first day, she walked by the table at the top of the stairs and shuddered. Once Josie explained what it was and assured her its inhabitants were friendly, she embraced it.

What she was looking for now, she'd told Josie, was someone like Derek—someone so closed off to the idea of the spirit world they would ignore all signs.

"By the way," Naomi said, "was there a kid in here?"

"I don't think so. Why?"

"Ling found tiny fingerprints in her piecrust."

A chill ran up Josie's spine. "I have no idea."

Naomi shrugged. "Anyway, she threw it out and started over."

"Well, don't tell Derek that. You know how he is about wasted product. I've got to get to the meeting. Specials?"

Naomi handed her a list. "If I like Eduardo, will you guys be able to meet him on Friday?"

"If you like Eduardo, we trust you. Just get references."

Downstairs, everyone had assembled in the barroom. This included Jerome, who ran the bar with Derek, and their servers—Ian, Lucy, and Twyla. The servers and busboys were Josie's responsibility, while Derek was the point person for bar staff and porters. He had the easier end of things—this waitstaff made Josie feel like a den mother in charge of an unruly group of scouts.

Jerome was an experienced bartender and voiceover artist whom the ladies loved as much for his mixology skills as his smooth baritone and deep hazel eyes. Ian was a boyishly handsome, naive kid from Wisconsin who had come to New York with dreams of being an actor—a staple in the restaurant world—and who Josie hoped would make a better thespian than he did a waiter. Behind his back, they called him Ian the Inept. Derek wanted to fire him, but Josie was determined to make a breakthrough, so she worked on him with Pygmalion-like dedication, patiently reminding him of the same things night after night, hoping they'd stick. What he lacked in competence he had an excess of in charm and looks, and he used that to his advantage whenever an attractive young woman graced the restaurant. Lucy, the best server they had, was a Bronx-born recent graduate of Pace University who lived with her parents to save money for grad school. She wanted a master's degree in hospitality, though Josie and Derek didn't think she'd need one to excel. Twyla was an ethereal blonde from Australia who did a little modeling and a lot of reading Tarot cards and astrological charts. Her dream was to meet the designer Marc Jacobs, who lived in the neighborhood and was, apparently, an Aries.

"Okay, guys," Josie said. "Specials. We've got char-grilled oysters à la Felix."

"Who's that?" Ian asked.

"Felix is a restaurant in New Orleans. Our soup today is corn and crab bisque, which we really want to push because we don't want leftovers. No one wants to be serving days-old crab."

"No gumbo?" Ian asked.

"We always have gumbo," Josie and Derek said at the same time.

"This is the soup du jour."

"I thought you said it was crab bisque?"

Josie glanced at Derek, who stared at the ceiling, his jaw clenched. She hurriedly continued. "Creole duck breast—"

"Oh, ducks are so darling!" Twyla was vegan.

"And delicious. Creole duck breast in a red wine glaze with fig stuffing. We can offer the fig stuffing as a side as well. Root vegetable jambalaya, which is vegan." She nodded to Twyla.

"Yay." She clapped her hands.

"Finally, catch of the day is snapper, served either grilled or Pontchartrain—which is what?"

"White wine, lump crabmeat, shrimp," Lucy said.

"Correct. Okay, what are the specials?"

Lucy raised her hand. "Char-grilled oysters à la Felix, corn crab bisque, which we're pushing the hell out of, Creole duck breast with red wine glaze and fig stuffing—also available on its own—vegan root-veggie jambalaya for Twyla, and snapper, Pontchartrain or boring."

"Perfect. Moving on, we're placing an ad for a manager, and Naomi may have found a sous chef."

"Also, guys, we need to talk about a few booze-related things." Derek looked at Ian.

Josie knew what was coming. They went over this often.

"In the interest of not wasting inventory, we need to push the wine that's already open when people order by the glass."

"How do we know what's open?" Ian asked.

"Like I said last week, brother, I put a check next to it on the chalkboard when we open one." Jerome had Josie's level of patience for Ian, whom he related to as a fellow aspiring artist. But where Ian was naïve, Jerome was shrewd and ambitious. Growing up outside the city in Mount Vernon, New York, he had joined every theater club and after-school program available to him and learned as much about the business as he could. He'd recently signed with a voiceover agent and went on auditions every week. On the opposite end of the spectrum, Ian was green. He'd moved to town with stars in his eyes, had no idea how to go about the business of becoming an actor, and didn't do much to find out. His real passion was women. Josie had no idea how far he took things with the ones he met on the job, but he did collect an impressive array of phone numbers.

"Another bartending note," Derek said. "I know it's not our favorite thing—and believe me, if we didn't have to, we wouldn't—but we've got to work on our upselling."

"Yeah, guys," Jerome said. "Stop giving me orders for 'vodka and soda' or 'gin martini.' We need to push the good stuff."

"What if we get the vibe someone can't afford the good stuff?" Twyla asked.

"If they're out to dinner at our place, they don't need to be drinking well vodka," Derek said. "If someone orders a vodka soda, offer them Ketel One or Stoli. Nine times out of ten, they'll agree because it's easier."

"Exactly, D, then you've gone from a four-dollar drink to a ten-dollar one."

"And if they really don't want it, they'll say so. No harm, no foul. Josie—anything else?" Derek asked.

"Nope," she said. "Okay, folks. Let's roll."

⚜

Josie placed the manager ad in *The Village Voice,* and by Thursday had twenty-three applicants to vet over the phone. She and Derek continued their upswing, enjoying more laughter, affection, and glimmers of hope at the prospect of having extra help.

On Friday, they had a full morning of interviews scheduled.

"What do you think the odds are we can find someone today?" Josie towel-dried her hair while watching the morning news on mute. The presidential elections were in November, pitting George W. Bush against Vice President Al Gore.

"This guy really wants to save the environment." Derek pointed to Gore, then pushed the plunger into the French press. "We should listen to him."

"Agreed." Josie clicked off the television at a commercial. "What do you think the odds are we can find someone today?"

"I don't know—did you get a good feel from any of them?"

"I did—and if we're lucky, we can check references tomorrow, and she can start as soon as next week."

"She?"

"Most of the people coming in are women. I threw in two guys for kicks."

"Fine by me. Women get shit done."

One of the myriad things Josie appreciated about Derek was his unwavering respect for women in an industry overrun by misogyny. Women in other restaurants made less than their male counterparts and tended not to have seats at the decision-making table. This was not the case at Miss Sylvie's.

They drank their coffee, then left the apartment. When they'd decided to move in together the previous year, they'd found—quite by chance and because Boodles and Bulleit knew a realtor—a sublet on the corner of Ninth Street and Fifth Avenue, one block from the restaurant. It was a former hotel, built in the twenties, with an ornate lobby of marble and carved plaster. The long corridors were windowless and some of the apartments haunted, a fact Josie learned when they toured the available units. She couldn't explain to the realtor why she chose the viewless one-bedroom on three over the spacious apartment on the top floor that looked onto Fifth Avenue, but she was adamant.

While Derek and the realtor were in the living room of the bigger one talking about air conditioning and track lighting, Josie stepped back into the bedroom to measure the closet. As soon as she did, she felt a burst of iciness. From the ensuite bathroom, she heard whispering and opened the door to see a woman talking to herself in the mirror. She was dressed in a navy-and-white floral dress with a full skirt, white pumps, and pearls. Her hair was in pink curlers. She didn't notice Josie.

"You are a good wife. You are a good wife." She started to cry, and makeup ran down her cheeks. An empty prescription bottle lay at her feet. The woman opened the cabinet and took out a straight razor.

Josie backed up and ran into the living room, startling Derek. Behind the realtor's back, she shook her head.

"I like the one downstairs better!" she said, her voice high and breathless.

"You do? But the light...." The realtor gestured toward the windows.

"I don't need light!" In fact, she did, and they would buy an absurd number of lamps for the apartment downstairs.

Before the realtor locked the door, Josie was by the elevators.

"What's going on?" Derek asked when he reached her.

"Ghost."

"I mean, Joze, it's an old build—"

"Unhappy ghost."

He didn't request details.

She and Derek came to embrace their viewless apartment on the third floor, and Josie tried to get to know the people who moved into the one upstairs. Her efforts proved futile. They left after a month.

⸸

THE FIRST PERSON they interviewed was a cocky young man named Scott who cracked his knuckles and directed all his responses at Derek.

"What do you love about the industry?" Josie asked.

"What's not to love?" he said to Derek. "Beats the hell out of sitting in an office. You get to sleep in. There are perks, if you get my drift."

His eyes slid to Josie's chest.

"Absolutely not," she said when he left.

The next two interviews were young women who didn't have enough experience and both of whom spoke in tones that would get tiresome quickly.

"What's with this phrasing every sentence like a question?" Derek asked after the second one left. "What am I missing here?

"I think it's a generational thing, old man."

"Easy there, sister—you'll be in your mid-thirties soon."

"I'll be thirty-four!"

"Exactly."

"How is that mid-thirties?"

"One, two, three are early-thirties. Four, five, six are mid."

"That's absurd."

Naomi walked through the front door, bike helmet under her arm. "Morning y'all!"

"Naomi, when do you think the mid-thirties start?" Josie asked.

"Thirty-four, baby."

"Shit."

"How are interviews?"

"Let's see, so far we've had a creeper and two valley girls."

"Nope. Maybe she'll be the one." Naomi nodded to the front door where a tall woman with a mane of blonde curls stood by the hostess stand, bottle of water in hand, big smile on her face.

"Hello!" Josie said. "Are you Charlotte?"

"I am. You must be Josie. What a beautiful space!"

Josie brought her to the table and introduced her to Derek.

"I see you're from L.A." He held up her CV. "What brings you to New York?"

"We came to be closer to my husband's family in New Jersey. I needed a break from Los Angeles. My last job was managing the restaurant at the Standard on Sunset, which, if you don't know it, is this ultra-trendy spot with tons of celebrities. It can get a little obnoxious. A *lot* of different personalities, but it was a fun place to work."

"I can only imagine what managing a restaurant in West Hollywood is like," Derek said.

"You figure out pretty quickly who wants to be treated like a star and who wants to blend in. But before that, I worked at a great little place that was brand new. I was their first manager and helped build their clientele. It was amazing to see them start to thrive. That's what drew me to this opportunity. I love to help new places grow."

"That's fantastic," Derek said. "We could use your talents."

"What qualities do you think are most important in a manager?" Josie asked.

"Flexibility, sense of humor, good memory for detail. People's names, their go-to drink, who likes what special. Treat every customer like a VIP. You need to have a photographic memory—or be good at faking it. Never let a returning customer think you've forgotten them."

"Amen," Josie said.

"Also—discretion."

"Discretion?"

"I learned that one the hard way early in my career—if a male customer comes in with a woman you've never seen before, don't ask after his wife."

"Uh-oh," Derek said, laughing.

"Yeah, not my finest moment."

"I mean, what kind of guy brings the other woman to a place he frequents with his wife?" Josie asked.

"Rookie move," Charlotte said. "But still, I should have known better."

Josie heard a high-pitched buzzing and tried to tune it out. She could tell Derek liked Charlotte, as did she. She was confident, personable, attractive....

"Would it kill her to wear lipstick?"

...and haunted. Icy fingers trailed down Josie's spine. She looked behind her as furtively as she could and saw a middle-aged brunette woman in an 80s-era royal blue silk suit, complete with shoulder pads, holding a martini glass in one hand and an unlit cigarette in the other. Her bangs were sprayed straight up, and she spoke with a strong Long Island accent.

"And that hair—it's so unkempt!"

"...and special events, where we bring in extra hands...." Derek and Charlotte were oblivious to the intrusion.

"How many people can you accommodate?" Charlotte asked.

"We're thinking if it's not a sit-down, about one hundred twenty-five."

"She'd be such a pretty girl if she just put some effort in. You'd think all those years in Hollywood would have made her less—what's the word—Bohemian. More glamorous. Her sister's the glamorous one."

"...my husband's schedule is a little unpredictable, but that shouldn't be a problem."

"Oy, that husband of hers. She should have married her college boyfriend. He's a doctor now. How are these two ever going to have stability? He works for this start-up and that start-up.... Here's an idea, work for a company that's already started!"

Derek and Charlotte looked at Josie, awaiting a response.

Sweat beaded on her forehead. "Sorry—what?"

"I just asked if you had anything to add." His measured response betrayed his fraying patience.

"No, no—I think you guys covered it all."

His eyes lingered on her a beat too long.

"Charlotte." Her voice sounded shrill. "Have you lived on the East Coast before?"

Derek arched a brow at Josie.

"No—lifelong west coaster. But I've spent a lot of time here. I used to come visit my aunt Shira every summer."

Bingo.

"*And over the December holidays. Don't forget the December holidays.*"

"And the December holidays," Josie said, ignoring Derek's puzzlement. "I mean, I assume. Where does Shira live?"

"Lived—she was on Long Island."

"*Massapequa!*"

"Massapequa. Sadly, she died when I was in high school."

"I'm sorry."

"She was a force of nature—always liked a party, loved her martinis." Shira held up her glass. "She's probably where I got my love of the restaurant world."

"*We went to the best!*"

"We went to the best ones—Quilted Giraffe, Côte Basque, Windows on the World—"

"*But we checked out all the new spots too!*"

"But we checked out all the new spots too. And the cool, off-the-beaten path places—Russian food in Brighton Beach, dim sum in Flushing."

"*With me, she dressed up.*"

"We'd get all dressed up—she was a very elegant woman."

"*I still am!*"

"I miss her a lot."

"*I'm always with you, bubbeleh.*"

"Oof." Josie sighed.

"What was that?"

"Sorry—I mean, I'm sure you do. But I believe she's always with you, somehow."

Derek shot Josie another loaded look. She avoided meeting his gaze.

"Yeah, it's funny, I've talked to a couple of mediums over the years, which of course I take with a grain of salt—"

"Of course."

Derek cleared his throat. Josie continued to stare intently at Charlotte.

"And every single one of them has said she's around me constantly."

"*I am.*"

"Constantly! That's"—Josie swallowed hard—"really comforting."

Charlotte smiled. "It sure is."

"Well, it was really great meeting you, Charlotte." Derek stood. "I have a feeling you'll be hearing from us."

"I mean, we still have a lot of people to see, but it was great chatting," Josie said.

After she left, they spoke over each other.

"She's really great!"

"I'm not so sure about that one."

"Josie, why? She's smart, funny, knows her stuff—"

"I don't know." Josie tried to adopt a casual and contemplative tone. "She seems like a very nice woman. I'm just not sure she's the right fit. Let's see who else comes in—our next interview's in twenty minutes."

She took a towel and rubbed at an invisible spot on the bar. When the silence stretched for an uncomfortably long time, she looked up.

He was staring at her.

"Okay." She exhaled with resignation. "I'm sorry."

He threw his hands in the air. "Let me guess, Sylvie got a bad vibe? Lana Turner's jealous?"

"Derek." She tried to remain calm but felt her ire rising. "If you want me to meet you where you are, getting mad at me for things that are out of my control is not going to help."

He folded his arms.

"My… whatever you want to call it is not going to disappear because you don't want to hear about it. It's not up to you. I need to figure it out, and until I do, I will try not to rope you into any of it. Okay?"

Josie paused so he could respond, but he didn't.

She drew a breath. "Yes, Charlotte is great, but she comes with… baggage. That aunt she mentioned? She was here. And she's a lot."

"Do you have any idea how hard it is to find someone who hits all the marks?"

The desperation in his voice tugged at Josie.

She closed her eyes and took deep breaths. "Yes, I know how hard it is to find someone great. And she was great in almost every way. But I'm telling you, if that aunt is around—"

"She was great, and she has exactly the right experience. Unless someone perfect walks through the doors, we can't not hire her because you have your whatever-you-call-it. We have a business to run. We make too many decisions because of your ghost thing. "

"My 'ghost thing' is real, Derek—"

She was saved by Naomi trotting down the steps from the kitchen.

"Y'all, that was some crazy spirit energy came in with that woman."

They both looked at her.

"It was like," she pantomimed choking herself, "I was being suffocated."

Derek puffed out his cheeks and exhaled. "I'm going to get some air."

Once he was gone, Josie turned to Naomi. "Thank you."

"For…?"

"For corroborating what Derek doesn't want to hear from me—that woman, Charlotte, came in *avec* ghost."

"Girl, you're lucky I'm me. How many people could you utter that statement to up here?"

"Not many, and that's one of the reasons I'm so grateful for you. Derek is not happy with me these days, and this kind of thing doesn't help. I was doing really well in not discussing it with him, and then that interview happened. He knew something was up when I hesitated on Charlotte because she was really great otherwise. God, I hope we find someone."

"You will. And when you do, I think things'll get better for you two."

"I sure as hell hope so. I miss him—the him I fell in love with."

The fifth candidate, a shaggy-haired fellow named Nick, arrived five minutes early. Josie chatted with him while they waited for Derek to return. Like Charlotte, Nick was a recent transplant to the city.

"Love Chicago but was ready for a change, so I decided to give New York a try."

"That's a big leap of faith. This can be a tough town for newcomers. I know—I was one."

Josie moved to New York right out of college and spent her first few years living with roommates, temping in corporate America by day while working for tips at highly trafficked cocktail bars by night. It was a tiring gig—most of the venues stayed open until 4:00 a.m.—and not having her own space was hard for her. Having had such a solitary childhood, solitude was her comfort zone. Her jobs required her to make small talk with and fend off the unwanted attention of over-served men with corporate credit cards. When she wasn't at work, she wanted nothing more than alone time.

When she turned twenty-five, Nanette gifted her money with the express purpose of her being able to live on her own. Her apartment in Brooklyn was tiny, but it was all hers, and she took great pride in it. She'd decorated it with wares she found throughout the city, jewel-toned bedding from an Indian shop in Jackson Heights, lush throw pillows from a Tibetan store on Greenwich Avenue. She'd always been good about keeping her space organized. Whenever life felt chaotic or unwieldy, this was one thing that remained entirely within her control.

"Well, I have some friends from college here, and I'm a writer. It's a great place for writers—tons of history."

"Absolutely! And this neighborhood is full of literary tradition. Have you been to Cedar Tavern yet?"

"No—what is it?"

"A cool old spot on University, a couple blocks from here. Huge hangout for writers and artists back in the day. There's also White Horse on Hudson—"

"Where Dylan Thomas drank himself to death!"

"Allegedly. Chumley's, Marie's Crisis—lots of literary ghosts roaming this neighborhood," Josie said, in part to see how he'd respond.

"Ghost writers?"

"Touché. Derek's a writer, that's why I know all this." She was so used to presenting him this way, so proud of his talent, that she forgot the topic was off limits. There were so many verboten subjects it was hard to keep track.

"Do you write?"

"No, I'm just a reader."

"Writers don't exist without readers."

"Well, that's not entirely true. Don't writers need to write the way runners need to run?"

"To some extent. But not gonna lie, I write with my reader in mind. What kind of stuff does Derek do?"

"I don't." Derek came up behind Josie, and she startled, the tips of her ears flushing. "Derek Magnus, former writer, current restaurant guy."

"Nick Halligan. Good to meet you."

Derek sat down, and the conversation morphed into an interview. His mood had improved, and things were going well.

Then Josie felt the tingling. She was stunned it was happening again, didn't understand why these visits were becoming so frequent, yet here it was. She closed her eyes. When she opened them, a pretty young woman in a 1997 Lilith Fair t-shirt stood behind Nick. She caught Josie's eye.

"*Oh, good! You can see me!*"

Josie sighed and muttered, "Damn it."

"What's that?" Nick asked.

"Oh, no. I just… I hear you. Been there."

"Well, yeah, I mean, it's got its pluses and minuses. Irregardless…."

Derek kicked Josie under the table, but when she didn't react to their longstanding joke, he turned to her, concerned.

She smiled what she hoped was a breezy, casual, there-is-totally-not-a-ghost-at-this-interview smile.

He turned back to Nick. "Did the place hold private parties or events?"

"*Don't hire him. Trust me, we dated for three years. He is NOT a good person.*"

Josie widened her eyes and looked from the woman to Nick and back again.

"*Oh, no no no—he's not a murderer. I OD'd right after the show.*" She gestured to her t-shirt. "*You think I'm spending eternity in an ill-fitting concert tee by choice?*"

Josie chuckled, then fake-coughed to cover it up, and they looked at her again.

"It was pretty serious," Nick said. "But we got through it."

"I'm so glad," she said.

"*He's in New York because his reputation in Chicago is shot—he's a full-on klepto. Stole from the last three places he worked. And he lies. He was never a manager. He was a bar back, then a waiter.*"

Nick was smiling now, a disconcerting grin that showed both rows of teeth.

"*Also, his writing? Totally derivative. He thinks he's Jack Kerouac. He's not.*"

"Well?" Derek asked after he left. "I thought he was pretty cool."

"He was nice." Josie searched for an excuse. "Do we have references for him?"

Derek looked at his resumé. "That's weird—it just says 'manager at top Chicago restaurants.' Huh."

"Huh."

Fifteen minutes later, their final interviewee came in. Stephanie Katz was a stylish brunette with short, slicked-back hair and dramatically lined brown eyes. She wore a navy-blue pinstriped pantsuit and white canvas sneakers. Josie said a silent prayer that she'd come alone and would be great. Unless this worked out, Derek would try to persuade her to hire Charlotte.

"My friends call me Steph," she said on introduction.

"Welcome, Steph." Josie gestured to the chair across the table. "Have a seat and tell us about yourself."

"Sure. I'm a born and bred Manhattan girl. Just moved to Bedford Street, so I'm in the neighborhood."

"I love that part of the neighborhood," Josie said.

"Me too. The BBC."

Bedford, Barrow, and Commerce Streets sat in the heart of the West Village and still boasted their original architecture. To Josie, they were quintessential old New York. The previous December, she and Derek had walked through the neighborhood in the quiet winter hush of a snowstorm, one that blanketed the cars and obscured the streetlights, masking all signs of the modern age. It was one of those moments she knew she'd remember forever—timeless and romantic—and she was nostalgic for it now.

"Where did you move from?"

"Brooklyn. Williamsburg. I'm a painter, and my studio's out there."

Derek scanned her resumé. "What made you leave Mary Franco Events?"

"Same reason I left Brooklyn. Mary Franco and I split up. But she's great at what she does, and I loved the work we did—everything from private dinner parties to huge galas. The relationship didn't work out, but she's an impressive woman. Built the company from scratch when she was in her twenties and grew it steadily each year. A lot of people don't last two years in this industry, let alone two decades."

"The fact you can speak highly of an ex bodes well for your ability to navigate the dysfunctional family of a restaurant staff," Josie said.

"I pride myself on my ability to work with anyone, to not take things personally. Best to leave that shit at the door when I leave for home. My version of *The Four Agreements*."

"I know that book!" Josie counted on her fingers. "Don't take anything personally, never make assumptions, always do your best, and—what's the fourth?"

"Be impeccable with your word, my friend."

"Right, thank you."

"So, what is it about our dysfunctional family you're drawn to?" Derek asked.

"I love the energy of this space. I've been here a bunch over the years. My parents had their twentieth wedding anniversary when it was *Blush!*"

"The infamous *Blush!*" Josie said.

Blush!, whose italics and exclamation point were an integral part of its identity, occupied the space in the 1980s and epitomized the decade with its Southwestern pastel color scheme and nouvelle cuisine.

"I'd also been to Bistrot a few times—"

"I thought you looked familiar!" Josie said.

"Yeah, I remember you. You look a lot… lighter. Happier. Is that okay to say?"

"It is." She looked tentatively at Derek, and he put his arm around the back of her chair. "I am."

"You guys are sweet. So yeah, I love the energy here, and I love New Orleans. I meditated to manifest my next gig, and *voila*—here you were in the *Voice*. It's funny though—I searched for your ad on Craigslist but couldn't find it."

"Yeah, we're a little low-tech here," Derek said.

"How are you with technology?" Josie asked.

"Pretty good, actually. I built Mary's website, automated her invoicing. I was a math and science nerd in high school, so I love this stuff."

"That's amazing. It's one of many changes we need to make here."

"What else are you thinking?"

"We need more traffic. We have loyal regulars, people we knew from Bistrot, but we're having a hard time getting newcomers. Or press."

"I took the liberty of reading up on your competition—other places with Creole and Cajun food, downtown spots with comparable price points, that kind of thing. Have you thought about live music?"

"Not really," Derek said. "We have a lot of mouths to feed as it is."

"Yeah, but if you got the right setup, it could be a huge draw. New Orleans is all about the music, right? You could easily fit an acoustic duo in this corner, move these tables back a few feet, have a happy hour, and bam, you've got a scene."

"Where do we find musicians?" Josie asked.

"I booked them all the time for Mary. Actually, I know these guys who would be a great test run—singer with guitar and bass. They play Zydeco, blues, all kinds of stuff. They'd be perfect."

"How much would they cost?"

"These guys—honestly, free food and drink and a tip jar would be fine."

"I wouldn't be comfortable with them just playing for tips." Derek shook his head. "And we don't have the budget—"

"We could figure something out!" Josie needed Stephanie to want the job.

"Just say the word and I'll reach out to them."

They talked for a few more minutes and before saying goodbye. Josie told Stephanie they'd have an answer early the following week. In truth, she hoped they could sort it out and hire her on the spot, but she owed Derek a conversation after her adamance against Charlotte.

"What did you think?" she asked when they were alone. "I liked her."

"I'm not sure. Something felt off."

"What do you mean 'off?'"

"I can't put my finger on it."

"Well, if you can't put your finger on it, maybe it's not there!"

"Josie, that's a pretty weak argument coming from someone who puts so much stock in the unseen."

"Fair enough. What if I call Mary Franco for a reference, then we take it from there?"

"I guess, but… I mean, this one's already spending money on a happy hour with live music?"

"She has a point, though, about New Orleans—music is a draw. Let me make the phone call."

She brought Stephanie's resumé back to the office, closed the door, and flipped through the phone book until she found her.

"*Mary Franco.*"

"Mary, hi, this is Josie Gray calling. I'm one of the owners at Miss Sylvie's Bistrot in—"

"*Right, the Cajun place in the village—*"

"Wow—yes, exactly!" She needed to play it cooler when someone outside the neighborhood knew the restaurant. She cleared her throat. "Do you have a moment?"

"*Yep, I'm stuck in traffic. Move, you idiot! Sorry.*"

"I'll keep it brief. We're hiring for a manager, and Stephanie Katz came to see us. She listed you as a reference, so I just want to confirm you worked together."

There was a confusing silence before Mary spoke. "*She listed* me *as a reference?*"

Josie looked at the resume. Mary wasn't listed under references—in fact, there were three other names there—only under work experience. But she talked about the work they did, so it was an easy mistake to make.

"She has you down as her most recent place of employment. Can you verify she worked for you?"

"*I can verify she worked for me, yes.*"

"Cool. And is there anything you think I should know about her as a candidate?"

"*Well, this is fucking awkward—pardon my French.*"

"Not a problem. You were saying?"

"*If I'm being completely honest, things ended on a fairly sour note, which is why I'm super surprised she listed me. But I don't want that to impact your decision because it was personal. I will say this—Stephanie is very smart and capable.*"

"Smart and capable—that's good. She said she built your website?"

"*She's very good with technology.*"

"Excellent, because we need that. Thank you so much for your time."

"*You're welcome. Just—I feel an obligation to say this as a fellow business owner—she's a people pleaser, and sometimes she gets confused about which people to please. But again, she is very capable, and I wish her, and you, the best.*"

Josie walked back to the bar where Derek was setting up.

"How was it?"

"She described Stephanie as very smart and capable."

He looked at the ceiling, then back to Josie and nodded. "Okay. What do I know about intuition? Fine—you can offer her the gig."

Chapter Four

Once Derek agreed to hire Stephanie, Josie was wracked with doubt, finally quelled with her powers of compartmentalization. Those powers were proving quite useful in protecting her from constant angst over Alex, Declan Kelleher, her relationship, and now Derek's misgivings about their new hire.

There were far worse traits than being a "people pleaser." Stephanie didn't come across as weak or malleable—if anything, what Derek had probably responded to was the fact she seemed so sure of herself, more a leader than a team player. This was a good quality in a manager.

This could be great for them because the pressure of the business was taking a toll on every aspect of their lives. Lately, there was no intimacy, a byproduct of stress and long nights, but now even affection had waned. Josie was optimistic they could find their way back to what they had, which had come as a surprise. Neither was an expert on relationships, and certainly neither had been in anything so serious. This was what Josie reminded herself when they argued—they were in this for the long haul and wouldn't disintegrate because of a fight.

When they first started working together, they became fast friends who occasionally crossed the line after a late night. They liked each other, but in addition to a shared love of jazz, movies, spicy food, and dark humor, they had in common an aversion to commitment. So they broke it off as quickly as it began, and it would take six years and one very strange summer for things to shift again. Josie was anxious to rekindle the blissful, early days.

Things remained tense through the weekend, but the idea of extra help on the horizon gave her hope. To do her part, she kept talk of spirits at bay and worked on being more present.

She spent time at Jefferson Market garden, meditating to channel Nanette's wisdom and strengthen the psychic blinders that would keep the spirit world from infiltrating hers. She had learned the previous summer it was possible to create boundaries, just as one would for a living person who took up too much time.

On the Tuesday Stephanie started, Josie and Derek met her for a late breakfast at a diner on Hudson Street.

"Let's talk happy hour," she said, diving into business.

Derek's jaw was tight, one of his tells.

"I reached out to the guys I mentioned, and they're available for an early gig Friday if we want to give this a trial run."

"How do you see it working, Steph?" Josie asked.

"I see us doing five to seven. Pick a red and a white to sell for half price, we'll do cheap pints, half-priced well drinks. I'll talk to the kitchen about doing some easy bar bites that we can offer—"

"This sounds like a hell of a lot of stuff to give away," Derek said.

Josie scraped her teeth over her bottom lip.

"We're not giving anything away," Stephanie said firmly.

"Wine, booze, food…?"

"We're giving discounts on alcohol and free food that's not the good stuff. Nothing that will ultimately impact the bottom line, I promise. There may be some trial and error, but I feel strongly, this is going to be a draw. People like deals, and happy hour is appealing for all the young professionals who live around here, students…."

"Not students." Derek slapped his hands on the table. "No underage drinkers."

"Of course not." Steph pushed back. "There are students of legal drinking age, grad students, and I'm assuming your bar has soft drinks too, right?"

"Right." Josie felt like a kid watching her parents bicker.

"Look, you guys hired me because I know what I'm doing, correct?" She directed the question at both of them, which Josie hoped was diplomacy and not defensiveness. She didn't share Derek's resistance to spending money for the possibility of growth, but she needed to respect his concerns.

Compromise, Nanette would advise.

"We hired you, Stephanie, because this restaurant is our baby, and we care deeply about what happens to it." Derek looked at her with unblinking eyes. "A manager *seemed* like a good move."

"Well, I wouldn't have taken the job if I didn't intend to care deeply about your restaurant too."

"How would we advertise happy hour?" Josie raised her voice an octave as she channeled her young self, interrupting her parents from the top of the stairs.

"I'll make up flyers to put around the neighborhood, in coffee shops, other places that will let me. And then a ton of word of mouth this week."

"Jesus," Derek said. "How much will flyers run us?"

Then again, Josie's peacemaking efforts had rarely worked in the past.

"One hundred dollars per flyer," Stephanie said with a straight face. "But I promise it'll be worth it."

Josie laughed louder than was called for.

"They're free. I used to do this for Mary. I have a kick-ass printer and a bunch of supplies. Just need something with your logo on it."

"I mean, nothing ventured, nothing gained, right guys?" Josie cringed at her own cliché.

He shrugged. "I don't know. Joze, if you want to, I guess we can give it a try, but no commitment for future happy hours."

"No commitment," Steph said, as a waitress placed their omelets on the table. She pulled a bottle of Cholula hot sauce from her bag, then poured a generous amount on her plate.

"You travel with hot sauce!" Josie was impressed.

"Always."

"A woman after my own heart."

"You guys want?" She held it out. "Most places only have Tabasco, and that's not my thing."

Josie handed the bottle to Derek. "My favorite is Crystal."

"Of course—the official condiment of New Orleans."

"Which reminds me." Derek shook some hot sauce onto his plate. "We need to order more. We move a lot of that stuff."

"Nectar of the Gods," Josie said.

"Order Crystal." Stephanie jotted a note on her pad. "On it. So what do I need to know about the crew?"

Derek sat back, trying to relax. He speared a forkful of home fries. "Josie, want to give Stephanie the rundown?"

"Sure. Chef Naomi is fabulous. You'll like her a lot, and she's putting together a great team in the kitchen. Jerome, Derek's right-hand man, is a gem."

"He's great," Derek agreed. "And it doesn't hurt he's a draw for the ladies."

"And some of the boys."

"Okay. A good-looking bartender can be an asset, as long as he behaves."

"Not that men in this business are ever held accountable, but he behaves." Josie took a sip of coffee. "Or if he doesn't, he's discreet. Waitstaff-wise, Lucy's the best. Twyla is lovely but exhausting."

"How so?"

"She's super into astrology and wants everyone to know she's vegan."

"We had to ask her to stop begging our guests not to order meat." Derek shook his head at the memory. "It was maddening."

"She's young. But her intentions are good, and she takes direction."

"Yeah, that won't fly." Stephanie made another note. "Who else?"

"Ian...." Josie looked at Derek. "Ian's a project."

He shook his head again. "He's your project. If it were up to me...."

"He's a very sweet kid who needs a lot of instruction."

"He needs a lot of the same instruction over and over and over. Talk about exhausting."

"Question." Stephanie held her pen up. "Why are you keeping on someone who's...?

"Totally inept? I ask her this every day."

"For one thing, young women love him too, which can be good for business. But more important, he tries, and to me that counts for a lot."

"Josie's a collector of lost souls." He meant it as criticism, but she liked the way it sounded.

"I get it." Stephanie chewed the end of her pen. "Mary was like that too, giving people second, third, nineteenth chances. It's a very kind trait, but not always a shrewd one."

"Exactly." Derek put his hand on Josie's. That this surprised her made her sad. "If the hiring and firing decisions are off our plate, could we make some changes?"

"Yeah," Stephanie said. "I have no problem taking that on."

"Maybe this'll be the week Ian pulls himself together."

"Maybe it will. But it won't."

He gave her hand a squeeze before letting go, a tiny gesture that gave her hope.

When they got to the restaurant, Josie brought Stephanie to the kitchen to meet Naomi.

"What's this?" Stephanie asked on the landing. She ran her hand over one of the chargers on the table. "This is pretty."

Josie hadn't had to explain in a while and blushed. "It's our ghost table—something I found in New Orleans and wanted to bring back here. A refuge for the spirits connected to this place."

"You really are a collector of lost souls."

"I know it's not everybody's thing. Derek wants nothing to do with it."

"I think it's cool. New Orleans has mad respect for the dead."

"Do you believe in ghosts?" It was a question she probably should have asked sooner.

"What's not to believe? Who are we to assume we know everything there is to know about consciousness and existence?"

"Exactly."

"I've never seen one, but I'm totally open to it. Maybe I should get back down to New Orleans. I love that town."

Josie pushed open the door to the kitchen, where Naomi was at the stove working on her gumbo.

"Thanks to this fabulous woman, you can get a taste of it any time you want. Chef, meet Stephanie."

"My friends call me Steph."

"Steph, this is Chef Naomi."

"Hallelujah, Steph!" Naomi gave her a fist bump. "We need you badly. These two crazy kids been trying to do it all themselves, and it damn near tore them apart."

"I'm here to ease the burden. And that looks like a hell of a gumbo."

"If I may say so myself. Oh, hey—Josie, is Eduardo here yet?"

"He wasn't when we came in."

"He'll be along. I have a real good feeling about him. The sous chef I just hired," she explained to Stephanie.

"My first-day buddy. What's his background?"

"He's worked in restaurants the past bunch of years, grew up in Arizona. Learned to cook from his mama, like me. Strong work ethic, knows his stuff. We had a ten-minute conversation about Dutch ovens."

"Okay, and the million-dollar question." Josie turned to Stephanie. "We've been having a hard time with sous chefs because of the ghost table, so Naomi has to vet extra carefully."

"Praise God, it's not an issue." Naomi clasped her hands together and looked up.

"How do you know?"

"I hinted this place might be haunted."

"How did you do that?"

"By saying a lot of people think this place is haunted."

"Subtle hint," Stephanie said.

"And I told him about the ghost table. He just shrugged it off. Asked about *mirepoix*."

"Excellent, my friend. Derek will be relieved, and I look forward to meeting him."

"I'm making a special staff meal to welcome you two tonight, Stephanie. Any allergies?"

"Just cats, Chef."

"Noted."

Josie led Stephanie back downstairs, then showed her the office off the dining room.

"We'll share the space. Derek doesn't spend a lot of time here, so you can have the second desk."

"I took the liberty of bringing a few personal items with me."

"Make yourself at home."

Stephanie wriggled her backpack off her shoulders, then pulled out a pink Himalayan salt lamp, a stress ball, a mug filled with pens, her notepad, and a Rolodex stapled with business cards.

"I know all this stuff is digital." She held up the Rolodex. "But I'm still old school with certain things."

"Not as old school as Derek and me." Josie nodded to the blinking answering machine. "Case in point. If you want to check those, the code is the last four digits of our phone number. I'll let you get settled."

Derek and Jerome were talking to a man Josie didn't recognize in the bar. He was in his early thirties with a build similar to Derek's—just under six feet tall, lanky and muscular. He was handsome, with dark hair, tan skin, and light brown eyes, and he wore a black bandana around his forehead. When he turned to Josie, he smiled, revealing a gap between his front teeth.

"Here she is." Derek put his hand on Josie's waist. "Josie, meet Eduardo."

"Eduardo, welcome! I've heard great things about you. Naomi is really excited you're joining us."

"Good to meet you, Josie." He held out his hand.

As she reached for it, the hair on the back of her neck stood on end. When she touched him, pins and needles shot up her arm.

"Eduardo comes to us from Flowers, in the Flatiron."

Derek furrowed his brow when he saw the expression on Josie's face. She took her hand from Eduardo's and tried to ignore what she was feeling.

"Yes, it was a great spot, a nice place to work…."

"*Help him.*"

She heard the woman's voice clearly and became overwhelmed by sadness. Plastering on a smile, she rubbed her neck and fought the tears stinging her eyeballs, waiting for their release.

"We're thrilled you're here, Eduardo." Her voice caught. "Excuse me a minute, guys."

Her legs felt like they would buckle at any moment as she climbed the stairs to the ladies' room. Once inside, the tears fell.

"What was *that*?" she asked aloud. The tissue box was empty, so she ducked into one of the stalls. When she came out, Ruby stood at the sink.

She would have to work harder on those boundaries.

"*Why are you crying, Josie?*"

"I don't know." She dabbed at the smudges of mascara beneath her eyes.

"*Is it because of the new guy?*"

"What do you mean?"

"*The new guy. Eduardo. He's sad, and now you're sad.*"

"How do you know he's sad?"

"*His eyes are sad.*"

"Were you downstairs?"

"*Just for a minute, but then I came back up here.*"

"Did you tell me to help him?"

"*No. Are you going to help him?*"

"I'm not sure how to." She put her hands on the sink and took long, deep breaths.

"*Are you mad at Derek again?*"

"Why would you think that?"

"*I don't know.*" She giggled.

"What, Ruby?"

"*You stopped dressing up and all.*"

Josie looked in the mirror and had to agree. She'd stopped putting effort into her appearance, reverting to the plain button-down tops and black pants that had been her uniform after Nanette died. At the time, she'd reasoned dressing up would be an affront to her sadness, which was deeply flawed logic. Nanette always looked beautiful, even in her final days. She'd lain in bed in white satin pajamas, her shiny dark hair tinseled with gray, olive skin barely lined after more than nine decades. Josie resembled Nanette's younger self and was grateful for those genes.

Now she was doing it again, letting her inner turmoil radiate outward. This needed to change. Derek deserved the woman he'd fallen in love with the previous summer. As her sorrow had begun to dull, she'd rediscovered the joys of dressing up, started wearing lipstick again—Charlotte's aunt would have approved. It wasn't coincidence that Derek's interest piqued as Josie started to care about her appearance.

"You're right, Ruby. I should dress up more."

"*You're so pretty when you do.*"

"Thank you."

"*I told Alex he can talk to you.*"

"Do you know what he wants to talk about?"

"*His mother.*"

"What about her?"

"*I'm not sure.*"

Derek was estranged from his parents and never spoke of them. Josie knew only the basics. His father was a captain of industry who immersed himself in affairs—both the business and extramarital varieties—after Alex died, and his grief-stricken mother spent her days in bed, shades drawn, a bottle of booze on the nightstand. He'd been essentially raised by the help and a much older sister when she was around, which wasn't often.

If Alex had a message about his mother, she'd have no idea how to convey it.

"If you get any details, will you let me know?"

Stephanie walked in and cocked her head at Josie. "Am I interrupting something?"

"Oh!" She waved her hand in the air. "No, I talk to myself."

"They say that's a sign of high intelligence."

"Or sheer madness. How's it going?"

"Good. I checked the messages. There were a couple of reservation requests, so I'll call back to confirm." She frowned. "Are you okay?"

"Yes, I'm fine." Josie wiped her nose with the tissue she was holding. "Allergy attack."

"Okay. Well, if there's anything else I can take off your plate, that's what I'm here for."

"I'll take you up on that."

Stephanie rubbed her arms. "Is it always so cold in this room?'

"*It is when I'm here.*" Ruby wiggled her fingers. "*Boo!*"

"No, not always. I'll talk to the guys about it."

Behind Stephanie's back, she mouthed, "*Stop it!*" then went back downstairs.

Derek was alone in the bar.

"Did Eduardo go up to see Naomi?"

"Yep."

"I think these two will mesh well with everyone."

"Josie, what happened before?"

"What do you mean?"

"When I introduced you to Eduardo, you got this really weird look on your face."

"I don't know what you're talking about."

"I don't believe you."

Determined not to cry again, she pulled her sunglasses from her bag. "I'm sorry you don't believe me, don't know what to tell you." She spoke with forced cheer. "I'm going to take a walk."

She dropped the smile as soon as she stepped outside. If Derek didn't want to deal with her "ghost thing"—his words—he had no right to try to force answers out of her. He was testing her and setting her up for failure, and if she failed, so would they. That wouldn't do.

They loved each other, and they were good together. They were just under extreme stress. Things would get better because they had to.

It was quite possible what happened with Eduardo was a figment of her overactive imagination. Between Ruby, Alex, the restaurant, and relationship stress, she wasn't thinking clearly these days.

She crossed Sixth Avenue, then turned the corner to the garden, where she greeted the volunteers at the gate. After visiting a few more times during the week, she'd begun to recognize them.

Most of the benches were occupied, but Josie's was waiting for her, illuminated by the sun like a beacon. Settling onto it, she closed her eyes, turned her face to the warmth, then concentrated on her breathing. She imagined herself inhaling positive energy, exhaling tension. Inhaling protection, exhaling chaos. She envisioned all the negativity of the past weeks melting away and evaporating.

Things were going to get better. She would make it so.

Inhale good intentions.

"You've got this," she said on her exhale.

All around her were the sounds of the city—cars honking, construction noises, people talking, laughing, shouting, an occasional dog—but she remained still, eyes closed, wrapped in her cocoon. She visualized it as white light protecting her, helping her to manifest the boundaries she needed. The sun felt good. This was her bench, her garden, her neighborhood.

"Excuse me?"

She opened her eyes. A woman stood before the bench with a notebook in one hand, coffee cup in the other, her face obscured by the sun in Josie's eyes.

"Do you mind if I sit?"

Josie moved her bag and jacket to her lap. "Sorry. Sometimes I forget I don't own this bench."

"You might want to reconsider. It's a nice one."

Josie smiled and closed her eyes again.

Inhale purpose....

"It's so beautiful here."

Josie looked at her. The woman had removed her sunglasses, revealing herself to be a striking brunette with prominent features—straight, shiny hair that fell below her shoulders, dark eyes fringed with thick lashes, an aquiline nose, and crimson lipstick. She wore a cropped leather jacket over a white tank top, jeans, and black Converse high tops. So many women in New York looked effortlessly chic. Josie just looked effortless. "It is a magical spot." She smiled and closed her eyes.

Inhale strength. Inhale calm. Exhale—

"Do you live in this area?"

Resigned to the fact she had company, she faced the woman and smiled. "I do. How about you?"

"I do now. I'm Ani."

"Josie."

"Pretty name."

"Thank you—yours too."

Perhaps this was part of Josie's spiritual work, being in the here and now, connecting with people. Having intentional interactions with the living might help her strengthen boundaries with the dead. Certainly making friends would stanch some of her loneliness, provide her with the extra mooring she needed these days.

"What brings you to the neighborhood?"

"An excellent housesitting gig for friends on Tenth between Fifth and Sixth. Across the street from Piadina."

"You're right near us. We live on Ninth and Fifth and own the restaurant Miss Sylvie's, just down the block."

"I've walked by it. It's a nice-looking place."

"I hope you'll stop in and try us sometime."

"I'd love to."

Josie checked the clock on the library's spire. "I should head back there, but it was really nice to meet you."

"You too, Josie."

"Welcome to the neighborhood!"

Despite the calm she felt as she walked over, Josie knew well a sideways glance or curt response from Derek could easily derail her. She needed a protective shield against his volatility.

He and Stephanie were seated at a table in the barroom when she arrived, and he looked at her with kindness in his expression.

"Hey, you." He held his hand toward the empty chair at their table.

"I need to go take care of a couple of things. How's it going so far, Steph?"

"Great. I've met Eduardo, Anthony, and Ling," she said, referring to a food runner and the pastry chef. "Derek's getting me up to speed."

"We'll introduce Stephanie and Eduardo to kick off our staff meeting, then let her take it from there, okay?"

"Sure. How are your kitten-herding skills?"

"Pretty solid."

Derek followed Josie back toward the office.

"How was your morning?" he asked when they got inside.

"Fine. I went to the park for some alone time, wound up meeting a woman, Ani, who's new to the neighborhood. Put in a plug for the restaurant, and she said she'd come by sometime."

"Nice."

"I'm taking our needs for more business seriously, you know."

"I know you are. Look, I'm sorry I said I didn't believe you."

"Okay."

"Joze, you know I love you even if we're arguing, right?"

"I don't know, Derek. Sometimes it feels like you've forgotten you do."

"I never forget. This whole thing is just—" He waved his arm around the room. "A lot. So many moving parts, this Kelleher situation is not going away anytime soon, and I'm stressed all the time. It's seeping into everything—I've been having weird dreams."

"About Kelleher?"

"Among other things."

"Well, the good news is you're not alone in any of this. Yes, it's a lot, but we're in it together. If you want to be…."

He pulled her toward him and kissed her. "I want to be."

Chapter Five

ADDING EDUARDO AND Stephanie to the mix made a quick difference. With a sous chef, Naomi could focus on the big picture, creating specials and refining the menu. A manager to keep track of the minutiae meant the ladies' room tissue box was replaced without Josie having to ask and a case of Crystal hot sauce arrived at the restaurant Wednesday morning. Best of all, Derek's wariness toward Stephanie abated enough that he let her take the lead on Friday night's happy hour. He was trying.

Since their first encounter, Eduardo had given Josie no red flags. Still, she remained vigilant.

"What do you know about him?" she asked Naomi.

"That he's fine looking. I mean, even Lucy commented, and she plays for the other team."

"Besides that."

"Besides that, I'm a fan. As for what I know about him, not much. He holds his cards way close to his vest, but he cooks with love. No formal training but good experience. Last job was at some joint in the Flatiron?"

"Flowers, which closed a year ago. Any idea what he's been doing since?"

"He made mention of taking some time off back home. Don't know why, but I get the sense it's kind of heavy. He's got this sadness to him."

"I feel that. Viscerally. Is it too much for us to take on?"

"No way. First of all, he strikes me as a guy who will leave that stuff at home, not bring it into his work."

"Compartmentalizing? I know a thing or two about that."

"It has its place. But second, even if he didn't, we can't discriminate against the sad. There'll be no one left. Everyone's got something."

Josie had no intention of discriminating, but if her empathy were to again reach the level it did when they met, it would be impossible to ignore. It was already proving to be. Knowing something was wrong and not being able to address it would be torturous. This had always been the case, which was why hearing indiscernible snippets of her parents' arguments was traumatizing and caused the malevolent magical thinking that it was somehow her fault—a feeling she hadn't entirely shaken. It was why the revelation after six years that Derek had a tragic past he'd never mentioned was hard for her to accept. She'd known he had something, knew his distancing himself from his family wasn't the result of a happy childhood, but she'd had no idea of the details.

It wasn't that she couldn't handle darkness, it was that she absorbed it and wanted to help everyone involved, living and dead. This was overwhelming, particularly when those involved didn't want her help.

Until she got to know him better, she'd have to stop trying to figure Eduardo out. She had uncanny abilities, but mind-reading was not yet one of them.

Before dinner service, she stood at the hostess stand looking through the upcoming reservations. Derek and Jerome added new wines by the glass to the chalkboard, the servers reviewed the specials, and the other porters did last-minute checks to make sure everything was in order.

Something compelled Josie to look in on her ghost table, so she climbed the back staircase, then stopped short. Perched on one of the seats was a bloated copy of the Nynex Yellow Pages. She checked the spine—1989. Someone had unearthed it from the basement, where they kept archival items they hadn't gotten rid of, like menus and cocktail napkins from the space's previous occupants. They'd cleared most of the junk out the previous summer when Bistrot was to be renovated, but Josie had felt a sentimental hold on certain souvenirs. To her, they were a way to honor the space's past. However, she did not recall hanging onto a dated phone book.

A prickly feeling crept between her shoulder blades as she recalled the phone books she'd sat on as a child in the homes of people without kid-friendly seating.

The book was on the chair she'd designated for Alex. According to Derek, his brother had been quite small for his age.

She pushed open the doors to the kitchen.

"What's good, girl?" Naomi looked up, spatula in hand.

"I'm not sure. Did any of you put a phone book out there?"

"Out where?"

"On the chair closest to the kitchen?"

"At the ghost table? I don't mess with that. That's sacred space."

"Me neither." Eduardo shook a colander of *haricot verts* under the faucet.

There were murmurs from the line and prep cooks. No one seemed all that invested in the matter.

Back on the landing, Josie looked closer at the place setting. The silverware had been moved about, and tiny fingerprints smudged the water glass.

"Alex, are you here?"

The air around her remained warm and still. She tried to think of what to say next, then jumped when someone called her name. When she leaned over the railing, she saw Mario, the head porter, holding a tray of glasses and looking up at her.

"*Qué paso*, Mario?"

A holdover from Bistrot, he was like an uncle to Josie. He wanted her to learn Spanish, a useful skill in the city and industry, and patiently corrected her attempts. She was getting better.

"*Tienes un visitant.* You have a visitor, Josita. Up front."

"Who is it?"

"*No lo se*—a man asking to speak to you."

"Be right down!" She looked back at the table.

Derek headed her off in the dining room. "Doctor Bannister is here."

"Why?"

"No idea. He's up front."

With a deep breath, she held her head high and walked through the room.

"Josie, hello," the doctor said when she approached. "My apologies for showing up unannounced. Perhaps I should have called first, but I was on the block—"

"Is there something I can do for you?"

"I wonder if we might sit and talk for a moment? Have a word in private?"

"I only have a few minutes before dinner starts...."

"I don't imagine this should take long."

Josie led him to the dining room, raising her eyebrows at Derek as she passed. He pointed from himself to her, silently asking if she needed his help, and she shook her head. She sat down in a booth.

Dr. Bannister took the seat across from her. "Josie, I'd like to apologize."

His halting cadence sounded different from his original demeanor.

"For?"

"For not taking you at your word when you came to see me."

It was far more than not taking her at her word. He had outright mocked her.

"I've never experienced what I did then, perhaps because I've never given much mind to the paranormal."

"I can appreciate that." She fiddled with a salad fork but kept her eyes on him. "However, I don't have the luxury to not give it much mind, as you may have realized."

"Yes, well, I realize it now, and what happened in my office was truly remarkable. I've since spoken with one of my colleagues—unlike me, Susan has always had a strong belief, and she explained it in such a way that even this stubborn old fool could start to follow."

Josie smiled. "I can't fault you for not understanding—I don't, though it's been explained to me in numerous ways through the years."

"I wouldn't say it's understanding I have either. More of an acceptance that there are things I *don't* understand."

"That's a good way to put it."

"I also wanted to tell you that I was very, very close to the grandfather who—what's the right term here?"

"Came through?"

"Came through, then."

"I understand. As I mentioned, I was very close to my grandmother. She was my anchor, and I miss her terribly."

"Are you able to have contact with her?"

"To an extent. It's not quite as literal as you may be thinking. But it took losing her for my abilities to come back after they'd been dormant for decades."

"I wonder if it might be possible for Grandfather Bannister to... come through... again? Because, you see, there are certain things, like the dog, only he knows. And there are answers to lifelong questions only he can provide. Do you think I could hear from him a second time?"

Josie tried to parse his question. "I really can't say. I mean, I can't predict when people come through for me. I'm not a medium."

"Aren't you?"

"*Aren't you?*"

She recognized the second voice as the man she'd heard in the doctor's office.

"No, I'm not. Mediums are professionals. They know how to focus to channel messages from the spirit world and can decide when and how to hear from them. And equally important, when and how *not* to hear from them. I'm not there. I can't control whether I'm going to hear from anyone at all, let alone decide who to contact. If I could, I'd be hanging out with my grandmother."

"Is this something you're interested in pursuing? Because, according to my colleague, there are all sorts of trainings and classes—"

"I don't think my relationship would survive that. What happened in your office alone caused a huge blowup."

"I'm sorry to hear that. If you think you and Derek might benefit from it, I'd be happy to recommend another therapist. I realize it wouldn't be appropriate at this juncture for us to work together."

"I will give that some thought. Thank you."

"Thank *you*, Josie." He gave her a smile so genuine it reached his eyes. He was handsome when he wasn't scowling or smirking.

"For what?"

"For opening my mind. I can be a right stubborn bloke."

"Well, you *are* male." Josie elicited a second smile. "Let me see you out."

Dr. Bannister nodded to Derek as they walked through the bar.

"You've done nice things with this space."

She stood in the restaurant's vestibule and watched through the window as he walked up the five steps to the sidewalk.

"Well, *that* was weird," she said.

"*Excellent work, lass.*"

"Thank you."

"For what?" Derek had stepped into the vestibule with her.

She turned around. "For encouraging me to talk to him."

"What did he want?"

"To apologize."

"For being a pompous ass?"

"More or less."

⸸

ON FRIDAY AFTERNOON, Derek had a meeting with the accountant he told Josie would get him to Miss Sylvie's in time for happy hour. She left the intricacies of finances to him as he had a better mind for them than she did, and he gave her the layperson's recap when there was something she needed to know.

While they got ready, she considered Ruby's observation and decided to dress up. From the depths of her closet, she extracted a vintage gold wrap dress she'd bought the previous summer and paired it with knee-high white suede boots.

"You look pretty." He ran his hand down her back.

"Just pretty?"

"You're always beautiful—that's a given. You're pretty in this dress."

"Thank you, Mister Magnus. You're fairly dashing yourself."

While she brushed her teeth, she studied him in the mirror and easily recalled what had attracted her when they'd first met, an attraction that came barreling back last August. He was handsome, if unconventionally so—light brown wavy hair that needed a trim, gray-green eyes, square chin, and a crooked smile she had always found sexy. In recent years, he'd developed crow's feet, which she adored—evidence that despite his pain, he'd done a lot of smiling in his thirty-seven years. And he was a deeply good human being, which made him all the more attractive. He was caring, smart, and an excellent problem solver with a great sense of humor—though one might not guess that from his demeanor lately. At his core, he was calm and pragmatic, where Josie had become a dreamy optimist, and when it worked, it was an excellent combination.

"What are you talking to the guy about?" She swiped mascara on her lashes.

"The general state of things. He's pretty conservative, so I don't know how he's going to feel about this thing we're doing tonight. We may be in over our heads."

"D, I think you're being overly cautious. Stephanie knows what she's doing, and we mark stuff up pretty high in the first place, right? So what's a few dollars off the price of drinks for one night?"

"That's not the point. One night isn't going to make or break us, but we have to think about the future. Kelleher is buying shit up all around us, closing in like Michael Corleone. If he makes the right offer on our building, he could quadruple our rent."

"Quadruple! Aren't we protected by our lease?"

"Josie," he said with practiced patience. "We have less than a year left on the lease we took over from Chef. No, we're not protected. Not even remotely, and quadruple was probably understating it."

"Okay, well, *irregardless*...." She waited for him to smile. He didn't. "Regardless, we've committed to tonight, so it's futile to lament it. You're taking all the happy out of happy hour."

"I'm not *lamenting* it. I'm being practical. Stephanie doesn't have the big picture, and not for nothing, but that's not really your forte either."

She ignored the dig. "What do you think of her so far? Do you like her more than you wanted to?"

"It's been three days. She seems pretty on top of things, I guess. I don't know. What do you think?"

"I agree, she's very on top of things. So maybe we can trust her on this?" She traced her lips with a plum pencil, filled them in, then pressed them together.

"Like I said when we met her, I can't put my finger on it, there's just something I'm not jibing with yet. Like we're missing part of the story."

"I think it's 'jiving.'"

"It's 'jibe,' as in agree. I love you, but you're wrong."

"Okay, Roget." She enjoyed the moment of levity. "Anyway, I like her. She seems like a pretty open book to me. Eduardo, on the other hand, is a tough read."

"Why do you need to read him? He's doing his job."

"I know, it's just—he seems like he has a lot of sadness. Naomi said the same thing."

"This is work, Josie. These are our employees. We've got to keep boundaries."

"I'm working on boundaries and just making an observation."

"I know you, and there's a fine line between 'observing' and 'trying to fix.'"

He wasn't wrong, but it irked her he was now monitoring her interactions with the living.

"Seriously, Josie—we have a business to run."

"Seriously, Derek, I know that, and I think valuing our employees and caring about their emotional wellbeing is part of it." It stunned her how quickly her warm feelings could dissolve.

"We don't know anything about this guy, and you're already worried about him. I saw the look on your face when you met him. I recognized it."

"No, you didn't. You don't know what that was, so stop assuming."

"Actually, you're the one who's making assumptions!"

"Derek. I'm very intuitive, and I can tell he's had a tough time. I cannot believe we are arguing again."

He threw his arms in the air.

"What do you want to do, tie him to a chair and make him tell us his life story so you can try to repair whatever damage he has? Live and let live. Stop trying to meddle and fix."

"Please stop policing me."

"I'm not policing you—this is ridiculous. Yeah, we are arguing again." He shook his head. "I'm going to midtown."

"Your appointment's in an hour!"

"I'll walk slowly." He mumbled a goodbye and left.

Josie groaned in frustration, so tired of ricocheting from affection to strife. "Damn it."

She dumped the coffee he'd poured her down the drain, a tepid act of defiance. He considered himself a connoisseur, selecting the best Jamaican or Sumatran beans he could find at McNulty's Tea and Coffee on Christopher Street, grinding them fresh every morning. To Josie, coffee was functional. It had a job to do, and she neither relished the taste nor appreciated its nuances. This was a departure from her otherwise sophisticated palate. Coffee was the one substance on which she and Derek had diametrically opposing views.

She emptied the rest of the French press, gathered her things, then left. On her way to Jefferson Market Garden, she stopped at her favorite bodega for her cup of choice—a large iced, light and sweet.

In the garden, she settled onto her bench and pulled out the book she was reading—*Tender is the Night.* On the rare occasions she made time to read and could lose herself in fiction, she was working her way through the American canon. Attempting to start a new chapter and utterly distracted by the disappointing end to her morning, she had to read the same paragraph twice.

"Damn it, Derek. Why do you have to do this?"

"Josie?" Ani stood in front of her, Met Museum tote bag over her shoulder and coffee cup in hand.

"Oh, hi! You caught me talking to myself." She flushed with embarrassment. "Nice to see you again." She moved her bag to make room, and Ani sat. "How are you liking the neighborhood?"

"I love it. Feels like home already. How's your week going?"

"How is my week going…?" Josie was too raw to lie. "Not well, actually. Running a restaurant is challenging enough. Running it with my boyfriend is a whole other level of tough."

"Yeah, that sounds like a lot."

"You have no idea."

"Have you two been together a while? Sorry if I'm overstepping, I'm not good with small talk."

"I'm in hospitality—I'm starved for real conversation. We've been together a year, but we've known each other a while. I knew relationships were tricky and running a restaurant was tricky, but the combination—" She shook her head. "Sorry. I've known you for approximately four minutes and am already airing my grievances."

"Please don't be sorry. We may not know each other yet, but I don't have a psych degree withering away in a drawer at my mom's house for nothing."

"Seriously?"

"Yeah. I thought I wanted to make a living out of listening to people air their grievances, but life took me in a different direction. Really, if you feel like venting, do."

Josie looked down at her ragged fingernails—she'd started biting them again. Talking about feelings was probably a better habit.

"I don't know, lately it feels like I have a roommate, not a boyfriend. A roommate who occasionally tells me he loves me. We can't get on the same page… I'm not even sure we're in the same book. We just had our, like, nineteenth argument of the week. Over nothing."

"They're always over nothing, aren't they? When really they're kind of over everything."

"It's exhausting. Do you have a partner?"

"Yes, but we don't live together, so I get breathing room."

"That sounds delightful. We're on top of each other, and I can't stop accidentally pissing him off. I love the guy, and I know he loves me, but this is not a fun stretch."

"Been there."

"And you're right, it is over everything—restaurant stress being the main issue. We have very different ways of viewing things. I won't bore you with specifics, but that's the gist of it."

"Can I offer some unsolicited advice?"

"I am very much soliciting it. Please do."

"When Steve and I argue, I ask myself what's more important—winning or getting along. Of course, that means I have to bite my tongue a lot, but it's usually worth it."

"I'll give that a try next time I need to, which will probably be in about twelve minutes. And then an hour later. And so on and so on."

"Been there too."

Josie pulled one of Stephanie's flyers from her bag.

"We're hosting our first happy hour tonight, yet another bone of contention. If you're not doing anything, come by. Live music, etcetera."

Ani took the flyer. "This sounds great. I have to be a bit of a homebody while I'm in town, but maybe I can come for a bit."

"This is a tough town to be a homebody."

"That it is. I'm writing a book, so I usually work all week and then go up to Connecticut, where Steve lives, late Friday or early Saturday."

"You're a writer? I love that!" Josie held up her paperback. "I'm a reader. Is it fiction?"

"Yes indeed. I'm working on the Okay American Novel."

"I'm sure it's much better than 'okay.' I can tell you're smart and insightful. Derek, that's my boyfriend—if he hasn't changed the locks—is a brilliant writer."

"He hasn't changed the locks."

"What's your book about?"

"If you're asking for plot, I have no idea. I'm much better at premise. It's a multigenerational family saga with a bit of time traveling, loosely anchored in my family's history."

"That sounds very cool. How's it going?"

"Let's see, this week we've run into each other twice in the middle of the day."

"You have to take breaks, right?"

"Yeah, I do. It's actually going pretty well right now, and I schedule these breaks to keep my sanity. Have to be proactive when it comes to finding balance."

It took Josie a moment to recall where she'd heard that phrase. Dr. Bannister. It was one of the wiser things he'd said during their ill-fated session. Being proactive was not always easy for her, and she needed to start playing the starring role in her life, being more deliberate about manifesting the things that were important to her. Right now, forging a connection outside of work was one of them.

"If you ever want to meet up on purpose during a break, I'm around. When I'm not at the restaurant."

Ani pulled a pen and leatherbound journal from her bag and tore out a scrap of paper, then scribbled on it.

"Here's my number. I have a great little backyard at my friends' place. Come by sometime."

"A backyard? How decadent."

"I spend a lot of time in it. The place is being renovated, and I'm there to keep an eye on things. If you don't mind construction, it's a lovely spot."

"I'm a New Yorker, I barely notice scaffolding anymore." Josie hoisted her bag onto her shoulder. "Maybe I'll see you tonight?"

"Yes—that'll be my motivation to make progress in the next hour. And otherwise, give me a ring next week. Anytime."

Josie left the park lighter than she'd arrived. Nanette would be proud of her for initiating a friendship. If she started weighing the serendipitous moments—brief levity with Derek, meeting Ani—as heavily as she did the challenging ones, the peaks and valleys that defined her life these days would seem less at odds with each other. She was off to a good start.

Feeling eyes on her, she spun around. A man stood just outside the gate behind Ani. With his baseball cap, beard, and mustache, it was hard to tell his age, but there was something sinister about him, even from this distance. He looked right at Josie, who turned quickly, heart pounding. Tears sprang to her eyes, bringing with them a surge of the sadness she'd sensed in Eduardo. Just as quickly as it came on, it was gone.

When she glanced back again, the man had retreated and was walking east on Tenth Street. She'd imagined danger where there wasn't any. All the conflict and uncertainty were making her paranoid.

She summoned those powers of compartmentalization and continued toward the restaurant.

Chapter Six

"THERE SHE IS!" Stephanie said when Josie came in. "Come meet the guys."

In the bar, two men were plugging cables into power strips. A guitar case covered in stickers leaned against a wall, and the enormous shell of an upright bass lay in front of the window.

"Josie Gray, meet Billy Duane and Hal Mundy. Gentlemen, the lovely Josie, who owns this place."

"Co-owns. Nice to meet you guys."

"Hello, Miss Josie." Billy took her hand and kissed it, which she didn't mind. "This is a fine establishment you've got here."

He had the southern drawl she loved and was rakishly handsome—black wavy hair spilling from a ponytail, soul patch, sparkling eyes. He wore a silk button-down shirt in a kaleidoscope pattern of blues, purples, and greens, and black leather pants. Hal was lanky, with kind brown eyes and dark blonde hair that dipped below his fedora. He had on a shiny blue sharkskin suit over a black shirt.

"I'm glad you approve. Who plays what?"

"Guitar for me, and harp." Billy held up a harmonica. "And Hal here's a monster on the bass."

"You're both monsters!" If Josie didn't know better, she'd think Stephanie was flirting. "Billy Duane and the Bayou Dogs—you're gonna love them, Josie."

"Today it's just the Bayou Dog." Hal tipped his hat to her. "Sometimes there are more of us."

"And every single one is fantastic." Stephanie giggled.

She was nervous, and Josie understood. The stakes were high for her with this event, and now Josie second-guessed whether they should be doing it at all, let alone on her fourth day on the job. But it was too late now, so Josie's role would be to champion her efforts regardless of the outcome.

"Steph tells me you have a taste for the music of New Orleans." Billy Duane licked his lips, rendering the comment more salacious than he might have intended. Or maybe he knew exactly what he was doing.

"I do—for all things New Orleans, as you can probably tell. We've tried to build a little slice of it here."

"You've done a fine job. And the menu's somethin' special—makin' me homesick just to read it."

"That's our amazing chef, Naomi. A native New Orleanian. Is that where you're from?"

"Not exactly, but close. Lafayette, Louisiana. I spent my formative years in Algiers Point," he said, referring to a riverfront neighborhood in New Orleans. "Hal here, he's a Yankee, a New York City boy."

"Born and raised in Brooklyn. Bay Ridge."

"And what about your fine self, Miss Josie? Where do you hail from?"

"Nowhere as exotic as Louisiana or cool as Brooklyn, I'm afraid. I'm from New Hampshire."

"Live free or die." Hal gave her a two-finger salute.

"Yep, official winner of the weirdest state slogan. But I've been in New York upward of a decade. It's home now."

"If you can count a place like this as part of your home, you're doing something right. What's your connection to New Orleans?"

Josie touched her fleur-de-lis pendant, and Billy took the opportunity to look at her chest. "My grandmother lived there for a bit and instilled a love of jazz and hot sauce in me."

"Your grandmother sounds like my kind of lady. I could see myself spending lots of time here, take away the blues when I can't get home. Get to know you some."

He was the quintessential frontman, handsome, charming, cocky, a little dangerous. It had been a while since Josie'd had this kind of attention and even longer since she acknowledged needing it. It felt good to be flirted with regardless of how disingenuous it may have been, but this would not exactly ease things between Derek and her.

"I'll let you guys finish setting up."

She walked through the bar, aware of Billy's eyes on her. Twyla and Lucy sat with Stephanie in a booth in the dining room.

"Everything good here?" Josie knocked twice on the table.

"Peachy," Stephanie said. "Just bringing the girls up to speed on how this is going to work tonight. Because if all goes well, happy hour's going to spill over into more covers for dinner."

"That would be fabulous. I'm looking forward to the music. The guys seem cool."

"Is he a Leo?" Twyla asked. "The singer?"

"I have no idea when his birthday is." Stephanie strained to keep a straight face.

"I bet he is. Or an Aquarius."

"Jesus, girl." Lucy had no game face and little patience for Twyla's obsession with the stars. "Stay on this plane for now."

"I'm thoroughly on this plane, Lucy. I just like to know who I'm dealing with."

"Okay, then—" Stephanie slid a piece of paper across the table. "Here are tonight's specials."

Josie climbed the front staircase to the ladies' room, where she scrutinized her face in the mirror. Making an effort paid off. She looked pretty, deserving of the attention she was getting. From her makeup bag she chose a shimmery crayon liner to touch up her eyes, followed by a second coat of mascara on her lashes. Her olive skin held remnants of a summer tan. She fluffed out her hair, its dark, beachy waves falling midway down her back. Sometimes it veered toward frizzy, but today it looked near perfect.

"Hi, beauty," she said to her reflection, then closed her eyes when she realized what she'd done.

"*Hi, Josie.*"

"Hi, Ruby."

"*There are some nice-looking fellows downstairs.*"

"Yes, those nice-looking fellows are the musicians playing tonight. Why don't you hang out at the table so you can watch and listen?"

"*Maybe. Or maybe I'll just stay in here and spook people.*"

"Ruby, please."

"*I'm just kidding, Josie.*"

Josie often tried to persuade her to leave the ladies' room but couldn't fault her for wanting to stay there. It was her domain. It was where she died in 1974 and where Josie encountered her in 1999. But it was problematic. Every now and then a customer would report strange happenings—unusual noises, uncomfortable feelings. Josie launched into her spiel about the building's age, old construction, and drafts often enough, she could recite the explanations in her sleep.

There was another reason she wanted Ruby at the table—to be there when Derek's brother came back around.

"Has Alex been here again?"

"*Yes, he comes by.*"

"I hope I can talk to him soon."

The door opened. Stephanie entered, then laughed when she saw Josie. "Holy smokes. You weren't kidding about Twyla."

"Would I kid about something as serious as what the bass player's rising sign might be?"

"You're funny. Hey, have you heard from Ian?"

"No." Josie sighed. "He didn't call to say he'd be late?"

"If he did, he didn't leave a message."

"Knowing him, that's entirely plausible."

"I don't know about that one."

"*I don't either,*" Ruby said. "*He's not a good waiter. Always flirting instead.*"

Josie ignored her while she and Stephanie primped. She reapplied her lipstick while Stephanie traced a perfect cat's eye onto her lids.

"You do that so well," Josie said. "You'll have to teach me your ways."

"Happy to, but I think you're doing fine on your own. Looks like you have an admirer."

"*Ooooh!!! Who?*"

"I bet he's like that with all the ladies."

"Not quite—he was definitely giving you some extra attention. But don't worry. Once he meets Derek, he'll back off. I think."

"Wouldn't be the worst thing in the world if he didn't. A little competition may be the spark we need."

"*Josie*!"

"Been there." Stephanie wrapped her arms around herself. "Jesus—it's freezing in here again!"

Ruby giggled, and Josie offered a tight-lipped smile.

"Wait—is this room haunted? Isn't that a thing, that it gets really cold when a ghost's around?"

"Steph, this is such an old building. It's been here for a century and gets drafty. I'd say we have more structural issues than ghosts."

Back downstairs, the guys were sound-checking with a riff of "Hey, Good Lookin'." Josie moved to the music, and Billy watched her while he sang.

"Sounds pretty good to me," he said when they stopped. Hal twisted a few knobs on his amp.

"Sounds great, guys."

"Miss Josie, want to come take a gander at the set list? Make sure it meets your approval?"

"I'm sure it does, but yeah, I'll take a look."

He slipped his guitar strap over his head, picked up a spiral notebook, then stepped around the mic stand. Placing his hand on the small of Josie's back, he leaned in. He smelled faintly of cigarettes and sandalwood.

"Now these two are originals, but you probably know most of the others. You seem to have good taste."

Josie's breathing shallowed while she pretended to read the list. "Looks like a great set!"

"I'm glad you approve," Billy Duane said, his lips so close to her ear his words vibrated.

"Josie."

Derek's voice startled her, and she darted away from Billy, which only made her look as though she'd gotten caught doing something illicit. "Hey, there," she said breezily. "Derek, this is Billy Duane and Hal Mundy. They're the musicians."

"No kidding." He nodded at the gear, then extended a hand to them both. "Derek Magnus—good to meet you."

"How you doing, man?" Billy shook his hand. "You've got a fine-looking setup here."

"Assuming you mean the restaurant, thank you."

To the untrained ear, it might have sounded as though Derek were being challenging, reacting with jealousy or suspicion. But that wasn't his style. He knew and said often that healthy flirtation was part of the culture in an industry that peddled food and booze and centered around socializing. Still, there was something about the look he cast in Josie's direction that felt different this time.

Fortunately, Jerome walked in the front door hauling big bags of ice, sparing her any further awkwardness. For now.

"Yo, D—this should be enough, right? Want to help me bring up the cases?"

"Sure." He nodded to the guys, then glanced quickly at Josie before ducking under the bar and following Jerome down to the liquor room.

"Is that your fella?" Billy asked.

"That's my fella."

"He's a lucky one."

"Yeah, well, he needs to be reminded of that every now and then." She immediately wished she hadn't said that.

"He shouldn't need reminding."

"Hey, Bill, you ready to hit?" Hal asked.

"Sure thing, boss." Billy strapped his guitar back on and winked at Josie before walking away.

The guys came up from the liquor room laden with bottles. To celebrate the kickoff, they'd decided to offer Prosecco as a happy hour special. They had a surplus thanks to a recently canceled engagement party for which they'd received a minuscule deposit.

Josie asked Jerome to pour her a glass. It was rare for her to have a drink on the job until after hours, but this was an unusual night, and her stomach was in knots. She ignored the puzzled look on Derek's face and walked to the end of the bar where Jerome placed her glass.

"Thanks, hon. If tonight goes well, we might make a dent in all this prosecco we've been sitting on."

"I think it's gonna be great." He poured himself a half glass and toasted her. "Cheers, boss lady."

"Cheers. Of course, with such short notice, we may not get much of a crowd this time, but if it goes well, word will spread, right?" She took a big sip of her drink and remembered she'd neglected to eat lunch.

"If we build it, they will come. Looks like they're already starting to. Check it—five o'clock on the dot."

"Wow. People really do love a deal."

She stashed her glass at the corner of the bar, where Jerome promptly refilled it and went to greet the first guests. The band started up, and people got drinks and seats. Stephanie flitted about, encouraging the complimentary bar snacks, which tonight included Andouille pigs-in-a-blanket, crawfish croquettes, and Cajun chicken wings. It did seem a fair amount to give away. Josie could see why Derek was wary.

Every time she looked his way, Billy Duane was watching her, singing to her. She found she didn't really mind.

At twenty after five, Ian rushed in frazzled and short of breath, his shirt misbuttoned in two spots and a purple hickey on his neck. Josie motioned him into the dining room so they could talk in private.

"Oh, hey, Josie. I overslept."

"It's evening, Ian."

"Yeah, I know—my roommates were having a party when I got home last night, and I stayed up way too late."

"You have to call when you're running late. That's protocol. We've talked about this."

"I tried the restaurant but got the machine, and I couldn't find your cell phone number."

Josie counted to five in her head. "First of all, Ian, if you call and get the machine, leave a message. Second, you should have our numbers stored in your phone. And finally, it's not me you should be calling now, it's Stephanie."

"But you're the owner!"

"Yes, and she's your manager, right? Please go tell her what happened. And pop your collar up—no one needs to see that."

He slunk away like a scolded puppy, and Josie returned to her wine.

"Looking good out there, boss lady!" Jerome shook a silver cocktail shaker and delivered a perfect pour into a martini glass. He speared three olives, then slid the drink toward a customer. "Enjoy!"

The martini drinker was a woman in her early forties, attractive with a wavy caramel bob, heavy-handed eye makeup, and far too much dark lipliner. Reflexively Josie rubbed her lips together, then held up her glass. "Cheers!"

"Cheers," the woman said joylessly, clinking Josie's glass.

"How are you doing tonight?"

"That's a loaded question. But this is cool." She waved her hand around the room. "Do they do this every week?"

"This is our first happy hour. Hopefully, it'll go so well we'd be foolish not to continue." Her smile was not returned. "I'm Josie, one of the owners here."

"Sidney Feist. I just moved into the neighborhood."

"You're the third woman I've met in the past week who's new to the area. What brings you here?"

Sidney Feist took a hefty sip of her martini, plucked an olive off the toothpick, then bit it in half. "I felt I needed a break from the Upper East Side after I walked in on my husband in our bed with the twenty-three-year-old dogwalker. Seemed like a good time to rent."

A couple standing nearby whispered to each other and walked closer to the band.

"Sorry for the bluntness. I'm kinda bitter."

"I don't blame you—that's awful. How long ago did you move here?"

"One week. Which means it's ten days since that fateful afternoon." She shook her head and plucked another olive. "I miss my dog."

"Jerome, take good care of Sidney, whatever she needs." She mouthed "water," and he nodded.

"Sidney needs a second drink." She held up her glass. "Soon as you see me get below the halfway mark."

"Josie," Derek called to her. "There are people here—where's Stephanie?"

"I don't know, I'm on it." She was grateful for the interruption from a woman well on her way to being overserved.

As she made her way to the front, Billy, who was singing an original song that included the lyrics, *Faisons l'amour, mon petit chou-fleur*—let's make love, my little darling—blew her a kiss, then launched into a harmonica solo. The zing to her stomach was both exhilarating and worrisome. It had been long enough she didn't know anymore where the line between harmless and wildly inappropriate blurred.

She looked at Derek, who was talking to a customer and hadn't noticed. Her mind jumbled and inhibitions fading, she could see the appeal in running away with a free-spirited musician—far more appealing right now than being tethered to serious Derek. It felt good to feel desirable. And desired. Not that she'd ever act on this. For better or for worse, she was loyal to a fault.

She went to greet the newcomers, whom she was thrilled to see included Boodles and Bulleit.

"Gentlemen! Welcome back!" She kissed them both on the cheek. "I thought you'd abandoned us."

"Never, honey!" Boodles said. "We've been soaking up Indian summer in P'town."

"And the Catskills," Bulleit said.

"And the Catskills."

"Well, it's great to have you here to christen happy hour with us."

"This is fabulous," Boodles said.

"Fab-u-lous," Bulleit repeated. "We needed this in the neighborhood."

"I mean, there are plenty of happy hours, but not a lot with live music." She glanced toward Billy, who was now singing in Sidney Feist's direction. "And there's only one Miss Sylvie's."

"True dat," came a voice Josie hadn't heard in a while. "Hello, Miss Thing."

"Curtis!" She threw her arms around her friend. "Oh my God, have I missed you!"

"It hasn't been *that* long."

"Long enough!"

Curtis Mitchell worked with Josie and Derek at Bistrot for six years, and the previous summer, he'd started to get cranky about being perpetually single and far from his goals. Like many in their industry, he had come to New York for a singular purpose—in his case, to go to school and become an interior designer—taken what was supposed to be a temporary restaurant job, and fallen into years-long inertia. The end of Bistrot had had a salubrious effect on many of its employees, though, forcing them out of stagnation and onto the next thing. For Curtis, this meant prioritizing his dating life. Shortly after the restaurant closed, he met a handsome, wealthy older man at a gallery opening. He and Henry, who owned the gallery in question, quickly moved in together, and Curtis enrolled at Parsons School of Design to get his BFA.

"You know I'm only a phone call away."

"Yeah, but you have a busy life."

"I'm never too busy for you guys. How are you lovebirds?"

"We'll talk. Come say hi to D."

Derek had spotted him and ducked under the bar.

"We're putting the band back together." Derek loved movie quotes, but Josie hadn't heard one from him in a while. The tiny act of familiarity was reassuring.

"This is something," Curtis said. "You guys look great."

"*You* look great." Josie cupped her hand on his cheek.

He did. He was a tall, Black man from Atlanta with the propensity to put on pounds when he wasn't paying attention. His frustration at being single had led him to a rigorous gym habit, then he met Henry. In love, he took care of himself.

"You do look great, man," Derek said. They talked for a few minutes until the bar got busy and Derek reclaimed his spot.

Josie held Curtis's hand while she surveyed the room. The music, growing crowd, and sounds of laughter and popping corks gave her hope. Maybe this was the start of something. They might not make a lot of money on this first go-round, but people were enjoying the scene and that meant they'd return. She tried to catch Derek's eye, but he was back to serious mode. It was almost as though he were intentionally avoiding her, but he wasn't one for pettiness or games. Then again, lately his behavior was as unfamiliar as it was unpredictable. For the second time that day, tears dampened her eyes, and she surreptitiously dabbed them away.

"Lady, your eye makeup's smudged," Curtis said. "Have you been crying? Do you need another hug?"

"No, but go introduce yourself to Sidney, the woman talking to Boodles—she *definitely* needs a hug."

She hurried up to the ladies' room, where the stalls were occupied by two girls barely out of college who'd been there for an hour. Josie had watched them sashay through the bar, seeking approval from the men they passed, and up the stairs. She wet a tissue to wipe at the smudges under her eyes and was about to head back down when the girls started talking.

"There's like, so many hot guys here. I want to meet the bass player."

"I like the bartender," her friend responded, and Josie mouthed, *Which one*?

"Which one?"

"I mean they're both, like, super hot, but I was getting vibes from the white guy—he's got this Ethan Hawke things going."

"No way—I think he's got a Jude Law thing."

Josie smiled at her reflection. If having a crush on Derek kept these girls coming back and maybe bringing their friends, she'd take it. Business was business. And despite all of her uncertainty these days, one thing she was certain about was that Derek was giving this young woman no vibes. He was a consummate pro behind the bar and equally loyal.

"I'm full from all those apps."

"They were so good. We're totally doing this again next week. We just saved like fifty bucks on dinner."

They exited the stalls at the same time and blanched when they saw Josie had overheard them. The one she guessed liked Derek was petite and very tan with straight black hair, her friend blonde and voluptuous.

"Oh, hi," the short one said. "You're the owner here, right?"

"One of them, yes. I'm glad to hear you ladies are enjoying happy hour. You should come in for dinner some night—we have a great menu."

"Oh—" She giggled. "Maybe next time my parents come to visit."

"Yeah, we're kind of on a budget? So we don't really go out to dinner? Unless it's happy hour?"

"All right then," Josie said with measured patience she wasn't feeling. "I'm glad you're having fun."

She went to push open the door, then called over her shoulder. "And I agree—the bass player and bartenders are hot."

She couldn't fault these girls. They were probably in entry-level jobs, and New York was expensive. When she was their age, she too gravitated toward bargains, the difference being she'd never have admitted to the proprietor of one of these spots that she was in it for the freebies.

As she started down the stairs, Billy Duane was making his way up. Her stomach fluttered.

"Hey, good lookin'." He stopped her mid-descent. "How we soundin' out there?"

"You guys are great!" She hoped it was dim enough he couldn't see her blushing. "You're not done, are you?"

"No, ma'am. Just takin' a quick break." He put his hand lightly on her waist, and she held her breath. "Listen, Miss Josie, if you ever need a friendly ear to talk about the problems you're having with your buck, I'd be happy to listen."

"My buck?"

"Your guy."

"Ah. Thank you."

"Anytime." He continued up the steps, and Josie shook her head to reset. This was definitely veering toward inappropriate, and she hoped she hadn't somehow led him on. She'd need to establish a firm but friendly boundary. It wasn't too late, but if they were to come back the following week, she'd have to do it fast.

At the sight of a tiny figure at the bottom of the stairs, she erupted in goosebumps. Alex. She had met him the summer before without realizing it, and then he'd shown back up when she first implemented the ghost table.

He was darling, with big eyes like his brother's and a mane of blond curls. He was dressed in a striped sweater and red slacks and clutching a stuffed bunny. As Josie rushed down the remaining steps, he recoiled in fright and ran into the dining room.

"Alex! It's okay—" She followed him, but by the time she got there, he was gone. Even in the dim light, she saw the landing was unoccupied.

She wanted to kick herself for scaring him off and scrambled to think how to fix this. How to fix all of it—Alex, Billy, Derek. She was surrounded by distraction, the wine hadn't helped, and she needed to refocus on her job before addressing any of it.

Curtis was seated next to Sidney, who'd reached the bottom of her second martini.

"Lady!" He put his arm around Josie's waist. "Will you please convince Sidney that there are plenty of fish in the sea?"

"Of course there are, Sidney! This just happened, you've got to lick your wounds. When you're ready, you'll get back out there and meet someone amazing. You're a beautiful woman!"

"I'm old."

"You are absolutely not old."

"I'm forty, for Christ's sake."

"Girl, I'm right behind you," Curtis said. "I'm not old."

"And wanna hear the kicker?" She was starting to slur her words. Josie nodded to Jerome, who shot soda water into a glass and slid it across the bar. "I turned forty a month ago. It's like I"—she puffed out her cheeks and made firework shapes with her hands—"reached my expiration date!"

"Well, that's nonsense, missy. I personally think women only get better with age." Curtis always knew how to make women feel beautiful.

"Me too, and I'm not just saying that because I am one," Josie said.

"One what?" Sidney held her empty glass toward Jerome.

"A woman. Are you sure you want another martini?"

"Yeah." Curtis eased the glass from her hand. "Maybe something a little less… gin? There's great bar bites here. Have you eaten anything?"

"Uh-huh." She held up a toothpick. "Olives."

"I'm making you a plate."

"Excuse me a minute, guys." Josie mouthed "thank you" to Curtis. "I have to run up to the kitchen."

She walked into the dining room, where less than a third of the tables were occupied, and ran into Stephanie.

"This is pretty great, don't you think?"

"The band sounds good and people seem to be having fun. I just hope we can turn the ones enjoying free food and cheap drinks into regulars who pay full price."

"I'm confident we can. I told you there'd be some growing pains. Trust me on this."

"I'll try to harness your confidence. Have to run upstairs, but I'll be back down in a minute."

"Is there something I can take care of for you?"

"No, thanks. I just have to ask Naomi something," she lied.

When she reached the landing, Ruby sat at the table waiting for her.

"I saw Alex."

"*I know.*"

"Did he say anything more to you?"

"*Just he wants to talk to you but doesn't want to spook Derek. I told him tonight is extra busy, so maybe he should come back another day.*"

"Thank you, Ruby. I appreciate that."

"*Someone can see me.*"

"Who?"

"*A lady downstairs with silver hair.*"

Josie looked out at the dining room from the railing. At a table in the center of the room sat an elegant couple, a man in a suit and a woman with an impressive head of silver curls.

"How do you know she can see you?"

"*She came into the bathroom and said hi and don't worry, I won't tell.*"

"Wow. Okay. I'm going to see who she is."

Josie walked around the room saying hello to the other tables before making her way to the center one.

"Hi, folks. How is everything tonight?"

"Excellent! My wife and I haven't had food like this since we were in Louisiana."

The woman gave her an inscrutable smile, then took a sip of red wine. Wearing a peacock blue kimono with silver rings on several fingers, she looked like someone who could see ghosts.

"I'm so glad you're enjoying everything. My name is Josie. I'm one of the owners here."

"I'm Philip Leventhal, and this is my wife, Dana."

"Very nice to meet you both. Do you live in town?"

"Santa Fe. We're here just tonight on our way to Paris." Philip beamed at his wife.

"Lovely! Vacation?"

"And business. Dana's giving a lecture at the Sorbonne on paranormal phenomena. She's a spiritual medium."

Bingo.

"How fascinating! I'd love to hear more about your work sometime but don't want to interrupt dinner."

"I'll leave you my card." Dana glanced toward the landing, then looked intently at Josie. "This place is something special."

Back in the barroom, Curtis had enlisted the help of Boodles and Bulleit. They listened attentively to Sidney, lips pursed in concern, heads shaking, murmurs of disbelief. Curtis slipped off his seat and came to Josie. "Wowza."

"Yeah, she's having a rough go of it."

"You are *definitely* gonna be seeing more of that one."

"God, I wish you still worked here."

"Honestly, girl? So do I."

"I thought you'd be happy to have moved on, working toward fulfilling your dream!"

"Yeah, yeah—that sounds utopian in theory, but I feel like a kept man."

"What do you mean? Henry's amazing! You guys are great together!"

"I know. He is great, and he's rich, and he's fine with me not working. And I feel like a kept man."

"You are not a kept man, honey. You're in school!"

"I wish I didn't have to rely on his generosity for every damn cup of coffee. Slight exaggeration." He pinched his thumb and index finger together. "Slight."

"Well, just say the word, and you can come work with us again a couple of nights a week." She gestured into the near-empty dining room. "It'd give us plenty of time to catch up."

"Maybe I will."

Over the microphone, Billy Duane announced they'd be playing their final song of the night. "But we will come back anytime Miss Josie will have us," he said before launching into Redbone's "Come and Get Your Love."

"Damn girl." Curtis growled like a dog.

"What?"

"Don't play coy. And he's hot."

She looked over to Derek who—arms crossed, jaw set—was finally watching the band.

Chapter Seven

HAPPY HOUR DID not, in fact, result in more covers, and the dining room remained sparsely populated. After making the decision to close early, Josie and Derek walked the block home in silence, the tension between them like a frayed wire. Neither said a word until they were inside.

"How did it go with the money man today?"

Derek's expression further darkened. "About as well as I expected. He didn't think happy hour was a good idea. At all. Calculated what a Kelleher buyout would mean in dollars."

"And?"

"It's rough, Josie. Rougher than I realized. We basically have until the end of the year to start turning profit or we're fucked."

"The end of the year?"

"Yes. That's three months from now."

"Well, a lot can happen in three months. We're surrounding ourselves with good people, people who care about us and our success because *we* care about *them*."

"Josie, for such a smart person, you're being incredibly naive about this. Kelleher doesn't give a shit that we're nice. He's a businessman."

"Yes, I know that."

"I need to get some papers to the accountant first thing tomorrow. More shit for him to tell us we're spending too much on."

Josie refused to let his negativity threaten her inherent sense of calm about the restaurant's future. Despite any second thoughts she'd had regarding the events of the night, she felt intuitively things would work out. With Nanette in their corner, there was no way they'd fail. She held her fleur-de-lis like an amulet and prayed for Derek to lighten up.

"We can't have a do-over of tonight."

"We were light on covers, but happy hour was great. Did you see how much fun everyone was having?"

"Free booze and food will do that."

"It's more than that, D. It was warm and festive, and people were socializing. It was like Bistrot in its heyday."

"Bistrot in its heyday had a waiting list for reservations. We had an empty dining room. This is a business predicated on sales."

"Yes, I know that too. But it certainly helps if people enjoy the place where they're going to spend money. Remember when Steph pitched this? She said it would be trial and error at first, but ultimately she thinks it'll translate into regular customers and turn a profit."

"Ultimately doesn't keep the lights on."

She started to respond, recalled Ani's advice about getting along versus winning, and held her tongue. Derek pulled out the kitchen trash bag to take down the hall to the garbage chute, something she'd meant to do before leaving the apartment that morning. Flopping onto the sofa, she noticed a tiny run in her tights, just above her boot. She pulled at it so it laddered up her thigh.

When he returned and went to the bedroom to change, she followed him, scavenging for something to say to reset the mood. She washed her face, then looked up to see him standing behind her in the mirror, leaning against the door frame. Flashing back to the days they were more than roommates, when he would wait in that same spot for her to come to bed, she smiled.

"Hi, you."

"Can I get in there?"

She stepped aside, embarrassed, and he closed the door. By the time he reemerged, she'd thought of an icebreaker. Ridiculous she needed one with her partner of over a year.

"I overheard some girls talking about all the guys there tonight. They're gonna come back next week. One of them mentioned how hot the 'Jude Law-looking' bartender was."

Derek smiled his adorable, asymmetrical smile. She'd conquered a tiny hill.

"I mean, Jerome's a good-looking guy, but I don't really see Jude Law." She smiled at her own joke.

"Speaking of good-looking guys…."

"Mm?"

"I think ol' Billy Duane is sweet on y'all, Miss Josie," he said in a surprisingly good Cajun accent.

"Oh, please. He was flirting with every woman in there. And probably some of the men."

"He was serenading you all night."

"Well, it's harmless."

"Then why are you blushing?"

"Wasn't it great to see Curtis?"

"Always."

"I feel bad he got saddled with Norma Desmond."

"Be nice. She's an excellent tipper."

"Did you hear her story? She's new to the neighborhood because she caught her husband getting it on with the dogwalker."

"Seems to be a dog theme happening here."

"That should help business, a boozy divorcée. Take that, Kelleher."

Derek smiled again, but this time it was flat and unconvincing. She regretted mentioning his nemesis by name.

"I'm beat," he said. "You coming to bed?"

Josie fell asleep quickly, thanks to the wine, then woke at 4:00 a.m., also thanks to the wine. During her summer of sorrow the previous year, she'd often woken at this hour and lain in bed yearning for her grandmother. Now when she thought of Nanette, which was many times a day, it was with a reflective sadness—anchored by regret that Derek never met her.

She worried working on those psychic blinders she was far from mastering would further distance her from Nanette, the last thing she wanted. Her goal was to hear Nanette's voice in her head when she meditated and know it *wasn't* her imagination, but she had a hard time trusting in that. Wanting to believe was one thing, doing so another.

Josie sat up and leaned lightly against the headboard so it wouldn't hit the wall. Her corner of the bedsheet had come unfurled during her restless hours of sleep, and she tried to pull it tighter.

As she told Dr. Bannister—and his grandfather—she was not a medium. She couldn't just contact Nanette when the mood struck, nor did she have control over how often Ruby or Alex or anyone else came through. People sought out mediums for answers and healing. What could she do with a message from Alex intended for someone who didn't believe in ghosts? Someone who would be anything but healed by hearing about his mother?

She slipped out of bed hoping to tiptoe into the living room. In the dark, she bumped into the nightstand. Something clanged to the ground.

"Watch it!" Derek shouted in his sleep. He mumbled incoherently, rolled over clutching a pillow, then resumed the low, steady breathing that would become a snore. He was both a heavy sleeper and a light one, which Josie wouldn't have thought possible had she not witnessed it on a regular basis. A childhood marked by his mother's erratic mood swings had left him vigilant to sudden loud noises at night.

The bedroom door reminded her it needed a few squirts of WD-40, but Derek didn't stir this time. Josie went to the kitchen and filled the electric kettle with water. While she waited for it to boil, she sat on the sofa and closed her eyes. Her body was exhausted, her mind wide awake.

If someone had told her a year ago what her life would look like today—that she'd see Ruby so often it barely fazed her, that Alex would be trying to contact her, that she and Derek would be in such a tough space—she wouldn't have believed them. The beginning of their relationship had felt so perfect, as beginnings often do. There was a way back to that feeling, and she knew what she needed to do to get there. She needed to stay calm when he was stressed about the restaurant, not take it so personally because it wasn't about her. And when his anger did feel personal, she needed to remember the source—the little boy living in trauma who had to constantly be on high alert and anticipate everyone else's emotional needs. Derek never shed that identity, he grew around it. Just as she never shed her misunderstood-by-most little girl but grew around her.

The kettle clicked off, and Josie returned to the kitchen. She pulled the "Goddess" mug Curtis had gifted her from the cupboard, poured water over a bag of chamomile tea, then leaned against the counter while it cooled.

Her feelings of being misunderstood as a kid were not helped by the realization she could commune with the dead. Nanette understood but that wasn't enough—this "gift" was not just scary, it was something else that made her *other*. There was plenty to set her apart from her peers in Keene, New Hampshire in the 1970s. A broken childhood home. A decidedly un-PTA mother. The fact she enjoyed music and movies from eras past—Billie Holliday and Jimmy Stewart—to the pop culture—ABBA and John Travolta—her classmates devoured. And her innate sadness, which stemmed from all of the above. Were it not for Nanette, her childhood memories would be fairly devoid of warmth.

Josie drank her tea and eased back into the bedroom. After she slipped beneath the covers, Derek rolled over and put his arm across her, pinning her down. The weight of his sleeping body comforted her.

Just as she began to drift off, she heard someone whisper her name and opened her eyes to darkness. Confused, she lifted her head but the room was still. She felt a creeping sense it was Alex reminding her he was out there, too shy to communicate with her yet.

"Come talk to me soon," she whispered.

Derek mumbled something in return.

On Saturday, the bar stayed busy enough Derek didn't obsess over happy hour. Josie weathered the moments of tension—of which there were plenty—as she'd intended. When she found herself waxing defensive, she visualized a childhood photo of him to remind herself of the little boy at his core. Of the fact he, like everyone, was shaped by the family he was born into.

They had in common a complicated relationship with emotion based upon two very different mothers. Derek's was prone to depression and histrionics, and he developed into a man with an aversion to feelings and a hard shell around his own. Josie's had her own hard shell—signaling emotions were weakness and weakness was bad—and her daughter learned early to pack away her feelings in a box, one she would only open in private or around the person she felt safest with. When that person—Nanette—left the earth, so too did Josie's ability to keep her emotions in check. It would take conditioning to reclaim that skill.

When they arrived at the restaurant Sunday morning, Josie left Derek and Jerome to set up the bar. As she made her way through the dining room toward the office, movement on the landing caught her eye.

Alex stood on the top step. As soon as she noticed him, he turned and ran.

"*Alex!*" she called in a loud whisper, taking the stairs two at a time.

When she reached the landing, he was gone. She swung open the kitchen door, yelping when she saw Eduardo at the stove. He startled and dropped a ladle.

"I'm so sorry!" She squatted to pick it up, but he'd already retrieved it and now stood inches from her face.

"Are you okay, Josie?"

"Yes!" Adrenaline coursed as she cycled through reasons she'd be in the kitchen. "Is Naomi here?"

"She's at the farmer's market. Is there something I can do for you?" He was smiling, his tone warm.

Josie felt ice-cold. "No, I just needed to tell her something."

"*How is he?*"

The voice came and went so quickly, Josie wasn't sure whether she'd heard it or thought it.

"How are you?" Her own voice sounded forced to her ears. "I mean, how are you liking it here?"

"I love it. Feels like home already."

He had an easy smile.

She feigned her own with quivering lips. "I'm happy to hear that. And I'm so sorry for startling you. I'll let you get back to work."

"No problem. If I see Naomi first, I'll tell her you want to talk to her."

Josie walked stiffly back through the doors feeling she'd failed. Now there were two elusive people in her life, Eduardo and Alex, both of whom she needed to help with no idea how to.

Brunch saw a steady stream of diners, never a full room but enough covers that she stayed busy and distracted. Toward the end of service, she spotted a young couple with a half-dozen picked-over dishes in front of them. The woman twirled her hair while the man scribbled in a notebook. Her suspicion aroused, she approached their booth.

"Hi there, folks. How is everything today?"

The man slid his arm over the page he was writing and looked at her with a self-satisfied smirk. "The *food* is good." His emphasis was not subtle. His date slurped through the straw in her Bloody Mary and blinked several times.

"Has something *not* been good about your experience?" She braced herself. They were seated in Ian's section.

"Well, since you asked, are you the manager?"

"I am not. I'm the owner. One of them."

He jotted something down. He was young, early twenties, in a Dartmouth sweatshirt and Red Sox cap—a pet peeve of Derek's, both the team and the fact he was wearing a hat at the table. The date was a meek blonde with chipped nail polish and an oversized sweatshirt emblazoned with plaid Greek letters.

"For starters, we had to ask our server for drinks three times." He wiggled three fingers in the air, and Josie cringed. "When he finally brought them, they were wrong."

"I'm so sorry that happened. How frustrating. I'll have a word with your server. In the meantime, your drinks are on us."

"And then my girl—babe, you want to say?"

She nodded.

"Go ahead."

She made a pouty face and spoke with a breathy lisp. "He brought me the wrong thalad. But I was tho hungry, I ate it."

"I'm sorry about that too. Of course, we'll comp you your salad."

"Full disclosure." Now the guy held both hands up as though being arrested. "I'm with CityEats."

Josie sensed this was meant to impress her. "CityEats."

"Babe—" He jutted his chin toward his girlfriend, still holding his hands in the air.

She opened her knockoff Louis Vuitton pocketbook, then pulled out a glossy yellow pamphlet. "ThityEatth."

"Okay. Well… welcome."

"We're basically Zagat, but hipper. Younger. Edgier. And"—he snapped twice and pointed finger guns at Josie—"we have a website. So this means you could be looking at your review as soon as next week. Which is why the service thing? No bueno. Right, babe?"

"No bueno," she repeated.

Josie squeezed her lips together and offered a wan smile. "Understood. I'm glad you enjoyed the food. We'll comp you those items, and I'll have a talk with your server about being more attentive in the future."

Ian was chatting up a trio of young women sipping mimosas at a corner table in the bar. He said something, and they giggled loudly. Josie looked over to Derek, who rolled his eyes and threw his hands in the air. She tapped Ian's shoulder, and he jumped.

"Oh! Hey, Josie."

"Can I talk to you?"

He turned back to the women and laughed self-consciously. "Uh-oh, the boss wants to talk to me!"

"Good luck!" one of them said, raising her glass.

Josie led him out of the room toward the front door.

"Ian, table five—"

"Oh, shit. The salad?"

"Yes, the salad. And the drinks."

"Yeah, I forgot to write those down. My bad on that. But the salad thing—there are like five different ones on the menu! If it were just the regular green salad, I wouldn't have—"

"There are two entrée salads on the brunch menu today. Frisée with poached egg and beet with goat cheese."

"Okay. I guess I thought I'd remember, so I didn't write that down either. Sorry, Josie."

"There's more to it. The guy is a restaurant reviewer. That's why they're here."

"Oh, jeez. I didn't know."

"You wouldn't have, but that shouldn't matter. This is a service industry. Every customer is important."

"Okay."

"Do me a favor. Go back and apologize for the mistakes. Tell them we're comping the entire meal—don't tell Derek—and if they'll give us another chance, we'd welcome them to come in for dinner, on us."

"Okay."

"And Ian, write down your orders, please. Every time. That's part of the job."

Between brunch and dinner, while most people took their break, Derek ran errands in the neighborhood, dropping off dry cleaning and getting an extra set of keys made at the hardware store. Josie stayed at the restaurant under the guise of having a chat with some of the waitstaff. In truth, she hoped a quiet stretch without others around would embolden Alex to look for her. She spent the better part of an hour sitting at the ghost table, silently inviting him to join, to no avail. This would require a lot of patience.

She gave up and went downstairs just as Derek returned.

"Hey, there. Did you get everything done?"

"Yeah. What were you doing upstairs?"

She pulled the elastic band from her wrist and scooped her hair into a ponytail, striving to come across as casual, unhurried, nothing to hide.

"Just waiting for Naomi. I wanted to ask her a question.'

She felt like a kid who'd been caught misbehaving and reminded herself this wasn't personal. Derek's aversion to the ghost table was not about her. It was about him.

That he wouldn't have to think about it were it not for her was beside the point.

"Why are you lying?"

"I'm not lying!" She followed him into the office.

"Josie, you've got a lot of tells—you're bright red, and you bite your bottom lip when you're lying."

"Well, why are you asking me questions you don't want answers to?" She asked it firmly, not defensively. "And why would I need to justify spending time anywhere I want in my own restaurant?"

He opened his mouth to respond, then closed it and remained quiet. After a moment, he said, "You're right. I apologize."

She tried to mask her surprise. "Great. Thank you for that."

"I just want to make sure you're okay."

"Why wouldn't I be?"

"I don't know, just, I want to make sure you're not grieving Nanette too hard and I'm being oblivious."

"Really?"

"Yes, sweetheart."

She believed him. More accurately, she believed this was one piece of it, that he figured Josie spent all her time at the table thinking about Nanette. His own model for grief was so askew, he didn't understand how normal it was to think about lost loved ones, how it was okay to reflect and feel your sadness. That grieving didn't have to look as dangerous as his mother's had or as avoidant as his father's.

"That's why it makes me uncomfortable, Joze. I don't want it to be this tangible symbol of your sadness. That's my intention, anyway."

"I appreciate that's your intention, but your execution almost always conveys anger and judgment, not concern."

"Doesn't intention count more?"

"In theory, but the execution is the part I hear."

"You're right. And I really do apologize. It's just, I worry you devote so much time and thought to people who aren't here anymore." He held his hand up. "I know they're here on some level, but I think you know what I mean."

"Yes. Of course I do."

"Okay, good."

"But I've been getting out there more. I'm talking to Curtis a fair bit, and that woman I told you about, Ani? I ran into her again, and she invited me over. She's housesitting for friends a block away during the week and in Connecticut with her boyfriend on weekends."

He'd pulled open the drawer to the filing cabinet and was flipping through folders, looking for whatever he needed to give the accountant. "That's cool."

Josie was fairly certain he had ceased paying attention.

"She's a writer, a novelist."

"Mmm." He pulled out a green folder and a blue one.

"So you guys have that in common."

"Cool," he said.

She was certain he wasn't listening.

He kissed the side of her head before going to the bar.

Ian slipped out for a break as soon as his last table finished—likely to avoid Josie, but she noticed. When he returned before dinner, she asked what had happened with the reviewer.

"I gave him the message, but"—he shrugged—"he's just the brunch guy, doesn't do dinner reviews."

"Okay. Well, we tried. And hopefully we learned something, yeah?"

"He did say they'd come in for dinner anyway."

"Oh, for fuck's sake. Of course he did. Don't tell Derek that either."

Derek would find out about the comped meals soon enough, but for now, things were better, and she didn't want to risk upsetting him. The restaurant had had a reasonably strong weekend after the lackluster turnout post-happy hour. He was being warm and affectionate. She felt connected to him again.

And yet, something was off. She could see it in his eyes.

She checked on him throughout the night, looking for clues. As usual, he was a professional and conveyed nothing on the job.

When dinner wrapped up, Josie stood at the bar chatting with Jerome while Derek tended to customers at the other end.

"How do you think Friday night went?"

Jerome drizzled olive juice into a martini—the "dirty martini" was having a renaissance—then slid it across the bar.

"Honestly? About what I expected. Decent crowd, we moved a lot of booze, didn't make a lot of money. But it'll get better."

"I'm so glad you think that. I wish he did." She tilted her head toward Derek. "*Señor* Moody over there."

Jerome laughed, and they looked at Derek.

He glanced up, broke into a huge smile, then called out, "Hey man!"

Confused, Josie spun around. She shrieked at the handsome, familiar face. "Johnny!"

Johnny Giardino was Bistrot's longtime sous chef. A tough-talking, streetwise Staten Island native, he'd spent much of 1999 espousing theories on the millennium bug, convinced when the clocks struck midnight on New Year's Day, the world would implode. Banks would lose everything, electricity grids would fail, airplanes would fall from the sky. When midnight came and went without much more than a ball dropping in Times Square and citywide drunken shenanigans, he had what he'd describe as his "come-to-Jesus" moment. He reevaluated his life, decided to follow in his father and brothers' footsteps, and joined the FDNY. He'd recently been assigned to a firehouse on Liberty Street in lower Manhattan.

"Hey, gorgeous!" He swept her up in a hug.

"I'm so happy to see you!"

"Likewise." He leaned across the bar and shook Derek's hand. "My man. Looking good, brother. You been working out?"

"When I can. Johnny, meet Jerome, my right-hand man."

"Johnny Giardino. Good to meet you."

"I've heard a lot about you, Johnny. Thought your last name was 'The Sous Chef.'"

"Used to be. What am I hearing about you guys rotating sous?"

Derek looked up from the drink he was pouring—a scotch on the rocks, Johnny's longtime libation of choice. "How did you hear about that?"

Johnny shrugged. "Small town. Word travels."

"Well, we were having a challenging time with it. Not anymore. We found a great guy." Josie avoided Derek's eyes.

"I was gonna say, I'm finally getting used to this crazy-ass schedule, so if you wanted me to check anyone out for you, I'm in."

"Where were you two weeks ago?" Derek slid his drink to him.

"Still getting used to this crazy-ass schedule." He held his glass up. "Cheers."

"I've missed you, Johnny," Josie said. "Are you happy?"

"Happiest I've been. Don't get me wrong, I fuckin' loved the Bistrot crew, but these cats I'm with now? These are my brothers." He thumped his chest twice, then held his fist in the air. "When you've been through the shit we have, the bonds are tight."

While they waited for the bar stragglers to leave, they reminisced about Bistrot and caught Johnny up on news about their former coworkers. After they locked up, he walked them down the block to their apartment.

"I'm happy for you guys, and I'm glad Curtis found someone too."

"So are we," Derek said, taking Josie's hand.

"What about you, Johnny? Is there anyone in your life?"

Johnny had always had his share of admirers, a group that grew in size as he took over the kitchen last summer during Chef's downward spiral, but he'd never brought anyone significant around. Josie had always thought that a waste of what she considered a great catch. He wasn't for everyone—he was rough around the edges and the conspiracy theory thing could be wearying—but he was kind, strong, and she had a feeling he'd be a loyal partner to the right woman. In joining the fire department, he'd added "intrepid" to his list of attributes.

Now he smiled almost shyly, something she'd never seen.

"There is." He spread his hands in the air as though showcasing a movie marquee. "Marie DiBenedetto."

"Johnny and Marie!" Josie said.

"Exactly. They used to tease us about that. She was my girl in high school, and I've been trying to win her back. It's kind of working."

"Keep fighting the good fight, brother," Derek said when they reached their building.

"I will."

"And please don't make it another two seasons before we see you again, honey!" Josie hugged him.

"I promise I won't. I love you guys."

Josie was so bolstered by Johnny's visit, she was surprised by Derek's quick return to the solemn, distracted mood that had confused her all night.

On Monday, he got up to go to the gym before heading in to do inventory. That this was a task Jerome could easily take on, freeing up an entire day they could spend together, was a suggestion Derek was not ready to hear. The bar was his baby, built exactly as he wanted. It would be hard for him to relinquish control.

Now that they had Stephanie, the few restaurant tasks Josie might have tackled on a Monday were out of her hands. At one point in her life, she would have treasured having several hours to herself. Today, she felt unmoored.

She rinsed the French press and coffee cups, put them on the drying rack, then walked around the apartment looking for more busywork. After making the bed, she set upon the clothing—all hers—piled on the chair in the bedroom, folding some and hanging the rest. In a jacket pocket, she found a tube of lip balm and the piece of paper with Ani's phone number on it.

Though Ani had told her to call anytime, and Josie knew it would be good for her to have friends outside of work, she could be shy initiating contact with people who weren't part of her restaurant world.

She twisted the cap off the Blistex, applied it to her chapped lips, then decided her hands felt dry too. A bottle of Kiehl's lotion was in the bathroom cabinet. Nanette had touted the importance of moisturizer from the time Josie was old enough to care about such things, and the habit had stuck. She retrieved it, then sat on the edge of the bed to slather on generous amounts, rubbing it into her arms and elbows and accidentally squirting some onto the duvet cover. After scraping up what she could with her fingernail, she was unsatisfied. Maybe it was a good day to stay home and do laundry.

No, this was the new Josie, the one with thicker skin who didn't take everything personally and could leap out of her comfort zone and make a new friend.

She unfolded the paper, flipped open her phone, then paced the apartment while it rang.

Chapter Eight

Ani invited Josie right over, and after a quick detour to her bodega for coffee, she headed to the apartment one block north of Miss Sylvie's. When she arrived, a pair of workmen in paint-splattered coveralls were seated on the front stoop taking a cigarette break.

"Here she is—" Ani came to the door as Josie walked up the path. "*Mi amiga Josie.*"

"Hola," Josie said, waving.

"*Hola señorita,*" the older of the two men said.

"*Buenos dias,*" said the other.

"No se si habla español," Ani said.

"Actually, *hablo un poquito y quiero aprender màs,"* Josie said.

The older man gave her a thumbs up. "Very good Spanish, miss," he said in accented English. He had kind, brown eyes and a chipped front tooth.

"Come on in, Josie. I'm so glad you called. It was perfect timing for a break."

"You must start early." Josie followed her into the townhouse.

"It varies. This morning's alarm was the garbage truck at five forty-five. Once I'm up, I'm up."

Ani explained that while the crew worked upstairs, her domain was the ground floor. Clear plastic tarp obscured the stairwell, and a drop cloth lined a path to the front door. From above them came the sounds of hammering and a radio playing. Even with the construction, one could see it was a very elegant home.

A workman shimmied through the tarp carrying a painting tray and roller brush.

"Buenos dias," Ani said.

"Hola." He gave Josie an admiring glance and nod as he walked out the front door. He was strikingly handsome, tall and broad-shouldered, with high cheekbones and a goatee.

"Is it hard to work with all the noise? And with guys who look like that walking around?"

Ani smiled. "Isn't he adorable? That's Hector. It's not that hard to work. The sounds kind of function as white noise. Sometimes I can't write if it's *too* quiet."

"Luckily, that won't be an issue in this town."

"No, it isn't. And it's kind of nice when the crew is chatting. It keeps me in the world of my book."

"How do you mean?"

"These guys are Latino, like the family in my book. I'm third-generation Mexican-American. I listen to what they talk about—people back home, their communities here, their *fútbol* teams. The specifics have changed over the years, but I imagine every generation that emigrates deals with similar themes. Found family and community, certain kinds of job opportunities. So every interaction I have with these guys is fodder. I'm constantly taking notes." She gestured to a coffee table strewn with legal pads and notebooks. "Anyway, let me give you the grand tour."

The apartment's ground floor featured a living room with a dark purple velvet day bed and goldenrod club chairs, a den with exposed brick, with built-ins lined with books and a rolltop desk, and an eat-in kitchen—a thing of luxury in the Manhattan Josie knew—with a farmhouse table and white wooden cabinets. A door off the kitchen led to a covered back patio and yard. It was a beautiful, eclectic space. A grown-up's apartment, one with good taste and ample resources.

They went out to the patio to sit at the wrought iron table.

"No wonder you love it here. It's great! Where are the owners?"

"They have a house upstate in the Hudson Valley. I'm living here rent free, which is amazing, to keep an eye on the work. It's a perfect setup for me."

"And the boyfriend in Connecticut? Steve?"

Ani offered a sad smile. "Keeping an eye on him too. He's a work in progress."

"Aren't they all?"

"How did you guys do over the weekend? I'm sorry I didn't make it by Friday. I'd love to see the restaurant and meet Derek."

"We'll be there. This weekend was a roller coaster, but I tried to follow your sage advice and choose my battles. There are just so damn many of them."

"Mostly restaurant stuff?"

"Mostly, but then it gets a little complicated."

"Tell me more."

It was an awkward topic to broach with new people, but Josie dove in. "What's your take on the spirit world?"

"On what aspect of it?"

"Whether it exists?"

"I one hundred percent believe it exists. I come from a long line of people who have the ability to communicate with spirits. That's part of my book, too, though lately I seem to have writers' block around the topic."

"Well, this is kismet. I have the ability too, and Derek wants absolutely nothing to do with it."

"Oh, wow."

"Yeah, I've had it on and off since I was a kid."

"Would you mind if I take some notes?"

"Not at all, if you think it'll be helpful."

While Ani went inside to get a notebook, Josie sipped her coffee and looked around the yard. It was enclosed on two sides by tall wooden fences and a third by a brick wall covered in ivy. A large ceramic planter sat in one corner, filled with red and magenta geraniums badly in need of water. In another corner, the broken figurine of a woman—dirty white marble, faux antiquity from the looks of it—lay on its side. Something metallic sparkled in a tree, and Josie walked across the yard to get a closer look. It was a string of purple Mardi Gras beads, like a message from Nanette. As Josie realized this, the scent of gardenia wafted through the breeze.

Ani returned carrying the notebook she'd had in the park, a chestnut, leather-bound journal embossed with the word *Write*.

"All right. Tell me anything you feel like sharing." She pulled the cap off a Mont Blanc pen and wrote the date at the top of a page she'd torn in half to write her phone number for Josie.

"Where should I begin?"

"At the beginning."

Josie launched into her backstory, how after her parents divorced she and her mother left Vermont and moved to New Hampshire to live with Nanette. Built at the turn of the century, Nanette's house was cobbled together from an eighteenth-century farmhouse and the surviving part of a paper mill that had been partially destroyed in a fire.

"I mean, how could it *not* be haunted, right?" Josie shrugged. "It's the perfect setting."

A labyrinthine passageway connected parts of the house and was rarely used in favor of the brightly lit hallways. Josie was intrigued by it and began to play there every day after school while her mother was at work and Nanette was downstairs giving piano lessons. She did this for months until the rainy day in June she met her first spirit. "It sounds so cinematic—a lonely little girl playing in the dark suddenly learns she can communicate with ghosts."

"What happened?"

"Nanette's downstairs giving a lesson, and I'm playing school with my stuffed animals. I hear footsteps, figure she's done teaching and coming to find me, so I call her name. Then I hear piano scales through the vent and am totally confused until this girl's voice starts singing behind me. I'm not confused anymore. I'm absolutely terrified."

Ani shuddered and held out an arm. "Goosebumps."

"I have never run as fast as I did down that hallway. I didn't tell anyone what happened. Hoped if I didn't talk about it, it would go away. Kind of how I deal with my problems today."

She paused, hoping for a laugh, but Ani was busy writing.

"Anyway, that was a one-off, and things stayed quiet for a while. A few months later, something else happens. Not as creepy this time, just weird." She waited for Ani to catch up in her notes.

"What happened?"

"One night, Mom and Nanette are cooking dinner. I'm setting the table and hear this knock at the door." She knocked on the table. "Clear as that. Not a branch scraping the window or the wind rattling or anything else. It was a knock. I go to the door… nobody's there. So I tell them what I heard, and my mom just gives me this look of pity. She did that a lot in those days because she thought everything I did was a cry for attention. After dinner, I'm extra sad because I'd been waiting in vain for my dad to call—something *I* did a lot of in those days—and feeling unlovable, exacerbated by what had happened earlier. Nanette pulls me aside and promises me she believes me, tells me she has it too. The whispers, she called it."

"Why 'the whispers?'"

"Because that was how they started for her. For both of us. These whispery voices—like the one I heard in the attic—that you could almost be imagining but definitely aren't."

"Did that normalize it a bit for you, that it was a bond with Nanette?"

"Not at all. I was already plenty bonded with her and didn't need this. She tried to convince me it was a gift, but it was too scary for me. Plus, she told me my mother wanted nothing to do with it, so that was another wedge between us."

"I take it she's a tough cookie?"

"More like a bitter cookie. She's mellowed out some. But I could only talk to Nanette about it all, and she taught me how to tune it out. It took a lot of practice, but I mastered it. Or so I thought. It all came back last year, after she passed."

She contemplated telling Ani about Ruby and Alex, but that seemed both too big to divulge and disloyal, as though she'd be betraying them, treating them like parlor tricks. Instead, she mentioned that Derek had a brother who died long ago and that this was one of the myriad complications in their relationship.

"He has a lot of unexamined pain, and he's like my mom—no interest in contemplating the spirit world."

"That's got to be hard for you."

"It is. Because where I was terrified as a kid, I now find it comforting. I still get freaked out sometimes, but it's just part of my life, and I accept it."

"Have you ever seen a ghost?"

"Yes. Several times now."

She described what happened during the manager interviews and, in hindsight, was able to laugh about it.

"How crazy is that, a ghost yenta? And a party girl? The aunt was a bummer because Charlotte was great otherwise and Derek really wanted to offer her the job, but I just couldn't handle that on a regular basis."

"Is it startling when they appear? I'm sorry for barraging you with questions—"

"Are you kidding? I'm starved for people to talk about this with." This wasn't exactly true. She could talk around the topic with Naomi, and Curtis was a believer, but it felt cathartic to tell the whole story of how it began and where she was today.

"It's not necessarily startling because I get these other cues just before I see them, like it might get really cold, or I get that creepy feeling in the back of my neck."

"Can you talk about the difference between a spirit and a ghost? My understanding is that ghosts haven't completed their transition because they have unfinished business on earth."

"Exactly. And once they complete whatever it is, however long it takes, they can move more permanently into the spirit world. And then they might not appear but can send signs. While you were inside, I was thinking about Nanette and got a whiff of her perfume."

"I love that."

"Me too. And I so appreciate this conversation. The more I can talk about it all with other people, the less likely it is to spill over into my relationship. But God, I wish he believed."

"Why is that so important to you?"

"Partially because it would cut down on the tension between us, but mostly because, like I said before, he's really never processed his grief. I get it, it sucks, but believing in an afterlife makes it much more bearable."

"Was he always aware of what happened to his brother?"

"He had no choice. It defined his childhood, which makes me want to go back in time and find the little kid version of him and just hug him tight. Sometimes now, when he's upset, I can *see* that little boy in him, and it breaks my heart."

"Poor guy. Both of them."

"I know. And by all accounts Alex was a great kid. Sweet, shy, funny, loved baseball...."

Josie zipped her jacket and hugged herself against the chill enveloping her. Alex was there, and this was an opportunity to get through to him, convince him she was safe to talk to.

"He was a wonderful little boy, and everybody loved him. They still do. Even Derek, who never got to meet him. That's his brother, and he loves him."

Ani paused, her pen hovering above the page. Josie was losing the thread. The air warmed again. She'd done her job.

"Anyway, their parents were obviously destroyed. The older sister wasn't in the picture much when Derek was growing up, though you can't really blame her. She was fifteen when Alex died. Apparently the mom had trouble conceiving the second time around, so here comes this miracle baby, then his life is snuffed out by a drunk driver."

"When did Derek come along?"

"Less than a year later, way too soon. He had a very confusing childhood because the way the other three responded to Alex's death was denial or worse, in the mom's case. The dad dove into his work—he was a pioneer of cable TV and traveled all the time. Probably had affairs. Mom was a wreck."

"Poor thing."

"She'd stay in bed all day, then come alive at night. When her husband wasn't around, she'd sob at Derek about things he had no control over—the war in Vietnam, the dishwasher malfunctioning, his father 'working late.'" On this, Josie used air quotes. "It makes me so sad to think about him trying to navigate all that."

"What a tragic environment for a kid to grow up in."

"I know. Part of why he's so particular about things is he grew up in chaos. He lived in his brother's shadow. At the same time, like I said, he loved him. It was like he had this guardian angel big brother he never got to meet."

"I get why you want him to believe."

"I think it can help us through the difficult times. Not just deaths. Breakups, major life changes—there are lots of ways to grieve."

"It's a universal part of the human experience. The one thing we all have in common."

"You sure you don't want to do something with that psychology degree?"

"Absolutely. That chapter ended."

"Well, you'd have made an amazing therapist. You have a very comforting energy."

"I get the sense that's part of your purpose too. You're a healer."

"I am?"

"Clearly. That's why you have a connection to the spirit world. That's why it's such a gift. And it's also probably why you're drawn to the restaurant industry. You've made a career out of providing a space for people to gather, be taken care of. You know better than anyone all the reasons, happy and less-so, people go out to restaurants. Doing what you do requires a ton of empathy."

"Thank you. I wish I could have articulated that years ago. When I first started in the service industry, my mother did her best to convince me it was frivolous. Once I let myself acknowledge I'm happy doing this work, my insecurity faded."

"I'm glad it did."

When a nearby church's bells chimed, Josie sipped the remnants of her coffee. "I should get to the restaurant and let you get back to work."

"Okay. I'm going to sift through all of these amazing notes and see what I can do with them."

"If you want any more details on any of it, just say the word."

Ani walked her back through the house, then outside, where the workmen were loading things into a van.

"Thanks so much for coming over. Let's do this again soon?"

"I'd love to come back and see you. This was great." She inadvertently caught Hector's eye.

He smiled, blushed, and looked away.

Ani nudged her. "Clearly, you are more than welcome."

Josie walked back toward her bodega, needing a second cup of coffee to power through the day.

As she waited in line, she felt a presence behind her and turned to see Sidney Feist, oversized sunglasses propped on her head, with a six-pack of Diet Coke in one hand and a bag of mint Milano cookies in the other. Her bloodshot eyes and blotchy, makeup-free face suggested she hadn't slept much the night before either.

"Hi, Sidney."

It took her a moment to place Josie. When she made the connection, she said, "Oh… I'm sorry, I don't remember your name."

"I'm Josie, from Miss Sylvie's."

"Josie. Right. Thanks for your hospitality the other night. I'm sorry I was messy."

"Absolutely no need to apologize." Having spent the previous summer anesthetizing her feelings, she could hardly fault a heartbroken woman for drinking too many martinis at happy hour.

"I'm mortified."

"Sidney, not a single person in my orbit would judge you for having a tough time with this and for doing whatever you need to dull the pain. Well, my mom might, but lucky for both of us, she wasn't there."

Sidney's smile gave way to her bottom lip trembling as her eyes filled with tears. She slid her glasses back down and dropped her cookies.

Josie heard, "*Grief*" when she bent to pick them up. "Okay if I give you a hug?"

Sidney nodded.

Josie put her arms around her for a few awkward beats. "I'm so sorry you're going through this." She handed her back the cookies. "Know you're welcome at Miss Sylvie's any time you want our company."

"Can I really show my face in front of your friends again? I feel so damn flawed these days."

"Believe me, once you get to know us, you'll see how beautifully flawed we all are."

Sidney took off her sunglasses and smiled. She was a surprisingly pretty crier. "I am so glad I ran into you. You have no idea how much I needed this right now. Thank you for being kind."

Josie walked the half block to the restaurant full of peace and purpose.

Chapter Nine

WHEN SHE GOT to Miss Sylvie's, Derek and Jerome were in the bar talking to a rep from Northern Spirits, their wine and liquor distributor. She said a quick hello, then went straight up to the landing.

She would not make a big deal of this, wouldn't try too hard. She'd simply concentrate on staying present and patient and hope Alex would appear again. Taking the seat next to his, she pulled her mobile phone from her bag. Despite the fact the whole world used them now, they were still a novelty to her, and she often forgot to check her voicemail. Now she saw she had two messages, one from Curtis, one from a number she didn't recognize.

"Miss Thing, it's me. I loved, loved, loved hanging with you Friday night and realize I need to see you more because you're my favorite person on this planet, don't tell Henry. Actually, you and my mama are tied for favorite people, but I digress. Anyway, I need me more Josie time, so let's make that happen. Love you."

Though it surprised her when he'd said it, she understood why Curtis felt like a kept man. His life finally looked on paper as he'd wanted it to for years. He was getting his degree and meeting all the right people, and none of this would be possible were it not for his wealthy partner. As best Josie could gauge, Henry was an excellent fit who offered far more than financial support, but money could be a sticking point in any relationship. Maybe coming back to the restaurant a few nights a week would be good for Curtis. It certainly would for her. And the way Ian was performing, there would probably be an opening soon.

She followed the prompts to listen to her next message, which began with a dramatic pause and the sound of a throat clearing.

"*Josie, this is your father....*"

It felt like a kick in the stomach.

Josie hit pause and fiddled with the butter knife in front of her. She'd not heard his voice in almost a year and was struck by the fact he'd identified himself as "your father" and not "Dad." When had that transition occurred?

Raymond Gray would call on birthdays and holidays. Even though he'd follow the script and say the things he was supposed to, there was a palpable emptiness to his words. When she had phoned to tell him about Nanette, he'd used pat expressions of sympathy, then quickly made the conversation and loss about himself.

She wiped both sides of the knife on the tablecloth to remove her finger smudges, then started the message over.

"*Josie, this is your father. I hope you're well. I'm calling to let you know Melanie and I will be in New York City on Wednesday for a couple of days. We'll be staying at the Sherry Netherland on Fifth Avenue and Sixtieth—*" Josie's stepmother said something in the background, her voice nails on a chalkboard. "*That's Fifth Avenue between Sixtieth and Sixty-First. We have several obligations and a dinner on Wednesday but should likely have some free time on Thursday.*" His use of the word "likely" was perfectly non-committal on his part, and quite typical. "*If you'd like to get together for a meal, give a call, and we can make plans.*" He recited his phone number. Melanie said something else in the background. He put his hand over the receiver, gave her a muffled response, then spoke into the phone again. "*Okay then, Josie. Bye for now.*"

When the call ended, she stared at the device in her palm. Amazing that this tiny thing could wield so much power, could bring decades of hurt bubbling to the surface. A person couldn't hide from the past anymore, not when anyone could reach anyone else at any time through something small enough to keep in a pocket.

She went to her address book, then tapped Curtis's name. When he answered, she said, "Hi, honey."

"*Lady! How was the rest of your weekend?*"

"A little better. We had a visit from Johnny!"

"*Swoon! How is he?*"

Though he knew Johnny was straight, Curtis had an unabashed and harmless crush on him.

"Great. He's very happy being a firefighter."

"Was he in uniform?"

"He was not. How was your weekend?"

"Ridiculous. Soft opening for the new show at Henry's gallery, and it was like a Who's Who of Who's That. New York socialites, art world darlings, Gucci heels, and Prada handbags. And that's just the boys."

"Speaking of ridiculous, guess who called me?"

"Patrick Moore."

"No! Jesus—bite your tongue."

Patrick Moore was a photographer with whom Josie had been involved the previous summer, until the day the wife he'd neglected to mention phoned the restaurant.

"Though this person does have a thing or two in common with him."

"Raymond Gray."

"Bingo."

"And what does Father of the Year want?"

"He and the step-monster will be in town this week, and if I'd like to get together for a meal, I may."

"How thoughtful. What are you going to do?"

"I have no idea. Nothing right now. I have until Thursday."

"When can I see you?"

"Whenever you want, but definitely Thursday if I wind up seeing them."

"It's a date. Keep me posted."

Josie hung up and closed her eyes, breathing in calm, breathing out father angst, willing away the sick feeling in the pit of her stomach. She would probably call him back. And if she did choose to see him, though she knew it was futile, a tiny part of her would not relinquish hope that this would be the visit that changed everything for the better. She was, above all, an optimist, despite the fact that in the nearly three-and-a-half decades he'd been her father, the one area in which Raymond had remained steadfast was his ability to disappoint.

On Tuesday, Stephanie was to lead the staff meeting. Derek insisted the three of them first have a conversation about happy hour.

"Don't be too hard on her," Josie said while they walked toward the restaurant. "It's not like she did this all on her own. We agreed to it."

"I know."

They were first to arrive and sat in the bar leafing through *The New York Times* while they waited.

"Let's hear her out before we start in on how we need to rethink this."

"We need to rethink this," Derek said the moment she walked in.

"Derek—" Josie put her hand on his arm. "Steph, take off your jacket and get settled. Then we can talk."

"Look, guys, I get that it seems like we lost money Friday." She dragged over a chair, then sat and pulled her scarf from her neck.

"That's because we lost money Friday." Derek slapped the table for emphasis.

"Yes, and I told you that could happen at first. Trial and error, remember that conversation?"

"Of course, I remember that conversation. I also remember saying I was not comfortable giving away so much shit for free and was concerned we'd take a big hit. I was right."

"As I knew you would be. People like getting things for free. But more importantly, and I mean this, the people who came in had a great time and realized what a cool spot this is. We had a scene going, guys!"

"We did," Josie said. "People had a good time."

"We have a business to run and investors to satisfy and fucking Declan Kelleher to dodge. People having a good time on the house doesn't do a damn thing for us."

"Actually, if I may play devil's adversary…." Stephanie said.

"Advocate," Derek said through gritted teeth.

"Advocate. People having a good time *will* do something for us. It'll translate into repeat customers even when it's not happy hour."

"We are not going to have a repeat of Friday."

"Nope, we are not. We're going to do things differently for this week's happy hour."

Derek raised his eyebrows and sat back in his seat.

Josie was equal parts impressed and nervous by Stephanie's audacity.

"Free apps were a major draw last week. Did you see those trays? They refilled them three times—bargain drinkers need something to soak up the fun, and we showed people how good our food is. We don't need to offer that much again, and not for free. How about we designate a server to the bar for those two hours and offer small plates just above cost? Four bucks for a couple of wings, six bucks for a combo, that kind of thing. Drinks wise, we were pretty generous last week. Two-for-one wine drinkers don't really care about vintage."

"Which is exactly what I told you when we were planning this."

"And you were absolutely right, so I'll leave those decisions to you. The one thing I will suggest is that you keep the drink prices what they were last week because that's the kind of shit people *will* remember."

"That's a good point," Josie said. "I mean, we can probably do that, right?"

"How many of these are we planning to test out before we decide it's not worth it?"

"Let's take it week by week. I think you might be pleasantly surprised by how quickly this catches on and how it *will* spill over into more business. Lots of crossover between the happy hour and brunch crowds, and it's a demographic that loves familiarity. You guys are a neighborhood spot first and foremost, right?"

"I like to think so," Josie said.

Derek offered a one-shoulder shrug.

"Cool. Also, the guys had a great time and are available again. Billy and Hal."

Josie avoided Derek's eyes. Instead, she waved to Lucy, who had just gotten to the restaurant, thus sparing any further conversation about Billy Duane and his Bayou Dogs.

Derek was uncharacteristically quiet while the staff trickled in, likely chagrined by Stephanie's forthrightness. To Josie's mind, she had handled her end of the conversation perfectly, acquiescing as needed while still holding firm.

"Okay, gang," Stephanie said once everyone was seated. "Derek and Josie have officially handed me the reins for these weekly meetings. Today, I want to go over my 'ten commandments of being a good server.' I've printed them out for each of you, so please look them over and commit them to memory."

She passed around slips of paper and offered them to Josie, who took one, and Derek, who didn't. Instead, he stood behind the bar with his arms crossed, observing.

"The first four commandments are from one of my favorite books—anyone besides Josie and me read *The Four Agreements*?"

Blank looks crossed over the crowd.

"I think my mom did," someone said.

"Highly recommend. Twyla, will you read them aloud? One through four."

"Be impeccable with your word," she read. "Don't take anything personally. Never make assumptions. Always do your best."

"Thank you. Questions?"

"What does impeccable with your word mean?" Ian asked.

"Good. What it means in the book is slightly different from what it means in the context of our work, so let's focus on that. Here, I mean choose your words carefully and with tact. If a customer asks about a dish that's not your favorite, spin your response. Say it's very popular or it's new, and you haven't tried it yet."

"You mean lie. I'm not very good at that. I'm a Sag."

"It's not really a lie, Twyla. Well, it's a white lie. We all know Naomi's food is excellent, but sometimes it's a matter of taste. Your preferences should never enter into the equation when we're trying to sell food."

"This isn't news, guys," Josie said. "It was part of your training, just phrased a bit differently."

"Exactly," Stephanie said. "It's nothing you don't already know, but I think it's helpful to see it written out. The other three are, I hope, self-explanatory. Moving on to number five—be a team player. We're all in this together, so let's help each other out. If one of us is in the weeds, the rest of us can pitch in and keep an eye on their section. A table shouldn't have to ask for water—or anything—more than once,"

"They shouldn't have to ask for water at all," Derek said. "Still, sparkling, tap—that should be your first question."

"Not 'how are you tonight?'" Twyla asked.

Lucy groaned audibly.

"It should be your first service-related question," Stephanie said. "Of course, you always greet them first."

Ian raised his hand. "Isn't it the busboys who pour the water?"

"It's whoever notices a glass is empty. If you see someone trying to get a server's attention, I don't care if it's clear across the room, you check on them. Every one of us represents the restaurant in its entirety."

Josie surveyed the group. Ian looked worried, Twyla confused, Lucy bored, and everyone else a combination of the three. This was serving 101, and while she'd thought she and Derek had ingrained it all into the staff, it was evident many of them needed to review the basics.

"Six—aperitifs. Within three minutes of being seated, water glasses should be full and drink orders placed. Twyla, you have a question?"

"What if they don't drink?"

Lucy groaned again. "Come *on*, girl!"

"Well, I'm sorry, Lucy," she said snippily. "But I don't want to tempt anyone into falling off the wagon."

"Twyla, dear." Stephanie was good at feigning patience. "This is not something you need to concern yourself with. Sober people dining out know how to navigate these questions, and the drink doesn't have to be a cocktail. Club soda with lime, Diet Coke, whatever people like to start off with is an aperitif. Seven, piggybacking on that, remember people's preferences. I can't stress this enough—this is what separates a fifteen percent tip from a twenty-plus, and what makes for return customers. People want to feel like VIPs, so remember names, table of choice, dietary restrictions, favorite cocktail. However—and this is important, see number three—never make assumptions. How do those two relate?"

"Easy," said Lucy, who excelled at remembering people's preferences. "Would you like a Bombay martini? Not, I had them make you a Bombay martini. Acknowledge that you know what they like, but give them the chance to try something new."

"Exactly. Brava. Eight, push the wine that's already open. This should be a no-brainer at this point."

Josie looked at Ian, who was tapping out a text message. "Ian, are you listening?"

He shut his phone and looked up.

"We've gone over this one a lot, guys."

"And it still bears repeating," Derek said in a game show announcer's voice.

"Nine, when you walk through that door, leave the rest of your life outside. We all have bad days and stress, but when you come to work, you're here to do a job. You're here to make sure everyone who joins us for a drink or dinner has a night of flawless service. *Capisce*?"

"*Capisce*," Lucy said.

"Ten, and this is the most important of all—if you retain only one of these commandments, make it this one."

"Make it all of them," Derek said.

"Right, but if you can master this, the rest will follow. Number ten—read the room. Read the nonverbal cues. When menus are closed, take the order. When a plate's pushed to the side, clear it. If someone is barely touching their food, ask if everything is all right and be prepared to offer a replacement."

"Sparingly," Derek said. "We're not a buffet."

His combativeness was wearing on Josie. "Luckily, the kitchen's so good this shouldn't be an issue. Please continue, Steph."

"If people are locked in intense conversation, don't interrupt. If a customer's had too much to drink, get them water. Your job—all of our jobs—is to give the customer the kind of night they want. So what does that look like? Vibe off them. Do they want you to be their pal or the help? Do they want an order-taker or an entertainer? It's not hard to figure out, and you guys wouldn't be in this line of work if you weren't good with people. How does all of this sound?"

"Basic," said Lucy.

Others murmured in agreement.

"Intuitive," said Twyla.

"It's a shit ton to remember," said Ian.

"That's why I made these cheat sheets. It's all on there. We open in twenty. Bring your A-games tonight, gang."

While everyone got ready for dinner—the servers memorizing the specials, Mario and his team running last-minute checks—Ian sat at a table in the dining room studying the list of commandments.

Josie relayed this to Derek. "He's taking it seriously, at least."

"The guy needs 'be a team player' in writing."

"I know," she said sadly. "What did you think of Steph's presentation?"

"It was pretty pedantic, but obviously some of these kids need it. Hopefully, it gave her some insight into the staff."

"Yeah, I have a feeling I'm going to be outnumbered where Ian is concerned."

"I have the same feeling. I'm still on the fence about Stephanie, but she is smart. She knows he's dead weight."

"I hate that. I really wanted him to figure it out."

"You gave him multiple chances, baby. Way more than most people would have. But enough is enough—we're running a business here, and the Ian Project has taken up too much time already. I think when we let him go, we can do it in good conscience. He'll find something else—he's handsome, likable, and we'll word our referral judiciously."

"Well, we can't fire him when he's actually making an effort. If there's another incident...."

"There will be another incident."

Throughout the night, Josie watched the staff for signs of improvement. What she saw was a lot more interaction with customers, fewer empty water glasses, and everyone pitching in more than the norm, which had Lucy scrambling to pick up the slack.

As Josie wended her way through the dining room, she passed two young couples seated in a booth with a high chair at the end of the table. Its occupant was an adorable Asian toddler with spiky black pigtails who was feasting on a bowl of noodles and green beans. She greeted the table. "I hope you're all enjoying dinner."

"It's wonderful," one of the women said. "I want the recipe for these shrimp beignets."

"I'll let Chef know they're a hit. She's just added them to the menu. And who is this little one?"

"This is Beatrice. She gives this place a rave review too!"

The little girl scooped up a handful of beans, then craned her body and started giggling and waving behind her. Josie's neck tingled as she followed her gaze.

Ruby and Alex stood at the railing looking down on the room.

"She makes friends everywhere we go," the father said. "Even imaginary ones. Who are you waving to, Cookie?"

"Hi hi hi!" she called, pumping her hand up and down.

Ruby motioned Josie to come upstairs.

Josie turned back to the table. "She's darling. Enjoy the rest of your dinner."

She trotted swiftly up the steps to them.

Alex clung to Ruby with one hand, his other arm hugging his stuffed bunny.

"*Thank you, Josie.*" Ruby sat, then scooped him onto her lap.

Josie sat facing the kitchen door, her back to the dining room. "Hi, Alex."

He was a beautiful child. It was like looking into the past and seeing his brother at this age. Derek's hair had been blonde too, and Alex had the same full lips and gray-green eyes. He looked at her now with more curiosity than fear.

"Thank you for letting me sit with you."

"*Go ahead, Alex. You can talk to Josie.*"

The kitchen doors swung open, and Anthony, a food runner, walked out balancing a silver tray laden with dishes.

"Hey, Josie. Whatcha doing?"

He was a talkative kid from Bay Ridge, Brooklyn, with a thick accent and a penchant for exaggerating. Josie found him endearing, in part because he reminded her of Johnny, the former sous chef.

"Just taking a breather." It was risky for her to be there during dinner, and this was the best she could come up with.

"We're sitting on five gallons of jambalaya if you want some." He trotted down the steps.

"Let's go to the office for some privacy," Josie said.

Ruby held Alex's hand as they followed her down the stairs, then through the dining room.

Baby Beatrice watched them and clapped her hands to the amusement of the adults at the table.

"She's smitten with you!" her mother said as they passed.

As Josie understood it, children that young were still receptive to seeing spirits. Everyone was born with the ability, but the more developed the rational mind and five primary senses became, the further removed many people got from it all.

Josie closed the door to the office. With Derek behind the bar and Stephanie on the floor, no one had reason to come looking for her. And if they did, it would be much easier to explain her presence here than on the landing.

She sat on the edge of her desk. "Do you want to tell me what's going on?"

"*It's Mommy.*" Alex looked down at his shoes. "*She's sick.*"

"I'm so sorry to hear that. Do you know what's wrong with her?"

He shook his head. "*She's sick.*"

"*Tell Josie why you wanted her to know this, Alex.*"

"*So Derek can see her.*"

Josie's stomach lurched. "Alex, do you recall when Derek was your age?"

He nodded.

"What was that like?"

He looked back at his shoes, twisting the hem of his shirt. "*Mommy was sad a lot.*"

"Of course she was, sweetheart. She missed you."

"*And she was mad.*"

"Do you know who she was mad at?"

He nodded again. "*Daddy.*"

"Why was she mad at Daddy?"

He shrugged and tugged on his bunny's floppy ear. He was old to be so attached to a stuffed animal, but it was well worn, like a security blanket.

"*Can I go back now, Ruby?*"

"*Yes, darling.*"

"Go back where?'

"*To Mommy.*"

"Is that where you are when you're not here?"

"*Yes.*"

"Is there something you want Derek to know?"

"*He should say bye to Mommy.*"

"I'll see what I can do, sweetheart. I'll try."

"But he has to!" he insisted, his face scrunched with worry.

"Okay. Okay. Then he will." She felt terribly promising something she might not be able to deliver, but it was what he needed to hear.

Ruby took him by the hand and led him to the door.

Before they left, he turned around. "*Bye-bye, Josie.*" At last, he smiled, revealing his dimples.

She sat for a few minutes, overwhelmed by the enormity of what Alex needed from her. She was the only person who could possibly make this happen. And while she'd been fiercely protective of Derek in all of the stories he'd told her from his childhood, for the first time, she wondered who his mother might have been outside of her darkest moments. Who she'd been before Alex died. She'd done a poor job weathering unthinkable tragedy and continued to face the consequences in the decades since Derek had left home. If she were sick, if this were among the last times he could possibly reconcile with her, Josie owed it to both of them—and Alex—to do everything in her power to make that happen. Even if it meant upsetting Derek in the short term for the good of the long term, because no matter what, this was his mother, the only one he had, and she deserved a final chance. Parenting did not come with a rule book.

In the morning, she would return her father's call.

Chapter Ten

JOSIE SAT AT the bar in the Sherry Netherland Hotel alternately flipping through the cartoons in an issue of *The New Yorker* and playing with cocktail napkins. Arriving twenty minutes early had seemed a good idea at the time, but as her anxiety simmered to a near-boil, it felt too long. Still, she preferred to be there before her father and Melanie arrived instead of walking in when they were already seated. It spared her from doing the awkward dance of looking for someone in a crowded room.

When she called Raymond back, she suggested meeting for breakfast—the safest, most finite meal. Derek had scoffed at the fact her father was making her trudge to his hotel in midtown rather than meeting her in their neighborhood, but Josie didn't mind. She preferred to let him choose. The specifics of their plans had always been up to him.

"Can I get you another stack of those?" the bartender asked. She looked down at the shredded pile of napkins in front of her.

"Sorry, Nervous habit."

"Maybe you should take up origami?" He handed her a fresh stack and collected the remnants of the first. "Have at it."

"Actually, I used to know some origami. Any requests?"

"Yes. I'll take a crane, a frog, and a flamingo." He winked at her. He was a handsome, middle-aged man with an Irish accent, sparkling eyes, and a lot of product in his salt-and-pepper hair. "Another club soda?"

"Please."

He slid her glass across the bar, filled it with ice cubes, then shot soda into it. "You sure you don't want something a little stronger to calm those nervous hands?"

"I absolutely want something a little stronger, but that wouldn't be wise. Got to keep my wits about me for the next hour."

"Blind date? Job interview?"

"Scarier. Meeting my dad and step-monster for the first time in… wow, almost two years. Maybe nineteen months?"

"That's a long time."

"I know. It's a long story."

"I hear you. I hadn't seen mine in nearly six years before he passed last December."

"I'm so sorry."

"You wouldn't be if you knew him," he said dryly.

When he went to fill another order, she tried to recall how to make an origami swan, something she'd learned while babysitting a very artistic little girl in the neighborhood she'd lived in during high school. She searched for the girl's name and came up short, recalling only that she was very pretty, with light brown ringlets and big blue eyes. What a happy child she was, always smiling and playing and doing crafty things. Sarah—that was her name. She'd be in her early twenties now. Josie wondered where she'd live, what she'd be doing, and mostly what it would be like to look back on such a happy childhood. She would never know, thanks in part to the man for whom she waited.

She folded a napkin into a tiny hat, then propped it atop a bottle of bitters on the bar in front of her.

One of Josie's earliest memories was of playing in the shallow end of the pool at a neighbor's Fourth of July party and wanting her father to help her float. She'd looked around and spotted him treading water, talking to the blonde woman sunning herself with baby oil and iodine at the side of the pool. The neighborhood moms stood in clusters, gossiping like extras on *Peyton Place*, and the blonde woman's husband looked on helplessly. Josie could picture him still, sandy hair, skin so pale his veins showed through, handlebar mustache, can of beer in hand—Schaefer or Schlitz, probably. She remembered feeling uneasy, though of course she lacked the life experience to verbalize why. But even then, she knew it was a good thing her mom was in the house and not watching her father talk to this woman.

She transformed a second napkin into a boat and placed it next to the bitters.

The blonde woman was Melanie, who had moved to the neighborhood that spring. She wore her hair in pigtails and wrapped her waifish figure in short, frilly sundresses and gingham bikinis. Most of the neighborhood men had harmless crushes on her. Raymond, whose crush would prove the exception to "harmless," was easily the best looking man in the neighborhood. A newly minted professor, he wore his hair long and, when not in swim trunks, dressed like a member of his favorite band, Led Zeppelin—silky shirts unbuttoned lower than they should be, tight pants. What he lacked in physical stature, he made up for in confidence. He knew how to talk to women, hold eye contact, ask questions, and remember answers. Melanie's husband was not a handsome man but was widely known to be incredibly wealthy from old family money, an heir to Entenmann's or Kellogg's, something pertaining to breakfast. Melanie embodied her role of wealthy wife as best she could in the suburbs of Burlington, Vermont, hosting dinner parties with multiple forks, aspic, and linen napkins. That she did none of the cooking herself, nor the cleaning, did nothing to keep the neighborhood men from thinking her the ideal woman in an era when the domestic arts were still the benchmarks of feminine perfection.

Two years later, in 1973, Melanie's husband would crash his Kawasaki motorcycle—the one thing, besides Melanie, the local dads envied him for—and spend three weeks on life support before widowing his wife at the age of twenty-six. Raymond went around regularly to comfort her until the night he didn't come home, and the rest was Josie's scandalous family history. And the source of her mother's bitterness. As far as Josie knew, Alice never so much as dated again.

Now Josie was sitting at the bar of an overpriced hotel crumpling napkins and trying not to think about all the reasons this was a bad idea.

"How's my menagerie coming?"

She looked down at the newly shredded pile in front of her and pointed to the hat and boat. "I'm warming up. It's a work in progress."

"I'm a patient bloke." He refilled her glass. "So what's your story? Why has it been so long since you've seen your old man?"

"We have an inconsistent relationship."

"Has it been consistently inconsistent?"

Josie thought about that. "Not entirely. The early post-divorce days were pretty consistent. But the woman he left my mom for doesn't like kids, and I was one, so we reached an impasse."

"Doesn't like kids?"

"Doesn't like messes of any sort, literal or figurative. And I was a messy kid with messy feelings."

"You were a kid. That's in the job description. But I hear you. My old man was the same in the not-liking-messes department. He was rather exacting."

"How did that manifest?"

"He wanted me to be a strait-laced, straight man with a career in banking, and I tried for a little while but ended up breaking my promises, moving to New York, falling in love with a man, and trying to be an actor."

"Sounds like a pretty great existence to me! And broken promises define my relationship with my dad, too, only it was always him doing the breaking. Hence, the visits tapered. I got tired of the cancellations."

"Nonetheless, here you are."

"Nonetheless, here I am. I guess I'm a believer in multiple chances."

"That's generous to the person on the receiving end, less so to you."

"Yes, but I can't seem to stop being generous."

Last summer Josie had had an epiphany. The notion that Raymond abandoned his wife and kid out of sheer selfishness was an outdated narrative drilled into her by her mother's unwavering condemnation of him. It would take her accidentally getting involved with the very married Patrick Moore to realize this. People didn't cheat in a vacuum. For reasons she could only surmise, her father was unhappy and found someone to fix that. You couldn't really fault a person for gravitating toward joy, regardless of how they came to find it.

She'd decided after all these years she could forgive him and strive for a new version of things, one that was civilized and adult. So she'd called him, only to learn he and Melanie would be leaving soon for a ten-month sabbatical in Europe and leaving Josie's relationship with him suspended in time.

But much had changed in the year since, and she was ready to try again. Besides, if she had any shot at urging Derek to reconcile with his parents, she'd have to lead by example. She'd felt fleetingly strong and virtuous making this plan, but now that it was here wished she could turn back the clock.

"Is this him?" the bartender asked, nodding over Josie's shoulder.

Her stomach twinged with dread, and she turned to see Raymond Gray walking toward them.

"Josie!

"Hi, Dad!"

He leaned in for what she expected to be a kiss on the cheek that instead became an uncoordinated hug. After separating, he said, "You're looking quite well."

"Thank you. So are you."

In fact, he looked older, wearier, the lines in his face evidence of decades' worth of tropical vacations. The rest of him was aging well, thanks in part to a regular swimming and bicycling habit and likely motivated by the coeds he taught, who grew relatively younger every year. He still wore his hair, now silver, on the long side, wavy and tucked behind his ears. Josie noted with relief that after keeping the Led Zeppelin look going far longer than he should have, he was finally dressing his age. Today he sported widewale tan corduroy pants and a tweed jacket over a navy blue flannel shirt. He looked every bit the history professor at a small college in Vermont that he was.

"Is your wife joining us?"

"Not just yet. She found a hot yoga class on the Upper East Side. She'll try to come by at the end for a coffee."

This was fine with Josie. After tipping the bartender—who mouthed, "*Good luck.*"—she followed the hostess to their table.

The crowd was very much what she expected—well-heeled and conservative, old money and expense accounts. As one of the younger people in the room, she received a fair number of second glances from the men they passed and scrutinizing looks from the women. She realized she could be mistaken for another segment of the population that frequented fancy hotel bars—an accessory to a much older man with money and power. With his looks and swagger, her father could pass for the type. In fact, most of his money was Melanie's, and his power was questionable.

They sat, and she ordered coffee, Raymond a pot of Earl Grey tea. He perused the menu, then moved his glasses down the bridge of his nose and gave her a tired smile. "How have you been?" He pronounced it as a statement, not a question.

"I've been great!" Her voice shot up half an octave. "Busy. You know, getting the restaurant going."

"How is it all working out?"

Unlike Josie's mother, slow to accept her daughter's career choice, Raymond had sounded impressed when Josie told him of her plans. Also, unlike Josie's mother—for whom food was a necessity, not a pleasure—he enjoyed dining out. In the early post-divorce years, where he fell short in reliability, he almost made up for it by taking her to the best restaurants in whatever town they met in. He used food as love, and, as an emotional eater, Josie was fine with this.

"It's going well," she said, squeaking out another lie and biting her lip. "I mean, it's not the easiest thing, owning a restaurant in New York City."

"Yes, I imagine the competition is fierce. But you've been in the game for a while, you must have a good handle on what works and what doesn't, no?"

"To some extent, but the city can be fickle with food trends and stuff like that. And it can be hard on new venues. It's a tough world to break into."

"Who does the cooking?"

"We have a great chef, Naomi, and she's putting together her team." Josie thought fleetingly of Eduardo. "She's from New Orleans. The whole thing is New Orleans-themed, with unique twists on some of the traditional dishes."

"One of your grandmother's favorite places, if memory serves." He poured a splash of the tea the server set down, assessing its hue before leaving it to steep longer.

"Indeed." Josie smiled. "She lived there for a while, you may recall."

"I do. She was a good woman, your grandmother."

"She was the best," she corrected him.

"She cooked a lot of those dishes too, and quite well. And now you're carrying on the mantle."

"Trying to, anyway. We have good days and bad, but I think we're putting together a pretty great team."

"Who is we? Do you have partners?"

"Well, we have a couple of investors, but they're pretty hands-off. Investing in a restaurant is, of course, not something you can rely on to make money."

"Of course."

"But the 'we' I was talking about is Derek and me." She had told him this in their last conversation, nearly a year ago.

"Derek…." He furrowed his brow.

"My boyfriend? We worked together at the old place for years and then started dating last summer. It got serious pretty quickly, and when Chef was selling Bistrot, we decided to buy."

"That's a bold move with a new romantic partner."

An interesting observation from a man who'd blown up his own life after a seven-week affair.

"I suppose it is, but we're a good fit and both passionate about the industry and what we're trying to build."

"Passion is important." Raymond had a glint in his eye and the hint of a smile.

"So, how have you been?" Josie cupped her hands around her coffee mug.

"Great, great. You know I was on sabbatical, and we spent most of the year traveling."

"Where did you go?"

"All over Italy—Rome, Florence, Murano, Venice—as well as Paris, Prague, Vienna, Madrid, Bruges. Your stepmother loves her treasure hunts."

Melanie collected expensive European glassware, some of which she sold through a shop she co-owned in Vermont, most of which adorned the mirror-backed glass shelves throughout their living and dining rooms. She was a high-end interior designer, and their house was large, beautiful, and unwelcoming due to the many objects one was afraid to sneeze forcefully near.

"That must have been amazing and exhausting."

"It was both. A lot of walking, a lot of old churches, a few great bookstores. Do you still love to read?"

"I do." She was pleasantly surprised he remembered such a quiet detail about her. "I didn't have much time when we were first getting the restaurant going, but now that we have more help, I'm getting back into it."

There was a pause, and Josie tried to think of something with which to fill it. She didn't know what else to ask about Europe, didn't want to talk about Melanie, wished he would ask her about Derek. It was a relief when he flagged down the server so they could order, then a buried memory flooded her thoughts.

She was fifteen years old and filling out. She never got fat, but her curves were starting to make themselves known, a sharp contrast to the skinny kid she'd been who could eat whatever she wanted. They were in New York City, belatedly celebrating her birthday, and had gone to Little Italy. After dinner, she'd asked if they could stop at Ferrara for cannoli, and Melanie pursed her lips, looked Josie up and down, and suggested they walk back to their hotel instead. Despite his love of good food, Raymond had a type—Josie's mother was nearly as slim as Melanie.

"And what would you like, Madame?" the server asked her.

"I'll have an egg white omelet with spinach and tomato. Rye toast, dry."

"Any bacon or sausage with that?"

"No. Thank you."

As he walked away, Raymond tapped out a text on his cellphone.

"What brings you to New York this week?" she asked when he finally looked up.

"One of Melanie's college girlfriends is getting married. Remarried. Small City Hall event in the morning, a lunch in Chinatown, then a reception tomorrow night at Tavern on the Green. It's going to be a long day, but it's important to Melanie, and you know what they say."

This was not something people threw together last minute, so plans had probably been in place for a while. It didn't surprise Josie she was an afterthought, but it still disappointed her. Disappointment was such a familiar feeling. It was the filter through which she viewed every single interaction with Raymond, though it had really never served her, never moved the needle.

A long-forgotten mantra of Nanette's popped into her head.

Forgiveness is not about accepting the past. It's about releasing its hold on you.

"Can I ask you something?"

A look of fear flashed over his face, and she felt a pang of sympathy, contemplated spinning it into an innocuous question, then decided she had nothing to lose. The only path forward was through the muck that had gotten them here.

"Why do you think our relationship has been so… hit or miss over the years?"

He cleared his throat. "How do you mean?"

She let out an incredulous laugh. "Seriously? I mean, I haven't seen you in practically two years."

"Well, we were away for a big part of—"

"Yes, I know that. But what about the three decades before?"

He fidgeted with his teacup, spilled a drop onto the tablecloth, then blotted the spot with his napkin. "Josie, do you remember the early days?" He raised his eyes to her. "After your mother and I went our separate ways?"

"Of course. We spent a lot more time together then. It got progressively less the older I got, and there were so many thwarted plans. So many. So much disappointment."

"Do you remember how difficult your mother made it for me to see you?"

"Not really. I mean, I wasn't part of the planning committee. I was a kid."

"You're right. You were. Your mother was very angry with me."

"Understandably."

"Understandably," he agreed. "But my shortcomings as her husband shouldn't have translated into my being barred from being your father."

"You weren't 'barred.' I mean, we did see each other."

"Yes, and then as you got older, you and Melanie started to have your differences."

"Dad, we didn't have differences. Your wife doesn't like children."

"That's not true."

"Well, she certainly didn't want to spend a lot of time with yours. Why else did almost every one of my school breaks coincide with a vacation she'd planned for the two of you to some adults-only resort?"

He opened his mouth to speak, closed it, then poured more tea. "Our breaks often overlapped."

Tears pooled in Josie's eyes, and she wiped them away angrily.

"And your mother—"

She cut him off. "Even if Mom made it difficult, she didn't make it impossible. You could have made a far greater effort than you did. I'm your daughter. I needed you. I deserved more of your time and attention than I got."

"You're probably right."

In his pocket, his phone buzzed. He pulled it out, flipped it open, and squinted at the screen. "Melanie. Let me just take this and see where she is." He leapt from the table to walk out of the room.

Watching him leave, Josie sat back, stunned. "You're *probably* right?" She punctuated her mockery of him with a guttural noise of disgust and turned her gaze to the lobby where he paced, frowning, while talking into his phone. Josie morphed into the young girl straining to hear her parents' argument, certain she'd caused it. She put her elbows on the table and her head in her hands.

The opening notes to "What a Wonderful World" came over the sound system.

She bolted upright and whispered, "Nanette."

This was their song, had been since the night of the phantom knock she'd described to Ani, the night she learned she and Nanette shared an unusual ability. Unnerved by what happened and upset by Raymond's failure to return her call—she'd wanted to tell him she'd passed her swimming test in camp, which, ironically, had involved treading water—she'd gone to her grandmother for solace. After assuring her she understood what had happened and shared this connection, Nanette took her to the piano and taught her this song. From then on, for Josie, it became inextricably linked to the comfort and wisdom her grandmother provided.

Now she was sending it her way for a reason. Nanette did not hold grudges or cling to the past, she met people where they currently were. Today, right now, Raymond was walking back to the table looking distressed. Josie couldn't expect him to answer for the past thirty-three years, nor could she forget them. What she could do was forgive him in the interest of releasing the past's hold over her.

"Unfortunately, Melanie can't join us after all." He sat back down and busied himself pouring tea with greater concentration than the task required. "The bride needs her help with some pre-wedding things."

"Okay."

"Josie." He looked up at her. A lock of hair had migrated down his forehead and gotten tangled in his glasses. "I'm sorry. I don't know what to say—"

"You don't have to say anything," she said gently as the server approached with their food. "Look, Dad, the past is the past, but we're here now, and I want to celebrate that. There's no reason we can't move forward and get to know each other better as adults, right?"

He exhaled, visibly relieved. "I would like that very much."

"So would I. Do you and Melanie have plans tonight?"

"As far as I know, we have no obligations until tomorrow."

"Then I'd love to invite you in for dinner, our treat, and you can meet Derek."

"I would like that," he said again. "Very much."

"So would I, so let's make it happen."

He put his hand on hers. "Thank you, Josie. Thank you. You have become a remarkable woman."

"I always was," she said with a smile.

Chapter Eleven

THEY PARTED WAYS with the plan that Raymond and Melanie would come to Miss Sylvie's when they opened to meet Derek before things got busy and to have an early dinner before their long day tomorrow. In fact, Josie had suggested the 5:00 p.m. start in hopes they would be in and out without realizing things *didn't* get busy.

She decided to walk home, a straight shot down Fifth Avenue that would take just under an hour and give her time to think.

For three decades, their relationship had been on Raymond's terms. Now she was an adult, a business owner. Raymond was in *her* town, and she got to call the shots. Melanie, too, would see her on her own turf, in her beautiful restaurant with her partner by her side. They'd finally witness her as the person she'd become, no longer beholden to her father's whims and broken promises.

The healing could begin. She needed this not just for herself, but for Derek too. She'd be living proof of the validity of Nanette's theory on forgiveness, that it releases the one offering it. If she could do this with her father, maybe she could convince him to make amends with his parents.

Of course, she had no idea how she would manage what felt like a Herculean effort.

Something that felt like chewed gum squished under her shoe. She cursed, looked at her sole, and laughed. It was a puffy sticker of an owl, Nanette's spirit animal. She chose to believe this was a sign confirming that she'd figure it out.

In her pre-breakfast anxiety, Josie had neglected to let Curtis know she'd returned Raymond's call. She pulled her phone from her bag to fill him in.

"Guess what I just did."

"You scaled the Empire State Building to swat at airplanes."

"I did not."

"You saved Gotham City from a malevolent penguin."

"Don't be daft."

"Then I give up."

"I had breakfast with my father."

"Tell me everything!"

"Do you want to meet him?"

"Of course I want to meet him! When? How?"

"He and Melanie—"

"You said her name," he said proudly. *"Look at you."*

"It's a brave new world. He and what's-her-name—"

"*Already*?"

"He and Melanie will be in tonight for dinner. Early. Are you guys free?"

"I wouldn't miss this for the world. Of course I'm free. Henry isn't, it's Thursday."

"Oh, right."

On Thursday nights, the Chelsea art galleries held evening hours. The blocks in the west twenties teemed with artists, collectors, fashionistas, and hangers-on carrying plastic cups of wine and moving from show to show. Josie had joined Curtis a couple of times before the restaurant opened and decided she preferred her art without a scene.

"*I will be there with bells on*."

"Excellent. I'll see you tonight, then."

She continued down Fifth Avenue, looking in windows of stores she couldn't yet afford for inspiration. Her birthday was close, and Derek wanted gift ideas. They'd also fantasized about going away for a couple of days, an impossibility before Steph but now almost doable. They could rent a car and drive north, see the autumn leaves, visit Burlington, meet Raymond and Melanie for dinner—but stay in a hotel. They could go for a hot air balloon ride, something she'd always wanted to do but only with a romantic partner. They could go to New Hampshire to see Alice. It would be sweet and nostalgic—she could show Derek where she came from and create new associations with these places.

She felt light, as though the cord tethering her to the past had been cut.

From the depths of her bag, her phone vibrated. She pulled it out. "Hello?"

"*Hi, Josie. It's Ani.*"

"What's going on?"

"*I'm ready to take a break and wondering if you want to meet up?*"

"I'd love to. I can only stay for a little while, but I'll be back in the neighborhood in about ten minutes."

"*Great! Door's open. Just come out back.*"

Josie cut over to Sixth Avenue to pick up a coffee at her bodega. It was far from the best coffee in the city, but she had a good rapport with the guys and knew they appreciated her loyalty.

On Sixth Avenue, she paused and looked downtown toward Manhattan's southernmost tip, from which the Twin Towers watched over the city like dutiful sentries. She loved this view, another touchpoint to Nanette. They'd come to New York during Christmas break when she was twelve—her first trip to the city—and they'd done it all. *Oklahoma* on Broadway. Ice-skating in Central Park. The tree at Rockefeller Center. The morning before they left, they took a tour of the World Trade Center, which was less than a decade old. On the South Tower's observation deck, while enthralled with its awe-inspiring views, Josie decided she would one day live in New York City. It was the moment she understood the world was so much bigger than her tiny corner of it and the things holding her back needn't define her. The towers symbolized boundless possibility and promise, and seeing them was a reminder both of that and of the fact Nanette was always with her.

She continued to Greenwich Avenue. It was warm in the sun with a crispness to the air that heralded autumn, her favorite season. Things were falling into place, and she had faith the restaurant would follow suit. If she could just get Derek to relax and let things unfold, life could be as good as it had ever been.

She'd stop by Ani's then find him and fill him in on the night's plans. Where Raymond was concerned, Derek was so protective of her she'd been hesitant to tell him about breakfast. When she did, he asked why she was rewarding her father for all the distress he'd caused, referred to him as an "entitled prick" before catching himself and backing off.

It was her fault he'd reacted that way. All he knew of Raymond was the bad stuff because that's all she'd told him. She'd basically done to Derek what Alice had done to her, colored his image of the man by reducing him to his worst behavior.

She'd glossed over the early days, the cozy memories, the fact that when she was a little girl, the sun had risen and set on him.

"Large iced, light and sweet," the man behind the bodega counter said when Josie walked in.

"Yes, please! I'm a creature of habit."

She paid for her coffee, then walked to Ani's. The front door was propped open, and two of the workmen were loading in boards and equipment.

"*Hola!*" she greeted them. Today she felt confident in her limited Spanish. "*Como está usted?*"

"*Bien bien gracias. Y usted?*"

"*Bien.*"

The cute painter, Hector, jogged down the steps and smiled.

"*Hola, señorita,*" he said, his face reddening.

"*Hola. Soy alli por ver mi amigo*!"

He looked puzzled, and she realized she'd butchered the phrase. Time for another lesson with Mario.

She shrugged apologetically and walked back to the patio, stashing her purse on the kitchen table.

Ani was leaning back in a chair, eyes closed, face to the sun, music playing on her laptop.

"Has my excuse for not working arrived?" she asked when Josie came outside, then opened her eyes and smiled.

"I'm only here for a minute. I don't want to keep you." Josie sat across from her.

"Where are you coming from?"

"Breakfast with my father, who's in town for a few days."

"That sounds nice!"

"I suppose it does in theory. Someday I'll bore you with the details. How's your morning going?"

"Not great. I'm taking a music break."

George Harrison's "My Sweet Lord" was playing.

"Can you write with music on?"

"Only instrumental. Nothing with lyrics, and I love classic rock—these guys, the Stones, Eric Clapton. I'm a bit of a dinosaur with my musical taste."

"Me too."

"These breaks are usually rewards, but sometimes, like today, they're incentives. I've barely written a word. I'm totally stuck."

"On anything specific?"

"Yes, actually. I need to figure out details of my B story. I need to decide why one of my characters is so tortured."

"Tell me more. If it helps, that is."

"It helps. My notes from our last conversation have already worked their way into the story. So this character is Robert. He's around thirty years old. From the outside, it looks like he has it all together—good job, friends, well-rounded life. But my protagonist is baffled by him."

"Who's your protagonist and what's their relationship?"

"Lila, and they're neighbors. She's just moved into the area where her family first settled when they left Mexico a few generations back. She's setting out to unravel a family mystery by writing about it."

"You're writing a book based on your family's experience about a woman writing a book based on her family's experience?"

"Write what you know."

"I like it. Tell me more."

"So Lila meets Robert soon after she arrives, and they become friends. She's attracted to him, but he keeps her at arm's length. He's hard to get to know, and the less he reveals, the more obsessed she becomes with the mystery of him."

"What makes her think there's mystery there?"

"She's intuitive, senses a lot roiling beneath the surface. She can tell he's haunted by something, and over time, it becomes such an obsession, it completely consumes her. It distracts her from her work and everything else in her life."

"I feel like you're describing something that's going on with me."

"How do you mean?"

Josie told her about Eduardo. "Distracting is a good word because that's what it feels like—I have the restaurant and my relationship to focus on, yet I'm finding myself distracted by this person I barely know because I feel like he has some unresolved trauma. Then I feel ridiculous."

"Why do you feel ridiculous?"

"Because, as my chef pointed out to me when this guy first arrived, everyone has something. Yet I don't wonder about everyone else to this degree. Some people are reserved, and it's not my business, so why am I so hellbent on knowing who Eduardo is and what happened in his past?"

"Because, like Lila, you're intuitive. And more than that, you're a healer. You can't yet heal what you don't understand. But maybe you and Lila don't need all the facts in order to use your skills. Maybe empathy alone is enough to heal those who need it."

"I feel like your fictional world and my real world are connected on some plane."

"Wouldn't surprise me at all. I'm a firm believer we meet people when we do for a reason. Maybe part of why our paths crossed is so we can figure out these two elusive guys together."

"Elusive and laconic. This guy doesn't give me a lot to work with."

"My Sweet Lord" ended, and "Bell Bottom Blues" by Derek and the Dominoes came on.

"Oh, this song!" Ani crossed her hands over her heart, closed her eyes, and moved her head to the music. When she opened her eyes, they were misty. "Sorry. It brings back vivid memories."

Josie waited for her to elaborate, but she didn't. "Don't be sorry. There are certain songs that bring me right back to the moment I first heard them. I just heard one, actually."

She told her about "Wonderful World" at breakfast. They talked music for a few minutes until Ani announced she was ready to get back to work.

"Slight chance I'm not going to Connecticut this weekend," she said as they walked into the house. "So if I have a productive few days, I'll swing by the restaurant."

"I hope you have a productive few days!"

Josie took her bag from the kitchen table and pulled out her phone to check the time. There was a missed call and message. As soon as it began, she heard the discomfort in Raymond's voice.

"Josie, hi. It was good to see you this morning and, uh, hear about the restaurant and what you've been up to. Thanks for the invite for tonight, it's much appreciated, um, but I'm afraid we're going to have to, uh, decline. There's a new sushi place Melanie's been wanting to go to and—what?" Melanie's voice droned incoherently in the background. *"Yeah, apparently it's hard to get a table, yet she managed."* He chuckled nervously. *"And tomorrow's the wedding, but let's make a plan to get*

together, either New York or Vermont or even Boston, like the old days, real soon." He paused. *"Okay, then, Josie. Again, nice to see you, and we'll talk soon."*

Her eyes burned. She took a deep breath and exhaled shakily.

"Everything okay, Josie?"

"Yep!" Her voice was high and tight. "Just some work stuff."

"All right. I will do my best to come by this weekend. Either way, see you very soon."

Josie walked home in a fog of humiliation. The talkative doorman was on duty, and she was grateful to hide behind her enormous Jackie O. sunglasses. As soon as she closed the door to her apartment, she burst into tears.

Derek wasn't home. Josie sunk down into the sofa while crying heaving body-shaking sobs. Three decades' worth of tears. Hugging a cushion, she cried for the little girl at the top of the stairs and the one who clutched her teddy bear while she and her mother drove off to begin their new life. For the lonely girl who feared the spirit world. For the child whose stepmother ridiculed her and whose own mother couldn't accept her feelings.

After so many years filled with self-doubt, she'd given up on the idea of happiness and strove for mere existence. Now she cried for all the versions of herself who had no idea her life would one day look like this—far better than she'd ever expected, while still deeply flawed. And she cried for the thirty-three-year-old who'd been bursting with joy only minutes earlier.

The sorrow Josie felt when Nanette died was bittersweet—bitter for her loss and sweet for the love they'd shared. It enveloped her like a hug from Nanette she'd never lose. This was entirely different. This was raw and jagged, and any connection to love was one-sided.

Derek's key turned in the lock. He entered in his gym clothes, red-faced and sweaty. "Hey, you." He took one look at her, then ran to her side.

She tried to speak but couldn't. He pulled her in tight and rubbed her back until her sobs grew shallow and her breathing slowed down.

"I'm an idiot."

"No, you aren't, baby."

"I actually thought it was different this time." She sniffled.

He got them each a glass of water from the kitchen. "What happened, Joze?"

"Where do I begin?"

"You met them at the restaurant."

"Him."

"Him?"

"I met *him*. It was just the two of us. Step-monster went to hot yoga instead."

"Of course she did."

"You'd have been proud of me. I confronted him."

"I'm very proud of you. What did you say?"

"Confront isn't the right word because I wasn't at all combative about it. But I asked him why things had been the way they had for so long, why our relationship was so uneven."

"Good for you. What did he say?"

"At first, he tried to blame it on my mom, then he blamed it on me not getting along with Melanie."

"Are you kidding me?"

"He was grasping, but when I didn't capitulate, he got… not apologetic, really, but…."

"Contrite?"

"Contrite. And nervous. So I let him off the hook and said we couldn't change the past but could move forward, get to know each other."

"Josie, that's incredible. You were compassionate and wise and the motherfucker doesn't deserve it. I'm sorry, I know he's your father, but he's a motherfucker."

"Well, not really. She hates kids."

Derek laughed. "I love you. And what you did was amazing."

"What did I do?"

"You forced him to look in the mirror. It was long overdue."

"Maybe so, but he covered his reflection back up so fast it was like he was sitting shiva."

"Tell me the rest."

"He claimed he wanted to move forward too and blah blah blah, and I asked if they're free tonight—oh yeah, that's the other thing—they're here for a wedding. A wedding!"

"Why does that matter?"

"Because I didn't know they were coming to town until two days ago, and this obviously isn't a spur-of-the-moment trip."

"Okay, well, disappointing but not surprising."

"I asked if they were free tonight—both of them, high road—and he said they were, so I invited them to come in for dinner to meet you. Not that he asked a single question about you. But he said they would love to come in. I'm sorry—I knew you wouldn't be in favor of that invitation."

"Josie, I'm in favor of anything that makes you happy. Doesn't matter what I think of the guy, he's your father."

"Well, it's a moot point." She flipped open her phone and cued up the voicemail, then watched the fury flash in Derek's eyes as he listened.

"Jesus Christ." He shut the phone, fuming. "What a bastard. What an absolute spineless coward."

"You see why I feel so stupid?" she wailed, burying her face in his chest and sobbing again.

He stroked her hair.

"Of course, I get why you feel this way, but I wish you wouldn't. You gave him a chance, baby. Christ, you've given him too many chances. He should fucking stand up to that woman."

She sat up and wiped her nose. "I mean, who knows what's going on there. She called while we were eating, and it looked like a tense conversation. Maybe there's something serious happening between them, I don't know. Maybe there's a reason he has to—"

"Josie, I don't care. You're his daughter, and you're amazing, and he clearly saw that today. He should be proud to come see what you've built."

"Oh, yeah. He told me I've 'become a remarkable woman.'"

"Become? You always were."

"He's rejecting me for a fucking California roll." She flopped her head in her hands. "This is a new low." She looked up when her phone buzzed.

Derek glanced at the screen, then handed it to her. "Curtis."

What time tonite, Lady Love?

"Oh, shit. He was going to come by to meet them. I totally forgot."

"Joze, listen. We're light tonight. Like, really light."

"I'm sorry. I know how stressful that is, but right now I just don't have the bandwidth to take on—"

"That's not why I'm telling you. Why don't you take the night off? Stephanie and I can manage things."

"Take the night off and do what? Lie around and feel sorry for myself?"

"First of all, you're not feeling sorry for yourself. Something really shitty happened, and you're sad and pissed off. Hell, I'm feeling those things. Why don't you get together with Curtis? Order in, chill, watch a movie."

"A night off?"

"A night off with your good friend."

"That actually sounds really nice." Her voice sounded tiny and sad, which only made her sadder.

"Then do it, okay? I'm jumping in the shower. Text him back." He leaned in and kissed her. "I love you."

"I love you too."

Curtis was every bit as pissed off as Derek and fine with the change of plans. He came over shortly after Derek left with a bouquet of dusty rose-colored dahlias and bottle of Veuve Clicquot. Josie had loaded the CD player with Billie Holiday, who was currently singing about stormy weather.

"You're playing your sad girl music." He pouted and held out the champagne. "I'm sorry, Lady Love."

"What the hell are we celebrating?"

"We are celebrating friendship and real family." He put the items on the kitchen counter, then gave her a hug. "Which is what we are. I love you, Miss Josephine."

"I love you too." Her voice was muffled against his shoulder, her eyes filling again. "Thank you so much for coming over."

"Thank me? Are you kidding? It is my pleasure to spend a night in with you regardless of the circumstances. We haven't gotten to do this in a dog's age." He set about snipping the flowers' stems.

Josie pulled a glass vase from the cabinet and took out two champagne flutes. She peeled the foil off the bottle, then twisted the wire caging holding the cork.

"Is there any sound more delightful than that?" Curtis asked when it popped. He filled the vase with water, then arranged the flowers. "Coffee table?"

"Sure. Anywhere. Thanks, honey." Josie followed him with the champagne glasses. They sat on the sofa.

"To us." Curtis held up his glass.

"To us." She clinked his glass, sighing. "Can you believe this bullshit?"

"Yup."

"I feel so dejected. Dejected and rejected."

"I know you do."

"I was finally ready to move forward."

"And you still can. You don't need his approval or participation to do that."

"How can I when so much of the stuff I've been mired in for decades is this exact pattern of behavior? I mean, sure, I'm in a better place now, but I'm still scarred, and now I have a fresh wound on top of that."

"Lady, first of all, you're in a *much* better place. You have a fabulous man who loves you. You own a business. You live in this beautiful apartment. You've got good stuff going on. You cleaned up your side of the street with Daddy Dearest, so yeah, you can move forward. It's his loss. This is no longer about you."

"It sure feels like it's about me."

"I know. Look, I have no idea who my real daddy is and no way of ever finding out. That used to haunt me—until I decided it was up to me to put it aside and move forward."

Curtis's mother had gotten pregnant by a man who fled town shortly after she told him she would keep the baby. His was a common enough name it would have been impossible, in the early 1960s, to track him down, and she didn't want to. She was an exceptional mother to Curtis, and when he was ten met and married the man who would eventually adopt him. It had never dawned on Josie he might wonder who his real father was.

"I'm sorry I've never asked you about that." She topped off their glasses. "I mean, I think of Darrell as your dad."

"I do, too, because he is, but that still didn't stop me from wondering about the man. Until I decided it wasn't doing me any good. I had to put it behind me so it stopped holding me back. I know it's a totally different situation here because yours disappointed you *after* you were born. A lot."

"More times than I could possibly count. And you know what else sucks?" She took a swig of champagne. "If the step-monster were a different person and I'd introduced you two, you could have talked about design. She's a horrible human being but has a good eye."

"Oh, please. I've got plenty of horrible New York-based designers to talk to. And some really great ones. Lady, we need to eat something. What do you feel like?"

"Not making any food decisions."

"Where are your menus?"

"Kitchen drawer by the window."

Curtis rifled through the stack of menus, suggesting things Josie rejected. He finally gave up on asking her opinion and ordered them Chinese food. While he was on the phone with the restaurant, Josie opened a bottle of Sauvignon Blanc.

"Steamed dumplings, moo shu chicken, orange beef, Buddha's Delight. Sound good?"

"Yes, honey. Thank you."

He settled back onto the couch and picked up his wine glass.

"All is not lost, Lady. There's plenty of good."

"I think that's part of why I'm so bummed too. Like you said before, my life *is* pretty good, finally, and this felt like another piece falling into place. I mean, believe me, it's far from perfect—"

"Perfect is the enemy of good. Count the wins."

"I also feel a little sorry for him because he's obviously at his wife's beck and call. And I can't help but think he's going to feel bad about this."

"Let him. I know you have a hard time with anger, but you have every right to it. You gave him a chance, and he squandered it."

In her buzzed state, the word 'squander' made her laugh.

"What?" Curtis also started to laugh.

That only made her laugh harder. She opened her mouth to explain and burst into another round of hysterics.

"I'm thrilled you're laughing but have no idea why!"

"Squander!" she said when she caught her breath.

"Squander?"

"I don't think I've ever used that word." She started laughing again. "Squander."

"Don't squander my use of the word squander!" Curtis said, and they were both in hysterics. Josie's cellphone rang—Derek.

"Hi," she said.

"*Joze, are you okay?*" He sounded panicked.

"I'm laughing. Didn't think I'd be doing that today.'

"*Oh, wow. You scared me. I'm glad you're laughing.*"

"Me too. What's going on there?"

"*Stephanie wants to fire Ian, and I think we should let her.*"

"What happened?"

"*Since dinner started, he's forgotten to put in the order—twice—and he spilled a glass of red wine on a man's Paul Stuart suit. Light gray Paul Stuart suit. Then he tried to blame it on the man.*"

"I hate this so much."

"*I know you do. But it's time. Do we have your blessing?*"

"Yes."

"What happened?" Curtis asked when she hung up.

"Were you serious about wanting to come back and work with us?"

"One hundred percent."

"You're hired. Let's call Derek back."

Chapter Twelve

JOSIE WOKE FRIDAY dehydrated, head throbbing. For a moment she forgot why she was hungover, then the previous day's events came flooding back.

"Damn it," she whispered. She was reminded of the weeks after Nanette passed, those peaceful few moments in the mornings when she forgot to remember.

It would be a lot easier to put her father out of mind if he weren't still in town, because although it was highly improbable he'd do the right thing, a tiny part of her still held hope. It would take such little effort on his part to make this better—maybe he didn't have time to come see her, but at the very least, he could call to apologize in earnest. He wouldn't.

As a child, she'd learned nothing was as deafening as the silence of a phone that was supposed to ring. That hadn't changed.

She dragged herself out of bed, rinsed her face, took the bottle of Advil from the cabinet, then searched for a cup. She wanted to lie back down, take another day off, but that wasn't an option.

Derek was pushing the plunger into the French press and looked up at Josie with bloodshot eyes and a five o'clock shadow. "How are you doing?"

"Not great." She slipped behind him to grab a glass. "How about you?"

"I didn't sleep well."

"Because of me?"

"No, you were out cold. Just weird dreams. You have a nice time with Curtis?"

"Weird dreams again? About?"

"I don't know."

She noted how quick he was to respond.

"How was Curtis?"

"He was wonderful. Comforting, maternal, made me eat."

"Good man. And he's serious about wanting to work with us?"

"Yes, he's thrilled. He feels bad he can't until next week, but they've had plans to go out of town for a while."

They would be short-staffed through the weekend but would make it work. Tonight was their second happy hour, and Josie was uneasy about seeing Billy Duane again. She and Derek were in a better place, the mess with Raymond having made him loving toward her, and she no longer craved the outside validation she'd needed the week before.

Still, something seemed off in Derek. He was in a mood Josie didn't recognize. He could usually manage on minimal sleep, and things like bad dreams didn't faze him, but today his mind was somewhere else.

Josie got to the restaurant in the early afternoon, wanting a couple of quiet hours there before things began. Much as she loved her night off, she wasn't yet ready to let Miss Sylvie's run without her. Before yesterday, she'd fantasized about being able to leave the restaurant in capable hands and go out of town. Now that the birthday trip she'd constructed in her head was off the table, she didn't want to go anywhere.

Then she remembered Alex. In her swirl of murky emotions, she'd managed to block out the rest of the Magnus family. Now the idea of trying to get Derek to Denver when she was feeling so blue daunted her.

She went upstairs, confident Derek would give her a pass on anything she did for the time being. Searching for a mantra to get her through her day, she sat at the table, closed her eyes, concentrated on her breath, and waited for the right words to come to her. When they didn't, she only resented her father more.

"Don't take this away from me too," she said, then startled as iciness enveloped the air around her. Her eyes flew open.

Eduardo was climbing the stairs, talking into his cellphone. He waved to Josie as he got to the landing. "Okay *mamà, hablo contigo después del trabajo. Te amo.*"

Josie repeated his words silently. He was talking to his mom, something about work. He looked handsome today in a white button-down shirt and black pants, an army green messenger bag slung across his shoulder. He pushed open the kitchen door with his hip. Josie closed her eyes and concentrated again to find her mantra, but still nothing came.

"*Talk to him.*"

She heard the words clearly. It was a woman's voice giving an instruction from the ether, one she had no inkling how to follow.

Eduardo was so guarded, she couldn't just "talk to him" and expect anything substantive to come as a result.

She followed him into the kitchen. He looked up at her from the large sink where he was rinsing peppers and celery in a colander.

"Josie—do you need something?"

"No, no. I just realized I haven't been up here in a while and wanted to check in. I used to spend a lot more time in the kitchen."

He nodded and continued his work.

"I love watching people cook," she said. "I find it strangely meditative."

"I hear that."

He picked up a stainless steel peeler and began destringing celery.

"Are you prepping those for the holy trinity?"

"I am. You know your stuff."

The holy trinity—a medley of finely diced onions, celery, and bell pepper—was to Creole and Cajun cooking what *mirepoix* was to French. It was the foundation to many dishes, as fundamental as a good *roux*.

He flashed her a quick smile, then looked down at the cutting board, his shoulders raised. Josie realized it was uncomfortable for him to work with his boss hovering. For all he knew, she was there to monitor—the opposite of what she'd intended. She had to quickly disarm him.

"This may sound weird, but I used to cook with my grandmother and miss it. Can I help with some of the chopping?"

"Okay." He sharpened a knife for her, then placed it on the cutting board. "I'll rinse and peel, you chop?"

Now she worried she was in over her head because it really had been a long time since she'd done this.

"Will you do a round first so I can see the size?"

He rinsed a pepper, then deftly trimmed and seeded it before chopping one half into tiny, uniform cubes. Josie took the other half and tried to emulate him to poor results.

"Here." He stood next to her and demonstrated how to chop quickly without picking the knife up from the cutting board, a much smoother and safer process than the one she'd attempted.

She tried another bit of pepper but couldn't match his technique.

"How about I rinse and peel, you chop?"

He smiled again, more relaxed this time, and they switched places.

A portable radio on the shelf above his work station played Santana's "Supernatural" over tinny, ineffectual speakers.

"We have to get you a better sound system up here!" Josie said.

"Nah, this is all I need."

They worked in silence while she searched for another entry point. She patted dry a pepper and handed it to him. "Are you having a good week?"

"Great."

More silence ensued while he chopped and she zipped the peeler over a stalk of celery.

"Was that your mom you were talking to before?"

He stopped chopping and turned to her. "Yes. Sorry. She gets confused with the time change and forgets that I'm—"

"No need to apologize! Moms are important! You can talk to yours anytime you want."

"Thank you. But better if I talk to her after work."

"Where does she live?"

"Tucson."

"Is that where you grew up?"

"Yes."

She waited for him to say more. This would not be easy, but if breaking through to him had felt important before, now that someone else wanted her to, she had no choice. She had to keep trying.

"Where did you learn to cook?"

"A lot from my mom and then some on my own, 'cause I did most of the cooking for her and my sisters."

"Lucky them. How many sisters?"

"Four. All younger."

"Four sisters—wow. You must have had your hands full."

This time Eduardo's smile didn't reach his eyes. "Our father passed suddenly, so I helped look after them. My mom worked long hours."

"I'm so sorry."

"Thank you. It's been years."

"What kind of work did your mom do?"

"Back then, she did housekeeping. Cleaned rooms in a hotel, The Arizona Inn. She's still there but works reception now."

"Arizona Inn. Why does that sound so familiar?"

"It's a pretty famous place. Been around since 1930. Lots of old-time movie stars stayed there. President Kennedy too."

"It must be a really special."

"It is."

"What made you move to New York?"

"I needed a change."

The decisive tone with which he made the statement implied there'd be no further questions.

"Well, we're so glad you did. You're a great addition to our family."

She felt silly now, embarrassed for having interrogated him. She rinsed the last of the peppers and was getting ready to leave him to his work when he finally reciprocated.

"You said your grandma liked to cook?"

"Yes. She was a great cook who loved New Orleans. I made a book of her recipes. I'll have to bring it in sometime to show you."

"I'd love to see it."

"Hey, y'all!" Naomi pushed through the door carrying shopping bags. "Are you our new line cook, Josie?"

"I'm a little bit of everything today. Not sure if you heard, but Ian's out."

"Out sick?"

"Out out."

"Damn spot."

"We're replacing him with my good friend Curtis—you'll love him. But he's away this weekend, so I'm pinch-hitting. Eduardo was kind enough to let me help him prep for nostalgia's sake."

"*Nuestra cocina es su cocina.*" Naomi put the food bags on the island in the middle of the kitchen. "We're going much simpler on happy hour tonight, per Mister D's request."

"Request? That's putting it mildly."

"Requested order." She took some items out of one of the bags, then headed to the walk-in, arms full. Josie followed her.

"Can I help you put stuff away?"

"No, girl. I've got a system. You go do your thing,"

"Okay." She stalled, as much to prolong her time in the kitchen as to hold off on seeing Billy Duane. She'd rather get downstairs just as he started playing, but that wasn't an option.

"Were you really nostalgic for chopping onions?" Naomi asked when Eduardo was out of earshot.

"Kind of?"

"Or do you have ulterior motives?"

"I really do miss cooking with Nanette, but yeah, I want to get to know Eduardo. Have you learned anything?"

"I know he's real tight with his mama. I overheard him talking to her the other day."

"He was today, too, but my Spanish isn't good enough to pick up on everything he said."

"Why are you so curious?"

"If there's something going on in his life that's impacting him emotionally, we should know about it, shouldn't we?"

"He's a hard-working dude. A machine. You see the way he preps? This guy's not gonna let anything impact him on the clock. Don't you worry."

"I'm not. I just want to make sure I'm sensitive to all of your needs."

"I don't think you know how *not* to be sensitive to us, Josie. You're one in a million. Now get out of here so I can get to work."

Josie passed Anthony, the loquacious food runner, on the stairs.

"Where have you been?" he asked. "I haven't seen you in a month!"

"Two days, my friend. I saw you Wednesday."

"Well, it feels like a month."

Downstairs, Jerome set up while Stephanie and Derek sat at the bar talking. Josie registered their body language—his back rigid, arms crossed, her gesticulating wildly, probably defending happy hour—and decided it was a conversation she needn't be part of. She bypassed the bar for the hostess stand just as the musicians walked in the door. Her stomach fluttered when she saw Billy.

"Hey there, beautiful."

It was a brazen thing to call someone who was essentially his employer, but she would let it bounce off her.

"Hey, guys. Welcome back."

Hal tipped his fedora. "Thanks for having us in again. Last week was a blast."

"I'm so glad you enjoyed it too. I'm looking forward to more great music tonight."

"Any special requests?" Billy touched her elbow.

"I'm sure whatever you have planned will be perfect."

"If you change your mind, just say the word. We aim to please."

"And please you do!" Stephanie swooped in and kissed Billy on the cheek. "How are my boys?"

Josie excused herself and went into the bar to sit by Derek, who was prepping the cocktail garnishes.

"Honey, if this doesn't work out tonight, we never have to do it again. But thank you for giving it another shot. It means a lot to me, and obviously it means even more to Steph."

"I'm doing this for you, not Stephanie."

"I know, and I appreciate it."

"How are you doing?"

"I'm okay. Glad to have things to distract me from my thoughts."

"I'm sure your Bayou Dog will be happy to keep you distracted, Miss Josie."

"He's not my type."

"Oh, yeah? What is your type?"

"Brooding, stoic, great writing chops, good with finances, kind of a cross between Jude Law and Ethan Hawke."

"If I see anyone that matches that description, I'll send him your way."

"Please do. I'll be waiting." She blew him a kiss, glad they still remembered how to flirt.

The band started up at 5:00 p.m., and shortly after that, people began to trickle in. Josie recognized some faces from the previous week and, as Stephanie predicted, some had brought larger groups this time. This included the young women Josie met in the bathroom, who now numbered five, and Sidney Feist, who had a girlfriend with her.

"I'm so glad you're back, Sidney."

"Thank you. And thanks for your kindness the other day."

"Anytime."

"This is my friend Melissa. I got custody of her in the split."

"No question," Melissa said. "Chicks before pricks."

"I'm going to stick to one martini tonight," Sidney said sheepishly. "If it'll put everyone's minds at ease, please let them know."

"Uh-oh," Melissa said. "Did Blanche make an appearance?"

"Yes."

"Who's Blanche?" Josie asked.

"My drunken alter ego. She was around a lot when Mel and I first met in the 80s, and she burned a lot of bridges. I thought I'd finally gotten rid of her, but she showed up last week."

"I promise you, she burned zero bridges last week. If anything, you're even more entrenched in the family now. I'm sorry to say, you're stuck with us."

Josie kept herself busy and avoided Billy, who continued to sing to her whenever she looked his way. She seated the tables that had come in for early dinners, went back to the office to check voicemail, then even went up to the ghost table to see if Ruby was there. She wasn't.

When she returned to the bar twenty minutes later, Melissa and another woman from the neighborhood were consoling a weeping Sidney, who had kept her pledge of one martini but was now drinking a Cosmopolitan.

"Oh, Sidney. I'm so sorry!" Josie put her hand on her shoulder.

"No, no. I'm sorry. No one wants a crying woman at the bar."

"It's okay, Sid." Melissa handed her a cocktail napkin. "You've got to let it out whenever it comes."

Sidney blew her nose, garnering a look of revulsion from the gaggle of young women standing nearby.

"What the hell happened to 'always?'"

"I promise it'll get easier." Melissa took the wet cocktail napkin and handed her a clean one. "There are a lot of great men out there."

"I thought Graham was one of them."

"Well, he wasn't. He's a shithead. You deserve better, and when you're ready, I'll introduce you to all of the decent single men I know."

"Thanks." She sniffled but perked up. "Maybe I need a one-night stand. Do you think I need a one-night stand?"

"Hell yeah, girl!" Melissa raised her cocktail glass. "There are much worse ideas!"

It sounded like a fairly terrible one to Josie, but she kept her mouth shut.

At quarter past six, the band took a break. Josie walked back through the dining room to check on the handful of tables. As she made her way toward the bar, she heard commotion on the front stairwell.

"Oh my God!" A friend of the young women from the previous week ran down the staircase shrieking, Billy Duane on her heels. "Oh my God!"

Josie rushed past bewildered diners toward them. The music playing in the bar was loud enough that no one there heard anything.

"What's going on?" She held onto the girl and led her to a booth, then looked fiercely at Billy, who couldn't meet her eyes. "What happened?"

She slid into the booth next to the girl. Lucy came right over and left a pitcher of water on the table for them.

"Billy, what is going on?"

"I don't know Miss Josie." He ran his hands through his hair. "I mean, we was—"

"It's not him!" The girl took a gulp of water and looked at Billy. "Sorry. It's not you."

"Oof!" He sounded relieved. "Jesus. Thank you. I don't know what happened up there, Josie. We were just having some fun in the ladies' room."

"You're at work."

"We were doing lines." The girl looked at Josie, wide-eyed and jittery. "I'm sorry. It's just—he offered me some cocaine"—Billy flinched—"and I had this really long week at work, and—"

"Never mind that now. What happened?" Billy started to answer, but she held her hand up to stop him. "I'm not asking you. What's your name, honey?"

"Whitney."

"Okay, Whitney. My name is Josie."

"I'm so sorry about the coke. I just—"

"Have some more water. Do you want to come back to my office so we can talk in private?"

"No, it's fine. He's fine."

She took a few shaky breaths, then downed the rest of her water. Josie refilled her glass and poured one for herself.

"Can I get some of that?" Billy asked. Josie slid the pitcher toward him but kept her eyes on Whitney.

"He chopped some lines on the counter…."

"Miss Josie, I—"

Josie shushed him. "Let her speak. Go on, Whitney."

"So I'm leaning over, and I get this really weird feeling all of a sudden. I don't know how else to explain it, but when I stood up, I saw something… someone… in the mirror, standing behind me." She shivered and wrapped her arms around herself.

Josie involuntarily did the same. "What did you see?"

"This, like, woman, but she wasn't really there. Like, I could see her, but I could almost see through her. It was like she was a ghost! Is this place haunted or something?"

"What did she look like?"

The strange look Billy gave her now was likely because she was less intrigued by the idea there was a ghost than she was curious about the ghost's appearance. But he was from the Gulf Coast, so he should understand.

"Pale, long red hair." She looked up at Billy who hovered awkwardly, his jaw twitching from side to side. "Did you see her too?"

"No, baby. I just saw the way you reacted and—"

"Was there something else in the stuff you gave me?"

"No way! Swear to God, Whit!" He held his hands up in defense. "I know my source. He's clean."

"Well, that's a relief." Josie's voice dripped with sarcasm. "Billy, your work here is done. You and Hal need to pack up your stuff and call it a night."

"Miss Josie, if you'll just let us finish our set, no charge for tonight. We'll keep going till seven."

"No, you will not keep going. Your work here is done. And you're correct, no charge for tonight, but I certainly hope you'll pay Hal for his time."

"I hope we can make this right. We're really digging these happy hours, and this place you've created is just like home—" He stumbled over his words. "I'm real sorry about the little kerfuffle but—"

"It's time for you to go."

She turned back to Whitney and, in her peripheral vision, saw Billy hesitate, wringing his hands, until he finally walked away.

"I'm sorry," Whitney said, her voice raspy. "About the drugs—"

"What's done is done. Just please don't do it here again, no matter who offers it to you."

She nodded. "I don't think I'll be coming back anytime soon."

"I'm going to get your friends to take you home, okay?"

She nodded again.

Josie found the other girls and suggested they meet Whitney in the dining room. "She's had a bit of a scare. I think it would be good for you ladies to get her home."

Stephanie was talking to Hal by the microphone. Josie asked to speak with her, and they walked to the hostess stand.

"Everything good?" There was a forced chipperness to her tone.

"No, everything is not good. We will not be compensating Billy for tonight."

"Why? What happened?"

"I'll explain later, but suffice it to say, this won't come as a shock to him. Nor will the fact he's no longer welcome here."

Stephanie's face crumpled. "Josie, I'm sorry if something happened. I didn't think he still—"

"We'll discuss it later." She took the front stairs two at a time, then pushed open the door to the ladies' room, where she found Ruby wringing her hands and walking in circles. "Ruby." Josie leaned against the sink and put her hand on her forehead. "Please stop pacing. You're making me dizzy."

"*I'm sorry, Josie.*"

"What happened?"

"*I didn't think she could see me. She'd been up and down a few times. And that fella was in here last week with a different girl—*"

"The musician?"

"*Yes. He was doing the same thing last week with a different girl—*"

"What were they doing?"

"*Well, last week he gave her cocaine and then tried to kiss her, but she didn't want him to.*"

"Are you kidding me?"

"*He was real pushy about it too. I was mad.*"

Josie's face flushed hot with anger. "Why didn't you tell me?"

"*I forgot because of Alex. I'm sorry, Josie! I'm so sorry!*" Her eyes filled with tears.

Josie wished she could hug her, but Ruby had once explained it took so much energy for spirit to be tactile that she had stopped trying.

"Don't be cross with me!

"I'm not, honey. I'm cross with him. What happened tonight?"

"*Well, he gave her some cocaine, and then he kissed her. She liked it. Then he gave her more cocaine. That's when she looked up and, well, I guess she saw me in the mirror.*"

"Okay. Okay." Josie closed her eyes. "How the hell am I going to fix this?"

"Fix what?" Sidney Feist staggered into the ladies' room.

"Sorry—just thinking out loud." Josie flashed a warning look to Ruby, who was now cowering in the corner. "Are you feeling a little better?"

"Yeah. Sorry about my meltdown. That wasn't Blanche. That was Sidney all the way."

"It was hardly a meltdown. You're feeling your feelings."

"I know. And what I feel is old and irrelevant."

"I'm so sorry you feel that, but you're neither of those things."

"You should see the dogwalker. She's so damn perky."

"You're beautiful, Sidney. I'll check in on you in a little bit, but I have to run down to my office right now." She nodded to Ruby, who understood. "Why don't you come back some night when it's not so crowded up front, and we can talk more?"

"Thank you, Josie. I will. I'm going to go home now and drown my sorrows in Häagen-Dazs."

"You deserve all the ice cream you want. Take good care." She pushed open the door, then ran back down the steps, stopping in the bar on the way to the office.

"What's going on?" Derek asked. "Why did those girls rush out of here?"

"Billy Duane is a total scum bag and no longer welcome here."

"I could have told you that last week."

"I know."

"What did he do?"

"Gave drugs to a customer and mauled her." No need to mention Ruby. Word would travel soon enough.

"That motherfucker." Derek looked over to where Billy and Hal were packing their gear while Stephanie stood by.

"I'm going over there." He slammed his fist on the bar and ducked under it.

"Derek, please don't!" Josie put her hand on his chest, which was heaving with anger. "The last thing we need is for one of us to make a scene. We've got to de-escalate things. We'll go through Stephanie."

"Didn't she say she worked with him before?"

"Yes, with Mary Franco, so if he had a reputation, she obviously didn't know about it."

As soon as the words were out of her mouth, she recalled Stephanie's odd choice of phrasing—"I didn't think he still"—and wondered how she might have finished that sentence.

"You sure about that?"

"Actually… no. I'll call Mary in the morning. For now, let's just let them leave, okay?"

"Fine." He glared in Billy's direction before reclaiming his spot behind the bar.

Ruby was in the office waiting for Josie.

Josie sat on the edge of her desk. "Thanks for telling me what happened tonight and last week."

"*I'm sorry I didn't tell you sooner.*"

"It's okay, I know now. But Ruby, what happened with the girl tonight—"

"*Oh, Josie. I didn't mean to scare her!*"

"I know you didn't. It's not your fault, but it does show that these things can happen and—" She didn't know how to say she was bad for business without hurting her feelings. "We just have to be careful. I don't think it's a great idea for you to hang out in the ladies' room anymore."

"*But Josie!*" Ruby's bottom lip trembled. "*That room is so important to me!*"

"I know," she said gently. "It's just that it's important to the restaurant too. If people are scared—"

"*But I didn't mean to scare her. Really I didn't! I'm so sorry.*"

"Sweetie, you don't need to apologize. But don't you want to move on from this place? I'd miss you a lot, but you can come back and visit. That's what the table's for, so you'll always have a place to hang out here. You don't need to be here all the time."

"*But Josie, I can't move on from you yet!*" She blinked back tears and looked surprised. "*Don't you know that?*"

"Why not?"

"*Because we have a soul contract.*"

"What's a soul contract?"

"*It means we have to help each other.*"

"How do you know we have one?"

"*They told me.*"

"Who's 'they?'"

"*The ones who met me when I first left here and got there. I can't move on till we work it out.*"

Chapter Thirteen

Before Josie could ask Ruby to elaborate, they were interrupted by someone needing help up front. When she went to find her before leaving for the night, she couldn't, so she fell asleep mulling over what it all meant. In a rare occurrence, she woke well before Derek after a hyper-realistic anxiety dream about Alex coming into their room while they slept. It was so vivid, Josie half-wondered if she'd dreamt it at all.

Of the many things making her anxious right now, currently topping the list was the conversation she needed to have with Mary Franco. It was too early to call, so instead she ground some beans and filled the French press to make coffee the way Derek liked it.

At 8:00 a.m., her phone chimed with a text from Ani.

GM. Hope it's not too early

She went through the laborious process of texting her back.

I'm up. All ok?

The response came a minute later.

Yes. Stayed here this w/e. Come by later?

B/t brunch & dinner? 2?

Perf.

Derek came out of the bedroom groggy, his hair sticking out in all directions.

"How did you sleep, my love?"

"Not well. I was up from two to five."

"I'm sorry. It was an awful night. I'm going to call Mary at nine."

He went to the kitchen to pour a cup of coffee.

"It's not as good as yours, but I tried."

"It's fine," he said dismissively, then added, "Thank you."

"Did you have bad dreams again?"

"Not bad, just—weird."

"Me too. Do you want to tell me about them?"

"It's too much to get into. Who are you texting?"

"Ani. I'm going to stop by her place later today."

"I thought she's in Connecticut on weekends?"

"You do listen!"

"Of course I listen," he said as though surprised she'd ever questioned him.

"She usually is, but not today. Maybe you can come meet her finally? After brunch?"

"I don't know. Let me just get through the next thirty minutes." He held up his cup. "Thanks for this, honey. It's a nice surprise."

She smiled but felt sad that her making the coffee was so noteworthy. It was time she start being more domestic. Derek showed his love through tangible action, while her strength lay in emotional caregiving, which he was seldom equipped to receive. So she'd find other ways to express herself, like getting up first to make coffee, or cooking dinner on their night off instead of defaulting to takeout.

They sat together on the couch reading the paper, Derek the front section, Josie *Arts and Leisure*. When she flipped through to find the book reviews, she glimpsed the lead story in the real estate section—*Declan Kelleher's Greenwich Village*. She pulled it out and surreptitiously buried it in the pages she was reading.

"Do you think it's okay to call Mary? It's just nine now."

"Should be fine. It's probably a workday for her."

Josie found her in the phonebook, dialed, then paced the apartment while waiting for her to pick up.

"Mary Franco."

"Mary, hi. This is Josie Gray from Miss Sylvie's Bistrot. We spoke earlier this—"

"Yes, hi, Josie. What can I do for you?" She was polite but direct, and Josie heard people in the background.

"I won't keep you. Just wanted to ask a quick question."

"*Shoot.*"

"Have you worked with a musician named Billy Duane?"

There was a pause, and Mary made a guttural noise. *"Please tell me you haven't hired him yet?"*

"Well, yes. He played a couple of happy hours, and there was an incident last night—"

"Of course there was an incident! There's always an incident, and that's why we stopped using him. Let me guess—he plied some college student with drugs and schtupped her in the coatroom? Pardon my Yiddish."

"Yeah, that's pretty close to what happened last night. Also, a week ago, when he apparently got aggressive."

"Shit—is the girl going to press charges?"

"I don't know, I don't know who it was."

"What? Don't tell me he *confessed—?"*

"No, another customer walked in on them and told me. So I take it you only worked with him a couple of times?"

"I wish. We hired him for a bunch of events. He made thousands of dollars from work we threw his way. He's a talented guy, I'll give him that. But once he got caught, we retraced our steps and found out he'd acted out pretty much every time."

Josie moved into the bedroom and lowered her voice. "Stephanie didn't know about any of this, right?"

Mary made a sputtering sound as though spitting out a drink. *"Are you kidding? Of course she knew! She was there when I went fucking ballistic on the dude. She's the one who called all the other people whose events we'd hired him for, so she probably knows more details than I do."*

"Wow."

"Please don't tell me she's the one who brought him to you."

Derek stood in the doorway listening. Josie shook her head at him.

"This is unbelievable. Yes, she's the one who brought them to us. Billy and Hal."

"Hal Mundy is a good man. Sorry you have to throw the babe out with the bathwater. And yeah, unbelievable, except totally believable. Stephanie has a skewed sense of loyalty, and I'm so sorry I foisted her on you guys."

"You didn't foist her on us."

"I gave her a solid referral because it seemed like the right thing to do. I honestly never thought she'd do something this fucking stupid and dangerous, pardon my English."

"I mean, what do you think her motivation could have been?"

"Honestly? Well, you might not know this, but we dated for a while."

"Yeah, she mentioned when we met her."

"Weird fuckin' thing to mention in a job interview, but that's Stephanie. Anyway, my point is I have some extra insight into her. She wants the seat at the cool kids' table she never got in high school, and for whatever reason, in spite of everything we learned, she thinks Billy Duane is one of the cool kids. I'm so unbelievably pissed at her right now for jeopardizing your business like this, and if I weren't about to set up for a bar mitzvah, I'd call and read her the riot act."

"Well, thank you very much for your time."

"It's quite literally the least I can do. Listen, feel free to reach out to me anytime. If you need vendors or entertainment, I've got a million contacts who I would *recommend."*

"Will do. Thank you again, Mary." She hung up and sat on the bed. "Derek, I'm stunned. This is exactly who Billy Duane is and why Mary stopped working with him. Stephanie knew all about it."

He sat next to her and dropped his head in his hands. "I'm gonna fucking lose it when I see her."

"Why would she do this to us?"

"Fuck it. I don't need to see her. Call her. Fire her."

That was what they had to do, of course, but Josie hated this part of things. More than that, she was hurt Stephanie would wrong them when they'd been so good to her, so trusting.

"But then we don't have a manager, and we really need one."

"Fuck it, Josie. She's fired. We figure out the managerial part later." He walked out of the room and shouted, "God damn it!"

Then came a loud thud.

Josie ran into the living room, where he was holding his fist and grimacing. "Honey, are you okay?"

"No, I'm not okay. I just fucking punched a wall and think I broke my finger!"

"Let me see it!"

He showed her his knuckles, which were red and swelling.

Josie pulled a bag of peas from the freezer—she'd bought them months earlier to make a chicken pot pie that never materialized—and wrapped a dishtowel over them. "Please sit down and hold this on your hand."

"I'm going to lose my fucking mind. Where's my phone?"

"I'll call her. Why don't you go to the gym and burn some of this off?"

"How the fuck am I going to do that if my hand is broken?"

"Derek, please stop cursing at me. This is an awful situation, but it's not my fault."

"I KNEW THERE WAS SOMETHING FUCKED UP ABOUT HER!"

She kept her voice measured. "And you were right. I see that now, obviously. I'm going to call her."

"No, let me do it—"

He dropped the peas on the sofa and stalked across the room to the bookshelf where his phone was charging. Muttering under his breath, he yanked the antenna, flipped it open, then pressed a few buttons. While he waited for her to answer, he wandered back to the coffee table and picked up the section of paper Josie had been reading. The real estate page fell out.

She closed her eyes and held her breath.

"Stephanie!" he said, holding the Declan Kelleher article in his hand. "Wait—damn it." He slammed his phone shut so hard Josie feared it would crack, then crumpled the newspaper into a ball and threw it across the room.

"What did she say?"

"She's calling me back."

"How's your hand?"

He held it up. "Not good. It's getting puffier."

"Okay, please sit down again and hold this on it for a few more minutes." She broke up the bag of peas to make it malleable, then rewrapped the towel around it.

He took it and just as he sat down, his phone rang. "Damn it!"

"I'll get it. We'll talk to her on speaker." She picked up his phone, relieved the screen was intact. "Hello."

"Josie. Hi. It's Steph." She sounded appropriately nervous. "*Listen, I am so sorry about what happened last night.*"

"Hold on, Stephanie. I'm going to put you on speaker." After setting the phone on the coffee table in front of them, she took Derek's good hand in hers. "Okay, we're both here."

"Hi, Derek. Listen guys, I'm so sorry and totally take responsibility for bringing Billy to you. I am stunned. I've known him for years, and this is the first time I've seen any—"

"Cut the bullshit, Stephanie," Derek said. "Just fucking quit while you're ahead."

There was a long pause before she spoke again. *"I'm not sure what you mean, Derek, but I'm being truthful. I've never known him to—"*

"You're FUCKING LYING!" he roared, his face reddening.

Josie had never seen him so angry, and she put her hand on his thigh to calm him.

But he wasn't done.

"Do you have any GODDAMN idea the kind of jeopardy you've put us in? You stupid BITCH!"

"Derek—" Josie said.

He shook her hand off and stood, bringing the ice pack with him. "I'm DONE, Josie. You deal with this idiot." He stomped into the bedroom, then slammed the door.

Josie took the call off speaker, determined to give her one final chance at honesty. "Stephanie, I know you knew about Billy's proclivities."

"No, Josie. I swear! I've never had an issue with him, and like I said, I've known him for years, so no one is more shocked by what happened than—"

"I spoke with Mary."

Another long pause.

"Mary—?" Her voice faltered as she said it.

"Mary Franco."

"Oh my God, Josie. If she claims I knew about whatever happened, she's lying! She's just trying to get back at me for breaking up with her. I swear!"

"What motivation would she have to lie to me?"

"*What motivation would* I *have*?"

"Only you can answer that."

Derek burst out of the bedroom, bellowing.

"QUIT WHILE YOU'RE AHEAD!"

On the other end of the phone, Stephanie began to cry. *"I'm sorry. I'm so sorry. I can't believe this—"*

"It's okay," Josie said out of habit.

"NO, IT ISN'T OKAY!" Derek grabbed the phone from her hand and spoke into it with chilling calm. "Stephanie, I don't ever want to see your face again. Come get your shit from the office at three o'clock this afternoon. Someone will be watching to make sure you don't steal anything. Leave your keys on the desk, don't ever contact us again, and if you don't come, we're throwing it all out." He flipped the phone shut. "Why the hell would you tell her it's okay?"

"I don't know. It just slipped out. Of course it's not okay."

"You're way too easy on people."

"I know."

"I'm going to get some air. I'll see you over there." He threw the bag of peas back into the freezer, then grabbed his jacket and keys.

As soon as the door slammed shut, Josie started shaking, her nerves utterly frayed. She had never seen him like this, had no idea how his anger might evolve, and it scared her. She was also unbearably sad his short-lived compassion had fallen away so quickly. On top of this, Raymond was a shit father, Stephanie had betrayed them, Declan Kelleher owned Greenwich Village, and she was stuck with Ruby, who had lost them a customer. All of that, though, paled in comparison to the fear she felt having witnessed Derek in such a rage. He had every reason to be angry, but it was devastating he'd taken it out on her so viciously.

The most immediate dilemma was they were out a manager, and it was her fault for pushing for Stephanie when he'd wanted Charlotte.

She needed to fix this, spearhead the search for a replacement. She'd get ahead of it, so by the time he brought it up, the search would be underway. This time, she'd do things as everyone else did in the twenty-first century and place the ad online. She went to Derek's desk and jiggled the mouse to wake his computer.

The screen lit up on an open Word document. She closed it, then saw it was titled *DM-Novel.* Biting her lip, she opened it again and read.

Chapter One

Jack Denton was conceived in grief and born in fear. He thought of himself as the phoenix that rose from his dead brother's ashes, an apt metaphor for the sibling of a kid killed in a house fire eleven months earlier. He was the replacement, and his mother never let him forget that.

Jack spent his first eighteen years trying to love her until he gave up and fled with three hundred bucks and a one-way ticket to New York.

She closed the file, panicked she hadn't saved it, then reopened it to check. It was intact.

"Oh my God." She put her hands to her mouth and paced back and forth across the room.

This was huge. He was writing again. And from an incredibly vulnerable place. Processing his trauma.

While, of course, this was something she wanted him to do, the timing scared her. The present was so fraught, she didn't see how revisiting the past right now could improve things. Maybe this helped explain his extreme reaction earlier. They'd weathered dishonesty in employees before, realized a little too late someone's moral compass was missing a magnet, and he'd never reacted so heatedly. Maybe this writing project was churning up too much.

She was too frazzled to think about the ad and instead took a long shower as hot as she could stand it. Afterward, she dressed in a pair of stretchy black jeans she'd forgotten about and as-yet-unworn suede boots from one of the shoe stores on Eighth Street. Nanette used to say if you looked the part, the mood would follow. In the back of her closet, she found a cashmere boat-neck sweater in winter white still bearing its price tag. She chewed the plastic thread to remove it.

She did her makeup, put on the diamond stud earrings Derek gave her for Valentine's Day, then opened the bottom drawer of her jewelry box where she faithfully placed Nanette's fleur-de-lis necklace every night.

It wasn't there.

Frantic, she slid the box across the dresser and rifled through all of its compartments—to no avail. When she remembered the adage about being less likely to find a missing item when looking in a panic, she began methodically searching the closet floor, bathroom, living room bookshelves, and sofa cushions. She dumped everything out of her purse, but the only extraneous items were a faded Duane Reade receipt, three pennies and a dime, and a mint Life Saver that had escaped its packaging.

The other place it could be was her office at Miss Sylvie's because sometimes she unclasped it and held it like a good luck charm. But she couldn't imagine leaving for the night without it, its delicate weight around her neck so familiar, its absence would be noticeable. It was part of her. Much as she wanted to get there and search for it, and much as she wanted to find

Ruby to continue their conversation, she'd have to wait. In this moment, it was most important Derek get to work first and have time to cool down before she showed up.

She took her phone from the coffee table and texted Ani.

Ok if I come now?

A return text chimed shortly after.

Yes! Come anytime!

After a final sweep of the apartment, she promised herself the necklace wasn't gone. She'd never lose something so dear, so it was just temporarily misplaced.

On her way to Ani's, she paused on Sixth Avenue to acknowledge the Twin Towers and ask Nanette to help her find it.

The man at the bodega greeted her effusively. "Hello, my beautiful friend! The usual?"

Just as she'd dressed in an effort to fool her sadness, she arranged her face into a happy smile. "*Si, mi amigo. Muchas gracias.*"

"*Con mucho gusto!*" He filled a cup with ice, prepared her coffee, then took a piece of banana bread from the glass case. "On the house. *Estás muy bonita hoy.* You look very pretty today!"

"Thank you."

It was stunning the impact a kind gesture or word could have on her these days. She held her back straighter as she walked down the block.

Ani's door was propped open, and the handsome painter was walking out with a large box.

"Hola, Hector! Como estàs?"

"Bien gracias."

He glanced fleetingly down her body, then caught himself and averted his gaze. Blushing, he brushed past her.

She walked through the apartment to the patio.

Ani was perched at the table, her *Write* journal in front of her. She looked up with a smile when Josie came outside. "Don't you look beautiful!"

"Thank you, but I'm really bummed out because I can't find my necklace."

"The one you were wearing last time? The fleur-de-lis?"

"Yes. It was my grandmother's and is one of the only things I own that I really care about. I'm hoping it's just at the office or somewhere obvious I've overlooked. How come you're not in Connecticut?"

"Wasn't worth it. Steve's working all weekend. Which is fine. I could use the extra writing time, and I'm finally in the zone."

"The writing zone?"

"Yes. One of those stretches where the ideas flow so fast I can hardly type them up. It's like creative autopilot. Which is why I'm happy to have this break because I've been staring at this screen for hours already."

"Have you made any progress with your character?"

"I'm starting to figure him out. I've decided he comes from a big family, lots of siblings, and he's the de facto man of the house because the father is in prison. Why, I'm not sure yet, but we'll get there."

"Well, that's a coincidence. My mystery man—"

"Eduardo."

"Yes, Eduardo. One of the few things I know about him is he has four younger sisters and no dad, so he was the man of the house."

"There you go. We're in sync."

"But I want to learn more."

"Give it time."

"What else have you figured out in your story?"

"I'm working with this idea that Robert's Achilles heel is his guilt over something that happened to his family, something traumatic he feels responsible for. Maybe his dad's imprisonment, maybe something else. Whatever it is, it's not his fault but…."

"Guilt doesn't care."

"Exactly. But enough about fiction. How's your weekend going besides the necklace? Which you're going to find."

"It's been pretty awful." Josie chewed her thumbnail. "We had an incident at the restaurant and had to fire someone, now Derek is mad at me again."

"I'm sorry."

"And here's something else—I accidentally found out he's writing again."

"Accidentally?"

"Yeah, I found the start of a novel on his computer. I didn't mean to, but he left it open, and I read the first couple of sentences. I feel horrible."

"You guys share the computer?"

"Technically, yes, but it's really his. The thing is, I was trying to do something good when I stumbled upon it, something to make the big picture better."

"The road to hell is paved with good intentions."

"I know. I feel awful, but I also feel a hundred other things."

"Like what?"

"I think I'm glad he's writing again, but I'm also sad he didn't feel he could talk to me about it, and I'm super nervous because what he's working on seems to be autobiographical fiction. And his biography is not pretty."

She gave Ani the gist of the sentences she'd read.

"There is so much else going on these days impacting his mood. I want to support him but don't know how. I mean, do I tell him I saw what he's working on?"

"Personally, I like to veer toward honesty even if it's not always comfortable. You weren't snooping. He left it open. So yeah, if it feels right, let him know you know. And beyond that, give him time and space. A lot of the work will happen when he's nowhere near the computer. Some of my best sentences come to me in the tub."

Josie's phone vibrated. She pulled it from her bag to see an incoming call from Curtis. "Hang on one sec," she said to Ani. "Hey, honey. Everything okay?"

"*Everything's fine, Lady Love. I'm back in town though—we had to cut our trip short because this Chilean painter Henry's been trying to woo is in New York. Do you think y'all could use me down at Miss Sylvie's? There's only so much conversation about stippling and chiaroscuro a guy can take.*"

"I'm not sure what you just said, but yes, come work brunch with me. We have a situation I don't want to face alone. I'd love to have you here."

"*You've got it. Let me just put my face on, then I'll shoot down in a cab.*"

"I'm at my friend Ani's, which is literally a block from the restaurant. Pick me up here!" She gave him the address and hung up.

"Is someone coming over?" Ani asked.

"Yeah, my friend Curtis, who's going to start working with us today. I'm sorry—I should have asked you first, but I really want you two to meet. Plus, I need a few minutes to brief him before we get to the restaurant. I can always meet him outside if—"

"Which one is Curtis?"

"I don't think I've mentioned him yet. He's my closest friend. He's basically the anti-Derek in that he totally believes and has been seeing spirits since he was a kid. He's one of the few people I can talk to about that stuff."

"Then I look forward to meeting him. Maybe I can interview him sometime."

"Oh, I'm sure you can. He's an open book too. Question for you—do you know what a 'soul contract' is?"

"More or less. My *abuela* used to talk about them. Why do you ask?"

As much as Josie wanted to be honest, she wasn't ready to explain. Bonding about a belief in spirit was one thing, discussing the specifics of her experiences another. It still didn't feel right to expose Ruby. Until now, she'd deemed their relationship so sacred, she'd not even told Curtis about her.

"Someone mentioned it in passing, and it sounded intriguing."

"The way my grandmother explained it, it's something that's worked out wherever we go between lifetimes. So the people 'they'"—she used air quotes—"say come into our lives for a reason? These are people we have soul contracts with. Does that make any sense?"

Josie mulled it over and shook her head. "Kind of? Not really."

"I guess the idea is everyone you cross paths with in a significant way—your mom, your third grade teacher, your husband, a friend, even a stranger you have a great conversation with and never see again—anyone who has any sort of impact on you is someone you know across lifetimes. You enter and stay in each other's realms because you have things to work out together. Like I said the other day, I believe we meet people for a reason. So if you and I have a contract, it's written in the stars we happen upon each other in the park, become friends, you help me work out some things in my book, I help you figure out how to approach Eduardo. We complain about our boyfriends, help each other through rough patches. It may sound minor, but we're fulfilling our contract. If you have a contract with someone, you have work to do with them, and if it doesn't happen in this lifetime, it'll happen in a future one."

"Do you think a living person can have a contract with a dead one?"

"That was what my grandmother believed, and that we have unlimited contracts. Ooh, that gives me an idea for Robert's dilemma."

She began scribbling in her notebook, filling one page and turning to the next. Josie sipped her coffee and looked around the yard. The geraniums still hadn't been watered, and now three deflated ballons lay next to the planter, as though they'd escaped a birthday party and met their demise. They looked pitiful to Josie, and she wondered at Ani's ability to focus in such an unkempt environment. Perhaps it was a byproduct of being in the zone. She hoped Derek could one day get there, maybe when some of the dust from Friday settled.

"Okay," Ani bookmarked the page with her pen.

"What was your idea?"

"This idea of a soul contract is going to be the thing that finally helps Robert release his guilt. I just have to figure out how to connect about a thousand dots."

"The whole process is fascinating to me, this ability to tell a story. How much of it is mined from your life and how much is pure imagination?"

"It's hard to say because the two start to blend. It's a weird kind of alchemy."

"Well, I have deep appreciation for storytellers and am excited to one day read your book."

"Be careful what you wish for. I'm going to need a beta reader soon."

"Meaning?"

"Meaning someone who'll read early drafts and give me feedback—general feedback or specific things they have questions on or opinions on particular issues I ask about."

"I'd love to do that for you!"

"Great! When I'm ready, I'll print out the first couple of chapters."

Josie's phone pinged in her hand. "That was fast. He's outside already." She scraped her chair back. "Thank you once again for an enlightening coffee date. I needed this one badly."

"I'm glad I can offer respite from the chaos. I'll come say hi to your friend."

Curtis stood on the front stoop with two iced coffees.

"Large iced, light and sweet."

"Thank you. It's a multiple-cup day. Curtis, meet Ani. Ani, my dear friend, Curtis."

"It's great to meet you, Curtis."

"You too! Any friend of Josie's, especially one as stunning as you are."

"See why I keep him around?" Josie asked.

"One hundred percent."

"Any chance you can come by the restaurant tonight, finally?"

"I'll do my best. Let me see how far I get, and I'll try to take a quick study break. Until then, I hope everything goes better than expected."

On the short walk to Bistrot, Josie filled Curtis in on the Billy Duane debacle, the ghost sighting, Stephanie's role in it all, and her missing necklace.

"Lady, that's horrible! Your fleur-de-lis?"

"Yes, and I'm trying not to panic."

"Don't panic about that. But that Stephanie sure sounds unhinged. And… we have a ghost?"

"You knew that! We have a ghost table."

"Well, yeah. I knew we had a ghost—ghosts—in theory, meaning the ones we honor, but we have a specific one that's scaring people?"

"We have a ghost, I don't know details." She'd tell him, eventually. "Derek doesn't know that part yet, but he's plenty livid about the rest."

"Understandably."

"Understandably. However, now we're down a manager again. We need someone soon or Derek and I are going to spontaneously combust. Want a promotion? You know the business as well as anyone."

"I can't. School has to come first. What about that Lucy? She seems pretty managerial."

Josie stopped walking and grabbed his arm. "That's actually a really good idea!"

"Maybe try to deliver the line sounding less shocked."

"No, but I mean, you hardly know her, and you can see it—she'd make a kick-ass manager!" She stood on tiptoes, and he bent down so she could kiss his cheek. "You might have just saved my relationship."

"My man," Derek said when they walked in, clapping Curtis on the shoulder. "I'm sure Josie filled you in on what's going on around here."

"Lordy. Y'all shouldn't have to be putting out fires like that."

"Curtis has a good idea for the manager position. What about promoting Lucy?"

Derek pursed his lips, looked up in the air while he thought, then nodded. "Wow. Actually, that's pretty damn smart."

"Again, guys, delivery is important."

"No, it's a really good move." He clapped him on the shoulder again. "Nice going. Great to have you back in the fold, man."

Curtis shrugged. "I aim to please. What do y'all want me to do first here?"

"Go say hi to Jerome, he's behind the bar. Joze, can I chat with you for a second? In the office?"

"Sure."

As she followed him back to the office, she did a sweep for Ruby but didn't see her. Derek shut the door once they were inside.

"How's your hand?"

"Bruised but not broken." He held it up to show her. "I'm sorry for this morning. I shouldn't have lost my temper at you and left like that."

"It's been a rough stretch, and this debacle is the icing on the cake we didn't order."

"There's more to it, to my mood. It's about the dreams I've been having."

"Okay."

He sighed and held her hand with his good one. "It's my brother."

"Your brother?"

"Alex. I'm dreaming about him every single night, and it's freaking me out."

Chapter Fourteen

THE ICY FEELING that crept down Josie's back was offset by the rawness of Derek's expression. She'd never seen him so vulnerable. "Sweetheart, of course it's freaking you out!"

"I'm sorry I didn't say anything until now. Turns out not thinking about these dreams won't stop them from coming."

"No, I imagine not."

His eyes misted, and she laced her fingers in his.

"Jesus. Sorry," he said. "Get a grip, man."

"You don't need to get a grip. This is a really big deal."

"I haven't felt like this in decades. And when I lose my shit over anything, like last night, I wind up taking it out on you. That's not okay. I'll try to do better."

"Please do. I can't stand walking around on eggshells with this pit in my stomach."

"Crazy thing is, another part of what's weighing on me is the bullshit with your father, and that's the last thing I should be lashing out at you for. I guess when you said 'it's okay' to Stephanie, it triggered something. Because what she did is *not* okay. What your dad did is *not* okay. It dredged up some of my childhood, where I had to pretend things were fine when they weren't, or swallow my feelings 'cause you're not supposed to be mad at your parents. Then the dreams started coming. And I haven't told you this, but I've been writing."

She cupped his face in her hands. "I know."

"You do?"

"Yes. You left your file open, and I went to look something up on the computer. I'm sorry. It was an accident."

"You never look stuff up. You hate that thing."

"I know." She threw her arms in the air. "And the one time I decide to use it, I invade your privacy."

"Did you read it?"

"Only the very beginning, and it was beautiful. It reminded me what a wonderful writer you are. And piecing it all together, of course you're overwhelmed, Jack Denton."

He gave her a half smile. "You like the name?"

"It's a good one."

"I started writing in the middle of the night after like, the third dream. That's what I do when I'm up in those hours. I thought maybe the dreams were my psyche trying to purge some of this stuff and writing it out would help, like if I took care of it while I'm awake, he'd stop showing up while I sleep. I was wrong, and I don't know what it all means."

"I have ideas. Maybe you'll indulge me later, let me bring up some of the stuff you don't usually like to talk about?"

He was quiet for a beat. "Okay. You can do that."

"Thank you."

"But first, we have to get through all five brunch covers."

What Josie really wanted was to look for her necklace, but she didn't want to pile on to Derek's angst by adding her own. She did a perfunctory scan of the desktops and surfaces, pledging to search deeper when she had time.

In the dining room, Curtis sat with Twyla and the other servers.

"Is Lucy here?" Derek asked.

"She's only working dinner tonight," Twyla said. "Something I can help you with?"

"No, we just need to talk to her. We'll do it tonight."

Josie put her hand on Curtis's shoulder. "Before the hordes come in, come upstairs with me to meet Chef."

"Twyla says I give off strong Capricorn vibes," he said as they climbed the stairs.

"Everyone says that about you. Crazy to think you're a Pisces."

"That girl's a trip." He gasped when they reached the landing. "Lady, I forgot how beautiful this table is." He put his arm around her waist. "Even if you accidentally drew in some mischief-making entity, you've created a perfect refuge for our departed loved ones."

Curtis was Josie's closest support after Nanette died and had been particularly fond of Sylvie for the eight years he worked at Bistrot. In her final summer, with her memory slipping and people noticing, he'd become protective, escorting her across the street to her apartment at the end of the night.

"This has been a bone of contention with Derek, but he's choosing his battles. For now, it stays."

"Good. It would be a strange hill for him to die on, but if he did, he'd have a beautiful place to hang out."

Josie brought him into the kitchen. "Hey, guys! I want you to meet someone."

Naomi paused on the pot she was stirring and rested the spoon to the side. She wiped her hands on her apron. "Hey, there! You must be the famous Curtis!"

"Bring it in, Chef." He held out his arms for a hug. "My fellow Southern transplant."

"You can take the girl out of the south.... Glad to have you on the team."

"Glad to be on it. And I can't believe I'm just meeting you. Your shrimp and grits make me swoon."

He did a double-take when he saw Eduardo, who came around the corner and smiled at Josie. "Back for more holy trinity prep?"

"Not today. I want to introduce you all to my dear friend who's working with us now. Eduardo, meet Curtis Mitchell. Curtis, Eduardo Quiñones, our sous-chef."

"Good to meet you, man." Eduardo extended his hand.

Curtis reached for it, appeared to short circuit, then quickly let go. "Nice to meet you." He turned to Josie, an unreadable look on his face.

"We should get back down. It's almost brunch time."

Outside the kitchen, Curtis paused at the table, his hands on the back of a chair. He stared into the air. "What in the hell just happened?"

"Talk to me."

"I touched his hand and got the weirdest vibe, like an electric shock of sadness." He shuddered.

"I had the same exact thing when I met him, and it's been plaguing me."

"He's so handsome and so sad."

"I really needed to hear this from someone else. I thought I was losing my mind. Derek told me not to pry into his life, but I've got to know what's going on."

"Something." He shuddered again.

"Can you make it your mission to get to know him?"

"Lady, you know I'd do damn near anything for you, but not this. I'll need to mainline Prozac to hang out with him."

"For what it's worth, I only felt it the first time. But since then, I keep hearing words around him, asking me to help him. It's like some higher power letting us know he's not okay and tapping us to figure it out."

"I need to leave this alone."

"I need your help."

"Can't do it."

"We'll discuss."

"End of discussion. Let's get on with this beautiful mess that is our livelihood."

It was a refrain Josie heard often when they worked together at Bistrot. It would take some effort, but she would convince him. He'd get onboard with the Eduardo mission.

Brunch flowed quickly, the room not desolate but empty enough Josie was embarrassed and hoped Curtis didn't regret his decision to join them. But he remained in high spirits and handled his duties with exemplary finesse.

"Sorry to leave you alone to deal with this." Derek zipped up his jacket. "But I know you'll do better than me. You won't punch any walls."

"Not looking forward to it, but no, I won't punch any walls. I'll call you when she's gone."

At 3:00 p.m., Josie waited in the bar, assuming Stephanie would be eager to get this over with and show up on time. She didn't.

"What do I do if she doesn't come?"

"Change the locks," Curtis said. "Meanwhile, can I tell you how grateful I am to be back here with you and D? I've missed y'all. And this place is great."

"It *is* great, though you'd never guess from the dozens of empty seats at every meal."

"Rome wasn't built in a day, Miss Thing."

Josie could hear Jerome rearranging things downstairs in the liquor room, clanking bottles as he moved them about. He probably couldn't hear them, but she lowered her voice anyway. "Miss Thing really needs your help with the Eduardo situation."

"Why me?" Curtis whined.

"Because you're the only one who gets it. Naomi sees his sadness but doesn't want to delve. Plus, I'm her employer."

"I don't want to delve either, and you're *my* employer too!"

"You don't count."

"The poor guy. The poor *hot* guy."

"I have never experienced anything like what happened when I shook his hand. Have you?"

"Not like that. But we're energy sponges, you and me. I pick up on strangers' emotions constantly."

"Have you picked anything else up from people here?"

"From customers, sure. Sidney Feist, even before she said a word. That bald guy at brunch. The little kid at happy hour."

"What bald guy?"

"Table twelve. He ordered the eggs Sardou and three mimosas, his friend had pancakes and water."

"What kid at happy hour?"

"The little guy running around looking for his stuffed bunny rabbit. At least, I assume it was stuffed."

"I don't remember a—" Josie stood quickly and widened her eyes. "What did he look like?"

"Cute little blonde fellow. Mop of curls. Big smile, dimples."

She grabbed his shoulders. "Oh my God—you saw him?"

"Why are you being weird?"

"About this tall?" She held her hand up. "Striped sweater?"

"Josephine you're freaking me out."

"That's Derek's brother!"

"Derek's—" His mouth hung open. He rubbed his arms. "Oh my God."

"I know!"

He walked in a circle, hands on his head. "Oh my God, oh my God."

"Did you interact with him?"

"I said hi."

"Did he say anything?"

"He said hi too." His voice cracked. "This is so sad and freaky."

"Welcome to my sad and freaky world. And now that I have your attention, I desperately need your help."

"With?"

"Getting Derek to call home. I have so much to tell you—"

Jerome emerged from the liquor room carrying four bottles of wine, a bar towel slung over his shoulder.

"Boss lady, you have company."

She turned with trepidation.

"Josie." Stephanie stood by the entrance to the bar, hands on her hips, jaw jutting forward.

Josie read body language well enough to know she was being challenged. She looked at her watch—fifteen minutes late. "Let's go to the back, Stephanie."

Curtis twirled around in his barstool and began talking intently to Jerome, so obviously pretending he didn't know what was going on, it was clear to anyone looking he knew everything.

In the office, Stephanie slid off her backpack and crossed her arms. Her hair, usually neat and gelled, hung in her face. "Look, Josie, I'm sorry about what happened, but I'm really not cool being blamed for something I had no control over."

"No control over? What are you talking about?"

"I wasn't up there! I didn't know Billy had drugs on him or was hitting on that girl or whatever!"

Derek was right—Josie was the person for this job because there was no way he'd be able to remain as calm as she was determined to. No matter how much Stephanie escalated, she'd keep her own voice and responses even.

"Stephanie. Whether or not you knew he had drugs or designs on that girl is irrelevant. No one's accusing you of premeditating this incident. But you knew who he was and brought him to us anyway."

"I didn't know who he was!"

"Mary *told* me you did. That you were there when she confronted him."

"Mary's a liar," she said coldly. She blew a strand of hair out of her eye and glared defiantly at Josie.

"Again, Mary has absolutely no reason to lie to me."

"What reason would I have?" Her voice shot up several decibels, and she flared her nostrils.

"To keep your job?"

"That is bullshit!"

"Don't shout at me, Stephanie. Please calm down."

Stephanie continued to stare at her, chest heaving. "It's Mary who's lying. I would never lie to keep my job."

"That's not how we see it."

"Who's 'we?'"

"Derek and me."

"Wow, Josie." She yanked open a desk drawer, then began shoving things into her backpack. Josie catalogued everything she removed, hoping to catch sight of her necklace—both to have it back and to have cause for firing Stephanie in the remote chance she were telling the truth and it was Mary who was lying. "I thought you were *so* much cooler than this. I would never have pegged you as one of those women."

"One of what women?" Josie asked wearily.

Stephanie arranged her mouth in a tight grimace, refusing to look at her. For the first time since Josie had met her, she looked deeply unattractive.

"One of those women who discredits herself and lets her man run the show."

"What on earth are you talking about?"

"Derek didn't like me from the start, that was clear, and he's trying to pin this on me so he has a reason to get rid of me. He's not the type of guy who wants women in charge. It threatens him."

Josie let out an incredulous laugh. "If it makes you feel better to believe that's what's happening here, go for it. I think if you find out who's replacing you, you'll realize how ridiculous you sound. Not to mention, I'm the co-owner here, and we have a woman running the kitchen. Your allegation is utterly absurd."

Stephanie's bottom lip trembled.

"Look, Stephanie, I'm sorry this didn't work out, and I believe you had nothing to do with what happened last night—of course you didn't. But I'm having a very hard time believing Mary's lying and you knew nothing of Billy's reputation."

"Okay, fine!" She huffed like a petulant teenager. "I knew there'd been an incident or two, but I didn't know details. He's a great musician, and I'm a big believer in giving people the opportunity to change. Because people do change. What happened to you being the one who gives second and third chances? You let Ian stay on and keep screwing up!"

"I believe people can change as well. But that, too, is irrelevant. Ian was not great at his job, but he never knowingly put our business in jeopardy. As Derek and I see it, if you knew there'd been any incident at all, then you jeopardized us. If you want to believe I'm just going along with him because he's the one in charge, so be it. I have zero interest in trying to convince you otherwise, and frankly, I don't care what you think of me."

Stephanie twisted a key off her keyring and held it out. When Josie reached for it, she pulled it back.

"You know, Josie, it would be a real shame if word got out this happened. Not just that there were drugs and all that, but that this place is haunted. That'd be pretty bad for business, wouldn't it?"

"Are you threatening me?"

"I'm just making an observation."

She dropped the key in Josie's palm and smiled. "There are lots of tabloids in this town that love restaurant dirt. I read Marcus Dreyer's piece on Bistrot last summer."

Marcus Dreyer was a gossip columnist for the *New York Mirror* who thrived on sordid tales from the industry. The previous summer, he penned a snarky account of Chef's spectacular public meltdown—the incident that marked the beginning of the end of Bistrot.

"You're a troubled person, Stephanie. I hope things get better for you." Josie shooed her out of the office, then followed her through the dining room to the front door. She watched her walk up the steps and away from the restaurant.

"My lord." She walked into the bar. "That was insane. That woman's issues are the stuff of legend."

"Yeah, I could have told you that from the start," Jerome said.

"I need another coffee. Curtis, will you take a walk with me?"

"We have coffee here!"

He was trying to avoid continuing their conversation, but Josie didn't care. She needed him. She bit her bottom lip. "I need a walk *and* a coffee. Jerome, do you want anything from the outside world?"

"All good."

Curtis made a face and hoisted himself off his barstool. "If I'm not back in thirty, send help."

"You got it, brother."

Once outside, Josie said, "I don't need coffee."

"I know that. You have so many tells."

"Let's walk around the block."

She took his arm. They made a left on Ninth Street, then another left onto Sixth Avenue. "So, this is fabulous. Stephanie's threatening to call Marcus Dreyer and tell him the restaurant's haunted."

"Honestly? That could be really good for us. That's the kind of thing that entices people. The ghost table is a draw, right?" He stopped and turned to her. "Oh my God. It's 'us' again! How great is that!"

"The best, but as for the ghost table, no one goes up there anymore. It had about three weeks of fame, and it's not like Derek's eager to advertise it. How could publicity about the other night be good? Between Declan Kelleher—and the only good thing about this Stephanie bullshit is that Derek's temporarily stopped obsessing over him—but between that and a ghost sighting, we could be really screwed."

They made another left on Eighth Street to walk the long block—an inelegant, well-trodden stretch anchored by a Gray's Papaya and lined with discount shoe stores and headshops—toward Fifth Avenue.

"Are you kidding?" Curtis asked. "People love this stuff! Why do you think there are so many books and TV shows about haunted hotels and restaurants? Ghosts are hot. There's even some medium with a TV show now. And oh my God, are you sure there wasn't a little kid running around happy hour?"

"If there was, I didn't notice, and the kid you described sounds like Alex right down to the bunny. I've seen him too. He came to find me because he has a message for Derek."

"Holy moly." Curtis tightened his grip on her. "This is freaking me out."

"You're the one person I know who's seen them before! I need you to normalize this for me. You can't be freaked out."

"Well, I can't help it. It's been a minute since I've seen one."

"Are you sure about that? Apparently, it hasn't."

"I'm not sure about anything. How are you so Zen about it all?"

"Because at this point, I don't have much choice. Once I started seeing them, I started seeing them. And the one from last night, I see her constantly."

"Her! The one who freaked out that girl?"

"Yes. Her name is Ruby. She's one of the waitresses who died at Dave's Continental, and she never really left the building."

"Oh. My. God."

"Yeah."

"Girl. One at a time, please. I worked in that building eight years and never once ran into Ruby, and I don't want to now."

"That alone is probably enough to keep her away. But she's the one who brought Alex to me, and I don't think he'll be coming back either. I think he's done what he came here to do."

"What makes you think that?"

"If I tell you, can you try to accept it at face value without getting all freaked out?"

"No. Tell me anyway."

"Like I said, Ruby's around a lot. And that makes sense—it's where she died."

"That's so sad."

"She's very troubled, very sweet, and we've forged some kind of friendship. She says we have a 'soul contract.' Do you know what that is?"

"Vaguely."

"According to Ani, it means we've known each other across lifetimes and have something to work out together. That we're contracted to help each other. Part of my contract with Ruby has to do with Alex and Derek, which will help them but also will help *me* because it'll allow me to reach Derek in a way I've never been able to. Ruby brought Alex to me because he has a message for Derek."

"Which is what?"

"Their mother is sick, and he needs to go see her. So, wild as this all sounds, I think now that he's told me that, he's back in Colorado, and I have to figure out how to get Derek out there too."

"What about your end of the contract? What are you supposed to do for Ruby?"

"I have no idea."

"How the hell are you going to get Derek out to Colorado?"

"Also no idea."

"Lady."

"I know. I learned this morning that part of what's been stressing him out so much is he keeps dreaming about Alex."

"Visitation dreams?"

"Probably, and they're taking a toll on him. Trying to get him to consider going home in the middle of all this feels nearly impossible. But I have to do it."

They turned north on Fifth Avenue and headed toward the corner of Ninth, where Josie and Derek lived.

"This ain't gonna be easy, Josie."

"No, it ain't. Because if there's one thing about Derek, it's that—"

"Incoming."

Derek was crossing the street toward them, waving a manila folder.

Josie had grown quite adept at quickly switching gears and greeted him with a smooth diversion. "I'm really, really glad you weren't there, D."

"Have we seen the last of her?"

"Seen, yes, but probably not heard."

"Meaning?"

"Let's just say I get the feeling she's not going to go gentle into that good night. What's in the folder?"

"Remember the Red Sox bro? I found his review and printed it out."

"Is it terrible?"

"Terribly written, but they liked the food."

"Who reviewed?" Curtis asked.

"Something you've never heard of. CityEats. Last weekend, this insufferable kid comes in with his girlfriend and waves me over, complaining their server forgot their drinks and got their order wrong. Any guess whose section they were in?"

"My esteemed predecessor's."

They went back into the restaurant and sat at a table in the barroom. Derek pulled out a sheet of paper. "Want to hear this?

"Of course."

"'*Miss Sylvie's Bistrot, contrary to its name, serves Cajun food in a spacious* endroit—'"

"*Endroit*?" Curtis rolled his eyes. "Bitch, please."

"'*This reviewer came here for brunch recently accompanied by a lovely companion with exquisite taste in food, not to mention dates, and while we can say some good things, the experience left us wanting a little je ne sais quoi.*'"

"Well, *JE sais,*" Curtis said. "This guy can't write for *merde.*"

"'*The food we wound up with—eggs Sardou, a staple in the Big Easy, and savory beignets, to name a few—were sumptuously prepared and flavorful, and our libations did the trick. Unfo we can't really speak to the meal we ordered, as what we got was not that.*'"

"I mean if you tried to write about a bad writer, you couldn't write this bad," Curtis said.

"Seriously," Josie said. "It's almost impressive."

"'*To say the service was lacking is like saying the Titanic hit a speed bump. Meaning there was no service.*'"

"Wait." Curtis held up a finger. "Is he an iceberg denier?"

"I'm totally lost."

"That's because it makes no sense. '*Nevertheless, they comped our meal and offered us a free dinner, which we will definitely take them up on.*'"

He shifted his eyes to Josie.

"Sorry, honey, I just didn't know what else—"

"'*Maybe the confusing name is one of the reasons there's no draw. Nothing about it matches the cuisine. Who is Miss Sylvie?*'"

"Oh no, girl." Curtis slapped the tops of his thighs. "Don't you go there."

"*And why a bistrot? Why not say it like it is—it's about New Orleans. Not the owners' friends. We give this experience, on the CityEats scale of Nope to Yay, an Eh with promise. Our roving dinner team will update this review once we go back for our comped meal.*'"

"Brilliant."

"If this doesn't get him a Pulitzer." Derek folded the page in quarters.

They sat in silence, digesting.

"I mean, the eggs Sardou *are* great," Josie said.

Derek shrugged. "He kind of has a point about 'bistrot.'"

"You know, y'all, maybe the name change thing makes a tiny bit of sense?"

"We can't do that!" Josie said. "Screw that guy. There's no rule that a restaurant name has to be literal! Tavern on the Green's not a tavern. Shun Lee Palace isn't a palace. Windows on the World is actually Windows on New York and New Jersey. We can't change the name!"

"It's something to think about," Derek said. "The word 'bistrot' is kind of misleading."

"Well then, can't we just name it Miss Sylvie's?"

"That sounds like we serve soul food," Curtis said. "We serve food with soul, but the real soul food is at places like Sylvia's in Harlem. Look y'all, I loved our Sylvie. But if anyone would want us to succeed, it's her. We could honor her memory with a photo or a plaque at her seat."

"Drink named after her," Derek offered.

"So, what do we call the place then?"

"How about Fleur-de-Lis?" Lucy breezed by, then said over her shoulder, "Sorry—I read it this afternoon."

Josie instinctively touched her clavicle, then remembered its bareness.

"Should we…?" Derek asked her.

"Sure."

"Hey, Lucy?" Derek called. "Can you come here a sec?"

"Uh-oh. Am I in trouble?" She pivoted on her heel, then walked toward them.

"Not at all. We want to promote you to manager."

Chapter Fifteen

LUCY ACCEPTED THE position with enthusiasm and resolved to find her replacement quickly. Confident she would dive headfirst into the role, Josie left her to handle the start of dinner service so she could search for her necklace. She looked behind the bar where found objects were stashed. All that was there were an abandoned pack of Lucky Strikes—neither bartender smoked—and two lighters, a Zippo engraved with the letter X and a fuchsia Bic. She checked the lost-and-found shelf in the coatroom but found only an umbrella, a single leather glove, and the keycard to a hotel room. Finally, she went back to the office, opened drawers, looked under seat cushions. Nothing. Dejected, she went back to the dining room.

Lucy stood in the entrance, keeping watch.

"How's it going?"

"So far so good," Lucy said. "And I'm not just saying this 'cause I get a new gig out of it, but I felt like there was something off about Stephanie from the start."

"So did Derek. I should have listened to him."

"No 'shoulds.' Regret is bullshit. Learn the lesson and move on."

Josie scanned the room, wistful for the halcyon days at Bistrot when every table was filled while people waited in the bar. "It would be easier to do that if she hadn't threatened to out us to the press."

"For what?"

"Having a ghost."

"Let her. Table's a draw, what's one more ghost?" Lucy nodded up to the landing, where people were milling about.

"What's going on up there?"

"Some girls wanted to see the table, so I sent them up. That okay?"

"I think so. It's just weird. It used to be a revolving door for photo ops, but no one's asked about it in months."

"Want me to see what's going on?"

"I will."

A quartet of young women flanked the table—one brunette in a cowboy hat, another with a pixie cut, a tanned blonde, and a redhead. They had a digital camera and were taking turns playing photographer while the others mugged, flashing peace signs and making kissing faces.

"Hi, ladies," Josie said when she reached the top of the stairs. "Can I help you with something?"

"Hi!" The redhead wiggled her fingers in a wave. "Do you work here?"

"Sure do."

"Cool. We wanted to check out your ghost table."

"May I ask how you heard about it?"

The girl in the cowboy hat wolf-whistled.

The redhead swatted her, then answered. "This guy I met last night? He used to work here too." She blinked several times and tucked a strand of hair behind her ear.

Josie knew what was coming.

"Do you know Ian?"

"Indeed."

"I met him at happy hour after class, and he said—"

"Class? How old are you guys?"

"You're not really supposed to ask a woman her age," the pixie cut said snippily.

"No, it's cool, Catherine," the redhead said. "We're legal. They checked at the bar."

"Okay. You met Ian last night, and he said what?"

"He said he quit because he didn't like the owners," the pixie cut said.

"Did he, now?"

"What can you tell me about him?" the redhead asked.

A dozen possible responses ran through Josie's mind. "I can tell you he has a robust social life."

"Ooh, Chelsea," the blonde said. "A boyfriend with a robust social life? That would be a change."

"As if, bitch." Chelsea laughed, then turned back to Josie, who hated when women referred to one another that way. "This is really cool. I totally believe in ghosts."

"I'm glad you think it's cool. We do, too, because we love and respect the people we created this table for. They're very important to us. Let's be mindful of that."

She gestured to the one with the cowboy hat, who was checking her lipstick in the reflection of a butter knife. The blonde elbowed her, and she put it down.

"*Josita*!" Mario came partway up the stairs. "You have a visitor. *El mismo hombre* from last time."

"*Quién, el medico*?"

"*Creo que sí*,"

She turned back to the girls.

"Okay, ladies. Time to wrap things up. Thanks for visiting."

"I'll tell Ian you say hi," Chelsea said. "What's your name?"

"Stephanie."

Josie followed them down the stairs and found Dr. Bannister by the entrance to the dining room studying the black-and-white Hollywood stills on the wall, hands clasped behind his back.

"Doctor Bannister."

He spun around.

"Josie. I hope you'll pardon yet another intrusion."

"No intrusion. Can I help you with something?"

"Well, this is rather awkward, but I wanted to know if you wouldn't be terribly bothered by my dining here."

"Tonight?"

"Yes. You see, my wife and I were on our way to the home of friends in the area when they called to say there was a change of plans. Their oven stopped working, and it was hard to find a table anywhere, so they made a reservation here."

Josie ignored the unintended—she hoped—slight.

"They're seated in the dining room, but of course I can explain this is a conflict of interest without saying why—"

"It's not awkward at all, Doctor Bannister. Please, come in and join us. I'll make sure you're well taken care of."

He unclasped his hands and smiled. "Thank you, Josie. This is very kind of you. Do you think Derek would be all right with it? And whatever I should tell my dining companions about how we know each another is your decision."

"Tell them the truth." She shrugged. "We had a consult, and it wasn't the right fit. It must happen all the time. As for Derek, honestly, he'll be happy just to have the business."

Josie kept an eye on their table throughout the night.. They seemed to enjoy themselves and in fact the dining room, while not full, maintained the comforting thrum of a festive night—conversation and laughter punctuated by the clinking of glasses and flatware to plates.

On one of her walk-throughs, she met Anthony carrying a tray of dishes down the stairs. "Hey, Anthony. Table fourteen are VIPs—"

"That's Twyla's section!"

"I know. Will you make sure they're not being inundated with talk of orbs and moon signs?"

"I'll do my best." He cocked his head toward the landing. "It's Grand Central Station up there tonight."

"Word seems to have gotten out."

"Whatever keeps the lights on."

She took the stairs two at a time to find another group of tipsy young women with a digital camera. Ruby was seated at the table, watching them. She held a finger to her lips, letting Josie know she knew to be quiet.

Josie was eager to talk to her. But first….

"Hello, ladies." She extracted a glass from one of the women's hands, placed it back in front of Nanette's seat, and made a mental note to have Lucy write up rules. "Let's keep the place settings where they are."

"Sorry!"

"How did you all find out about this table?"

The three women talked over one another.

"Some guy we met at happy hour told us you have great cocktails and that this table's here, and we should come see it."

"We're having drinks downstairs but wanted to come up and check it out. I'm like, super into the whole ghost thing."

"So am I! I swear the house I grew up in was haunted—"

"Who was it that you met?" Josie asked.

"Some guy who used to work here but quit because he hated the—"

One of the girls nudged the speaker with the subtlety of a leopard-print thong. "What's your name?" she asked.

"I'm Josie, I'm one of the owners here."

They looked at each other, clearly privy to Josie's reputation as one of Ian's unbearable bosses.

"Cool. Well, thanks! Let's go downstairs, guys. I need another—what am I drinking again?"

"A *Vieux Carré*," her friend said, butchering the cocktail named for the French Quarter.

"Thank you so much for coming in. If you see Ian again, please give him my best."

"Will do!"

"Bye, Jody!"

As the women retreated down the stairs, Ruby giggled, then clapped her hand over her mouth. When they were alone, she said, "*Hi, Josie.*"

"Hi, Ruby. Listen, I want to talk to you more about the whole soul contract thing."

She was interrupted by Anthony, who bounded up the stairs so quickly she had little warning until he was standing in front of her.

"Yo yo. Your VIPs are on dessert. Thought you'd want to know."

"Thank you."

She wanted to say more to Ruby, but Anthony lingered, so she nodded and went back down.

Dr. Bannister's table was strewn with the detritus of a meal enjoyed. A near-empty wine bottle nestled amidst coffee cups, a French press, and two plates bearing the remnants of the beignet profiteroles Ling, the pastry chef, invented.

"I see you've ordered my favorite dessert!"

"They're fabulous!" Dr. Bannister's wife said. "This has been a sensational meal, start to finish."

With her English accent, gray bob, and wide, pleasant face, she was her husband's perfect physical counterpart. Together they reminded Josie of a pair of novelty salt-and-pepper shakers.

"Have you lived in New Orleans?" the woman from the other couple asked.

"No, but I've spent some time there. It's one of my favorite places on the planet."

"A magical city." Dr. Bannister, who'd given no indication in their initial conversation that he had any connection to it at all, beamed at her. There was a glob of chocolate sauce on his yellow and blue necktie.

"We've spent a lot of time there over the years," Mrs. Bannister said. "This food is as close to the real thing as I've had."

"Our chef is a proud New Orleans native, and as my partner says, you can taste the love in her food."

"Here, here!" Dr. Bannister said, hoisting an empty wine glass.

"I'm so glad you all enjoyed your meal."

"If you'll have us, we'll happily return."

"With pleasure, Doctor Bannister."

"Please, call me Quentin."

This festive gentleman—chocolate-smudged, red in the cheek—was a very different man from the one she'd met in his office. Twyla brought over a tray of cordials and set them and the check on the table. She gestured toward Mrs. Bannister. "This lovely lady is a Sagittarius just like me."

"What are the odds? No rush at all on the check. Enjoy your drinks!"

Josie spent a few minutes chatting with the table next to theirs, and when she turned around again, her eye was drawn to movement on the landing. She jogged up the steps and found Ani circling the table, admiring its settings. Ruby sat watching her.

"Ani! You came! Does this mean writing went well?"

"Well enough that I needed a break. I wanted to say hi and see the famous ghost table, but you were busy, so Curtis brought me up."

"I'm not sure how famous it is, though a disgruntled former employee seems to have made himself a one-man PR machine for it. And on the subject of disgruntled former employees, I have so much to tell you."

"Come by tomorrow or Monday when you're off?"

"I'd love to. I'm so glad you're finally seeing the restaurant. And the table."

"It's really special." Ani stopped at the setting next to Ruby's and ran her hand over the charger. "The details are exquisite."

"The guests of honor are worth it."

"Josie," Ruby said. "*I need to talk to you—*"

Ani shivered. "Really strong energy here too."

"You feel it?"

"How can you not?"

"*Please, Josie!*"

"Want to come downstairs for a drink or a bite? On the house?"

"I wish. I still have a chapter and a half to finish tonight. It's beautiful out, so I decided to take a walk, but I should get back. Want to walk me down and introduce me to Derek?"

Ruby shook her head frantically. "*It's an emergency!*"

"I have to check in with the kitchen, but introduce yourself on the way out."

"Okay. Come by tomorrow. You know where I'll be."

"I do, and I will."

Josie walked Ani to the top of the stairs and said goodbye. When she turned back, she startled. Standing next to Ruby was a facsimile of Quentin Bannister dressed in Victorian attire, clothes for which Josie could only guess the names—waistcoat, ascot, some sort of long fitted jacket. And a top hat, that one she knew. Her initial shock gave way to curiosity. "Grandfather Bannister?"

"*Yes, Josie. This is why I've been trying to get your attention! He needs to talk to you but didn't want to scare you so he asked me to help. He has a message, and the doctor's about to leave!*"

Josie looked over the railing where, indeed, the party of four were standing and exchanging the "great evening, we must do this again" pleasantries one did.

"Sir? I'll try to reach him before he goes. What do you want me to tell him?"

"*Tell him this, lass. Despite what he's always thought, his father did love him and was so very proud of him.*"

Josie felt a burst of tenderness toward Dr. Bannister and a pang of resentment toward her own father.

"*Tell him his father confided in me he was tough on him because he didn't want him to turn out like his brother, that he always knew he'd be the successful one. And tell him his brother is safe and happy on the other side.*"

"I will deliver that message as soon as I can."

"*Thank you, lass.*"

"Thank you. And thank you, too, Ruby, for being here."

Naomi stuck her head out the kitchen door.

"Oh, hey. I thought I heard voices. You talking to yourself?"

"Always."

"Hard to tell, there've been so many people up here lately."

When Josie reached them, the doctor and his group were headed out the door.

"Doctor Bannister!" she called. "Quentin!"

He stopped in the vestibule while the rest of his party went up the steps to the sidewalk.

"Josie?"

"I have a message for you."

"A message?"

She took a deep breath.

"From your grandfather."

She stepped into the vestibule with him and closed the door.

"He wants you to know your father loved you and was very proud of you."

Dr. Bannister opened his mouth and stared at her, so she continued.

"He says your dad was only tough on you because he knew you'd be successful."

He cleared his throat.

"And he wants you to know your brother is safe and happy on the other side."

His eyes glistened. He cleared his throat a second time, then took her hands. "Thank you, Josie. Thank you so very much. You are a remarkable woman."

At 10:00 p.m., Josie sat at the bar bleary-eyed, trying in vain to process all that had transpired, all she still needed to do, and how she was feeling. Grateful as she was to deliver the message Dr. Bannister needed to hear, it had dredged her hurt and anger about her father back to the surface. This was not where she needed to direct her mental energy right now.

Oblivious to most of what was on her mind, Derek leaned across the bar and held her hand, equally spent.

"You guys should go home," Jerome said. "I can close."

"You sure, man?"

"Absolutely."

"I'll help," Lucy said.

"Thank you. I'm pretty damn beat. And I know this lady is."

There were still a few people in the bar, including the trio of young women Ian had sent their way. This was, Josie suspected, a partial impetus for Jerome offering to stay.

Derek put his arm around her as they walked the block to their apartment. "Thank you."

"For?"

"Putting up with me."

She shrugged. "You put up with me too."

"Yeah, but you don't take all your shit out on me when you're stressed."

"You're right, I don't. Things are challenging, but again, we can't wait for perfection to be nice to each other. The restaurant impacts both of us."

"I know. I just can't tell if you realize how dire this Kelleher situation could be, and I don't want you to be blindsided by the worst-case scenario. This is our baby."

"Of course I realize how dire it could be, but I'm trying to be optimistic. And tonight was decent. Isn't it better if one of us stays positive?"

"Yes. You're much better at it."

"I try. Did you finally meet Ani?"

"Maybe? You're right, we were uncharacteristically crowded, and I'm so tired I don't know who I talked to."

Josie tried to mask her disappointment.

"I'm sorry, baby. I'm glad you made a friend, and I will meet her. But no, I would have remembered."

They greeted the night doorman, then rode the elevator to the third floor.

"Honestly, these dreams have my head swimming twenty-four seven. So much that I haven't been able to fall asleep without a nightcap most nights."

"Are you ready to hear my thoughts on what they might mean?"

He unlocked their apartment door, then sighed in resignation. "Okay."

They sat on the couch. She put her hand on his. "I think with dreams, sometimes something is trying to get your attention. Like there's a deep-rooted question or problem you're trying to work out, so deep you may not even be aware of it."

"So, how do I access it?"

"Do you remember any details about the dreams? All you've told me is Alex is in them."

He moved her hand and stood. "Night cap?"

"Okay."

She'd force herself into a second wind if that's what it took to have this conversation.

He pulled a bottle of bourbon from the liquor cabinet, poured two glasses, then added ice cubes. "They're kind of mundane." He swirled the glasses before handing her one. "I'm in the basement doing inventory, and he comes to see me. I'm taking a walk, look down, and he's next to me. It's never shocking or even surprising."

"Does he say anything?"

"That's what's so frustrating. He starts to. Or he waves like he's trying to get my attention. And then I wake up. Every damn time."

Josie sipped her drink. She needed to handle this with kid gloves. "I'm wondering—could this be subconscious concern about your family? It's been a long time since you've had contact with anyone besides your sister."

"That's by design."

"I know, but after everything I've gone through this past year—losing Nanette, attempting to smooth things over with my mom, this mess with my dad—isn't it possible it's all triggered thoughts about your own parents, even if you aren't aware?"

He mulled this over, then nodded. "That makes sense."

"You haven't been home in twenty years. Think about the future. I know it's not fun to contemplate, but the natural order of things has you outliving your parents. I wonder if, when all is said and done, you'll wish you'd had some closure. I would hate for you to walk around with that kind of regret."

"How the hell am I going to get closure? It's not like I can go drop in on them."

"Why not?"

He swirled his glass and watched the ice move. "Well, for one thing, the restaurant. But mostly, going back there, it's all just horrible memories."

"Honey, please hear me out. You left as soon as you could and never looked back, which leaves room for a lot of unresolved trauma. Unresolved everything."

"It's hard to resolve the childhood I had."

"I know. But awful as they may have been, they're your parents. You're hardwired to love them even if you hate them. Trust me, I know of what I speak."

"I don't hate them. I don't really think about them."

"Maybe on some level you do. I don't want to overstep, but I'm going to make a suggestion. Maybe you should call home, see what's going on."

He bounced his leg up and down.

She put her hand on it. "If there is an issue, wouldn't you rather get ahead of it than find out something happened when it's too late?"

He took her hand in both of his and stared straight ahead.

She'd wait as long as she needed for him to respond.

Finally, he spoke. "Okay if I sleep on it?"

"Of course, my love."

He fell asleep with his arms wrapped around Josie, who lay awake, mind racing.

Despite her insistence she wasn't a medium, where Dr. Bannister was concerned, she was as good as. Among the reasons people sought mediums were validation and closure and, as best she could tell, that's exactly what she'd offered him. She couldn't control when spirits came to her, but she could pay attention to why they did and use this knowledge to help the living.

Derek's was a much more complex set of circumstances than the doctor's. He hadn't yet agreed to call home, but Josie had a strong feeling he would. If and when he did, she'd have succeeded in the first part of her mission to get him back there.

Chapter Sixteen

SUNDAY CAME AND went with no mention of Derek's calling his parents. Josie knew not to bring it up. It had to be at the forefront of his mind, and she'd need to let things unfold. However, she had the dubious advantage of knowing time was not on their side.

She told everyone on staff about her misplaced necklace, asking them to keep an eye out for it but say nothing to Derek. Nobody questioned this. His stress was common knowledge.

On Monday, she walked to the travel agent on Eighth Street, whom she'd used for visits to New Orleans. His name was Per, he was from Oslo, and unlike others in his industry, he still didn't charge the customer a service fee, working only on commissions from airlines and hotels.

"Heading back to the Big Easy?" he asked when he saw Josie.

"Not this time. I want to look into options for a couple of nights in Denver. We're not quite ready to pull the trigger, but maybe we can put something on hold?"

"How soon?"

"It's hard to say. Could be as soon as tomorrow, could be next week."

Josie's birthday was the following Tuesday, and though this wasn't the trip she'd hoped for, it was the one they needed to take.

"Business class?"

On her first trip to New Orleans, she'd flown up front, having just inherited money from Nanette. She hadn't flown in years, had never had the money for first class, and so she treated herself. That wouldn't work this time around, Derek would never go for the splurge.

"Coach."

He tapped some keys on his computer and after a few minutes presented her with a package—round-trip flights and a two-night stay at a new boutique hotel, the Rialto, that was running a deal. He agreed to hold the package for twenty-four hours, which Josie hoped would be long enough.

She returned to the restaurant. Derek was doing inventory, and Lucy, seated in the barroom with a stack of resumés in front of her, was between interviews.

"How's it going?"

"One no-show, one latecomer, two people with weird energy, and one person who asked if she could have weekends off."

"Oh, dear."

"Nah, I'm not worried. We'll find someone."

Josie walked back to the office to do a deeper search for her necklace and was on her hands and knees beneath her desk when Derek walked in.

"Josie?"

She stood quickly and hit her head. "Ow! Sorry."

"What are you doing under there?"

She sighed. "I didn't want to burden you with this, but I can't find my fleur-de-lis, and I'm trying not to freak out."

In fact she was freaking out, but it was clear Derek needed the floor.

He closed the door, then leaned against it. "I'm sure it'll turn up."

"What's going on?"

"I think you're right. I think I need to call my sister. See what's happening with the family."

"What's changed your mind?"

"This overwhelming sense of guilt for staying away all these years. Dread too, but guilt is winning."

"I wish guilt weren't part of it at all. You did what you needed to do to protect yourself."

"Yeah, but ultimately this is the right thing to do. "

"And it's your nature to do the right thing, even if it's hard."

"Would you stay with me if I call her now?"

"Of course."

He sat at his desk, flipped open his phone, scrolled through the contacts. Josie pulled the other chair around to sit by him. She could just make out the tinny ringing of a faraway phone, then a woman answered.

"Hey, Vanessa? … Oh, sorry. This is her brother Derek. Is she available? … Do you know when she'll be back? … Okay, thank you."

He closed his phone, tapped it on the desk twice, then gave her a loaded look. "She's out of town. In Denver."

"Maybe you need to call your dad."

"My dad? Why my dad and not—"

"I don't know," she said quickly, casually. "I guess I figured that's an easier call than your mom?"

He thought it through for a moment, then nodded. "Okay."

"You've got this, honey."

Derek opened his phone again, scrolled, then pressed a button, bouncing his leg up and down the whole time.

"Yes, hello. Is he available?" He sounded ten years younger than he was. "This is Derek Magnus. His son…." He picked up a pen and drew zigzags on the notepad in front of him. After a pause, he said, "Hi. This is… I'm okay. … Yes, still in New York. … Um, I know it's probably weird to hear from me after so long, but I…. What? … No, I just tried her, and they said she was in Denver. Is she visiting? … No, not for a couple of months, that's why I called her…. What's going on?"

There was a long pause during which the disembodied voice on the other end droned.

Derek's expression grew increasingly grim.

"How long has this been? … Okay. And Vanessa's at the house with her…. Okay. Um, maybe we'll come out to see you guys…. Yes, with Josie, my girlfriend…. I don't know. Later this week, or next? … Oh. Okay. Sorry to miss you then…. Yes, I remember…. Thanks, you too…. Bye."

He closed his phone and cupped both hands around it. "My mom's not well."

"I'm so sorry."

"And it doesn't sound like she's going to get better. Fuck."

"How was talking to him?"

"All business. Cut me off because he got another call. And has a work trip sometime in the next couple of days that will 'probably overlap with' our trip. We don't even have a trip planned and already he's…." His voice trailed off. "Anyway, my sister's there now but leaving in the morning."

"Call her."

"That means I have to call the house phone. She still doesn't have a cell. If I can remember the number." He flipped open his phone again, tapped some keys, deleted, tapped again, then drummed his fingers on the desk while he waited.

"Hey, Vanessa? … Yeah, I just spoke to him…. No, I called…. Not particularly…. Can you tell me what's happening?"

Josie could hear Vanessa speaking quickly but couldn't make out her words.

"How come you haven't called? … When? … The restaurant? … Who did you talk to? Both times? Yeah, she doesn't work here anymore."

"Stephanie?" Josie mouthed.

He nodded.

"So, tell me, does she know who you are? … Like, not talking at all?"

At this, Josie choked up, recalling those final weeks with Nanette when she was no longer verbal and how desperately Josie wished she could read her thoughts.

"Okay. I guess we will then…. Yes. Twenty years exactly." He shook his head. "Wow. I wish you were going to be there…. I'll call you once we make a plan. I love you too."

He hung up and stared at the desk in front of him.

Josie rubbed his back. "What do you want to do?"

"I really don't know. What do you think?"

"You know what I think."

"Then I guess we're going to Denver."

"When?"

"Soon as possible, get this over with."

"You're okay to leave Lucy in charge?"

"I don't think I have a choice. I'll try to muster some of that Josie Gray optimism."

⚜

Less than twenty-four hours later, they were on a flight from Newark to Denver. Lucy assured them that between her, Curtis, Naomi, and Jerome, they'd have things covered.

Now they sat wedged into the middle and window seats of Continental Airlines flight 513 watching the in-flight movie, *Erin Brockovich*. At least Josie was watching, Derek looked out at the clouds, his headphones barely covering his ears.

When the movie ended, they sat in silence, Josie alternating between *Marie Claire* and F. Scott Fitzgerald and Derek still staring out the window. As they got closer to Denver, the flight got bumpy, and when they hit an air pocket, Josie yelped and grabbed his hand.

"I hate turbulence," she whimpered.

"You're okay, babe. It's always like that out here. It's the mountains."

He rubbed his thumb over the back of her hand and pointed out the snow-capped Rockies. They commented on how vast everything looked. Derek's nerves seemed to subside because he had a job to do now, keeping Josie calm.

They hit another pocket, and she tried a breathing exercise. Once she heard the landing gear come out, she relaxed.

"We're really doing this," he said.

"We're really doing this, and we'll get through it."

He peered out the window. "So weird they moved it."

The Denver International Airport had relocated since he'd lived there, a fact Josie learned from Per that Derek hadn't known. He'd worked hard over the years to block Colorado from his thoughts.

"Welcome to Denver, folks. Local time is one fifty-three p.m., and the temperature is hovering just around seventy-five degrees."

"I guess I didn't need to pack all those warm clothes," Josie said.

"You'd be surprised how quickly things change out here."

As they walked down the aisle, Josie saw a copy of the *New York Mirror* abandoned on a seat. In the bustle of leaving town, she'd forgotten Stephanie's threat to call Marcus Dreyer, whose column ran Tuesdays. She grabbed the paper and tucked it under her arm.

While they waited for baggage claim, Derek went to the men's room. Josie skimmed the paper until she found what she was looking for.

Waiter, there's a ghost in my gumbo! We hear strange things are afoot at Miss Sylvie's Bistro on West Ninth Street. Sources report an incident that occurred Friday evening involving a salacious staff member, a just-this-side-of-legal-aged patron, and a ghostly entity. While engaging in after-hours—and illegal—activities in the ladies' room, the patron looked into the mirror and saw what she swears was the ghost of a young woman. The Dreyer Report sent one of our ace reporters undercover Sunday night, and indeed other patrons have felt a presence inside the 100-year-old building, which boasts a ghost table on its second floor. We guess the team at Miss Sylvie's won't need to do much decorating for Halloween.

"What are you reading?" Derek asked, startling her. He looked down at the column before she could hide it. "Oh, shit. She actually leaked it."

She sighed and handed him the paper. "They spelled 'bistrot' wrong."

He read through it. "Staff member? Great."

"That scumbag. Marcus, not Billy. But Billy too."

"Dreyer's just doing his job. It's on Stephanie."

The buzzer sounded, and the baggage carousel churned into action.

"If it's any consolation, Curtis thinks this might be good for business."

"It's not."

"Good for business?"

He shook his head. "A consolation."

He stepped up to the carousel to wait for their bags, and Josie flipped over the paper. There was an article about Declan Kelleher buying up an entire block on Bleecker Street, steps from the restaurant. She rolled up the paper and dumped it in the nearest trash can.

Maybe it was the lack of sleep, the turbulent flight, the fact she was nervous about this visit but couldn't admit that as it wasn't her trip to be nervous about, but she was finally fearing Kelleher and the very real possibility he could cause them major problems. Beyond that, she was disgusted with Stephanie, whose childish behavior was infringing on their time in Denver where there was already so much at stake. But she needed to ignore all of this now and focus on Derek.

He carried their bags and held her hand as they headed to the car rental counter.

"I can't believe you pulled this together on such short notice," he said.

"This is an important trip."

Josie had rented an SUV. They put their luggage in the back, then climbed in. Since living in New York City and driving infrequently, she'd become a nervous passenger on the road too. She had no idea how mountainous their drives here would be and figured she'd feel safer higher up off the ground.

Derek pulled out of the airport and onto the highway. Though it wasn't the route he knew, his muscle memory of driving through Denver kept them from having to use a map. He was quiet as he drove, and Josie held his free hand, her turn to provide the comfort.

She looked out the window at the Rocky Mountains ringing the horizon. The sky was vast, a rich blue streaked with white—colors she knew, yet you could see so much more here that it looked especially vibrant. Focusing on the beauty of the landscape helped stave off her sense of foreboding about what was in store for this visit. The last thing Derek needed right now was for her to be on edge. As they drove, she noticed little tufts of grass pop up at the side of the highway.

"Prairie dogs," he said, without taking his eyes off the road. "I used to love seeing them."

"How cute!"

They reminded Josie of the munchkins that popped up after Dorothy landed in Oz, and this seemed an apt metaphor for something she couldn't quite pinpoint.

They drove forty-five minutes to their hotel in the Cherry Creek neighborhood. Josie had chosen the area because, according to Per, it was convenient and walkable with ample food and drink options. That it had apparently changed a lot since Derek lived in town gave her hope that it wouldn't be a minefield of painful memories. The house he grew up in was in an affluent neighborhood called Country Club, a fact he was sheepish to admit that they wound up laughing about.

The Rialto was as Per had described, shiny, upscale, filled with modern art and more amenities than they could possibly use in their brief stay. Their room was tastefully appointed, with Frette linens on a king-sized bed that perched on a raised platform, plush robes and slippers, a well-stocked mini bar, and floor-to-ceiling windows with sweeping western views of the mountains.

"How much is this costing us?" Derek asked, taking it all in.

"A fraction of what you'd think. They were running a special. It's kismet."

"Not much about Denver feels like kismet, but this is a nice room."

"It really is lovely." Josie flopped down on the bed.

Derek lay down next to her, arms folded behind his head.

"I wish we could just stay here and order room service," he said. "Watch movies and sleep."

"We'll plan a stay-in-and-order-room-service trip once we get through this one, okay? Maybe we can even do that for my birthday?"

"I don't think we can take another vacation next week."

"No, of course not. It doesn't have to be on my actual birthday."

"I'm sorry, Joze."

"For what?"

"I didn't even think about that. This trip means we aren't doing anything big for your birthday."

"This is way more important."

"No, it isn't. You're the most important to me. Your birthday's Tuesday. Can we have a party Monday night? A little something at our place?"

"We don't have to do that. I'm not a throw-a-party-for-myself person."

"Please? It'll be fun, and I'll do everything so you're not throwing a party for yourself. You haven't really celebrated your birthday in the years I've known you."

"All right. I can cook—"

"Absolutely not. I'll take care of it."

"Thank you. I'll try not to feel too weird about it."

"Good. You deserve a nice night, Joze."

From her vantage point, Josie could see across the room to the round glass breakfast table and its silver sculpture centerpiece that reminded her of vacuum cleaner attachments. According to Per, the Rialto took its artwork quite seriously. It hardly needed to. The magnificent mountain views were enough.

It occurred to her now how special this was, being away from home in a new-to-her city with the man she loved. She wished they didn't have to leave just yet and thought about suggesting a nap—their euphemism for not napping.

"It's so weird being here," Derek said, yanking her back to reality.

"It must be."

"I don't know if I thought I'd ever come back. I guess I knew I would have to eventually, for something like this, but it always seemed like it would happen in some hypothetical future."

"It's been a long time coming, and I'm proud of you." She put her hand on his chest.

"I couldn't do it without you. I don't want to do it all."

"But, I mean, we don't have to run right out, do we?"

She drummed her fingers lightly down his torso.

He sat up. "Yeah, I think I need to get this over with."

Josie sat up too, feeling silly for thinking he could possibly relax enough. If he couldn't get in the mood two thousand miles from his childhood home, he surely couldn't from two miles away.

They changed out of their airplane clothes and Josie refreshed her makeup. She followed Derek's lead and dressed casually, jeans and a short-sleeved blouse.

"Bring a jacket," he said.

"It's seventy-five degrees out!"

"I'm telling you, this place is full of surprises."

Derek pulled out all his nervous tics, pressing the elevator button multiple times, dropping the keys the valet handed him, almost forgetting to tip. After getting into the car, he tilted his head back and closed his eyes. "I wish I still smoked cigarettes."

"No, you don't, babe." Josie tuned the radio to classical music. "Why don't you take the long route? Give me a tour before we go to the house?"

"Okay. We can do that."

He began driving through the streets of Cherry Creek. "Wow—none of this was here."

"None of it?"

"The shopping mall was—I hated that place—but all these cafés and shops and things, no. That's the third yoga studio we've passed in two blocks."

Derek narrated as they drove, marveling at the new stuff, explaining how things used to be, and pointing out the changes. Whether or not he realized it, he was finally acknowledging the city was more than just his worst memories. He showed Josie his high school, the former arts center, the hotel where his senior prom took place. This was a side of him she'd never seen, one that smiled about the past. After a while, he announced they were entering Country Club.

Josie squeezed his hand.

"Fucked up I'm not going to see my old man."

"I'm sorry."

"It's okay. Would probably be too much right now. I wish you could meet my sister too, but she has to get back for something with my nephew. I had no idea how on-point she's been for my parents the last couple of years, but she has. It's like we were raised by four completely different people."

"So who's with your mother if your dad is traveling and Vanessa's not there?"

"Who else? The help. That's the Magnus way."

They drove through a gated entry to a wide street lined with elegant homes and gardens. Most of the houses had multi-car garages. The vehicles parked on the street were either landscaping trucks or modest cars that belonged to housekeepers and nannies.

They turned down a side street. Derek paused in front of a stately brick house set back on a sloping front lawn.

"Jeremy Adler's house."

"Who's that?"

"He was my best friend in high school. I think he wound up in California."

He turned down another street lined with grand elm trees and homes, each one bigger than the last, in a blend of architectural styles.

"This really is a beautiful neighborhood," Josie said.

"Lots of old money."

He made another turn, then pulled in front of a three-story Mediterranean-style house, white with a terracotta roof, arched entryway, and large, manicured front lawn. Two gardeners were out front, one riding a mower, the other trimming hedges lining the red brick walkway to the front door.

Derek put the car in park, turned it off, then turned to look up at the house. "Home sweet home," he said grimly.

"It's gorgeous. I can't believe you grew up here."

"I can't believe I made it out."

They climbed from the car. Josie held his arm as they made their way up the walkway. Derek nodded to the gardeners, paused in front of the door, then rang the bell.

"Coming!" a woman called from inside. The sound of footsteps moving swiftly toward them followed, then an attractive older woman in a nurse's uniform opened the door. "May I help you?"

Derek cleared his throat. "I'm Derek Magnus."

"Oh, Derek, yes! Your father mentioned you'd be in town. I'm Pauline, one of your mother's nurses." She had a lilting Jamaican accent that Josie loved.

"This is my girlfriend, Josie."

"Hi, Pauline." Josie shook her hand.

They stepped through the front door into a large foyer with marble flooring and an ornate gold mirror on one wall.

"Your mum is in the sunporch."

"The sunporch?"

"Yes, they built it some years back. Maybe you haven't seen it."

"I haven't been home in a very long time, so I don't really know what to expect. From the house or my mother."

"Well, she has good days and bad days. She isn't talking anymore, but she's still there."

"Yeah, that's how my sister described things."

Pauline led them through a formal dining room and living room. A Chagall hung above the living room sofa, and smaller paintings of equally impressive pedigree were arranged salon-style on another wall.

"They've rearranged a lot. Wow—that whole wall used to be photos of my brother." They entered a spacious kitchen with chrome appliances and a granite-topped island in the middle. "This is all new."

"You have a visitor, Lenore," Pauline called. She led them toward the screened-in porch in the back of the house.

Josie held back, letting Derek walk in first. She watched him react to the sight of his mother. Then the back of Josie's neck tingled as she stepped over the threshold.

Lenore was seated on a pale yellow flowered couch, a cup of tea in front of her. Beside her, holding her hand, sat Alex.

Chapter Seventeen

LENORE MAGNUS HAD been quite glamorous in her younger days, and one could see traces of this in the woman who sat on the porch dressed in a silky cerulean robe, staring through her living son. She looked older than her seventy-eight years, older than Nanette, who had been more than a decade her senior. Lenore was fragile and pale, and by the shock on Derek's face, it was clear she'd changed quite a bit in twenty years. She was still attractive—thick white hair in a braid, nails painted rose-petal pink. Her doe eyes were the same color as Derek's, a beautiful gray-green Josie had never seen on anyone before him.

And there was Alex, tow-headed and darling, one hand holding his mother's, the other clutching his bunny. He jiggled his leg—same nervous habit as his brother—and looked from Derek to Josie and back again. Of course he'd be there. Josie didn't know how she'd lost sight of that.

"Lenore, this is your boy, Derek." Pauline massaged her shoulder. "And his lady friend, Josie. They've come all the way from New York City to visit with you."

Derek looked at Pauline for guidance.

"You can talk to her, honey. She hears you, and she understands. Isn't that right, Miss Lenore?" Pauline picked up her teacup. "Drink your Darjeeling before it gets cold. Would you two like some tea?"

"That would be lovely, thank you," Josie said.

Derek stared at his mother, searching for words. "Hi, Mom." He glanced at Josie, who nodded her encouragement, then cleared his throat. "It's been a while. I haven't been to Denver in a very long time."

Josie coaxed him into a chair, then perched on an ottoman to his left.

"It's weird to be back here, but it's nice to see you, Mom."

"*He thinks I'm a terrible mother.*"

Josie startled.

Lenore looked at her now, eyes focused. Her mouth didn't move. "*That's why he left.*"

Josie's jaw hung open as she tried to understand what was happening.

"*Can you hear Mommy?*" Alex asked. "*Can you hear her?*"

She nodded.

Derek looked at her, then back to his mother. "I brought my girlfriend, Josie." He put his hand on her knee. "We own a restaurant together. In New York."

Lenore's eyes shifted to him, then back to Josie.

He began talking about the restaurant and their lives in New York, filling what he thought was silence with words Josie only half heard.

"*It wasn't all bad. He can't remember.*"

"We're figuring it out, though. Right, Josie?" He laughed self-consciously.

"Right!"

"*I loved him very much. It was just so hard after Alex—*" She looked down at her young son, petting the top of his head.

"What is she doing?" Derek asked Pauline when she came in carrying a teapot and cups.

"She does that sometimes. They had a cat until last year. Is that your kitty cat, honey? Are you petting Ferdinand?"

"Pauline, can I talk to you for a minute?" Derek asked.

"*Maybe I was terrible.*"

"I have to pay the gardeners. Take a walk outside with me." She put the tea on the sideboard, filled the cups, then placed them on the table.

"Josie, will you come?"

"You guys chat. I'll sit with her."

Once they left the room, Josie spoke.

"You weren't a terrible mother, Lenore! It must have been really hard."

"*You are a great mommy.*"

Lenore looked at Alex, then back to Josie. "*Maybe he blames me too.*"

"Blames you?"

"*Like his father, for what happened.*"

"*It wasn't your fault, Mommy!*"

"Oh my goodness, no. He doesn't blame you for what happened to Alex! I promise you that."

"*He forgets the good things. He forgets he was my bear cub.*"

"He's here now because he wanted to see you."

"*Will you tell him I'm sorry? Will you tell him I love my bear cub?*"

She looked so sad, Josie would have promised her anything.

"Yes, I will. He knows you love him."

This was never the problem where Derek was concerned. It wasn't that he doubted she loved him, it was that her dark emotions overshadowed everything. She loved him as well as she could, which, unfortunately, hadn't been enough.

"*Will you take care of him?*"

"Yes. I promise."

"*Will you take him to the ship?*" Alex asked.

"To the what?"

"*The ship.*"

"What's the ship?"

He looked at her, wide-eyed with fear.

"*Please! You have to! The ship at the Palace.*"

"Is that a place here in Denver?"

He nodded.

"Like a hotel?"

She thought of the Palace Hotel in New York. Alex shrugged and Josie tried to recall where she'd glimpsed a phone on their way through the house—the kitchen counter. There must be a phonebook close by.

Pauline and Derek walked back into the room, and Derek sat by his mother again. A hint of a smile flickered over her face.

"You're happy to have your handsome boy visiting, aren't you Lenore? He looks like you. And remember, Vanessa will come back next week." Pauline said to Josie, "We just talk to her same as we always did."

"*My bear cub.*" Lenore yawned wide, and her eyes started to close. "*Derek. My bear….*"

"Nap time." Pauline pulled a throw blanket from the back of the sofa and draped it over Lenore. "I'm sorry, I know you just got here, but this is a sleepy time of day for her."

"We'll head back to the hotel," Derek said.

"Pauline, is there a powder room I can use?" Josie asked.

"Right off the kitchen."

Josie brought her teacup to the sink. Outside the powder room door, on a shelf above the telephone, she spotted the phonebook. She pulled it down and flipped through the white pages until she got to "P"—but found no listing for a Palace.

Something was wedged farther back in the yellow pages. When Josie flipped to it, she gasped. It was her fleur-de-lis necklace, bookmarking a listing for the Brown Palace Hotel and its restaurant, Ship Tavern.

In the bathroom, she clasped the chain around her neck and looked at her reflection, practicing her poker face. Now she knew where she needed to take Derek, though she had no idea why.

He was talking to Pauline in the hallway, car keys in hand. "Ready to go Joze?"

"I'd like to say goodbye to your mother."

"She's resting."

"Then I'll just look in on her."

She slipped past them and went to the sunroom.

Lenore was asleep, and Alex stood by the screen door, hugging his bunny. She showed him the pendant on her collarbone.

"Did you leave this for me to find?"

He nodded.

"Did you take it from my room one night?"

He nodded again.

"Why?"

"*So you could find the ship.*"

"That's the place, then? The Ship Tavern at the Brown Palace hotel? Can you tell me why you want us to go there?"

"*Someone there knows him.*"

"Someone who works there?"

"*Yes. She can remind him.*"

"Remind him of what?"

"*Good things.*"

"Okay, sweetheart. I'll do what I can. Thank you for giving me back my necklace. You're a very good boy."

Finally, he smiled.

Josie held Derek's arm as they made their way down the path toward the car. He pulled away from the curb, drove slowly down the street, then turned onto the next and shifted to park. He looked at her with tears in his eyes.

"Oh, sweetheart!" Josie unbuckled her seatbelt, then leaned across the console to wrap her arms around him.

"I'm sorry."

"Derek, you have nothing to apologize for! I can't imagine what this is like for you."

"Being back in that house was so fucking weird." He sniffled and wiped his eyes with his sleeve. "At least we were in a new room and not upstairs, where all the magic happened. But seeing her again, so frail.... Not just fragile, she was always fragile, but frail.... I don't even know if she knew it was me. Do you think she knew it was me?"

"I am certain she did."

"The fucked up thing? I could still access my anger. I don't hate her, and it's been decades, but I could still feel it, still remember what it was like living under that roof."

He pulled down the visor to look at his reflection, then flipped it back up. "Can't believe I was sitting there babbling about the restaurant scene in New York to a woman who's practically a ghost. But what was my other choice? Let her know how I really feel about her?"

"Do you think it's possible the past wasn't *all* bad? That maybe you've suppressed some of the better memories?"

"Why would I have done that?"

"Maybe because it was easier to walk away if you could turn your back completely. Self-preservation."

He took this in, nodding, then restarted the car.

"You're a wise woman, Josie Gray."

"You're a wise man, Derek Magnus."

"I don't know if I want to go back there tomorrow. I made my point. I showed up."

"We don't need to decide now."

"What do you want to do for dinner?"

Here was her chance.

"The travel agent made a few recommendations."

"Yeah, maybe we should ask at the hotel for something nearby."

Josie didn't know where anything in Denver was, she just knew where they needed to be that night.

"Do you know something called the Brown Palace Hotel?"

"Sure—that place is a legend. But it's kind of a haul. Let's look for something closer—"

"This might be my only trip to Denver for a long time. I wouldn't mind checking out a legend."

Not only was she pressing her luck, it was out of character for her to push for anything when this trip was for Derek. To her surprise, though, he gave in.

"You're right. Sure. There's a few restaurants there, from what I remember—a fine-dining one—"

"Mmm, I don't really have fine-dining clothes."

"This is Denver. You don't need them. But there's also the tavern, which is an old-school, upscale pub. Or used to be. A martini and prime rib type of joint."

"I'm in a martini and prime rib type of mood."

At the hotel, they asked the concierge to make them a reservation, then went upstairs. While Derek was in the shower, Josie texted Ani. They'd left town so quickly, she hadn't had a chance to let her know they'd be gone.

Hi from Denver. Here w D. Much to tell.

Next, she texted Curtis. Dinner service would be well underway, it being two hours later in New York.

Checking in. Hope all is fine. Let me know how it goes there.

Her phone sounded almost immediately with a return text.

Slammed!

Slammed as in busy? At restaurant?

When no response came, she went into the bathroom where Derek was brushing his teeth, a towel wrapped around his waist.

"I just checked in with Curtis, and it sounds like they're busy tonight."

He gave her a thumbs up, then turned. "You found your necklace!"

"I did." She touched the pendant. "Believe it or not, it was right there in my jewelry box."

He held her eyes for a beat as though he weren't sure he believed her.

"I was searching so hard, I completely overlooked it!"

"Glad you found it."

They dressed, then went to the lobby. The hotel called a taxi to take them to dinner. Derek offered to drive, but Josie wanted him to be able to relax as best he could, have a drink or two, stay open to whatever the night had in store.

"Pauline seems pretty great," she said as they rode through Cherry Creek toward downtown Denver.

"My dad's always hired good help."

They pulled up to the hotel, which reminded Josie of the Flatiron in New York, narrow and angular. The street out front teemed with bellmen, doormen, and guests. They walked up the steps into the lobby, and Josie immediately felt the spiritual energy intrinsic to old hotels. This wasn't why they were there, though. There was another reason, a living person Alex needed them to encounter.

The lobby was a large skylit atrium with arched entryways, wrought iron balconies, and grillwork extending several stories to the ceiling. It felt stately and important, rich with a history of prominent guests. According to signs, the hotel itself opened in the late 1800s and their destination, Ship Tavern, in the 1930s to usher in the repeal of Prohibition.

"Do you know much about the history of this place?" she asked.

"I used to. I think there was a murder at some point." He flashed her his crooked smile. "So, right up your alley."

"There is strong energy here."

"Is that why you wanted to come?"

"We have enough of that at home. I wanted to come because of its amazing history. You know I love that stuff."

In fact, it was Derek who was the history buff, but he accepted her explanation.

Ship Tavern looked as Josie imagined a pub in London might. It had dim lighting, dark wooden wall panels and ceiling beams, and tufted leather seats and banquettes. Large, multi-paned windows let in the waning afternoon light. Committed to its nautical theme, the tavern, with its long wooden bar, was decorated with model ships, old sailing maps, and had a full-sized mast and crow's nest in the middle of the room.

The hostess led them to a table by the window, then offered a drink from the bar.

"Two Boodles martinis, one with an olive, one with a twist." She walked away, and Derek winked at Josie. "Right?"

"Perfect. You're splurging on premium gin?"

"How often do I go out to dinner with my wise and hot better half?"

"Not often enough."

"Not to mention things here cost half what they do at home."

"Okay, Cyrano, I prefer the romantic explanation to the frugal one."

"I'm the total package."

"Indeed you are."

Despite the heaviness Josie knew he was feeling, Derek was making a concerted effort to treat the night like a romantic respite. While he studied the menu, she studied the room. Unless he recognized the person they were there to see, and after so long that was unlikely, she'd have no idea if they were in the right section or even here on the right night.

"*Patience.*"

The voice was one she recognized. She'd heard it the previous summer at a time, like now, when she was searching for clarity in an unknowable situation. She reached across the table for Derek's hand.

He squeezed hers three times—their code for "I love you," which she thought he'd forgotten.

Their cocktails arrived, and Derek ordered dinner. The server was in her fifties with a pierced nose and perfect streak of silver in her otherwise black bob. She'd introduced herself as Jennifer and shown no signs of recognizing Derek, nor he her. Same with the hostess who seated them and the bartender, whom he spoke to when he retrieved a wedge of lemon for Josie's water.

Patience was her only option.

"Cheers, love." She held her glass up.

"Cheers to you, love."

They sipped their drinks.

"Ooh that's nice," she said. "I'd forgotten."

Derek was far away.

"What are you thinking?"

"That what you said before makes some kind of sense. Maybe I repressed some of the good stuff to make leaving easier."

"It would be totally understandable if you did."

"I keep having these flashes of memories that feel like they belong to someone else."

"What kinds of things?"

"Nothing I can describe in detail. Just bursts of *déjà vu*. That yard out back—while we were sitting on the porch, I had this lightning-quick image of running around with her, which is weird because I have no actual memories of doing anything fun together. You know *The Runaway Bunny*?"

"Of course—it's one of the greatest books ever written about a parent stifling their kid's freedom. But it's beautiful."

"It was that kind of scene, mother and kid, some kind of make-believe game."

"Oh, how I wish you could access those memories!"

"Who knows? They could be wishful revisionist thinking. There aren't a lot of charming Magnus home movies from that era."

"Do you think your sister could offer insight?"

"She was hardly around."

"Your dad?"

"Never around. Which makes me sad. Because some of what she—my mother—wallowed in all those years, it wasn't just about my brother, it was about him too. It was all jumbled together for her, so I guess it was for me too."

They paused the conversation when their food arrived, and Derek ordered a bottle of red wine. Josie took a hefty forkful of mashed potatoes, ravenous from skipping lunch and heady from the gin.

The meal was perfect for the occasion—rich, comforting, and evocative of the time warp they'd stepped into, as though the dining room, hotel, and nearly all of Denver had ground to a halt decades earlier and come alive again with Derek's return.

For much of dinner they spoke of happy things, trips they wanted to one day take, movies they wanted to watch, things they'd done in their wilder days. It felt like a real date. Inevitably, though, the conversation turned to the reason they were visiting Denver in the first place.

"Do you think Pauline's right that my mom understands what we're saying?"

"I think so. My only frame of reference is Nanette, and she understood us long past the time she stopped communicating verbally."

"How do you know?"

"We could tell. Her facial expressions, where her eyes would wander while we spoke, Plus, we'd been with her so much right before she stopped talking, so it was a continuum. You didn't get to do that."

"Because I left."

It was unlike him to need repeated reassurance, but he did.

"You left because you had to," she reminded him. "Your mom wasn't making it easy, even if she had a really good excuse. And your father—I mean, he wasn't making it easy for either of you."

"Honestly, I wouldn't know. I barely saw the guy. He was always traveling or working late, which is probably the cliché it sounds like."

"I know."

"When I think about it that way, it makes me really sad. She was alone in her sorrow. It's not like I could really do anything. He should have been there helping her, going through it with her, instead of plowing into work. And his secretaries."

"Do you think your mom feels guilty over what happened?"

"I don't know, but I can't imagine she doesn't on some level."

"What do you know about the circumstances of that day?"

"The day he died?"

The word was so blunt it jarred her. It sounded so final, which Derek still believed it to be.

He swirled his wine glass.

"It was after school, I know that. My old man was at work. Mom was in the middle of something—I guess she had a life back then, there were things for her to be in the middle of."

"What kind of things?"

"Rich lady nineteen sixties stuff. She was on 'committees.'" He used air quotes. "So she was busy, and Alex was bored. He took his bike out for a spin." He paused and watched the wine in his glass. Quietly, he said, "You know the rest."

"Putting myself in her shoes, thinking of all the stuff that would haunt me, I wonder if her guilt over what happened to Alex kept her from being as consistently loving to you as she should have been. Maybe she was scared to love you too much out of fear."

"Fear of what?"

"Losing you too."

The suggestion seemed to derail him. He swallowed hard. "We'll never know. And really, what difference does it make now?"

She reached for his hand. "I don't know. I just wish I could fix this for you, take away every bit of pain you've ever felt."

"Well, you can't do that, Joze, but being with you makes up for all of it. I'm really lucky I left Denver and came to New York and found you. Especially that part."

He looked up when the waitress approached.

"Are you still enjoying your meal?"

"Everything was great," Josie said. "Just what we were in the mood for."

"Room for dessert?"

"Not tonight," Derek said. "We've been traveling all day. I could use a nap." He winked at Josie.

"All right, then. I'll have someone clear your table and bring you the check."

Derek pulled out his wallet, then handed her a credit card. "You can run this."

She started to walk away, then turned back to them. "Derek Magnus?"

"Yeah?"

"Oh my God. I can't believe this. I'm Jennifer Laight. I was your babysitter!"

"Jennifer…." His face lit up. "Jenny?"

Anesthetized by the cocktail and wine, it took Josie a moment to realize what was happening. When she did, she got goosebumps.

"Yes! I was strictly Jenny then." She turned to Josie. "I babysat this guy for five years!"

"That's amazing!" She rubbed her arms. "When he was how old?"

"Starting right around the time you were two. Or no, older than that because we had your third birthday a few months after I started."

"I remember you. Wow, I haven't thought about you in years. No offense."

She held her hand up. "Please. You were a little wisp of a thing. I wouldn't expect you to remember me as well as I remember you."

"This is my girlfriend Josie."

"Nice to meet you, Jennifer. And to have a connection to someone who knew little Derek!"

"Yeah, I moved away for a bit when he was seven or eight, but wow, Derek, I always wondered what became of you. You were my favorite kid."

He smiled but his eyes were sad. "I wish I remembered those years better."

"You still have that adorable lopsided smile."

"Can you join us for a minute?" Josie asked.

Jennifer looked around the room. "Sure." She pulled a chair from another table. "Tell me everything. Where are you guys these days?"

"We live in New York. In the city. I've been there since I left Denver."

"We own a restaurant in the Village."

"Awesome. I knew you'd wind up doing something cool. "

"Well, I'm not sure how cool it is," he said modestly. "We're just getting going, and it's stressful."

"What was this one like when he was little?" Josie asked.

"The sweetest. So smart and creative."

"You haven't changed, my love."

"And when you were really little, you had an imaginary friend."

A high-pitched buzz enveloped the room, though Josie knew she alone heard it.

"I did?"

"Sure. Whenever you went for a nap, I'd hear you giggling and talking and singing. I always wondered—" She stopped herself and waved the thought away.

Josie leaned forward. "You always wondered...?"

"I guess part of me always wanted to believe it was your brother."

Chapter Eighteen

SOMETHING FLASHED ACROSS Derek's face, a look of confused recognition that gave way to shock.

"I'm sorry if that was weird to hear," Jennifer said. "You've probably forgotten all about it. You were really little."

"Do you remember anything?" Josie asked.

"Maybe? I think I remember people asking me about an imaginary friend when I was older, but I didn't know what they were talking about." He shook his head. "Wow. I haven't thought about that in years."

"What made you think it might have been Derek's brother?"

"There was this strong energy in that house. Not scary, just… persistent? And then when I'd overhear you, Derek, I swear it sounded like you were talking to someone. Little kids babble, but this was different. I know it sounds crazy—"

"If you knew the stuff Derek and I have been dealing with back home, you'd realize how not crazy it sounds to me."

"Well, I would listen. I couldn't make out what he was saying, and a lot of it was kid gibberish, but the rhythm always sounded like an actual conversation. Questions, pauses, responses. And, you know, he was at an age where, if you believe in these things, kids are still receptive to spirit energy."

Derek clung to her words.

"Once I asked what your friend's name was. You shook your head like it was a secret and giggled at the empty space behind me. I've told that story so many times."

"Did you ever say anything to my mom?"

"I didn't. She had enough on her plate. How is your mom?" Jennifer's tone conveyed sympathy.

"She's not well, which is why we're back here."

"I'm sorry."

"Me too. It wasn't an easy relationship. To put it mildly."

"I know she could be tough to deal with—I mean, I never saw it, but there were rumors. You remember how our neighborhood was. But you guys had a sweet connection from what I could see."

"I'm not so sure about that."

"Oh, you absolutely did when I knew you."

"What was it like?" Josie asked.

"I have these images of you two cuddled together on the couch with a pile of books. She loved reading to you. It was her calm and happy place."

"Why would you have been there if she was home?"

"She had me come every day after school, and I'd stay in the evening if she and your dad had something. I lived two blocks away, you probably don't remember that. But this one day she was really sad—"

"And drunk?"

"I never saw her drinking. But yeah," Jennifer admitted. "I know that was how she dealt with her pain."

"What happened that day?" Josie asked.

"Your mom had fallen asleep on the couch, and we went outside to the yard. You wanted to pick flowers."

Derek's eyes glistened while she spoke.

"There were wildflowers growing in your yard. You told me you wanted to bring some inside so your mom would have something pretty to wake up to 'in case she had sad dreams.' That always stuck with me. You were so compassionate. And you sometimes had this sadness too, which of course made sense, but you tried to hide it."

"Oh, honey!" Josie said. "That makes *me* sad."

"I'm sorry."

"Don't be sorry. I want to know this part of his life."

"It's just so amazing to see the grown-up version of that beautiful kid." She turned to Derek. "Do you remember what your mom used to call you?"

He shook his head. "I don't."

"Bear cub."

⸸

DEREK WAS PENSIVE in the taxi back to the hotel, so Josie quietly watched the city go by. He proposed a nightcap, and she agreed. At the hotel bar, she ordered a tawny Port, he a Calvados.

"What are the odds we wind up in the spot where my childhood babysitter works?"

"The universe moves in mysterious ways."

"And your travel agent told us to go there. Crazy. So many new places in town, and he picks that one."

"Are you glad we ran into her?"

"I don't know. I guess it's comforting to know you were right, every second wasn't awful. But it also makes me sad I stayed away for so long. My mom was a complicated woman. Is."

"Do you remember her calling you 'bear cub?'"

"I do now. That was the game we played in the yard. She was mama bear, and I was baby." He smiled reflexively at the memory. "Crazy, I haven't thought about that in decades either. And I probably never would have."

"What about this imaginary friend?"

He shook his head.

"I don't know. I probably pretended it was my brother or something. Coping mechanism."

"Maybe."

"You don't believe me."

"I don't know, my love. I wasn't there. But you know where my beliefs lie. And the thing is, what she said about little kids is right. Little kids and animals have the ability to see things most of us don't. I think it's beautiful."

Loose from the booze, he ran his palm up her thigh. "I think you're beautiful."

She clutched his hand to hold it still. "What do you want to do tomorrow?"

"Sleep in. Order room service."

"Do you want to go see her again?"

"I don't know. I don't think so. I'll decide tomorrow."

That he wasn't absolute in his refusal gave her hope, as well as determination to help him uncover more decent memories.

"Can I ask you a question, D?"

"Shoot."

"Do you think it would be cathartic to take me on more of a tour tomorrow? I'd love to see your elementary school, where your friends lived, anything else you might want to show me."

"Can I ask *you* a question?"

"Of course."

"Can we stop talking about my childhood and go take a nap?"

A long-dormant feeling twinged in the pit of her stomach. Derek signaled for the check.

In the morning, Josie woke to the housekeeper knocking at the door. Traveling, the two-hour time difference, and finally ending their drought had worn them out enough they slept later than they ever did at home.

Derek asked housekeeping to come back, then ordered room service. When the food arrived, he signed for it and wheeled the cart into the room.

Pillows propped behind her, Josie turned on the TV. She flipped through the channels until finding a good music station.

Soon she was sipping coffee and eating an omelet while they listened to a medley of contemporary artists—Macy Gray, Moby, Lauryn Hill.

"I don't care what anyone thinks," Josie said, though in fact she cared quite a bit what others thought. "There is a lot of decent music being made nowadays."

"There's some good stuff. But I'm old-school. I like music that came out before 1980. On vinyl."

"We have so much in common."

"We should go out sometime."

"I'll think about it."

He was finally relaxed enough Josie felt she could speak her mind without upending things. She had to because there was no way they could leave Denver without one more visit to the house.

"Honey, I just have to say—I get why you feel the way you do about your mom and why this trip is bringing it all back up. But I also know part of you has compassion for what she went through and who she is now. She has to know she wasn't a great mom to you, right?"

"She's not an idiot, so yeah, I'm sure she knew. And if she didn't, I imagine my twenty-year absence sent a strong message."

"Do you want her to spend whatever time she has left feeling sad and guilty? Or do you want to give her grace at the end of her life, accept she didn't handle things well but is not an evil person? Clean up your side of the street so you can have some peace when she's gone?"

He ran his hands through his hair and held his head. "I don't know. I don't know what the move is here. What should I do?"

"I can't decide for you, but I can tell you this—regardless of the outcome, I can rest better knowing I tried with my dad. I was ready to move forward."

"He fucked that one up."

"He did, but I can still move forward. I got my closure. How is your life these days?"

"All things considered, it's pretty fucking great. I mean, neither of us is winning awards in the parents department, and the restaurant's a mess—"

"It's not a mess. It's a work in progress."

"You're right. And like you've been saying all along, we can get through the bad times together. We're a good match."

"Maybe you can find a way to let your mom know you're okay. Because I think that's what every parent ultimately wants—for their kids to be okay."

"That's pretty much what I told her yesterday. I'm not sure there's anything else to say."

Josie dropped the conversation while they finished eating. Soon they performed their morning ablutions, and when Derek got out of the shower, he gave her a look of resignation.

"We can go back to the house. We can say goodbye."

"I think that's a really good idea."

Without the scenic route, the drive from the hotel was quick. Derek parked in front of the house. They walked up the path and before he could ring the bell, Pauline opened the door.

"I'm sorry, Pauline, I should have let you know we were coming by."

"No need. She's been so excited to see you!"

"How do you know?"

"I told her this morning you might be coming back around, and she got a big, pretty smile on her face. She's been fidgeting, watching the door, and she heard you pull up before I did. I swear that woman's got a sixth sense."

They followed her through the house to the sunporch where Lenore and Alex were seated together as they'd been the day before.

Derek cleared his throat. "Hi, Mom."

"Hi, Lenore."

Josie winked at Alex, then pulled two chairs around.

"*Did you go to the ship?*" he asked.

"Lenore, we went out to dinner last night, to the Ship's Tavern," Josie said, and Alex smiled and shook his fists in the air. "And something really crazy happened."

Derek began jiggling his leg.

"Why don't you tell her what happened, D?"

He kept his eyes on her for a beat before turning to his mother. "We ran into Jenny Laight."

Alex clapped his hands and bounced up and down.

"*The babysitter.*"

"You remember her, she lived in the neighborhood and babysat me for a bunch of years after school?"

"*Did she remind him how we used to be?*"

"Do you want to tell your mom some of the memories Jenny brought up?"

"She reminded me we used to read together. On the old couch. The green plaid one? You got rid of it—I guess it would be pretty out of style now." He laughed nervously.

Lenore shifted her eyes to Derek, startling him. Josie put her hand on his shoulder.

"Remember what she said about the flowers?"

"Yeah, she reminded me I used to pick flowers for you."

Something flickered in Lenore's eyes.

"*He tried. He always tried.*"

"She reminded me what your nickname for me was. Bear cub."

"*Bear cub.*"

Now Lenore's eyes welled.

Derek reached for her hand. "Don't be sad, Mom!" His voice caught. "These are the nice memories."

"*But he has so many bad ones. Because of me.*"

"Jenny brought up all these sweet memories you shared," Josie said. "It was really lovely to hear."

Derek just held his mother's hand while she cried.

Josie rubbed his back. "Anything you think she might need to hear from you?"

"I love you, Mom." He said it so quietly, he might have whispered it.

"*You do?*"

"I know you probably think I don't because I stayed away for so long. I'm sorry I haven't come back before now."

"*Tell him I understand.*"

"I think she probably understands why you haven't. I'm sure she feels badly about the unhappy times."

"*I do.*"

"Maybe let her know how you feel now?"

"We had some tough times, of course we did."

"*He was such a good boy.*"

"But I always loved you. I mean, all teenagers are rough on their parents, but our tough times were harder than most… I just want you to know I have no anger about them at all anymore. That's not where I am now. I know you were doing your best and were so sad, and it had to be really hard to be a parent again so soon after Alex died."

"*It was.*"

"But I forgive the bad times, and Jenny helped me remember the better ones."

Though tears continued to run down Lenore's cheeks, she smiled. She put her other hand on top of Derek's, then pulled it toward her and kissed it.

Josie could see him fighting back his own tears.

"*My bear cub.*"

Pauline came in with a prescription bottle and a glass of water.

"Time for your meds, honey. She usually naps before lunchtime. One of these pills makes her sleepy."

"Okay. We'll take off soon, then."

Derek held his mother's hands for another moment, then excused himself to use the restroom. After Pauline gave Lenore her pills, she went to the kitchen to prepare the afternoon meal.

"I hope you're feeling better, Lenore."

"*He remembers.*"

She was smiling now, her eyes bright, and looked years younger and more vibrant than she had the day before.

"*Does he remember me?*" Alex asked.

"Is that why you wanted us to find Jenny?"

He nodded.

"Well, honey, I'm not sure he's ready to remember yet, but we'll work on it."

Josie heard Derek talking to Pauline and held her finger to her lips. Lenore stretched her mouth into a contented yawn and murmured something Josie couldn't make out.

"Mom," Derek said, coming back into the room. "We're going to let you rest, but maybe we'll come back for another visit soon."

He took his mother's hand again, leaned in, then kissed her on the cheek. "I love you."

"*I love you.*"

He put his hand on Josie's shoulder. "Ready, Joze?"

"Is there anything else you might want to say?"

He frowned. "Did I leave something out?"

"What if what Jenny thought was true?"

"Oh." He nodded and cleared his throat. "Yeah, okay. Alex, if you're around and can hear me—"

He looked at Josie, unsure of himself.

"Go ahead, honey."

"I love you, too, buddy."

"*You do?*"

"I always have. I always will."

Alex broke into a toothy, dimpled grin, then ran over to his brother and threw his arms around his legs. Derek staggered and shot a bewildered look at Josie before shaking it off.

"Okay, then, little man," he said in the wrong direction.

As they left the room, Alex was back on Lenore's lap, nuzzling her as she drifted off.

The quiet ride back to the hotel afforded Josie the chance to replay what had happened. That Derek sensed his brother's presence was obvious, what he would do with that experience was unknown. Most important, though, they'd accomplished what they'd come to Denver to do.

After they parked, she suggested they take a walk before settling in to their night of movies and room service. Living in New York City, it was easy to lose sight of the fact most of the country didn't move around quite so much every day, and she was restless.

Derek took her hand, and they started down Milwaukee Street. Without warning, the sky darkened and erupted into marble-sized hailstones. Josie shrieked as lightning crackled across the sky and a heavy rain fell. They ran toward the hotel, darting under awnings with other wet, surprised people.

Once they were in the lobby, she laughed. "That was insane!"

"Welcome to Denver. Our weather contains multitudes."

"You aren't kidding! I'm sopping wet. And cold."

They rode the elevator to their room, where they toweled off and listened to the hail pelting their window.

"It's a perfect night for room service," Josie said.

"Let's start with an aperitif. I'll go to the bar and get us some wine."

Josie changed into her black cashmere pajamas and curled up on the sofa, grateful for a night in with her love, an entire evening without the distraction of the third member of their relationship—the restaurant. They were thousands of miles away, and if there were a crisis at Miss Sylvie's, there wasn't much they could do about it.

It was strange, though. They'd not heard from anyone since leaving town. She opened her phone and texted Curtis.

Checking in…

Then texted Ani.

Everything okay?

Curtis texted right back.

Slammed again

Either he was lying so she wouldn't worry, which didn't stop her from worrying, or they were missing their restaurant's most successful two nights yet. Either way, it was odd he wasn't saying more. It was also odd that Ani, usually so quick to respond, had gone silent.

Something hovered just out of reach of Josie's consciousness. She closed her eyes to try to grasp it and her mind went to the unsettling man she'd seen outside the Jefferson Market garden the first day she and Ani had really talked, the man she'd convinced herself was just passing by. A sense of foreboding washed over her.

She walked to the window, trying to keep her focus on the strange, beautiful moment at hand. The sky was a pearlescent gray with dark bands of rain in the distance. Elsewhere, muted sunbeams peeked through the clouds, illuminating patches of blue. Derek was right about multitudes—the weather was doing everything it could all at once.

She heard the click of his key card in the door before he walked in carrying two bottles of wine with their corks sticking out and a pair of stemmed glasses.

"I didn't know if you wanted red or white, so I got one of each. Dinner's coming up in a bit."

"Why are those uncorked? Did you get a head start in the elevator?"

"Bartender offered. I open wine for a living. It was nice to take the night off." He poured two glasses of white and handed her one. "To life."

"*L'chaim.*" She clinked his glass. "This is spectacular. I've never seen anything like it."

He put his arm around her. "I forgot you've never experienced these skies. I'm glad you are now."

"Objectively speaking, it's a beautiful part of the country."

"Hard for me to really be objective."

"Do you think you'll want to come back out again to see your mom?"

"Probably not." He stared at the horizon. "I said what I needed to. I'm glad I did, but maybe it was hard for her. She was crying at the end."

"Could they have been happy tears? Or relieved ones?"

"They could, but like you said, she's got to have a lot of regret too. And I hate to say this, but she should. Of course there were nice moments. I'm her kid. I was there for eighteen years, and she's not a monster. But the trauma was real."

"I know."

"By some miracle, I turned out relatively okay. But I can't just transition into the loving son taking care of his mom in her final days and pretending everything was fine. It wasn't. And I don't know that I need to be stirring up those memories while she's winding things down."

"That's fair."

"Also—" He stopped and turned to Josie.

He looked beautiful in the flat light of stormy skies coming through the windows. Beautiful and sad.

"What is it, honey?"

"So much happened there. So much tragedy and trauma. It feels like it's still imprinted in those walls. The darkness. And, yeah, the ghosts."

"The ghosts—"

"I don't know. I don't know if he's there or if he was there when I was a kid, and I don't think knowing would really help me. This part of my life is over, the Colorado part and all it represents. I think to keep moving forward, I need to leave it behind me."

Chapter Nineteen

THEY TOOK THE first flight out of Denver in the morning, returning to New York in time to drop their bags and get to the restaurant an hour before opening. When they arrived, Lucy and Curtis were in a booth in the dining room with the reservation book open in front of them. Josie cringed—it was a tangible symbol of their success or lack thereof on any given night.

"Does the fact you're looking at that thing mean there's something in it?" Josie asked.

"Yes!" Curtis said. "Welcome back. How did it go?"

She looked to Derek to answer.

"It was intense," he said. "Really fucking intense. How's everything here?"

"You have no idea," Lucy said.

"We don't." Josie squeezed into the booth next to Curtis and poked his arm. "The only word this one gave me was 'slammed.'"

"We were." Curtis shrugged. "And despite the chaos, Lucy is the best manager this building has seen."

"Thank you. We can chalk the chaos up to Stephanie Katz being impeccable with her word." Lucy held up a copy of *The New York Mirror*. "Marcus Mother-Effing Dreyer. Oh, and Ian."

"Ian?" Derek asked.

"I forgot to tell him," Josie said. "Yeah, turns out Ian the Inept is a pretty good flack. Even before Dreyer's column came out, he'd been impressing young co-eds by talking up the ghost table."

"Called it!" Curtis made an elaborate snapping gesture. "People love this stuff."

Lucy slid the book toward them. "Best part is these same people end up raving about the food. Raving. I had four tables ask me about making future reservations after dinner last night."

"That's incredible. Isn't it?" Josie nudged Derek, who was running his finger down the page.

"Is this a table for sixteen?"

"Yah, D. Some young thang is having her bachelorette dinner here next weekend," Curtis said. "And it's all about the ghosts. Everyone wants to see the table, take pictures with it. It's gotten so we have to bring people up in shifts once an hour so it doesn't get too crowded outside the kitchen."

"I've literally had people call up and ask if we're the 'ghost table place,'" Lucy said. "Oh, and I hired my replacement. His name is Jack, and he's a snarky Brit with excellent referrals."

"Fabulous."

"Happy almost birthday, Josephine," Curtis said. "We got you a packed restaurant and a snarky Brit."

Derek looked up from the book. "Speaking of, we're having a party at our place Monday night to celebrate this gorgeous dame."

"Yeah, Derek's insisting on throwing me a birthday thing, and I want everyone here to come."

"All of us?" Lucy asked.

"Of course—why?"

"Twyla at a birthday party sounds exhausting."

"Heard that!" Twyla chirped, walking in from the bar.

"Kidding!"

While people set up for dinner, Curtis pulled Josie aside. "You'll be proud of me, Lady."

"I'm glad, but next time I'm out of town, if that ever happens again, you have to give me more to work with than monosyllabic texts. I was worried!"

"Sorry. We were all in the weeds. It was a good thing, why were you worried?"

"It was a pretty emotional trip all around, and I couldn't reach you, and then I couldn't reach Ani either. Have you seen her?"

"Not since the weekend. But she's busy with her book, so what's to worry about there?"

"I don't know. I just feel kind of fragile. Between the trip and the birthday. Thirty-four!"

"I know that, young lady."

"So why am I going to be proud of you?"

"Because I'm working on befriending Eduardo."

"And?"

"Well, the good news is, like you promised, I'm not having those crazy-ass emotional sponge reactions to him anymore."

"That sounds promising."

"The bad news is, yeah, he's been through some shit."

"How so? And how did you manage to talk to him while you guys were 'slammed?'"

"We were so slammed, the entire staff needed to slam back drinks after all the ghost enthusiasts left. A bunch of us stayed late last night—Jerome, Lucy, Naomi, Jack-the-new-guy—and Eduardo was on his way out, but I batted my lashes and invited him to join."

"I'm pretty sure he's straight."

"My lashes don't discriminate."

"What did you learn?"

"He grew up in Arizona, oldest of five kids, all sisters."

"I knew that part."

"Dad was groundskeeper at the university—died in a worksite accident when Eduardo was twelve."

"That's awful."

"I know. Mom had to work multiple jobs—which was how I got him to open up. Once we got through the 'how long you been in New York, where you from' chatter, I brought up my childhood with Mama working all those jobs. So his mom's working a lot and he's basically the caregiver to his *hermanas*, has to get home first from school every day, help them with homework, make dinner, no extracurricular activities or time with friends or anything."

"That makes me sad."

"Yeah."

"What else?"

"That's it. He did say there was more to his story. But that's all I got."

"Okay. Well, thanks for trying. We still have a ways to go because that doesn't really explain anything."

"I know, but then Jerome started making shots, like premium shots—"

"Don't tell me this."

"Right. Sorry. Generic shots."

"Don't lie."

"You're not leaving me many options here, Lady."

"Okay, fine. Just don't tell Derek he used the good stuff."

"Of course not. Anyway, it turned into a party, so ain't nobody telling sad childhood stories. We played drinking games."

"Dude, you're almost forty."

"I know. It brought me back. I think it was good for him to talk though, 'cause he thanked me on the way out. He probably doesn't talk about personal stuff. That stoic, macho Latino thing."

"Right."

"What happened in Denver?"

"I can't get into it now, but we'll talk. It was an important trip, and I'm really glad we went. I think it was cathartic for Derek in a lot of ways, but of course it was also really hard."

"I bet."

"We did well, though. We were totally bonded for the first time in a long while."

"Did you get some lovin' in the mountains?"

"I'm going to ignore that and go say hi to Chef."

"Ooh, that sounds like a yes!"

"Don't be so gross."

"Don't be such a prude!"

"Welcome back!" Naomi said when Josie walked into the kitchen. "Girl, we've been in the weeds. I'm sure you've heard—"

"I did hear. Looks like Derek and I need to leave town more often."

"This is gonna be the new normal. I'm planning to double up on everything at the market tomorrow."

Josie turned to Eduardo. "How are you managing with our sudden popularity?"

"Great. I knew this would happen, just a matter of when. That table may be the draw, but our food's too good not to keep people coming back."

His mood was light, though he still bore dark circles of sleeplessness under his eyes.

Throughout the night, Josie fielded questions about the ghost sighting in the bathroom and redirected people to the table. Each time she went upstairs, she expected to find Ruby there but never did. She was both surprised and somewhat relieved to have fewer distractions on the busiest night the restaurant had seen since they opened. It was a test for the staff, who handled it all with aplomb. The new hire, Jack, was a nice addition—quirky and affable.

Josie basked in the night's success while it unfolded, enjoying the choreography of the servers and busboys navigating the room, the festivity in the air. It was a perfect reminder of why she loved this business, why she'd wanted to own a restaurant in the first place—to create a space for people to gather, enjoy a meal, spend time together for all the myriad reasons people dined out.

"This is fabulous." Curtis sidled up to her while she stood in the dining room entrance. "Reminds me of Bistrot's glory days without the side of crazy that Chef added to every meal."

"Chef was a complicated man. Excellent cook, though. I'm recognizing some faces tonight—do we actually have regulars?"

"We do. Including our friend Sidney Feist, who's on a cocktail date. And he's hot. He looks like a Bollywood star."

Josie found Sidney sitting at the corner of the bar, holding hands with a handsome South Asian man. "Hey, Sidney. I didn't see you come in. We're so packed tonight."

"Josie, this is my friend Anand. Anand, this is Josie."

With her hair and makeup toned down, she was a softer, prettier version of herself. Her eyes had a sparkle that was missing the first few times Josie saw her.

"Very nice to meet you, Anand."

"Pleasure," he said in a British accent.

When his phone buzzed in his jacket pocket, he kissed Sidney on the lips, then excused himself to take a call.

Sidney grabbed Josie's wrist. "Isn't he gorgeous?"

"Very handsome."

"And he's a doctor. A pediatrician." She held her hands over her heart. "How dreamy is that?"

"Where did you meet this dreamy pediatrician?"

"Ready for this? On a dating website. Match dot com. Never thought I'd say those words out loud."

"They're becoming really popular. Seems as viable a way to meet someone as anything else."

"You have to click past a fair number of frogs."

"I've never been on a dating website, and I've kissed more than my share of frogs. I'm happy for you, Sidney, and hope he's good to you."

"He's great so far. This is only our second date, but he's really nice. And funny. And laid back. My actor husband was way more uptight and took himself way more seriously. I hope it lasts."

"Whatever happens, you're back out there, and that's a big step."

"Yeah, and of course, now that I am, Graham is begging me to come back. Begging—phone calls, texts, carrier pigeons. But I'm not doing it. Even if I don't see this dude again after tonight, I've come to the conclusion I'd rather be alone than lonely in a marriage."

"Amen, sister. By the way, we're having a little party at our place Monday night for my birthday, and I'd love for you to join. Feel free to bring Anand… or anyone else!"

She walked to the other end of the bar where Derek was shaking a cocktail pitcher. He looked up at her and winked.

"How are you doing, my love?" She leaned forward so he could hear her over the delightfully crowded room.

"Insanely busy in the best possible way."

"I like that."

"I like you."

He tipped the pitcher into a pair of glasses, then slid them across the bar to a customer impatiently waving a twenty-dollar bill. At one time, Josie would have found this behavior abhorrent. Tonight, she viewed it as a sign of success. They were *almost* too busy to keep up with demand, and this was a good thing.

By eleven o'clock, the dining room had emptied, and the waitstaff was ready to unwind.

"Guys, join us for a nightcap," Curtis said to Josie and Derek. "For old time's sake."

"Not tonight, honey. We're exhausted—it's been a whirlwind couple of days."

"Amazing job, though, everyone," Derek said.

"Thank you, Stephanie Katz!" Lucy hoisted her beer in the air.

The new hire, Jack, raised a glass. "To Stephanie Katz! Who in the bloody hell is Stephanie Katz?"

"No one you need to concern yourself with."

Derek yawned. "Sorry guys. I'm beat."

Jerome told him to go home, assuring him he could handle the bar alone. "I did it the past couple of nights. And if we need, Curtis knows his way around a cocktail menu."

"Shirley Temples on the house," Curtis joked. "Seriously, y'all, go get some sleep. You deserve it."

"Thanks, guys," Josie said. "You're all amazing."

She held Derek's hand as they walked down the block.

"That almost doesn't seem real, how busy we got. Thanks for your vengeance, Stephanie. And your ineptitude, Ian. Poor guy can't even properly badmouth us."

Derek nodded and smiled but was clearly distracted. Having hit the ground running the moment they walked into the restaurant, Josie had managed to fully re-immerse herself in New York while she knew half his mind was probably still in Denver.

She got ready for bed. When she came out to say goodnight, he was sitting on the sofa with a glass of scotch in his hand.

"Aren't you exhausted, honey?"

"I don't think I'll be able to fall asleep."

"Talk to me."

"A really weird thing happened yesterday."

"You know I understand 'weird' better than most."

"When you told me to say something to Alex, and I did, I got this—I don't know—this sensation. Like I could feel him there, sense his presence, and it was familiar."

He held his glass in both hands, rested his elbows on his knees, then looked at her. "Josie, was he there?"

She sat on the arm of the sofa and put her hand on his shoulder. "Yes, sweetheart. He was."

"Oh, wow," he whispered. "Wow."

"Is it upsetting to know that?"

He sipped his drink while he contemplated the question.

"Upsetting? No. No, it's some weird kind of comforting. Part of me wants to know more—like did you see him, did you talk to him, is that how we found Jenny—but then mostly I think maybe I don't need to know."

"Well, if ever you want to hear more about my experiences, you know I'll tell you."

"And the shit with the restaurant—you were right, it is good for business."

"The ghost stuff?"

"The ghost stuff. I'm sorry I doubted you for so long."

"You don't need to apologize for that."

"I do, though. I fought you hard on this. I didn't want anything to do with it. I'm still not sure I do, and I can't say I understand at all, but…."

"But?"

"I guess part of me wishes I could have contact with him too. But maybe just knowing he's there, maybe that's enough. Knowing he'd been there all along, and I was never really alone."

⚜

In the morning, after Derek left for the gym, Josie finally heard from Ani, who invited her over. A hint of autumn chill hung in the air. When she arrived, Ani was sitting on the patio listening to music, wrapped in a navy-and-white Navajo-print blanket.

"Welcome back! How was your trip?"

"It was a lot of things, but mostly I'm glad we went. I was worried when I didn't hear from you. Is everything okay?"

Ani tilted her head back and forth. "Not really. Steve isn't doing very well, so I went to Connecticut to keep an eye on him.

"What's going on?"

"He's not taking very good care of himself these days. Some old habits are showing up. He has a lot of trauma and doesn't handle it well."

"I'm sorry."

"I realized this week I probably need to make his place home base for now instead of just going up on weekends."

"Will that be okay with the friends you're housesitting for?"

"Yeah, now that everything's underway and we know we can trust these guys, I don't have to be here quite as much."

"I'll miss seeing you so often! I love hanging out with you, and you've helped me through an especially rough patch."

"You've done the same for me, Josie. I'm really glad we met."

Josie kept a smile on her face in hopes of tricking her sadness. She hadn't known Ani long, but the friendship had come at the right time, and goodbyes, which had always been tough for her, had become exponentially harder since Nanette died.

"What happened in Denver?"

"I think Derek finally got some closure."

"I'm really glad to hear that."

"Yes, it's been a long time coming."

"That's what Steve needs, closure from the past. It's the only way to start healing from trauma."

"How are things in your fictional world? Have you made progress with your traumatized character?"

"I have, actually. Still ironing out details, but I'm getting there. And you? Any updates on his real-life counterpart, Eduardo?"

"Curtis and I are starting to unravel bits and pieces. Doesn't sound like he had much of a childhood—his dad died when he was young, he helped raise his sisters, didn't get to do much else besides school and home. He told Curtis there's more to it all, but we haven't gotten there yet."

"Sounds like he's been through a lot."

"Yeah, I think we need more opportunities outside of work to really get to know him. Oh, by the way, my birthday's Tuesday, and we're having people over Monday night. Will you be in Connecticut?"

"I'll just be coming back from the weekend to pack my stuff but probably won't go up again until Thursday. Give me your info and I'll come by if I can. If I'm back too late, we'll do a belated something soon."

"Bell Bottom Blues" came on the radio, and Josie recalled how emotional it had made Ani the last time they heard it.

"Should we change the station?"

"No, I think I need this right now."

Josie listened to the lyrics, to Eric Clapton telling the woman he was singing to that if he could choose a place to die, it would be in her arms. "Can I ask you a question?"

"Of course," Ani said.

"Is the person this song reminds you of an ex?"

She shook her head. "Not a boyfriend, no. But someone very important to me. We grew up together, and this was our song when we were teenagers. We would belt it out every time it came on."

She smiled wistfully at the memory.

"What happened?"

"We had a falling out."

"I'm so sorry."

"Me too."

"Do you think it's mendable?"

"Sadly, no. It's too late."

She gave Josie a loaded look and Josie understood this person was no longer with them. Ani didn't seem to want to elaborate, and so she let it rest. They spoke for a few more minutes, then said goodbye with promises to talk soon.

"If you're still open to it, Josie, I'd love to have you read some of my draft."

"I'd be honored."

"Then you'll have those chapters as soon as I can get them to you."

Ani hugged her so tight that as Josie walked toward the restaurant, she was overwhelmed by the sense they wouldn't see each other again. She didn't understand why, or what it meant. She just had a feeling.

Chapter Twenty

ANI'S IMPENDING DEPARTURE and Ruby's absence had Josie feeling blue all weekend. She'd grown accustomed to both of them. Where Ruby was concerned, not only did she have genuine affection for her, she'd come to play an important role in connecting Josie to the spirits whose messages she needed to impart. The air was heavy without her, yet Josie knew she wouldn't just slip away. She couldn't. They had a soul contract.

While the restaurant's burgeoning popularity should have made her happy enough, she couldn't shake the veneer of gloom. So she kept going, going, going, telling herself the more she moved her body, the more the endorphins would take over. She ran up and down the steps to the kitchen every chance she got, circled the dining room making small talk, did everything she could to shake her mood until eventually, it began to work.

In his own efforts to cheer her up, Derek added to the guest list for her birthday party with every familiar face that walked through the door. In theory, she appreciated this, but as she'd told him, being the guest of honor made her anxious.

"Lady, you deserve this and more," Curtis said on Sunday when they gathered in the bar between shifts. "People love you. Let's celebrate you."

"It's not my comfort zone. I'd rather be behind the scenes, not on display. Having a party for myself feels so self-indulgent."

"'Kay, but you're not having a party for yourself. We're having a party for you."

"And I hate to break it to you," Lucy said. "But you may need to practice being on display. I just fielded a call from some online outfit that wants to do a profile on you guys."

"On us? Why?"

"We're a hot ticket. Word travels fast."

On Monday, Josie woke to breakfast in bed, a bouquet of apricot- and cream-colored flowers, and a gift certificate for the Tranquility Day Spa in Soho.

"It's not even my birthday yet!" She yawned and stretched. "This is too much!"

"Never too much for you, baby. You have a facial, massage, and whatever else you want starting at noon. Lunch and mimosa included."

"Mimosas on a weekday? How decadent."

"Mimo*sa*. Save some energy for tonight."

Derek waited on her all morning, and Josie knew it was as much about her birthday as it was his appreciation for Denver. That trip was the thing he'd been dreading for decades, even if he hadn't fully realized it, the thing he wasn't sure he'd ever have the courage to do. With her help, he'd done it and survived.

The spa was a twenty-minute walk downtown. Josie set out after breakfast, passing through Washington Square Park on her way to Soho. It was her final day of thirty-three, and though birthdays ending in four weren't considered significant, this one felt it. She looked at the people she passed and tried to ascertain who was younger than her, who was older. Most fell into the former category.

She had a strange relationship with her birthday, largely because of the tradition of disappointment it held. All those years wanting from her father what he'd inevitably fail to give her, time and attention, which would lead to her mother's bitterness casting a shadow on the day and Nanette's attempts to keep everything light feeling forced and embarrassing. There'd be poorly attended parties where only a fraction of the classmates she invited would show, the popular kids not wanting to associate with the weird loner from the broken home.

Raymond sent gifts, and the guiltier he felt for letting her down, the more extravagant they were—expensive dolls and toys when she was young, designer clothes and accessories as she grew. One year it was private ice-skating lessons she didn't need. Another time he offered to pay for dinner out for Josie and five of her closest friends. She didn't have five friends at the time.

Once she was out on her own, she tended to work on her birthday, let it pass by with minimal acknowledgement. Last year was the one that finally allowed her to rewrite the day's narrative. She and Derek were a new couple on a hiatus from work and had driven upstate to go hiking and stay at a bed and breakfast. It was the best birthday she'd had, though admittedly the bar was quite low.

Now here she was, one year older, somewhat wiser, and with an existence that looked very different than it had twelve months earlier. She was a business owner in a serious relationship. Her life had substance, and her future, while uncertain as any future was, had greater potential than she could have once imagined. Derek assured her that by this time next year, the restaurant would be in such good shape they'd be able to go on a real vacation to celebrate her thirty-fifth. It was so refreshing for him to be the starry-eyed optimist, she went along with it despite being well aware there were no guarantees.

She reached the spa just before noon and spent the next several hours being pampered and prettified, enjoying a single mimosa and several cups of herbal tea in the candle-scented waiting room between treatments. The woman at the front desk talked her into a "Chakra Balancing" massage, whatever that meant, and Josie was suggestible enough she felt more aligned as she walked home. She loved the way the facial made her complexion glow when she saw her reflection in storefront windows.

By the time she reached her building, it was nearly 5:00 p.m. Guests were due to arrive ninety minutes later. Derek had left a note that he was running pre-party errands, so she had the place to herself while she showered and got ready, opting for the gold wrap dress he loved. She put Billie Holiday on the stereo and sang along, and when he came in thirty minutes later with Curtis and a case of wine, she serenaded them with the closing lines of "Crazy He Calls Me."

"Happy birthday, Lady Gray!" Curtis handed her a magenta double orchid in a square glass vase. "These are for you, and Henry and I want to take you two to dinner somewhere stupidly expensive."

"These are gorgeous. Where is Henry?"

He rolled his eyes. "Where else? Entertaining a client. This one's an uber-wealthy art collector from Berlin." He said this in a German accent.

"And he didn't want to bring him to a house party in a Greenwich Village one-bedroom?"

"Crazy, right? I, however, would much rather be here than at some five-hour tasting dinner with tiny portions and tinier pours of wine."

He complained liberally about his new lifestyle, but Josie knew him well enough to know he secretly loved it—the fancy dinners with wealthy Europeans, the fact his partner was a big deal in the art world who was sought after for his taste and expertise. Curtis wanting the autonomy he got working at the restaurant made sense, but Josie knew it wasn't the trappings of life with Henry he objected to.

"You guys can put on party music," she said. "Something more festive than Billie."

Curtis put the champagne and white wines on ice, then opened a couple of reds. Derek pulled out his books of CDs, meticulously arranged alphabetically by genre, and chose a few. Soon, the sounds of Portishead filled the air.

"Derek Magnus!" Josie said in mock disbelief. "What are you doing? This music doesn't predate the Carter administration."

"I'm dragging myself toward the twenty-first century. So far, it's not so bad."

"I'll take your word for it. What are we doing for food?"

"Sushi. Having it delivered from Blue Ribbon."

"Are you kidding? You're spoiling me!"

Blue Ribbon was a high-end sushi restaurant in the Village she'd been to once—when someone else was treating.

"No, I'm not, baby. I'm celebrating you."

He kissed her before going to the bedroom to change. Josie helped Curtis arrange the bar, cut lemon and lime wedges, and put out dishes of nuts and chips and salsa.

"He's right, you know. We're celebrating you, and you deserve to be celebrated."

"This is a weird birthday. It's an in-between age, but it feels big somehow."

"Thirty-four is a great number. You're in a great place, aren't you?"

"I'm in a pretty decent one," she admitted, "now that Derek and I are better and the restaurant's doing okay. But who knows how long any of that will last?"

"Nobody, which is why we need to enjoy it while it does. We spend so much time trapped in the past or worrying about the future, waiting for the other shoe to drop. So much time. All we have is this exact moment."

"You sound like Nanette. When did *you* get all Zen?"

He shrugged. "I'm working on it. Thinking about how cranky I was last summer, how once I decided not to be, or to fake it, anyway, everything turned around."

"I'm glad it did."

"For both of us. Doesn't mean it's all smooth from here on out, but it never hurts to embrace the good moments."

"Except then I miss them when they go away. It's like losing someone you love. Or a new friend." She had told him of Ani's leaving, and he understood her sadness.

"You don't get a limited supply of good, Lady. There will be more."

At a quarter to seven, the doorman buzzed to announce the first guests. Boodles and Bulleit walked in carrying flowers, wine, and a gift bag. It hadn't occurred to Josie people would bring presents, and she felt even more self-conscious that this was all for her.

Curtis popped open a bottle of champagne. "Now it's a party, y'all!"

People continued to arrive—Naomi and her roommate, Twyla, with a date she introduced as "an Aquarius with a lot of Gemini," and some people they knew from the building and neighborhood. There were more gifts and cards, boxes of chocolate, bottles of wine wrapped in silver mylar bags.

Josie's glass never neared empty before someone—usually Curtis—refilled it. She felt light and happy as she chatted with Bulleit about the restaurant.

"Did I hear you're considering a name change?" he asked.

"We had one conversation about it—my God, word travels fast in this town. Some reviewer wrote that the name doesn't make sense, and we're wondering if he has a point. Lucy suggested Fleur-de-Lis, which would at least clue people in that it's NOLA cuisine. But I have very mixed feelings about removing Sylvie's name."

"No, you can't remove Sylvie," Bulleit said emphatically. "Just because some hack doesn't understand the restaurant's name."

"I have an idea," Boodles said, stepping into the conversation. "What about incorporating the fleur-de-lis into your signage? It can be the *t* in Bistrot. *T*s."

"That's only effective if someone sees it written." Bulleit petted him on the head. "You're lucky you're handsome."

"I know I am, but it could work. Remember *Blush!*"

"How could I forget?"

"I like the idea of adding it to the design," Josie said. "I'll suggest."

Lucy brought her over a plate of sushi and gyoza, which she devoured. Playing hostess with unlimited refills was a prelude to skipping dinner, and she was grateful someone had reminded her not to. She flitted around the room and in and out of conversation. Every time she turned around, there were more people to talk to. She waved across the room to Eduardo, who was chatting and laughing with Jerome, Curtis, and Sidney Feist's friend Melissa.

"No Anand tonight?" Josie asked Sidney when they met by the ice bucket of champagne.

"He has an early day tomorrow." She smiled. "But he's taking me to his friend's party in Woodstock this weekend. An overnight!"

"That's a big step!"

"Told you, girl." Melissa came up and draped her arm around Sidney. "You were always way too good for that schmuck."

"I don't know about that, but this guy's pretty great so far. Isn't he, Mel?"

"Yeah, so don't fuck it up."

Josie continued to make her rounds, keeping an eye on Eduardo. He was being particularly social, and every time they were about to speak, one of them was intercepted by someone else. Now he was talking to Bulleit.

"Lady, look who's here!" Curtis said, his arm around Johnny Giardino. "Reunited, and it feels so good."

"Happy birthday, gorgeous!"

He held out a bouquet of roses, the handling and arranging of which Curtis promptly took over.

"Thank you, gorgeous!" Josie kissed him on the cheek, then looked behind him. "Did you come solo?"

He smiled. "Yeah. But we're getting somewhere, me and Marie."

"She's a lucky gal."

"I'm a lucky guy."

Johnny walked over to say hello to Derek, and Josie went to see who had spilled into the bedroom. She found Sidney and Melissa standing by the window holding a joint.

"I hope this is okay." Sidney carefully exhaled a stream of smoke out the window. "I brought party favors."

"It's fine. We have a good fan in here. Worst case, we'll sleep on the foldout in the living room."

Josie breathed in the sweet, pungent smell.

"You want?" Melissa held the joint toward her.

"God, no. You don't want me touching that. It makes me way too paranoid."

"Funny, it used to make me way too paranoid, but I think it was the combo of weed and being married to Graham that did it. Now I just feel mellow and happy."

Melissa poked her rib. "You're still married. Call the lawyer."

"I will, I will. I just want him to suffer a little longer, hold out hope so he has farther to fall." She exhaled another stream of smoke. "Wait—is that too vindictive? Am I vindictive? I thought I was the high-road type. Have I totally changed? Is this stuff making me paranoid?"

"Have fun, guys," Josie said.

In the living room, guests mingled. Derek and Lucy were leafing through the CD books. Johnny and Naomi sat on the covered radiator by the window. Her roommate was in animated conversation with Boodles and Jerome. All of these people had come to celebrate Josie and, in the moment, it no longer felt uncomfortable to be the guest of honor—quite the opposite.

"Lovely Libra!" Twyla called from the corner where she chatted with her Aquarius, Curtis, and Eduardo. "What a great party!"

"I'm so glad you're here!" Josie put her arm around Twyla. "It's so much fun having you all in our humble abode."

"Wouldn't miss it. I love birthdays!"

"You don't say." Curtis bumped her with his hip.

Eduardo laughed, draining the remnants of a gin and tonic. He was relaxed, off his guard. This seemed an ideal opportunity for Josie to try.

"Eduardo, can I borrow you for a minute? I want to introduce you to someone."

"Sure thing."

He followed her over to where Johnny and Naomi sat.

"Boss!" Naomi said. "We were just trading war stories."

"Having worked at Bistrot, I assure you Johnny's been to battle far more often than you or your sous chef. Johnny, meet Eduardo. Eduardo, your predecessor, Johnny."

Johnny stood and held his hand out. "Naomi says your knife skills are off the charts."

"Thanks. You still in the business?"

"You haven't heard the legend of Johnny?" Naomi giggled, touching his arm, and Josie flashed back to the summer before when tipsy girls vied for his attention at the end of the night. "He's FDNY now."

"Thank you for your service," Eduardo said.

"Aw, man, bring it here, brother." Johnny hugged Eduardo. "That's so beautiful to hear."

"I mean it. You guys are heroes."

"I'm gonna bring my girl in for dinner sometime soon and try your and Naomi's food. Good cooks are heroes too."

Josie knew if she didn't interrupt soon, she'd have a hard time getting Eduardo alone, which was what she needed to do.

"Oh, Eduardo, before I forget, can I show you that cookbook? My grandmother's recipes?"

"Yeah, of course! I'd love to see it. Good to meet you, Johnny."

"You too, man. You'll be seeing a lot more of me in the future."

Josie went to the bookshelf, then slid her finger across the spines until she found it. With nowhere to sit in the living room, she brought him into the bedroom. Melissa had rolled a fresh joint, and now Bulleit was partaking along with Lucy, who winced when they came in. "Sorry."

"For what?"

"Consuming illegal substances at my boss's house?"

"Personally, I think they should just legalize it already, but besides that, compared to all the crazy things that go on in this industry, you're fine." Josie perched on the edge of the bed.

Eduardo sat beside her.

"Thanks for indulging me. I'm very proud of this." She handed him the book.

"You should be. It's beautiful."

He ran his hand over the cover, which was gold foil with a fleur-de-lis pattern and the words *Chez Nanette* printed in purple. "You made it?"

"I did. In high school."

In her senior year, Josie took a photography class. This was her final project, a joint endeavor with Nanette. Nanette wrote out her recipes, and Josie pasted them along with photographs she took and developed of the cooking, baking, and final dishes. It made her nostalgic to see all the grainy black and white pictures of Nanette rolling out dough or stirring a pot, then posing with the food, her dark hair often flecked with flour.

"*This* is how you make red beans and rice," Eduardo said, reading through the list of steps. "Your grandma knew her stuff."

"A classic Monday dish."

"Why Monday?"

"That's the tradition in New Orleans, according to Nanette. I think the idea is you use leftover bones from Sunday supper and then let the dish simmer all day while you do your chores for the week. Or something like that."

"I love food traditions. We had a bunch in my family too."

They were getting somewhere. He turned the page and read through Nanette's recipes for étouffée and shrimp and grits. He turned another page. "Creole *and* Cajun gumbo. Most people do one or the other."

"Nanette marched to the beat of her own drum."

"You must have eaten good as a kid."

"I did." She paused while he read. "I bet your sisters ate well too, right? Did they like your cooking?"

"Yeah. Least that was something we never had to worry about. I can whip up a good pantry meal."

"What are they like, your sisters?"

"Four girls, four different personalities. Lots of arguing. I mean, we all loved each other, but you know how it is."

"That's a lot of girl energy under one roof. What are their names? And what are they doing these days?"

He crunched an ice cube. "Rosa's the youngest. She's a dancer. And a diva." He chuckled. "The one above her, Veronica, is studying to be a veterinarian."

"That's a noble pursuit."

"Yeah, she's the gentle one. Used to collect stray cats and baby rabbits she found in our yard. Then there's Luisa, the wild child. She's a bartender, talks about opening her own spot."

"Do you think she will?"

"Maybe. She has a history of dating old guys with money."

"I imagine that's not something you'd necessarily choose for your little sister."

"Not exactly, but this new one sounds better than the others. Sounds like he treats her right."

"I bet you're a good protector."

He pulled at a thread on his cuff. "I try."

"And the fourth one? What's she like?"

The question hit a nerve. He was quiet for a moment, staring at the book in his lap. "We were real close. Year and a half apart, same humor. Liked the same music, movies, most things. Tons of inside jokes. It was just the two of us for a while, before the other girls were born. That was a lot of details." He held up his drink. "Liquid courage."

"I don't mind detail. What's her name?"

"Diana."

"Pretty."

"First in the family to go to college."

"Did you go?"

"I was never great in school and started in restaurants soon as I could. Didn't really leave time for much else, then I came east three years ago."

"What made you move to New York?"

"More opportunities, better pay."

"Better pay but higher cost of living, I bet."

"Really, it was a change of scenery I wanted. The girls were grown, and I needed to do something for me. Just for me."

"I get that. It must have been hard to leave them, though. Do you talk to them a lot?"

He cleared his throat and drummed his fingers on his knee. "Diana and me, we had a falling out." He took a sip of his gin and tonic.

"Over what?"

"Do you really want to hear this now? It's your party."

"And you're one of my guests. I'm happy to talk to you. We don't really get the chance to at work."

"She had this boyfriend. Esteban. I couldn't stand him."

"Why not?"

"Everything a big brother wouldn't want for his sister—drug problem, gambling problem, couldn't hold a job, bad track record with girls. Women—"

Curtis peeked his head in the door and held up a bottle of champagne. Josie waved him away.

"After years of this on-and-off thing, she finally breaks up with him for good, and we're all happy. I move to New York. Last year, she decides she needs a change too, wants to try the east coast. I'm thrilled. Offer to fly back and help her pack her stuff up and drive out here together." He took another sip of his drink, stared at his hands.

The people by the window had left, and now they were alone.

"Eduardo, if this is too much for you right now, we can change the subject."

"No. I got to get better at talking about this stuff. And you're easy to talk to."

This was the best compliment Josie could ask for. More than anything else, it was how she wanted people to see her. "Well, I have a fair bit of practice with talking about the tough stuff. I did a lot of it last year."

"Is it okay if I smoke a cigarette?"

"Sure."

She followed him to the ashtray by the window. He pulled a pack of Parliaments and a lighter from his shirt pocket, shook one out, then lit it, careful to exhale through the screen. He offered it to her.

"You want?"

"Yes, but I'm going to resist."

She had quit smoking the previous fall after her habit grew heavy post-Nanette.

"This gets pretty dark."

"If you feel comfortable sharing with me, I can handle it."

Curtis came back in with a fresh gin and tonic for Eduardo and a glass of white wine for Josie, wordlessly removing their empties.

"Great guy," Eduardo said.

"The best."

He took a pull of his cigarette and sip of his drink. "Couple weeks before I'm supposed to fly back and help her move, I learn the truth from Rosa, our baby sister."

"The truth about?"

"Why she wanted to come east. Why she dropped out of school. The ex—he lives here now, begged her to come back to him."

"Oh, no."

"Yeah. I called her up and went crazy. I never talked to any of my sisters like I talked to her that day. She's crying, screaming back at me, telling me he's changed, no more drugs, got a good job, he's a new person. She promises." He let out a shuddering sigh. "But here's the thing, Josie. I knew him longer than her—he was my grade—and this guy was always trouble. So even if he's changed, I mean, how much can someone change?"

"I don't know. I think people can, but they have to really want to."

"Yeah. And she's a sucker for the broken ones. The wounded birds. Always has been. So she tells me she's moving out here to be with that *perdedor*… loser."

"I know the Beck song."

He smiled joylessly and took another drag of his cigarette.

"I call my trip off, cancel my ticket. No way I'm gonna make this easy for her, stubborn idiot I am."

"You were trying to protect her."

"She asks her friend to help her move. At the last minute, the friend has to work, so my sister decides to make the trip herself."

Tears pooled in the corners of his eyes.

"I didn't know any of this 'cause she wouldn't take my calls. She was stubborn too, and pissed. I wanted to apologize for how I spoke to her. Wanted to hear her out. I never got the chance."

"Not for lack of trying, though," Josie said.

It was clear how the story would end and clearer still he needed to keep telling it.

"She sets out on her drive, alone. Not half a day in, falls asleep." A strangled sob escaped from his throat.

"Oh, Eduardo. I'm so sorry."

His chin trembled. He gripped the windowsill and stared out into the night.

"You don't have to hold back your tears with me—"

"No, that's the problem, Josie. I can't cry. I wish I could just let it all out. But it's in my DNA. Men in my family don't cry. I know it would help, but I don't know how. It's just so hard, the guilt I feel."

"But it's not your fault! It was an accident."

"Yeah, but if I hadn't reacted so bad, she'd have let me know she was coming out alone. No way I'm letting my sister drive across the country by herself. Only she shut me out. I know we'd have made up eventually, but she was mad, and like I said, she could be stubborn as hell."

"I get why you feel guilty, but I hope you can forgive yourself. No brother wants to see his sister wind up with the wrong guy, and this sounds like the wrong guy."

"Crazy thing, he tracked me down. Don't know how. My other sisters swear they didn't tell him where I was working, but he came to see me last month right after I started with you guys."

"You talked to him?"

"Told him I had nothing to say. He tried to apologize for how he treated her before, swore she was telling the truth, he'd changed. I made him leave. I didn't want anything to do with it. Him apologizing so he feels better doesn't bring her back."

"I get that."

"Thing is, I feel for him. He loved my sister, and he was grieving hard."

"I'm sure he did love her. Doesn't mean he was right for her."

"Maybe I did the wrong thing. Maybe for her sake, I should hear the guy out."

"There's no right answer here."

"Can I ask you something?"

"Of course."

"Curtis says you can sense spirits, communicate with them. Is that true?"

"Somewhat. I can't predict when or how it'll happen, but I've gotten messages here and there."

"Maybe you'll get one from her someday. I just want proof she's okay." He rested his cigarette in the ashtray.

"I hope someday you'll get it. She sounds like a very special person."

"I got a tattoo in her honor. Want to see?"

"Absolutely."

He unbuttoned his cuff to roll up his sleeve, then looked down at his bicep. Before Josie could register what she was seeing, her heart pounded, the high-pitched buzz filled her ears, the air left the room. Josie's wine glass slipped from her hand and shattered on the floor.

Inked on Eduardo's upper arm was an image of Ani.

Chapter Twenty-One

Despite her long day and copious amount of wine, Josie was wide awake when the party ended. She dust-busted every last shard of wineglass, then insisted to Derek she wanted to clean the living room, have quiet time to reflect on the evening.

"I'm so glad you let me talk you into doing this, Joze."

Dressed in a short satin robe, she leaned against the doorway to the bedroom where he was already under the covers. "It was amazing having so many friends in the same room."

"Everyone had a good time. Great to see Johnny too."

"He's in a good place."

"Don't stay up too late, baby. I sleep better when you're next to me. Especially when you're wearing that."

"I won't. Just need a little time to decompress." She blew him a kiss, then closed the door.

As soon as she did, her heart pounded. The truth was, right now she needed to sift through her scrambled, booze-addled thoughts and make some semblance of sense out of what she'd seen.

She had made this mistake once before, when someone she thought she knew and considered a close friend turned out to have crossed over years before they met. That this could happen twice was astonishing. When she'd learned the truth the first time around, her initial response was a feeling of betrayal that she'd been lied to. But she quickly came to understand there was a reason this friend chose her when she did—she'd needed something only Josie could provide.

That meant Ani needed something from her, and she'd have to stifle her conflicting feelings to figure it out. In part, it was to help Eduardo come to terms with his grief, that much was clear, but how she could possibly do that was a mystery.

Like the friend last summer, Ani hadn't deceived her with malintent. She'd done what she needed to do to reach Josie. Tonight, her predominant feeling other than shock wasn't betrayal. It was sadness.

In the movie version of this scenario, there would be a clear-cut message for her to deliver—all was forgiven, Eduardo wasn't at fault, Ani was in a better place. Instead, Josie was given no instruction, no clue on what to do next.

Most of the cleanup was done, an advantage of having friends in the service industry attend the party, but a few dirty glasses remained. Josie emptied the drying rack, then set about washing the rest, meditating on the sound of running water. A melody popped into her head, and she started humming before realizing what it was—"Bell Bottom Blues." That song was Ani's connection to someone she'd known as a kid and cut out of her life. Her brother. Her brother who'd described the sister he'd lost as someone with whom he shared a taste in music. The puzzle pieces were fitting together with devastating accuracy.

In a burst of wishful thinking, she told herself this could be her overactive imagination at play. After all, she'd only glanced at Eduardo's arm, and there were lots of beautiful women with dark brown hair and big brown eyes. Plus, she wasn't the only person who interacted with Ani—Curtis had, never mind he had some of the same abilities as Josie—and the workmen. The workmen talked to her, she was sure of it. She'd become so tethered to her connection with the spirit world, her mind was playing tricks.

She knew what she had do in the morning—go to Ani's house. If she weren't there, she'd find evidence she existed. But she would be there, sitting out back on her laptop. They'd talk and she'd tell her all about Eduardo and the fantasy she'd concocted. Ani would understand and have insight into how and why she'd felt the need to connect the dots as she had. Yes, that was what would happen. Josie repeated this, drowning out the doubting voices in her head as she turned off the lights to tiptoe into the bedroom.

In the morning, Derek brought her coffee in bed.

"Two days in a row?"

"Of course. Today's your birthday."

She'd woken anxious to get up and out of the house but would have to be patient.

"Can we have breakfast in the other room? Two days in a row eating in bed makes me feel like the grandmother in *Willy Wonka.*" She'd have to stifle her anxiety with lame attempts at humor,

"Fair enough, Veruca. Want to open your presents?"

"As long as no one brought me an Oompa Loompa. Those guys scared the hell out of me when I was a kid."

"Damn it. Twyla brought one, and I forgot to poke holes in the box. Hope the little guy's not too pissed."

"That would be a very Twyla gift."

"He's a Gemini."

The presents were piled on the coffee table, and Josie opened them while they drank their coffee. Boodles and Bulleit had gifted her a certificate to the MAC makeup store on Christopher Street. Curtis brought Li-Lac chocolates and wrote a card with a long message she would read later. From Lucy, a blank journal with a peacock on its cover and a sparkly pen that said *Queen*. Naomi brought a book on New Orleans's hidden history and a tin of Café du Monde coffee. And from Twyla, a deck of Tarot cards. Everyone else had brought enough wine and champagne to last through two more parties.

"I have a little something for you too."

Derek handed her a small wrapped box. She peeled off the paper and recognized the name of a high-end jeweler in Soho.

"Do we need to take out a loan?"

"No, but let me explain. I got this when we thought your pendant was missing. You can exchange it."

She pulled out a burgundy velvet pouch and spilled a white gold chain with a diamond fleur-de-lis pendant into her palm.

"Oh my God. This is so beautiful!"

"I thought so, but since you found Nanette's, you don't have to keep it. They have a lot of cool things there."

"No, I love it. I'm going to wear them both, two fleurs-de-lis from my two greatest loves."

She went to the mirror and clasped it around her neck. It was longer than Nanette's necklace, and she loved the way they looked together. She spun around and gave him a kiss. "I love you."

"I love you. Happy birthday, Joze."

Josie said she had to run errands before work, so after breakfast she showered, dressed, and left the apartment. As soon as she closed the door behind her, adrenaline flooded her system. She walked a few blocks north on Fifth to take an extra-long route to Ani's.

She was of two conflicting minds, both of which came at a cost. On one hand, of course, she wanted to have been mistaken, for her friend to be there in the flesh and in her life. On the other, a tiny, niggling sensation deep inside her felt if she'd been right and Ani was Eduardo's sister, she'd have confirmation of her life's mission. Her connection to the spirit world would be an unequivocal gift, her role as a healer verified. She had spent so many years doubting herself and her purpose—and having it doubted by others—that maybe she needed the universe to validate her once and for all, even if this came with a terrible truth at its core.

She turned down Eleventh Street and walked west to Sixth Avenue, stopping to take in the grounding comfort of the towers. Someday, she'd revisit that observation deck.

The closer she got to Ani's, the more she decided she had enough validation from the universe, and what she needed most was for her to be there. When she reached the apartment, Hector was outside.

"*Hola, Hector, mi amiga està aqui?*"

"*Tu amiga?*"

"*Ani, la mujer que vive aquí. . . .*"

"*Què mujer?*"

Shivers ran down her spine.

"Can I?" Her voice quivered as she gestured to the open door.

He stepped aside to let her pass.

The apartment looked as it always did. Josie walked through each room, heart pounding, until she reached the back patio. She pushed open the door and stepped outside. Folded onto the back of Ani's chair was the Navajo blanket she'd worn the last time Josie saw her, and on the table were her *Write* notebook and pen. Josie's hands trembled as she picked up the notebook and flipped it open to a blank first page. She shuffled through the rest of it, all blank—and no torn paper where she'd scribbled her number. Written on the very last page were the words, *Thank you, Josie.*

Josie put her hand to her mouth. Had she suspected all along but talked herself out of it? Is that why the last visit felt so final?

She ran her hand over the blanket and let the tears fall.

"I'm so sorry, Ani," she whispered, hugging the journal to her chest. "I promise to look after your brother."

Josie walked through the apartment and out onto the street in a haze, getting to the restaurant on autopilot. She was relieved no one was on the floor yet. In her office, she sat and breathed deeply, asking for clarity.

She combed through all of her interactions with Ani as best she could recall them, including the night at the restaurant. It dawned on her then—Ani said she'd wanted to see the ghost table, yet Josie had never mentioned it to her. She'd intentionally left it out so as not to have to divulge anything about Ruby or Alex. She'd come by to look in on her brother. For all Josie knew, she'd come many times before.

With a start, she remembered the man outside the garden from whom she'd sensed sadness and pain. This was shortly after Eduardo started. Josie now felt certain it was Esteban—Steve—coming to find him, unknowingly walking right past Ani. This made her even sadder—Ani had come east to see the two men she loved, neither of whom was at peace, both in need of closure that would be nearly impossible to come by.

"Ani, what does it all mean?" she asked aloud. "What am I supposed to do now?"

Eduardo needed a sign to assure him his sister was all right. Telling him they'd met without the ability to offer something tangible was pointless and unkind. No, until she figured out how to translate her experiences in a way that could help him, she'd need to keep it to herself. Eventually she would tell Curtis, but today she needed to grieve privately.

She walked upstairs to the ghost table and touched the beautiful setting at Nanette's spot, craving the scent of gardenia or the appearance of a discarded owl sticker. Without such obvious signs, she'd just have to keep faith that Nanette—and Ani—would help guide her through this.

"Hey y'all," Naomi said, climbing the stairs. "Great party. Thanks for including me and Julian."

"I'm so glad you could join. Thank you for my gifts."

"You're welcome, enjoy them. That a new necklace? It's beautiful."

"Yes. Derek's done good."

"Derek's done great. What special treat can I make for you today? Dinner or dessert?"

Josie ran through dessert possibilities.

"How are your rice pudding skills?

"Stellar, but I can do something fancier than that!"

"I know you can, but I'm craving comfort food. Reminds me of Nanette. We made good use of leftover rice in the seventies."

"Then I'm gonna make you the second best rice pudding you've ever tasted. Let me get a jump on everything."

She swung open the kitchen door, and Josie went back downstairs.

"Lovely gathering last night!" Twyla chirped. "Your home is darling!"

"Isn't that broker speak for tiny?" Derek asked.

"No, that's 'charming' you're thinking of. Thank you Twyla, for the compliment and the Tarot cards. I've never owned a deck before."

"You know you're only supposed to use a deck that was given to you. Never buy your own."

"In fact I did not know that."

Eduardo walked in, and Josie felt a deep pang of sadness in her stomach. He looked as he had when they first met, rugged, handsome, black bandana on his head, and at the same time he was entirely different. A weight had been lifted from his shoulders. He smiled easily at her.

She followed him into the dining room. "Did you get home okay?"

"I did. Thank you for the party, and the talk. I guess I really needed it."

"You can talk to me anytime, Eduardo. And I'd love to learn more about Ani, anything you want to share."

He stopped short and turned around. "How did you know we called her that?"

"What?"

"Ani."

"You told me last night," she ad-libbed.

"Must have been the gin—everyone called her Diana except the family and a couple really close friends. "

"Then I'm honored to know her as Ani."

"You're a good person, Josie."

"So are you."

He looked at her for a beat before turning and heading up the stairs.

Dinner saw a steady flow of guests, a decent crowd for a Tuesday night. Josie led a couple of groups to and from the ghost table. When asked, she explained the settings were for "people who were important to this place over the years." Now there was someone else who would have a seat there whenever she wanted it.

As it was early in the week, service ended by 9:30, and the staff gathered in the bar. Naomi came down from the kitchen with a large dish of rice pudding in which she'd placed birthday candles.

"Ready, guys? Happy birthday to you…." she sang, and the others joined in a cacophony of pitches.

"Don't quit your night jobs, y'all," Curtis said.

Josie closed her eyes and made a wish.

May I find clarity in my abilities, and may this year be filled with happy surprises.

She blew the candles out in one breath.

"Thanks, everyone. And thanks, Naomi, for not using as many candles as the occasion calls for. The FDNY appreciates you."

Lucy wrinkled her nose and stared into the dish. "The hell kind of birthday cake is that?"

"It's rice pudding, just like Josie's grandma used to make. Special request."

"Yeah, sorry. I'm kind of caked out after last night."

Naomi scooped out dishes.

"Anyone want to bring one up to Eduardo? He volunteered to start cleanup."

"I will," Josie said. "I'm sure we're all ready to make it an early night."

She took two dishes upstairs. Eduardo was scrubbing a pot and singing along to "Every Breath You Take" on the radio,

"I come bearing weird dessert."

"Not weird—I was happy Naomi was making this. It reminds me of home too."

They sat on opposite counters and ate.

"This is different from Nanette's—there's a flavor I can't pinpoint."

"Cardamom."

"Yes! Thank you."

"You having a good birthday?"

"I'm having an important birthday. An unusual day with a few unexpected life lessons. I guess that's a good way to start a new year. What about you? What kind of day are you having?"

"I don't know. I spent so long trying not to think about my sister, and now I can't stop. Maybe I'm getting closer to finally crying. Maybe not."

"You will eventually. Grief has no timeline."

"I feel guilty, like I'm wronging her by not crying. But she'd think that's stupid. She'd probably say the same thing you did. You two would have liked each other."

"I'd welcome the chance to get to know her, so keep the stories coming anytime you want to share."

He smiled.

"You said she was a writer?"

"Yeah, she was working on a book about our crazy family. She was a really good writer."

"She sounds wonderful."

"That's why I was so hard on her about Esteban—she deserved someone better, someone more like her. But I don't know. Like I said, maybe I was too hard on the guy when he came by."

"Do you have any idea where the book she was working on is?"

"I have the first bunch of chapters—she sent them to me before our fight. Wanted me to give her my opinion, which is crazy 'cause she was so smart and talented. What would her dumb brother's opinion matter? But she wanted to hear it."

"Have you read them?"

"Not yet. I don't know if I can handle it."

"I get that."

"You think maybe—would you want to read them sometime?"

"I would love to. I'd be honored."

"I don't know, Josie, maybe there's something in those pages that could help me. Maybe there's, somehow, some kind of message she didn't die mad at me, that she understands why I reacted like I did. Or maybe there's the opposite message. That's what I'm afraid of. I know it all sounds stupid. It's not like she knew what was gonna happen when she wrote them. "

"It doesn't sound stupid to me. At all. You believe in signs, right?"

"Signs?"

"From people on the other side. Sometimes, instead of specific messages, they'll send numbers or songs or other things you associate with them."

"Sure, I guess, but I haven't gotten any. Or I don't think I have. Maybe coincidences here and there."

"Keep your mind open. She'll send you signs. I promise."

They finished dessert, then Eduardo went back to his cleaning. Josie was about to leave the kitchen when the slow-tempo opening strains of "Bell Bottom Blues" came on. She spun around.

He was standing still, gripping the edges of the sink, the water running. She went over and touched his arm, and when he turned, he looked stunned.

"Oh my God. This song."

"I know," Josie said.

"How?"

"I just do."

She hugged him tight while he cried.

Chapter Twenty-Two

Josie left the kitchen feeling a sense of calm that was foreign to her. Nanette and Ani were right—it was a gift, and Josie a healer. Finally, she accepted it.

When she got to the ghost table, she found it occupied.

"Ruby!"

"*Hi, Josie.*"

"I've missed you the past couple of days."

"*Well, there are so many people around now, and they're all coming up to see the table. I didn't want to make more trouble.*"

Josie sat next to her. "I appreciate that. But this is your place—you don't have to stay away!"

"*Is today your birthday?*"

"It is."

"*Happy birthday.*"

"Thank you. And thank you, too, for helping Grandfather Bannister. It was really important that I heard that message from him."

"*You're welcome.*"

"Do you remember the woman I was talking to that night?"

"*The one who visits her brother.*"

"Yes—*visits*? Had she been here before?"

"*She comes here a lot.*"

"Do you talk to her?"

"*Only once, and she told me not to tell anyone. That's why I never said anything about her. I'm sorry, Josie.*"

"It's okay. She had a good reason to ask that of you, and you kept your word."

"*Josie, there's another reason I stayed away since that night.*"

"What is it?"

"*I love it here. I love you. But I think maybe you're right, and I need to move on.*"

"Yes, I think you do, honey. Much as I will miss you."

"*But there's one thing I need. If only….*"

She waited for Ruby to elaborate. When she didn't, Josie prompted her. "If only what?"

"*Remember I said about the soul contract?*"

"Of course I remember. I know part of it was about Alex and Derek, and I think I fulfilled that."

"*You did. Alex can move on now. Well, he can after he helps his mom through the next part.*"

"What about you?"

"*I have something I need from you too.*"

"Okay."

"*This makes me real sad.*" Her eyes brimmed with tears, and Josie wished she could take her hand. "*When I was twenty-six, one year before—*"

She stopped, put her head in her hands.

"What happened?" Josie asked gently.

"*I got involved with a fella, but we didn't really know each other, and then he moved away. That was fine with me, but then I found out I was having a baby.*"

"That must have been really hard, Ruby."

"*It was. And even worse, I didn't know how to find the guy to tell him. I didn't know where he went. I had the baby, though, a little baby boy, and he was so beautiful. I just didn't think I could raise him right. So I gave him up for adoption.*"

"It sounds like you did the right thing."

"*I don't know about that because maybe if I kept him, I'd still be here.*"

"Do you have any idea where he is?"

"*I've looked in on him over the years, but I lost track.*"

"What do you need from me?"

"*I need you to find him. Tell him I loved him. Explain I needed to give him a better life than I could have done. I don't know if I'd have been a good mom. And he's had a real nice life, far as I can tell. But he's still hurt. He still wonders why.*"

"How do you know this?"

"*He went to a medium once. He believes. Only that man wasn't really a medium, so he didn't see me. I was right there, trying to get his attention.*"

"Does he know what happened to you?"

"*No. He went to see if maybe he could find me that way. Or find anyone who could give him answers. But the man was a phony.*"

"That's terrible."

"*This is what I need from you. I need you to find him and tell him I'm sorry, and I love him.*"

"I can try."

"*Please, Josie,*"

Her pleading brought Alex to mind, how much he'd needed Josie to get Derek to Denver and then to the restaurant.

"Do you know his name?"

"*Lucas. Lucas Fiorello.*"

"Okay, sweetheart. I will do everything in my power to find Lucas. If this is what you need to hear so you can move forward, please know I will fulfill my end of our contract as best I can."

"*Thank you, Josie. That makes me feel hopeful, and like maybe I don't need to stay here forever.*"

"I will miss you very much, but I agree, you do need to move on."

"*Can I come back and visit?*"

"Of course you can. And you can communicate with me in other ways. Want to think of a special sign you can send?"

"*Well, I do love that song about seeing clearly without the rain.*"

Josie smiled. "'I Can See Clearly Now.' That's a beautiful song."

"*I used to sing it all the time when he was in my belly, so it makes me think of him. And now we're talking about it, so it'll make me think of you too. That and the song about if you could read my mind. Do you know that one?*"

"I do. Those can be our signs."

"*I'll think of more, but if I do, how will you know it's me?*"

"You're a very special soul, Ruby. I'll always know it's you."

"*You're a very special soul, too, Josie.*"

"Honey, I have to go back downstairs—but know that I love you and I'll miss you and I'll think of you always. I'll look for those signs any time you want to send them my way." She pushed her chair back, then stood.

"*Can I hug you?*"

"I thought you said that was too hard?"

"*I said it's for extra special occasions.*"

She embraced Josie, and it was surprisingly warm and tangible.

"*I love you too.*"

Josie started down the stairs when Ruby called out to her.

"*Oh—and Josie?*"

"Yes?"

"*I know why you wanted rice pudding so bad.*"

"Why is that?"

"*You're having a baby.*"

Epilogue

I KNEW THINGS would start to fall into place. I didn't know how or when, but I knew Josie would be the key. How lucky we are that my brother took this job. They needed him, and he needed Josie's help to move on. Grief is complicated enough without guilt. I should know. I have both.

What happened to me was nobody else's fault. I've been stubborn my whole life, held grudges to prove a point, and where has it gotten me? We know the answer.

I made the choice to stay angry with Eduardo. I made the choice to take that drive alone. As I got farther and farther from home, every part of me knew I'd made a bad decision, and I was mad at myself for it. Eduardo wasn't trying to upset me. He was being protective, and for good reason. I should have listened to him. Sure, Esteban changed. He was trying, but he just wasn't right for me. Doesn't mean I didn't love him or my heart doesn't break that he's hurting so bad, but I think my brother will do the right thing—reach out and forgive him and help him find peace. I need that for both of them. I need that for me.

I was with Eduardo constantly after I died, searching for the person who would walk into his world and help me reach him. I was at the restaurant the day he met Josie, and I saw the look that crossed her face. She was the one, and not just because I realized she might be able to see me, but because she's able to really see Eduardo. She knew what he needed even before she knew why. I knew she'd get him to open up. Ruby's right. She's a very special soul.

And that little girl she's carrying? She's a special soul too. You'll see.

Author's Note

I was always going to dedicate this book to my father. What was not part of the plan was completing a draft at his bedside during his final weeks here. One of the last things he said to me was how proud he was that my first book, which he read in manuscript form, was being published. As I allude to in my dedication, when I told him how relieved I was he loved it, he responded, "Not as relieved as I am."

He knew I had finished a very rough draft of this book. After he left us, I asked a friend how on earth I could throw myself into revisions now. She advised me to use my feelings, let them fuel my writing. So I did. The fact that grief in its many manifestations is central to this trilogy certainly made that possible.

Like Josie's grief for her beloved Nanette, mine for my dad is "pure and uncomplicated." Josie's sorrow is offset by her gratitude for the time she had with her grandmother and the eternal bond they share, just as gratitude topped my list of unexpected feelings in the aftermath of my loss.

Josie and I share a keen awareness of co-existing emotions. Less profound than the conflation of grief and gratitude were my dichotomous reactions to learning I'd be writing follow-ups to *The Coat Check Girl*. I was as excited as I was daunted. Excited because I love these characters and their world and I get to spend more time with them. Excited, too, that for once I'd know exactly what creative project I was supposed to be working on. Daunted because I'd never written a sequel, let alone one for a book intended as a standalone. And daunted that I had a very short window to write this, compared to the decade-plus during which I worked on its predecessor. Learning to navigate co-existing feelings, which at times requires compartmentalizing, is part of Josie's arc in this book.

Once I turn this note over to my publisher, it will be time to dive into book three. Bolstered by the continued support of my writing and reading community and feeling my dad's spirit walking beside me, I will write the next story. I hope you enjoy this one.

Acknowledgments

To acknowledge the people who've been a part of this book, I must first thank everyone who supported *The Coat Check Girl* from its inception until now. Coaches, writing groups, betas, readers, reviewers, bookstores, book club hosts, and so many others—because of you, I'm inspired to continue honing my craft.

For this book, I owe thanks to the following people:

Jessica Reino, Stephanie Hansen, and the Metamorphosis team for guiding me on the path from writer to author.

The Roan and Weatherford family for welcoming me into the fold and my editor, Staci Troilo, for your encouragement, patience, and extraordinary talent.

My three beta readers—Kelly Nugent, Claudia Zuluaga, and Maggie Buchwald—for tirelessly reading, suggesting, and re-reading, until we got this where it needed to be. Your astute observations and excellent eyes were an invaluable part of this process … and I thank you in advance for reading drafts of book three…

To all the writers in my life, my three betas, as well as John Matthews, Richard Grant, Elena Perez, Jorge Rivera, Jamie Boud, Louis Spiegler, Roz Esposito, Hannah Bos, Jack Grace, Devin Burnam, Michel Morin, Brian Niemietz, Erik Lieblein, Leslie Rasmussen, Pooneh Sadeghi, and so many more—thank you for being part of my writing community. This can be a lonely pursuit, and it's rewarding to have friends with whom to vent and celebrate.

To the people I spent time with on my Western writing retreats—in Tucson, Richard, Mariah, and Izzy Grant, Dave Poplar, Bonnie O'Brien, and in Denver and Boulder, Melissa Bigarel, Laura Herrmann, Tracy Miller Perez, Jamie Emmons, Alan Feldman, Michi Sakurai, and cousins Madeleine, Russell, Donna, and Paris Hogan—thank you for welcoming me to your beautiful hometowns and rewarding me with fabulous meals and conversation after days spent writing.

To my family, Mom, Jules, D, Scarlett, Sebastian … boundless love and appreciation.

The same goes to my wonderful in-laws, the Smith family—with special thanks to Bill for plotting my next couple of books for me…

The dogs—Pago and Banksy—you are very good boys even when you stare at me while I'm working.

And finally, to Bryan, thank you for infusing my world with music, adventure, great food, and creative pursuits. Here's to much more of it all. oxoxox

About the Author

Laura Buchwald is a New York City native who travels when she can, finding creative inspiration at home and away. Her first novel, *The Coat Check Girl*, was published in October 2024. She lives in Manhattan with her husband and dog, both of whom are very supportive of her work.

www.ingramcontent.com/pod-product-compliance
Lightning Source LLC
Chambersburg PA
CBHW030424310726
48979CB00009B/1611/J

* 9 7 9 8 8 9 2 9 9 0 7 7 6 *